HAVE YOU READ THEM ALL?

Discover the entire Robert Hunter series ...

'Carter is now in the Jeffery Deaver class'
Daily Mail

THE CRUCIFIX KILLER

A body is found with a strange double cross carved into the neck: the signature of a psychopath known as the Crucifix Killer. But Detective Robert Hunter knows that's impossible. Because two years ago the Crucifix Killer was caught. Wasn't he?

THE EXECUTIONER

Inside a Los Angeles church lies the blood-soaked body of a priest, the figure 3 scrawled in blood on his chest. At first, Robert Hunter believes that this is a ritualistic killing. But as more bodies surface, he is forced to reassess.

THE NIGHT STALKER

When an unidentified victim is discovered on a slab in an abandoned butcher's shop, the cause of death is unclear. Her body bears no marks; but her lips have been carefully stitched shut. It is only when the full autopsy gets underway that Robert Hunter discovers the true horror.

THE DEATH SCULPTOR

A student nurse has the shock of her life when she discovers her patient, prosecutor Derek Nicholson, brutally murdered in his bed. But what shocks Detective Robert Hunter the most is the calling card the killer left behind.

ONE BY ONE

Detective Robert Hunter receives an anonymous call asking him to go to a specific web address – a private broadcast. Hunter logs on and a horrific show devised for his eyes only immediately begins.

AN EVIL MIND

A freak accident leads to the arrest of a man, but further investigations suggest a much more horrifying discovery – a serial killer who has been kidnapping, torturing and mutilating victims all over the United States for at least twenty-five years. And he will now only speak to Robert Hunter.

I AM DEATH

Seven days after being abducted, the body of a
twenty-year-old woman is found. Detective Robert Hunter
is assigned the case and almost immediately a second body
turns up. Hunter knows he has to be quick, for
he is chasing a monster.

THE CALLER

Be careful before answering your next call. It could be the
beginning of a nightmare, as Robert Hunter discovers as he
chases a killer who stalks victims on social media.

GALLERY OF THE DEAD

Robert Hunter arrives at one of the most shocking
crime scenes he has ever attended. Soon, he joins forces
with the FBI to track down a serial killer who sees
murder as more than just killing – it's an art form.

HUNTING EVIL

Lucien Folter, the most dangerous serial killer the FBI has
ever known, has just escaped. Now, he's hunting for Detective
Robert Hunter – and he's going to make him pay...

WRITTEN IN BLOOD

When Angela Wood gains possession of a book
containing horrific descriptions of multiple murders, it
becomes clear that a serial killer is on the loose – and even
DI Robert Hunter might not be able to stop him.

CHRIS CARTER

GENESIS

**SIMON &
SCHUSTER**

London · New York · Sydney · Toronto · New Delhi

First published in Great Britain by Simon & Schuster UK Ltd, 2022

Copyright © Chris Carter, 2022

The right of Chris Carter to be identified as author
of this work has been asserted in accordance with the
Copyright, Designs and Patents Act, 1988.

1 3 5 7 9 10 8 6 4 2

Simon & Schuster UK Ltd
1st Floor
222 Gray's Inn Road
London WC1X 8HB

Simon & Schuster Australia, Sydney
Simon & Schuster India, New Delhi

www.simonandschuster.co.uk
www.simonandschuster.com.au
www.simonandschuster.co.in

A CIP catalogue record for this book
is available from the British Library

Hardback ISBN: 978-1-4711-9757-4
Trade Paperback ISBN: 978-1-4711-9758-1
eBook ISBN: 978-1-4711-9759-8
Audio ISBN: 978-1-3985-1357-0

Typeset in Sabon by M Rules
Printed and bound by CPI Group (UK) Ltd, Croydon, CR0 4YY

Dedication

I would like to dedicate this novel to all of us who every day struggle with mental health issues, fighting one of the hardest fights there is to fight – the fight against our own minds . . . against a darkness that no one else sees.

Please, stay in the ring.
This fight is worth fighting.
This life is worth living.
Those happy moments are worth finding.
We deserve our right to make mistakes.
We deserve our right to try again.
We deserve to be here.
Please, don't give up.

Warning

This novel contains themes that some readers
may find upsetting. For more information
and support, please see page 531.

One

With concerned eyes, the taxi driver watched as a relatively drunk Melissa Hawthorne opened the back door to the silver Mazda 3 and awkwardly stepped out onto the sidewalk in front of her house. The time was coming up to 2 a.m., on a Sunday morning and Melissa had been drinking since around 9 p.m. the night before. She didn't usually drink a lot. She didn't usually get that drunk either, but it was her best friend's twenty-eighth birthday, which was celebrated at the Broken Shaker, a pool deck cocktail lounge, with a very relaxed South Beach vibe, located on the rooftop of the historically unique Freehand Hotel in Downtown Los Angeles. Fruity cocktails followed by Jägerbombs added up to quite a lethal combination, Melissa had found out. Though she'd had a great time, she wasn't looking forward to the mammoth hangover that she knew would be coming her way when she woke up.

'The door ...' the driver called out. 'Could you please close the door?'

'Oh, yeah. Sorry!' Melissa replied in an unsteady voice before shoving the Mazda's back door with her hip. The effort was cumbersome and not quite powerful enough for the door to shut properly.

'Nope, it didn't close,' the driver announced, pulling a face.

Melissa gave the driver a silly smile and tried a second time, but instead of simply giving the door a quick bump, she fully opened it again before repeating the shoving movement, this time with even less strength than before.

'Oops!'

'It's OK,' the driver said, with a shake of the head. 'I'll do it. Don't worry.'

As the driver got out of the cab and rounded the car, Melissa slowly stumbled toward her front door, where, in between trying to find her house keys and managing to properly slide the correct one into the keyhole, she spent the best part of two and a half minutes.

Once finally inside, she closed the door behind her, poured herself a glass of water and made her way into her bedroom at the back of the house. She dropped her handbag on her bedside table and took a quick shower before at last getting into bed. As she did, she checked her cellphone. The time was 2:28 a.m.

No messages.

Melissa would have been lying if she didn't admit to herself that she felt a little disappointed. At the Broken Shaker cocktail lounge, she had met someone who she felt quite attracted to. His name was Mark, and after several cocktails, a few shots and plenty of laughs, they had exchanged phone numbers.

At the bar, just before she left, Mark had asked Melissa if she wanted him to come back with her. Melissa had been tempted. Very tempted. It'd been over six months since she had shared her bed with anyone, after catching her boyfriend of two years cheating with someone he worked with. However, despite how drunk she'd felt and how attracted she'd been to Mark, Melissa hadn't wanted to appear too keen – in her book, taking someone to bed on the first night was never a good look.

'Maybe next time,' she had replied, sending a disarming smile Mark's way.

Secretly, Melissa was half hoping that he would text her before she went to bed. Nothing extravagant. Maybe just a 'Hope you got home OK' message, or even a simple 'It was nice meeting you tonight.' Something to let her know that he was still thinking of her. Mark didn't seem the type who played the conventional 'waiting until at least Wednesday before messaging' game.

2:30 a.m.

No messages. No missed calls.

'Mel, you're reading too much into this,' she told herself. 'This isn't your first rodeo, remember? He'll message you tomorrow.'

She put down her phone, turned off the lights and buried her head into her pillows, but as she was just about dozing off, she heard her phone vibrate on her bedside table, followed by the distinctive beep that announced a new text message. She blinked awake, smiled confidently and reached for it.

Did you have fun at the party?

Melissa's smile brightened.

I sure did. Melissa was one of those who could cell-phone type with both thumbs. And she was lightning fast at it. *Did u?*

I wasn't at the party

Melissa frowned at the reply. Still feeling somewhat drunk and fully expecting the message to have come from Mark, she hadn't checked the name.

'Unknown.'

The smile faded from her lips.

Who is this? she quickly typed back. *My phone didn't recognize your number.*

It took about fifteen seconds for a response to come back.

Oh, your phone wouldn't recognize my number. I'm definitely not in your contacts.

Melissa sat up against the bed's headboard, reached for the bedside lamp and turned it on.

So who are u? she typed back. *And if ur not in my contacts, how did u get my numb?*

Who am I? Well ... to you, I'll be a Mentor, Melissa. A teacher of sorts.

Melissa's forehead knitted with doubt. Not quite the reply she was expecting.

A mentor? she typed back.

That's correct. I educate. I teach. And this is all part of a big lesson, Melissa.

That was when the penny dropped for Melissa. She remembered that Mark had told her that he was a high school teacher. If she remembered correctly, he taught algebra.

'Oh, I see,' she said out loud, nodding at herself. Mark must have turned off caller ID so her phone wouldn't recognize his number, and this was him, probably still half drunk, trying to be charming, or funny, or mysterious, or something.

Cute, she thought. *But I hope he's not trying to be funny only to ask me for some nudes.*

Though she felt tired, Melissa decided to indulge him, at least for a little bit.

A lesson, is it? she texted back. *Ur going to teach me something, huh? So what r u going to teach me?*

It didn't take long for Melissa's phone to beep and vibrate with a reply.

The first lesson, Melissa, will be about fear.

Melissa's eyes squinted at the message.

'Fear?' she asked herself.

Was that an autocorrect word swap? Did he mean to type something else?

The message was quickly followed by a second one.

Then I'll teach you about pain...

Melissa's squint turned into a frown.

And yet a third message.

And once you finally understand what those two really mean, Melissa, I'll teach you about death.

Melissa's eyes widened in surprise and disgust at the words on her screen. If this really was Mark, he had a pretty horrible sense of humor.

What the hell? she typed back. *Mark, is that u? That's not funny at all. In fact, that's quite disturbing. Even more so at this time at night. U R drunk. Go to bed.*

The reply came a few moments later.

Mark? Who's Mark? Is that who you're fucking at the moment, Melissa?

'What?' Melissa gasped, her head jerking back slightly.

No, this couldn't be Mark. She was now pretty sure of that. Back at the cocktail lounge, Mark had come across as a sweet, polite, intelligent and quite funny individual. This didn't sound like him at all, drunk or not.

Melissa had had enough.

Listen, she quickly typed. *Whoever U R, that was just rude. I'm blocking ur number right now.*

Wait . . . The reply came back almost instantly.

Melissa paused.

There really is something that you should know.

She stared at her phone's screen like a mother waiting for her kid to apologize.

Are you still there?

Yes, I'm here. I'm waiting. What is it that I should know?

Instead of words, the next message Melissa received contained four Emojis. The first was that of a moon. The second, of a car. The third, of a door. And the final one was of a house.

Melissa shook her head at her phone before shrugging.

'What the hell is that supposed to mean?' She spoke the words as she typed them.

It means that tonight, Melissa, after you got back from your little soirée and stumbled out of the cab . . . about half an hour ago . . . you forgot to lock your front door.

As she read those words, Melissa felt a shiver of fear kiss the back of her neck and instinctively, her anxious eyes darted in the direction of her bedroom door.

'Was this a stupid prank?' the rational part of her brain tried asking her.

Maybe.

But if so, then the next two questions really worried her.

Who did she know that would be capable of such a distasteful joke?

'No one,' she concluded.

And – worst of all – how would anyone know that she had stumbled out of the cab and into her house about half an hour ago? The timeframe was too accurate for it to have been a guess.

Was this the cab driver?

No, Melissa thought, quickly discarding that idea. *It couldn't have been.*

The moment that followed was filled with hesitation, but it didn't last long, as it was interrupted by yet another message.

But it's OK, Melissa. Don't worry. I've locked your front door for you.

Melisa was completely unsure of what to do. Should she reply? Should she block the person? Should she go check her front door? Should she call the police or someone? What?

Ding, ding. A new message

Here, have a look.

This time, the message came accompanied by an eight-second-long video clip.

Melissa hesitated for just a split second before her curiosity got the better of her. She tapped the attachment and the video clip immediately started playing on her screen. It began by showing her house keys dangling from the keyhole on the inside of her front door. A second later, a gloved hand appeared. It reached for the keys and turned them to lock the door before removing them from the lock itself.

'What the fuck?' Melissa murmured to herself, but the video wasn't quite through yet. As the keys were removed from the lock, the camera panned right into her kitchen and onto the digital clock on her counter, by the fruit bowl. It read 2:24 a.m.

Melissa's eyes shot to the top left-hand corner of her phone screen – 2:38 a.m.

Fourteen minutes ago. That meant that she was in the shower when that video was shot.

Just before the video ended, the sender whispered something into the microphone, but not loud enough for Melissa to understand what was said. She immediately rewound the video a few seconds, turned up the volume on her cellphone, and brought it to her ear, but she never got to hear what was said.

As she brought her phone to her ear, Melissa angled her head slightly right, in the direction of her bedroom door, which she always left ajar.

That was when she finally realized that she wasn't alone in her house.

Hidden in the darkness of her hallway, in the gap between her bedroom door and the doorframe, she saw a face smiling back at her.

Two

'Hi there,' the tall, olive-skinned woman said, as she pulled open the door to greet the new guest. 'You must be Robert.'

Detective Robert Hunter of the LAPD's Ultra Violent Crimes Unit was a little surprised, but his expression gave nothing away. Instead, he smiled politely as he nodded.

'I am, yes.'

The woman's jet-black hair fell far beyond her shoulders and perfectly complimented her intense golden brown eyes. The delicate features of her youthful face were further accentuated by two very charming dimples, one on each cheek, that appeared every time she spoke.

'I'm Denise,' she said, returning the smile and offering a perfectly manicured hand, where her nails shone in crimson red, a color that matched her lipstick. 'I'm an old friend of Anna's.'

'Pleasure to meet you,' Hunter replied, taking her hand.

Denise wore white sneakers and a white T-shirt tucked into faded blue jeans, which had a natural tear over the left knee. The silver chain around her neck had a small but very detailed anatomical heart as a pendant.

'There you are,' Detective Carlos Garcia, Hunter's partner at the UVC Unit, said as he appeared behind Denise wearing a long and dark apron. Across his chest, in large white letters, were the words: 'Kiss the Chef'.

'I'd rather not,' Hunter commented, nodding at the words.

Garcia chuckled. 'A present from Anna,' he clarified. 'As if you wouldn't have guessed it.'

'Shall I take that for you?' Denise asked Hunter, already reaching for the shopping bag that he had with him. The dimples on her cheeks twitched into being and then out just as quickly.

'Sure.' He handed her the bag. 'Thank you.'

'Come on in, man,' Garcia said, gesturing Hunter inside with the grill spatula he had in his right hand.

'I'm going to go put this in the kitchen,' Denise announced, before disappearing into the house.

'Perfect timing,' Garcia said, as Hunter stepped into his partner's small entry lobby and closed the door behind him. 'The first batch of picanha has just come off the barbecue. Anna is slicing it now.'

Picanha was Brazil's most popular cut of beef. Due to its almost perfect marbling and tenderness, it was considered by many to be the perfect barbecue-grilling steak. Hunter had never heard of it until several years ago, when Garcia first invited him to a barbecue at his house.

Garcia, who was born in Brazil but had left at the early age of ten, after his parents' marriage collapsed, had inherited his barbecue grilling skills from his father, and truth be told, he was great at it.

'Everyone is outside,' Garcia informed Hunter, with a jerk of the head. 'Go right ahead. I have to grab something from the kitchen. I'll see you out there.'

Hunter wasn't exactly shy, but he also wasn't the most extrovert of people, especially when it came to social gatherings.

'Robert,' Anna called, as soon as Hunter stepped outside and onto the backyard.

Garcia had married his high school sweetheart almost immediately after their graduation. Always an optimist, totally supportive and sharp as a spear, Anna was also the sweetest woman Garcia had ever met. Her beauty, despite being unconventional, was nonetheless mesmerizing.

With a bright smile parting her lips, Anna walked up to Hunter and gave him a kiss on each cheek. Her short black hair was a little disheveled, mainly from moving her sunglasses from her eyes to her head, then back to her eyes again. As Hunter stepped outside, she had just moved them to her head.

'You made it,' she said.

Hunter frowned at her surprise. 'Don't I always?'

Anna laughed. 'For barbecues you do.'

'Thank you for having me again.'

'Always a pleasure, Robert, you know that, but come, let me introduce you to the ones you don't know.'

Three other people were leisurely sitting around a circular patio table. A fourth person was standing by the impressive brick barbecue that Garcia had built himself.

'This is Martin,' Anna said, indicating a tall and skinny man. He looked a few years older than the woman he was sitting next to. 'And his partner Charlotte,' Anna proceeded.

'Pleasure to meet you,' Hunter said, shaking their hands. 'I'm Robert.'

'You remember Paulo, right?' Anna continued, now indicating the person standing by the barbecue, flipping sausages over. 'You met him the last time you were here.'

'Yeah, of course we did.' Paulo said, turning and greeting Hunter with a head gesture and a bright smile. 'Hey man, how you doing?'

'I'm alright. Yourself?'

'I'm doing great,' Paulo replied, his Brazilian accent still very noticeable. 'You should try some of these sausages. Argentinian chorizo. So good it gives you goosebumps.'

'And of course you've met Denise,' Anna said, nodding at her childhood friend who was sitting to Charlotte's left.

'I have. Yes.'

Once again, Denise smiled at Hunter, but this time the smile came accompanied by a subtle wink.

'Let me get you a plate and some picanha to start you off,' Anna said, indicating an empty seat. 'Drinks are in the kitchen.'

'Thank you so much, Anna,' Hunter said back, before addressing the rest of the group. 'Can I get anyone a drinks top-up?'

'We're good, thanks,' Martin said, indicating his and Charlotte's cans of beer on the table.

'I'm good too, thanks,' Paulo said, returning to the table with a plate full of chorizo sausages.

'Anna?' Hunter asked.

'Thanks Robert, but Carlos is in there making me a caipirinha.'

'Oh, nice,' Hunter commented before allowing his eyes to settle back on Denise.

'Sure,' she replied. 'If you don't mind.'

'Of course not. My pleasure. What can I get you?'

'Red wine please.' She handed Hunter her empty glass.

'Coming right up,' Hunter said, as he turned and re-entered the house.

On the kitchen counter, Hunter found three bottles of red wine, together with a small selection of spirits. Garcia had just finished squeezing limes for a jug of caipirinha.

'Want one of these?' he asked, nodding at the jug. 'You know how good my caipirinhas are.'

'I do,' Hunter agreed, as he reached for a new glass and a bottle of Argentinian Malbec. 'I also know how lethal they are, but maybe later. I think I'll start with some wine.'

Garcia paused while his eyebrows arched at his partner. 'I assume the other glass is for . . . Denise?'

'No one else wanted a drink.'

Garcia smiled. 'She's nice, isn't she?'

'Who, Denise?'

Garcia chuckled and leaned against the kitchen counter. 'You know that that doesn't suit you at all, right?'

'What doesn't suit me?' Hunter finished pouring the second glass of wine.

Garcia pointed at him. 'Exactly what you are doing right now, Robert. Playing dumb. It's not your style and you suck at it, so just drop it.'

Hunter turned to face Garcia, holding a wine glass in each hand.

'She's single, you know?' Garcia pushed.

'Who?'

'Get out.' Garcia pointed to the kitchen door.

Outside, Hunter handed Denise her wine glass. 'Malbec OK?'

'Perfect,' she replied, before indicating the seat next to her. 'Have a seat.'

As Hunter took the seat, Garcia came out carrying a tray with the freshly made jug of caipirinha and several glasses.

'Get ready to get woozy,' he said, placing the jug on the table. 'This is strong.'

As Garcia poured the caipirinhas, Hunter's work cellphone rang in his trousers' back pocket. He reached for it and checked the display screen.

Unknown Number.

'Excuse me for a sec,' he said and saw the expression on Anna's face change.

'Everything alright?' Garcia asked, his tone now dead serious.

Hunter's reply was a coy tilt of the head before getting up and putting some distance between him and the other guests.

'Detective Hunter,' he said as he took the call. 'Ultra Violent Crimes Unit.'

'*Detective Hunter,*' the voice at the other end of the line retorted. '*This is Detective William Barnes, LAPD Southwest Division. I'm sorry to have to bother you on your Sunday off.*'

'It's OK,' Hunter replied. 'How can I help you, Detective Barnes?'

'*Well, I'm just really trying to save everyone some time and paperwork.*'

Hunter frowned at the reply. 'How so, Detective?'

'*About forty minutes ago, I received a call from dispatch concerning a body found inside a house in Leimert Park. African American female. Twenty-nine years of age. My partner and I arrived here about twenty minutes ago to find two ghost-faced uniformed officers standing outside the house. Both of them had already puked up their lunch, their breakfast and probably their dinner from last night too.*' There was a short pause. '*What I'm trying to say, Detective Hunter, is that no matter which way you look at this crime scene – and I don't think anyone is really able to look at it for longer than just a minute – this will be escalated to Violent Crimes. Of that, I have no doubt. So like I said, I'm trying to save everyone some time and paperwork because you guys are going to end up here, no matter what.*'

Hunter breathed out before shaking his head ever so slightly. His eyes lifted from the floor to meet Garcia's, who was still standing by the table full of guests.

'What exactly do you have?' Hunter asked.

Detective Barnes chuckled. '*I don't think words can describe what's in there, Detective. You'll have to see it to believe it.*'

'What's the address?' Hunter asked.

Garcia wasn't a lip reader, but he didn't have to be one to know that for him and Hunter, this barbecue was over.

'*Detective Hunter,*' Barnes said after giving Hunter the address. '*Do you believe the Devil exists?*'

'Excuse me?' Hunter's expression contorted into a quizzical one.

'*The reason I ask, Detective Hunter, is because if you don't . . . you might change your mind once you get here.*'

Three

With its vast number of independent galleries, music venues, bars, and even an open-air museum, Leimert Park, which was located in South LA, was better known for being the center for both historical and contemporary African-American art, music, and culture in the city of Los Angeles. Several internationally famous singers, musicians, and artists had started their careers in one of the many back-alley clubs and theaters in Leimert Park. The neighborhood was also a mere twenty-five minutes' drive from Garcia's house in West Hollywood.

Hunter tried urging Garcia to stay at his barbecue. After all, it was their day off and Garcia had guests in his house, but Hunter knew that his partner's work ethic was just as rigorous as his own, and both of them understood the importance of experiencing a crime scene in situ, instead of studying it through photographs and written reports. So when Hunter suggested that Garcia stayed with Anna and their guests, Garcia's reply was a simple 'As if.'

Anna, who always understood the kind of commitment that her husband's job required, had smiled kindly at him and Hunter as she read the 'I'm so sorry' expression on their faces.

'Go make the world safer for everyone, boys,' she said, putting on the bravest face that she could muster.

After turning left onto 4th Avenue from West Martin Luther King Boulevard, Garcia had to drive another block and a half before he saw the flashing police lights ahead of him. He parked on the road, just behind one of the three black-and-white LAPD cruisers that had practically barricaded the dark gray fronted house on the right.

The property in question had a three-foot-high brick wall surrounding it, with an old wood gate that was definitely in need of some restoration. The wall was there purely for aesthetic purposes, not security.

As they stepped out of Garcia's Honda Civic, both detectives couldn't fail to notice the uneasy tension that showed in the faces of all three uniformed officers standing by the black and yellow crime-scene tape that had been raised around the property. Whatever they'd seen inside that house, it had clearly disturbed them.

The perimeter extended all the way to the road, including the stretch of sidewalk directly in front of the house. As always, a large group of curious onlookers had already gathered around the perimeter, every single one of them with their smartphones in hand, eager to capture something a little more exciting than just crime-scene tape and uniformed officers.

With their badges clipped to their belts, Hunter and Garcia zigzagged through the crowd. At the perimeter's edge, one of the officers greeted them with a head nod before lifting the tape for them to stoop under. As soon as they did, a tall, skinny man in a light-gray suit approached them. He had been standing by the house's front door, idly staring at nothing at all, as if questioning existence itself.

'Detective Hunter?' he asked, as his evaluating gaze settled on the two new arrivals. His tie was loose and his collar button undone.

Hunter nodded.

Garcia adjusted his sunglasses on his nose.

'I'm Detective Barnes,' the man announced. 'We spoke on the phone.'

Hunter introduced Garcia and they all shook hands.

'Forensics hasn't arrived yet?' Garcia asked, failing to spot any forensics unit vehicles parked in the vicinity.

'Like I said on the phone,' Barnes replied, 'this crime scene has UVC written all over it. I didn't want to step on anyone's toes here. Some detectives can be very particular about that. Plus, we all know that UVC can get a forensics team out to a scene a lot faster than regular Homicide, so I called you . . .' he nodded at Hunter, ' . . . and no one else. This is your show. You run it in whichever way you want. I was called to this scene by mistake. What I did do was set a perimeter so that the social-media vultures would keep their distance.' He turned to look at the crowd on the other side of the tape. 'Nowadays everyone is a cameraman . . . everyone is a reporter . . . everyone is a critic.' Barnes shrugged disapprovingly. 'None of us need any of that hassle.'

Hunter and Garcia nodded their understanding before Garcia reached for his cellphone. Barnes was right. The LAPD Ultra Violent Crimes Unit was at the very top of the priority chain when it came to certain requests.

Garcia quickly placed a call to the LAPD forensics unit.

'The victim seems to be one Melissa Hawthorne,' Barnes continued. 'Twenty-nine years old, resident at this address. She lived alone.'

'Seems to be?' Garcia questioned.

Barnes's lips stretched thin as he angled his head to one side. 'I'm playing safe here because no proper tests have been conducted yet,' he explained. 'But you'll understand once you get inside. Facial identification, done purely by sight, is damn near impossible, even for her sister.' He paused to correct himself. 'Stepsister, actually. She found the body.'

That was about to be Hunter's next question.

Barnes breathed out before his squared chin jerked in the direction of one of the LAPD vehicles parked on the road.

'Her name is Janet Lang,' he said. 'She's sitting in that cruiser with a female officer. We had to give her something to calm her down. Hysterical doesn't even begin to describe it.' Barnes shook his head, as his eyes saddened. 'What a total mind-fuck having to have that as the last image of your sister. I am so sorry for that girl. She's only twenty-six.'

Hunter turned to face the cruiser that Barnes had indicated. Through its window, he could see an African-American woman with her face buried in the palms of her hands. Even at that distance, Hunter could see that she was shaking. Sitting next to her, with a comforting hand on her shoulder, was a female LAPD officer.

'The officer at the door can provide you with shoe covers and latex gloves,' Barnes informed them. 'Nothing was touched. The scene is as in situ as it can be.' He checked his watch. The time was coming up to 2 p.m. 'Look, I need to get going. Just before you guys arrived, a call came in about a shooting in Baldwin Hills. That's more my department.'

'OK,' Hunter said. 'Thank you for your help here.'

Barnes took one step in the direction of the road but paused before turning to face the two UVC detectives again.

'Good luck with this one,' he said, in a tone that made it clear that he was happy that this would not end up being his investigation. 'I really hope you guys catch this sonofabitch.'

Hunter and Garcia watched Detective Barnes duck under the crime-scene tape and jump into a blue Toyota Camry that was parked across the road. As he drove away, both detectives turned to face the house.

It was a small, single-story structure with a tiled hip roof and dark blue window frames. There was no porch. A curved walkway, made up of squared concrete slabs, led from the wooden gate at the three-foot brick wall to the front door. Surrounding the walkway was a well-cared-for lawn patch. There was no garage.

Despite the front door having been pulled almost to a close and the curtains on the two large windows at the front of the house being drawn shut, Hunter and Garcia could easily tell that the lights in the house's first room were on. Credentials in hand, they walked up to the uniformed officer guarding the front door, who, just like Detective Barnes had told them, supplied them with elasticated plastic shoe covers and latex gloves.

As Hunter reached for the door handle, the officer, a short and stumpy man with a thick moustache and matching sideburns, took a step to his right and quickly crossed himself, reciting something in Spanish.

The front door opened straight into the house's humble living room. One step was all that Hunter and Garcia managed before they saw her, just a little to their left, as the living room gave way to the open plan kitchen area. As they did, both detectives immediately came to a halt.

Garcia pulled his sunglasses from his face, his unblinking eyes nearly the size of poker chips.

'What the actual fuck?'

Hunter stood completely still, while an uncomfortable knot began tying itself inside his throat.

'In all your years in the force,' Garcia asked Hunter, without breaking eye contact with the body, 'detective or not, have you ever seen anything like this?'

Hunter's reply came as a simple whisper.

'No.'

Four

Melissa Hawthorne's living room was a modest one, both in size and in furniture items. Rectangular in shape, it had a three-seater, red-fabric sofa and two mismatching armchairs facing a medium-sized flat-screen TV that hung from the north wall. On the floor, a worn-out shaggy rug and a glass coffee table centered the room. The kitchen, which was located to the left of the entry door, was small but well equipped, including a modern dishwasher and a five-burner stove with a double oven. The walls in the living room were adorned by colorful framed prints that differed in sizes. A couple of vases with fake flowers added a tranquil and homey feeling to the room, but without a doubt, the main features of that open-plan living/kitchen area were the two thick wood beams that ran parallel to each other, high above their heads, about a foot or so from the ceiling. And that had been where the killer had left the victim's naked body. Hanging from the beam closest to the kitchen.

This wasn't the first time that Hunter or Garcia had attended a crime scene where a victim hung from the ceiling, but what had made both of their skin crawl was the fact that the body wasn't hanging by its neck.

The killer had used a climbing rope that had been thrown over the beam. At one end, the rope had been looped several times around the thick metal handle that ran across the front of the stove, before being secured in place with a triple knot. At the other end, the killer had attached a stainless steel, extra-large shark hook, and that was where things went from the crazy to the totally insane because the body hung from its mouth – as if the victim were a prized fish.

The hook had completely perforated the underside of the victim's chin, savagely rupturing through skin and muscle, as it severed arteries and ripped nerves apart, before coming out through the mouth and suspending the body about two feet off the ground, via the mandible. That had been why Detective Barnes had mentioned that facial identification, done purely by sight, was practically impossible.

Being suspended in mid-air merely by her lower jaw forced the victim's head back, making it look like she was staring at the ceiling and at the climbing rope that seemingly emerged out of her mouth. She was a petite and slim African-American woman who couldn't have weighed any more than one hundred and twenty pounds at a push, but that had still been more than enough weight pressure to cause her jawbone to completely dislocate. One didn't need to be a doctor to clearly see that both lower jaw joints had detached from her skull so severely that ligaments, nerves, tendons, and muscles had been shredded and torn, allowing her mandible to move gruesomely forward and out of line with the rest of her head. Her chin now sat about two inches past her nose.

From her open mouth and the wound under her chin, blood had cascaded down her neck, torso and legs to create an ugly and viscous pool of blood on the floor, directly beneath her feet. Her face was also completely covered in blood splatters.

To keep her from fighting and reaching for the rope, her hands had been tied behind her back, which made Hunter's stomach churn, because it indicated that she was still alive when the killer pulled at the rope to lift her from the ground.

The second indication that she was still alive while that

insanity had taken place was the swelling to her face and neck. It looked like someone had stuck a small balloon down her throat and then inflated it. The swelling, coupled with the weight pressure due to the fact that she was hanging from her jaw, meant that the skin and flesh around the lower half of her face had strained to such a degree that it was starting to tear, especially at the corners of her mouth.

'Why do something like this to someone?' Garcia asked, finally letting go of the breath that he'd been holding on to for quite a while. 'This is just sick.' He shook his head, as he tried to make sense of something so senseless. 'It's . . . pure evil.'

Hunter's gaze broke away from the body at last, as he began taking in the surroundings. He also let go of a sad and tired breath.

'That is the problem, Carlos,' he replied, taking a couple of steps to his left to reach the kitchen area.

Garcia walked the other way, into the living room. Though he tried studying the rest of the room, he found it hard to break eye contact with the victim.

'This does go way past being sick,' Hunter continued. 'Way beyond being evil. Someone would only take the time do something like this to someone else if the whole act had a meaning.' He reached the stove and began studying the climbing rope that knotted around the oven handle. 'She was murdered this way for a reason . . . and that reason . . . has to be something very specific . . . very personal.' From the stove, Hunter allowed his eyes to move along the rope and on to the fishing hook in the victim's mouth. The hook, which looped through her chin and came out through her mouth, had also cracked and broken off several of her lower teeth.

'This whole scene,' Hunter said. 'The murder, the staging, the props, all of it . . . was thought of, prepared, and executed with a lot of precision. Unless she was a climber and a fishing aficionado at the same time, these aren't regular household items,

Carlos. The killer wouldn't have found these in a drawer somewhere in here.'

Garcia crossed to the other side of the living room.

'He would've brought them with him,' he said in conclusion.

Hunter nodded and Garcia knew exactly what that meant – this hadn't been a spur-of-the-moment attack. All that savagery had been intentionally planned. Everything about this crime scene had a meaning.

Five

While they waited for a full forensics team to finally arrive at the house, Hunter and Garcia checked the rest of the property for signs of a break-in. They didn't find any.

None of the windows were broken and none seemed to have been tampered with either. The front door, together with the one that led from the kitchen to the small courtyard at the back of the house, also seemed intact.

Inside Melissa Hawthorne's bedroom, they did find her handbag on the bedside table. It contained a purse with eighteen dollars in cash, a few makeup items, her driver's license, a packet of gum, two credit cards, a hairbrush and a couple of old shopping receipts – no cellphone. They checked every drawer, every pocket of every item of clothing in her wardrobe, and every handbag they could find inside the house – no phone. They checked under the bed, under the sofa and under its cushions – still no phone. Hunter and Garcia both found that very interesting.

They had just stepped back into the living room, when Dr. Susan Slater walked through the front door, immediately followed by three other forensics agents, all of them suited up in white, hooded coveralls. As their eyes found the victim hanging in mid-air by her mouth, all four of them stopped dead. Despite all their experience and all the terrifying brutality that they had seen over the years, they all seemed shocked.

'Jesus!' the youngest of the agents murmured, slowly placing the tools case he had with him on the floor. 'Is that a fishing hook?'

'That's correct,' Hunter replied.

'Let's get all this photographed, quick,' Dr. Slater said, turning to address the team photographer.

'I'm all over it,' the young agent replied, adjusting his glasses on his nose and rounding the pool of blood on the floor to face the victim.

'Robert, Carlos.' Dr. Slater greeted both detectives with a simple head bob. 'How long have you guys been here?' She too approached the body.

Dr. Slater was one of the best and most accomplished lead forensics agents in the whole of California. In the past few years, she had led more forensics investigations for the UVC Unit than any other lead agent.

The other two team members began quickly setting up two powerful spotlights.

'About forty minutes,' Garcia replied. 'Give or take.'

'Single victim?' the doctor asked. 'Or are there any others?' She gestured to indicate the rest of the house.

'No, this is it,' Hunter replied, taking a couple of steps back to allow the agents to do their jobs.

'Any blood anywhere else?' Dr. Slater asked, angling her head to have a better look at the hook protruding from the victim's mouth. 'Signs of a struggle?'

'Not exactly,' Garcia said. 'The bed is unmade, which suggests that the victim didn't make the bed in the morning, was in bed when she heard a noise and went to investigate, or she was attacked while she was in bed, but that's all. No mess anywhere else, except for this.' He gestured toward the victim.

'This is ... pretty grotesque,' the doctor said, still studying the fish hook and the victim's viciously dislodged jaw. A moment later, she allowed herself to slowly examine the rest of body. 'Poor girl.' She shook her head. 'Just by looking at the swelling on her face and neck alone, I can tell you that she was still alive when that hook was pushed through her jaw.' She paused and peeked at both detectives. 'But you knew that already, didn't you?'

'I don't see much of a reason to tie her hands behind her back,' Garcia replied, 'if not to stop her from fighting.'

The doctor agreed with a nod.

'Lights on,' one of the agents announced, as they finished setting up the two forensics lights. He flicked a switch and the room burned in ultra-bright whiteness.

Dr. Slater carefully rounded the body. 'We are lucky to have the body in one piece.'

'What do you mean?' Garcia asked.

'Her mandible is severely dislocated,' she indicated as she explained. 'Both of her jaw joints have completely come undone, which isn't surprising, given that her whole body is being held up in mid-air exclusively by her lower jaw. The significant swelling indicates that ligaments and muscles have also ruptured around her neck and lower half of her face, and right here ...' The doctor indicated where the victim's lower jaw was supposed to be attached to her skull. 'You can see signs that the skin and some of the flesh are tearing.'

'If she were any heavier,' Hunter said, understanding what Dr. Slater was referring to, 'maybe by about twenty more pounds, or so – there's a chance that her jaw wouldn't have held for as long as it has.'

'That's right,' the doctor agreed. 'But even at her low weight, I'd say that we aren't that far from the total rupturing of muscles and ligaments, and tearing of the skin and flesh. If that had happened already, the body pressure would've caused her entire lower jaw to rip from her face and the body would've come crashing to the floor. No doubt an even more horrifying scene than what we already have here.'

Garcia cringed at the mental image.

'Do you think that was the killer's original intention?' he asked, but immediately lifted his hands in surrender. He knew that Dr. Slater had no way of knowing that. 'I'm sorry. Stupid question.'

'Who knows,' she replied anyway. 'But it wouldn't surprise me if it were. What I *can* tell you is that what seems to have kept it all together in the end was rigor mortis, which as we all know, toughens the muscle and ligament fibers. That hardening of the fibers has added a new resistance layer against all the tearing and rupturing.' She used her thumb and forefinger to lightly squeeze the victim's left biceps. 'Rigor mortis is well on its way. Ballpark guess – I'd say that she's been dead for at least ten hours. She was definitely murdered in the early hours of the morning. Not last night.'

Instinctively, Garcia consulted his watch. 'I'll instruct the officers outside to start a door-to-door,' he told Hunter. 'This road and a few of the neighboring ones as well. Maybe someone has noticed something out of the ordinary – a vehicle . . . someone wandering the streets . . . either late last night, or in the very early hours of this morning.'

Hunter nodded his agreement.

'I'm done with the body,' the photographer announced. 'I'll move on to the scene details.'

'Great,' Dr. Slater replied. 'Let's get her down.' She turned to face the tallest of the agents in her team, who stood at six-foot one. 'Shaun, while Mike and I hold her up, you unhook her from the rope.'

Shaun nodded and moved around to face the body.

'Need any help?' Hunter asked.

'Nah, we'll be OK,' the doctor replied.

Hunter and Garcia stepped out of the way, while Dr. Slater and Mike lifted the body up to ease the pressure on her jaw. As they did, Shaun reached up to the hook.

'Easy, Shaun,' Dr. Slater cautioned him. 'I'm sure that the hook has fractured her jaw in more ways than one. The bone might easily splinter.'

Shaun was as careful as he could be, and even so, it took him around a minute and a half to finally unhook Melissa Hawthorne from the rope. As the hook came free, a slab of flesh of about two squared inches fell onto the pool of blood, splattering some of it in all directions.

'Damn,' Garcia said, as he cringed.

'We need to bag that,' Dr. Slater said, nodding at it. 'That's her tongue.'

Six

Hunter and Garcia stayed with the forensics team until they were done processing the crime scene and the rest of the house. After that, instead of returning to Garcia's barbeque, Hunter stepped outside to try to get as much information as he could out of Janet Lang, Melissa Hawthorne's stepsister, while Garcia moved on to helping the uniformed officers with the door-to-door enquiries.

Forensics did find a couple of sets of fingerprints in the house. The first set was found in every room, clearly belonging to the victim herself, which was confirmed after a quick on-site analysis. The second set was found mainly in the living room/kitchen area, and though it was still to be confirmed, the assumption was that the prints belonged to the victim's younger sister, Janet Lang, the person who had found the body.

Forensics had also collected a few different hairs and fibers that were found on the floor inside the victim's bedroom and on her bed, but other than that and the props that the killer had used to hoist the victim up in the kitchen, nothing else was found that they deemed of any significance.

They also confirmed that there were no indications of forced entry anywhere – not on the doors, front and back, or on any of the windows.

The door-to-door had, so far, proved to be fairly unsuccessful. No one, not the next-door neighbors or anyone else on the victim's street, had seen anything or anyone that they considered suspicious, either on Saturday night or in the early hours of Sunday morning. The next-door neighbors also reported hearing no loud noises either. No screams or sounds that could've been the result of a struggle.

'This can't have been this killer's first crime,' Garcia said, as he and Hunter got back to his car. 'It's too clean . . . too elaborate . . . too well thought out.'

Hunter paused and looked up at the star-filled sky. He couldn't quite disagree with Garcia. It was a well-known fact that serial killers tended to refine their methods through time, escalating as they got more confident. Their first crimes, murder or not, tended to be a little sloppy . . . most of the time impulsive and badly planned. Very, very rarely would a killer go from 'no murder at all' to something sophisticated and well planned, like what they'd seen inside that house. When that happened, it almost always indicated a severe level of detachment in the perpetrator.

The lack of evidence left behind – fingerprints, DNA, footprints, forced entry, etc. – wasn't that much of a surprise. With so many films and TV shows out there themed around CSI and forensics, anyone could learn the basics of suppressing evidence in one sitting.

True, there was no evidence at the moment to suggest that this had been the work of a serial killer, and both Hunter and Garcia hoped to high heaven that that was the case, but the principle was the same. Nothing in the crime scene looked like this was the killer's first ever crime.

'I know,' Hunter said back.

'Maybe we should check the national database,' Garcia suggested. 'Cross-referencing murders for anything similar . . .' He thought about it for a heartbeat. 'Or even remotely similar.'

Hunter nodded in agreement. 'I'll get Research onto it first thing in the morning.'

Seven

By nine o'clock the next morning, Dr. Carolyn Hove, the Chief Medical Examiner for the Los Angeles County Department of Medical Examiner – Coroner, had already scrubbed up and made her way into Autopsy Theater One, at the end of a long and brightly lit corridor, down in the basement of the main coroner's building.

The LA County Department of Medical Examiner – Coroner was one of the busiest coroners in the whole of the USA, and despite its team of pathologists performing anywhere between twenty to forty autopsy examinations every day, the workload would still inevitably accumulate, especially over the weekends.

Most bodies, as they arrived at the LACDC, would be added to the back of the post mortem examination queue, but there were some exceptions to that rule. Cases marked as urgent by the investigating officers would usually take priority over certain other cases, but that priority would still be at the discretion of the Chief Medical Examiner. Another exception would be new arrivals that belonged to an investigation conducted by the LAPD UVC Unit. Due to the nature of their investigations, those would always take precedence even over urgent cases sent in by any other department, and that was why Melissa Hawthorne's body had already been brought into Autopsy Theater One and transferred onto the second of the two large, stainless-steel autopsy tables at the center of the large sterile room.

Her body was lying on its back, uncovered, with her arms loosely resting by the sides of her torso. Livor mortis, the discoloration of the skin due to the gravitation of blood after death, had made her legs look significantly darker than the rest of her body. Her skin appeared waxy and rubbery, which indicated that she had been brought into the morgue and stored into a cold-storage locker just a little under twenty-four hours after her death.

'Wow!' Dr. Hove said, as she paused by the autopsy table. 'This is . . . certainly something different.'

Though Melissa's head was lying flat against the table surface, the damage to her jawbone, together with the rupture of her facial muscles and ligaments had been so severe that her chin was resting against her chest.

Nathan Reese, one of the three junior pathologists who usually assisted Dr. Hove, was standing to the left of the autopsy table.

'How does something like this even happen?' he asked, his eyes fixed on the body's facial deformation. 'I mean . . . did somebody just rip her mouth open until she was dead?'

'She was hung by her mouth,' Dr. Hove told him, reading from the admission file that she had with her. 'The perp used a fish hook to do so.'

'Jesus!'

'I know.' Dr. Hove put down the admission file and gloved up. 'I take it that all the joints have been flexed, right?'

To make sure that rigor mortis had already come and gone, joint flexing was a normal procedure when dealing with new arrivals, where their post mortem examinations had been brought forward for one reason or another.

'Yes, the orderly who brought her in has flexed them. We're good to go, Doc.'

'OK, let's make a start.'

Nathan adjusted the microphone that hung from the ceiling,

directly above the examination table and switched on the digital voice recorder.

Dr. Hove began by stating the date and time, followed by the assigned case number. Next, she spent a couple of minutes describing the general state of the body, before moving on to a much more detailed external analysis, where she began by studying the victim's neck.

No strangulation bruises.

A quick touch-examination revealed that neither the larynx nor the trachea had collapsed. The hyoid bone in the victim's neck also didn't seemed to have been fractured in any way.

Dr. Hove used her thumb and index finger to pull open the victim's eyelids. With the help of a magnifying glasses headset with a directional light, she carefully studied the victim's ocular globe. As expected, her cornea was cloudy and opaque, but what the doctor was looking for was a phenomenon called petechiae – minute red specks that could be dotting the victim's eyes and eyelids. Those signified tiny hemorrhages in blood vessels that, for a number of different reasons, could occur anywhere in the body, but when found in the eyes or eyelids were usually due to a blockage of the respiratory system, consistent with suffocation or asphyxiation.

The victim's eyes and eyelids were both dotted with them.

'Death resulted from lack of oxygen,' Dr. Hove announced to the microphone. 'That lack of oxygen did *not* derive from strangulation.'

'Poor woman,' Nathan said with a shake of the head. 'No one deserves to die like this.'

Dr. Hove sent him a judging stare.

'I know,' he said, lifting both gloved hands. 'I'm not getting emotional, Doc. I'm just making an observation that no human being deserves to go this way, that's all.'

The rest of Melissa's body's external examination lasted another five minutes or so. It revealed no further surprises.

Next, the doctor needed to check all of the body's cavities for signs of aggression, sexual or otherwise. She started with the vagina.

The skin all around the vulva, including both of the upper thighs, showed no bruises or hematomas – nothing that would give Dr. Hove any cause for concern.

Her next step was to examine the vagina's internal walls, but she didn't get that far.

As she used her thumb and index finger to spread the walls, she paused, her eyes squinting at something.

'Hold on a sec,' she said, angling her head to one side to get a better line of vision.

'Something wrong?' Nathan asked, repositioning himself around the autopsy table.

'I'm not sure. Can you pass me a pair of locking forceps, please?'

'Would you like the speculum as well?' Nathan asked, handing Dr. Hove a pair of surgical locking forceps.

'Maybe in a minute,' Dr. Hove replied, as she inserted not much more than the tip of the forceps into the vagina. 'It looks like a foreign object was left inside of her,' she announced, for the benefit of the digital recording.

Behind her, Nathan bent over at the waist, trying to look over the doctor's right shoulder. As he did, he heard the instrument in her hand click.

'Got it,' Dr. Hove said, before slowly extracting whatever it was that the forceps had clipped on to.

Securely gripped at the tip of the surgical instrument was a small, transparent, grip-seal plastic bag of about two square inches. It was clear to see that the bag wasn't empty.

'Are those drugs?' Nathan asked.

Dr. Hove straightened up her body and lifted the forceps up to the light.

'I'm not too sure.'

Once again, for the benefit of the digital recording, Dr. Hove dictated what she had retrieved and from where.

Nathan tilted his head left then right, trying to better understand what they were looking at.

Still keeping the bag at the tip of the forceps, Dr. Hove gave it a little shake.

'It looks like we have a folded piece of white paper inside a plastic bag.'

'A small paper envelope, perhaps?' Nathan again.

'I don't think so.' Dr. Hove shook her head, after looking at the bag through her magnifying glasses. 'But let's find out, shall we?'

She flipped the glasses back up onto the headset then turned around and placed the small bag on a stainless-steel worktop.

Nathan quickly joined her.

From the instruments tray, Dr. Hove retrieved a second pair of locking forceps. It didn't take her long to pull open the bag's grip-seal and extract the folded piece of paper from inside.

'It doesn't look like a drugs envelope,' Nathan commented.

Dr. Hove's eyes moved to him.

'I'm just saying.' Nathan gave her a shrug.

'It doesn't look like an envelope at all,' she agreed before using both forceps to finally unfold the strip of paper, which had been folded three times. As she undid the last fold, she paused.

'What the hell?' Nathan said from behind Dr. Hove. 'What does that even mean?'

'It means that we better call the UVC Unit.'

Eight

For Hunter, that Monday morning started with a trip back to Melissa Hawthorne's house. He got there before the sun was up.

Albeit necessary, the forensics circus provided a craziness of movement, people, noise, and lights that was a whole world away from what the original crime scene would have been like. Hunter wanted to walk the scene alone, no distractions, with the lights out and with the house as quiet and as still as it would've been just before Melissa was killed.

He didn't really believe in premonition, omen, clairvoyance, or whatever name people liked to call it. He also didn't believe that by revisiting the crime scene on his own, he would somehow get abrupt visions of what had really happened in there. What he did believe in, what he knew existed was evil ... the human kind ... the kind that could lead someone to rip the life out of a young woman in one of the vilest ways Hunter had ever seen. And evil, sometimes, would leave clues behind.

That morning, Hunter spent almost two hours inside Melissa Hawthorne's house. Most of that time was spent in the living room/kitchen area. The pool of blood had been cleaned from the floor, but a stain still remained, marking the exact location where a young woman had been robbed of her life. The room now also carried a particular smell that came with the aftermath of every crime scene. It wasn't the putrid smell of decomposition. That was a very different smell all together, and Melissa Hawthorne's body had been days away from entering that stage when found. No, this was a peculiar smell – part sweet, part heavy iron, and part disinfectant agents. The crime scene clean up team had, once again, done their job well.

Standing in the exact spot where Melissa's body had been found, his feet at the center of where the pool of blood had once been, arms sunk to his sides, Hunter looked up at the ceiling, stretching his neck until he couldn't anymore. He held his head in that position for a few seconds before moving his chin forward as much as he possibly could to also stretch his lower jaw. As he did, he felt a pull under his tongue, followed by his throat constricting.

Hunter held himself in that new position for several seconds, trying as best as he could to imagine Melissa Hawthorne's agony ... her desperation ... her pain ... her panic ... her terror ... because she knew that no one was coming for her. She knew she would die.

All of a sudden, the skin on both of his arms turned into gooseflesh and he felt as if something was trying to dig a hole into his stomach.

And there it was, as if Hunter could sense it – evil. Its ugly, invisible presence somehow still lingering in the air ... still embedded in those walls, like some sort of 'catch me if you can' tease.

Hunter lasted less than a minute in that position before he had to let go.

He stepped back from the bloodstain on the floor and looked around the kitchen one last time.

The gooseflesh didn't go away.

The pit in his stomach didn't go away.

True, death and evil had stained that house for ever, but what had really left Hunter with a very bad taste in his mouth was that he knew from experience that that sort of evil, personal or not, very rarely came in a single dose. More often than not, the urge to hurt . . . to kill again . . . was too strong, practically impossible to contain. It was just a matter of time.

Nine

The LAPD's Ultra Violent Crimes Unit's office was located at the far end of the Robbery Homicide Division's floor, inside the famous Police Administration Building in Downtown LA. When Hunter got there, about half an hour after leaving Melissa Hawthorne's house, Garcia was standing before the picture board, which was pushed up against the south wall. He had just finished pinning up the last of the forensics photos they had received from CSI.

'Morning,' Hunter said, placing his jacket on the back of his chair and firing up his computer.

'The more I look at these,' Garcia replied, his eyes never leaving the board, 'the less sense they make.'

Hunter didn't join Garcia by the board. He didn't take a seat at his desk either. In silence, he simply looked at the photos from where he was standing.

'Yes,' Garcia continued, 'I know that every murder, especially the ones assigned to our unit, are in essence, senseless, but I'm not talking about the crime itself, or the motive, or the fact that this kind of sadism has to be a personal affair. I'm talking about the method.' He shook his head as his eyes slowly moved from one picture to another. 'This killer didn't strangle her, he didn't cut her into pieces, he didn't gut her, he didn't even eat her flesh. No, he really did string her out by her mouth ... like a fish ... in her own living room. "Senseless" doesn't quite cut it here.'

Before Hunter could say anything, the captain of the LAPD's Robbery Homicide Division, Barbara Blake, pushed open the door to their office and stepped inside. Without acknowledging either detective, she walked straight up to the picture board and paused next to Garcia, her eyes taking in the photos, her brain trying to understand them.

'What in the hell of hells?' she murmured to herself.

'Good morning, Captain,' Garcia said, his stare moving to her for just an instant.

The captain's long, auburn hair was elegantly styled into a twisted bun. She wore a white silk blouse that was neatly tucked into a black tube skirt and black low-heel shoes. Her makeup was subtle, professional, and still very feminine. Her dainty earrings matched her black beaded necklace. In her right hand, she held a case file.

It took her a few more seconds before she looked back at Garcia, then at Hunter.

'What the hell is wrong with humanity?' she said, her voice sad and angry in equal measures. 'Why? What would be the point in doing something like this to another human being?'

'Because it means something to the killer,' Hunter replied, finally taking a seat at his desk.

'What does?' Captain Blake pushed.

'All of it, Captain,' Hunter replied before his gaze moved to Garcia. 'All that senselessness. Everything you see on those pictures. It all means something to the killer.'

She allowed her eyes to study on the horror displayed on that board for a moment longer. 'Including the victim?'

'Especially the victim,' Garcia was the one who replied. 'This is too up close and personal, Captain . . . too intimate.'

'Personal as in – the killer wanted her in particular?' The captain pointed at a photo of Melissa Hawthorne. 'Or are we talking about what the victim represents?'

Hunter sat back on his chair. 'Are you asking us if we think this is a hate crime?'

'I am,' the captain confirmed, broadly gesturing at the board. 'Because to me, this is the image of "hate" … pure hate … pure ignorance. The kind of hate and ignorance that very few people are capable of, and among those who are, I can't discard race fanatics.' She paused, taking a breath to steady her voice. 'Since the Black Lives Matter movement, a lot of good in this country's racial divide has occurred, but at the same time, little pockets of ultra-extreme racists have sprung up just about everywhere. Many of them right here in LA. You both know that. And this exact same question will be asked by the press, by the Chief of Police, by the Mayor, and probably by the Governor of California as well, so let me ask you again because we won't be able to escape it – do you think that this is race-related?'

'Right now, nothing can be discarded, Captain,' Garcia replied first. 'We don't know much at this point. It's been less than twenty-four hours since she's been murdered, but we're working on it.'

Captain Blake's attention returned to the board. A few seconds later, her slim index finger pointed at a specific photo. 'What sort of oversized fishing hook is this? Can it be traced?'

'It's a giant shark hook,' Garcia replied. 'Also used for alligators. Stainless steel. It can withstand in excess of nine hundred pounds of weight.'

The captain pursed her lips as she looked back at her detective. 'People fish for alligators?'

'They do.' Hunter, this time.

'In California?' she challenged.

'That's just it, Captain,' Garcia took the lead again. 'The hook can be used for alligators, as well as sharks, or any large fish – tuna, swordfish, you name it – and those, we've got plenty of over here.'

'So tracing the hook is out of the question?'

'Practically impossible,' Garcia informed her. 'It could've been bought online from any fishing shop anywhere on the planet, not to mention a private sale via eBay, or any of the many private sale sites that can be found online.'

Captain Blake took a step back from the board. 'OK, so who is she? Do we know that much?'

Hunter reached for his notepad.

'Her name was Melissa Hawthorne,' he read from it. 'Twenty-nine years of age, born right here in Los Angeles and a resident of Leimert Park. She lived alone and was a hairstylist. Worked for a small independent hair salon called Hues of Curls on Crenshaw Boulevard. Not that far from where she lived, actually. Her mother, Joanna, passed away a year and a half ago – cancer.'

'How about her father?' the captain queried.

'Her biological father has been out of the picture from the get-go,' Hunter told her. 'From what we understand, Melissa never met him. For the next five years, Mrs. Hawthorne had a string of different live-in boyfriends, until she remarried Clayton Lang.'

Captain Blake shifted on her feet. 'Any history of abuse by any of the live-in boyfriends?'

'We're looking into it,' Hunter informed her before moving on. 'Mr. Lang also had a daughter from a previous relationship – Janet – three years Melissa's junior. Despite the two girls not being blood sisters, they got along as if they were twins. Janet was the one who found the body.' Captain Blake momentarily closed her eyes and used the tip of her index finger to lightly rub between her eyebrows. 'When was that?'

'Yesterday at around 11:30 a.m.' Hunter flipped a page on the notepad. 'Melissa and Janet were supposed to have gone jogging in Kenneth Hahn Lower Park, prior to going out for brunch around the same area. Meeting time was 11 a.m. After a few text messages and a couple of unanswered calls to her sister, Janet got worried and decided to drop by. The front door was left unlocked.'

'Anybody else had keys to her house? Boyfriend?'

'According to her sister, only Janet herself had a copy. Melissa had no boyfriend. At least not anymore.'

'And that means what, exactly?' Captain Blake asked, frowning at Hunter.

'It means that she did have a boyfriend, but they split up some time ago. Janet wasn't exactly sure when, but it was less than a year ago.'

'Do we have a name for this ex-boyfriend?' the captain pushed. 'Maybe he had a key and never gave it back. Do we know why the relationship ended?'

'His name is Kevin Garrison. The information we got from Janet is that the relationship ended because he was cheating on Miss Hawthorne.'

Captain Blake pulled a face that practically spelled the word 'typical'.

'That's all we have on him so far,' Hunter continued. 'But we'll find him. There are a lot of people we need to talk to.'

'Who are you starting with?'

'Janet and Melissa were both at a friend's birthday party on Saturday evening,' Hunter read from his notes. 'The friend's name is Kelly-Ann Teller. According to Janet, Miss Teller and Melissa were best friends.'

'What time did they leave the party?' Blake asked. 'The two sisters?'

'They didn't leave together,' Hunter explained. 'Janet was there with her boyfriend and they left sometime after midnight. Melissa stayed behind.'

'How did she get home? Did she drive?'

'No. She doesn't own a car. We suppose she took a cab, but we don't know for certain yet. We'll be talking to Kelly-Ann Teller today. Hopefully we'll get a list of all the guests that were at her party on Saturday evening and then talk to each one individually.

Also, since she was Miss Hawthorne's best friend, Miss Teller might know a little more about Kevin, the ex-boyfriend.'

'Did the victim go to this party by herself?' Captain Blake looked at Hunter. 'Or did she take a date? Do we know?'

'According to her sister, Miss Hawthorne went to the party on her own, but here comes the kicker: she mentioned about going to the party on her social media . . . several times. In fact, she first mentioned it over a week ago. She even posted the date and the location.'

Captain Blake allowed her head to drop, as if defeated. 'Unbelievable. When will people learn to stop publicizing their lives?' She breathed out disappointment. 'How about her phone? Any calls to or from her phone on that night?'

'We don't know yet. Her phone hasn't been found.'

Captain Blake's brow creased as she looked back at her detectives.

'We looked everywhere,' Hunter reassured her. 'The phone is gone. We tried tracing it last night. The signal is dead.'

'So it's been destroyed.' Captain Blake didn't phrase it as a question.

'Most probably,' Hunter confirmed. 'We're getting in touch with her network provider for a copy of everything – text messages, phone calls, whatever we can get.'

'OK,' Captain Blake nodded at Hunter before facing Garcia again. 'Go on.'

'That's it,' he informed her. 'Janet Lang was in shock and could barely put a sentence together, which is no real surprise.' His head tilted slightly towards the picture board. 'It took Robert over an hour and a lot of patience just to squeeze this much information out of her.'

'I'll try again either later today or tomorrow morning,' Hunter said.

'How about this Clayton Lang?' the captain asked. 'Janet's father, any history on him?'

'He's also passed away around four years ago,' Hunter said. 'Heart attack. From what we understand, he was a great stepfather to Melissa.'

Captain Blake's gaze returned to the board. 'This ex-boyfriend of hers . . . Kevin, right?'

Garcia nodded.

'Any idea if he was involved in gang activity?'

Both detectives knew the reason for the captain's question. She was correct about the fact that the kind of hate and ignorance that the pictures on that board depicted was indeed a special kind. The kind that very few people were capable of, and certain LA gangs were internationally known for the brutality and sadism of some of their acts. Especially when those acts were intended as a lesson to others, or as revenge.

'Like Robert said, Captain,' Garcia said, 'we know basically nothing about this Kevin Garrison character, but we already talked to Captain Carmona of the LAPD Gang and Narcotics Division.' He shook his head as he indicated the board again. 'He's never seen or heard of anything like this before. If this is the work of a gang, it's something brand new.'

Right then, Hunter's desk phone rang.

'Detective Hunter,' he said, bringing the receiver to his ear. 'UVC Unit.'

'*Robert, it's Carolyn.*'

Dr. Hove's velvety but strong voice was no stranger to Hunter's ears.

'*I'm done with the autopsy of case . . .*' She read the case file number to Hunter. '*African-American female – I understand that this is your investigation?*'

'That's correct, Doc. Any interesting findings?'

Dr. Hove chuckled, but it carried no humor. '*Yes, I'd say so. May I suggest you drop by to have a look?*'

'Have a look?'

Garcia and Captain Blake's stare asked Hunter the same silent question.

'*It appears that whoever strung your victim up by the mouth left you a little present.*'

'Such as?'

'*We found a note.*'

'A note?'

Hard frowns from Garcia and Captain Blake.

'Where?' Hunter asked.

'*It was left inside of her.*'

Hunter knew exactly what that meant.

'OK, we're on our way.'

Ten

The main building at the LA County Department of Coroner was, in every sense, an impressive piece of architecture, clearly influenced by the Renaissance style. The façade of the old hospital turned morgue was a stylish combination of red bricks and light-gray lintels. The extravagant entrance stairway was flanked by a couple of gothic-looking lampposts, which added an extra pinch of charm to a beautiful building that ironically sheltered nothing but death.

In morning traffic, the short drive from the Police Administration Building to the LACDC took Hunter and Garcia just under ten minutes. As they stepped into the entrance lobby, Martha, the Jamaican receptionist with kind eyes and plumb cheeks, nodded courteously at them. She had perfectly mastered the art of the solemn-respectful face. Her greeting smiles were always gentle and polite, her facial expressions showed compassion and understanding, and her tone of voice had an almost soothing quality to it.

'Detectives,' she greeted Hunter and Garcia as they approached the reception counter, already placing two visitor badges on it.

'Martha,' Hunter replied, returning the courteous nod. 'How are the kids?'

'More expensive than ever,' she replied with a roll of the eyes. 'I hope you've been keeping well.' She pushed the visitor badges toward both of them. 'Dr. Hove is expecting you. She's in Autopsy Theater One, down in the basement.'

Hunter and Garcia had been to the LACDC so many times that they could practically navigate every corridor . . . in every floor . . . in every building . . . blindfolded.

Martha buzzed them through the security gate and they made their way to the staircase just past and to the right of the reception counter.

In the basement, they turned right at the end of the first corridor then left at the end of the following one. Directly in front of them was a set of double swing-doors.

The plate above the doors read: 'Autopsy Theater One'. Hunter pressed the button on the intercom and waited. Three seconds later, the door buzzed open and Hunter and Garcia stepped inside the large, winter-cold room, illuminated by two rows of fluorescent lights that ran the length of the ceiling. Two stainless steel autopsy tables dominated the main floor space – one fixed, one wheeled. Each was occupied by a body, covered by a white sheet. The two circular surgical-lights above both examination tables were switched off. A hospital-style gurney was parked next to a wall of body fridges. Dr. Hove was standing by the second examination table – the fixed one. She wore blue latex gloves and a long, white lab coverall over her regular clothes.

'Robert, Carlos.' She greeted each of them with a subdued head bob.

'We have a note?' Garcia asked, losing no time.

'Come have a look and I'll guide you through everything.' Dr. Hove gestured them closer as she spoke.

Hunter and Garcia gloved up and approached the autopsy table. Dr. Hove reached over, grabbed the two top extremities of the white sheet that covered the body and pulled it down to the body's waist.

'Oh Jesus, Doc!' Garcia gasped, his head jerking back slightly.

Hunter didn't flinch.

The body on the table in front of them was that of Melissa Hawthorne, but her face was now incomplete. The entire lower jaw was missing.

As part of the post-mortem examination, Dr. Hove had to cut through what was left of skin, muscles, tendons and ligaments, and remove the mandible in its entirety to determine the extent of the damage caused by the fishing hook and the pressure exerted on her jaw.

'What?' Dr. Hove asked. 'I thought you were at the crime scene.'

'I was, but so was her jaw. Dislocated and hanging by a thread, but it was still there.'

'You've seen . . . similar. I know that.'

'Similar, yes,' Garcia accepted. 'But even you have to admit that this is something else.'

The doctor's lips squeezed into a thin line. 'Yes, this is definitely something else.'

'So what have we got, Doc?' Hunter asked.

'Well,' Dr. Hove began. 'Just like Carlos mentioned, her mandible was severely dislocated. It was also fractured in nine different places.'

Garcia grimaced again.

'I'm going to skip the whole anatomical explanation about ruptured muscles and what have you because none of that would really interest you, but this will.' Dr. Hove guided their attention to something on a stainless steel worktop to her left. 'Her tongue was deliberately severed. Not by the hook that was forced into her mouth, but by a sharp instrument, something like a scalpel or a pair of scissors. The cut was clean.'

Garcia peeked at Hunter, who kept his full attention on Dr. Hove. They both knew that a victim's tongue being deliberately severed by a perpetrator could signify an act of revenge – payback for something that the victim had maybe said, or could've said.

'What's the official cause of death?' Hunter asked.

'It's actually a combination. She half suffocated, half drowned – both in her own blood.'

'Fuck!' Garcia breathed out, momentarily closing his eyes.

'The wound to her lower jaw was brutal,' Dr. Hove explained. 'Savagely so, and unfortunately, as I'm sure you already know, she was alive through it all.'

Hunter nodded once.

'I have no doubt that she passed out from the sheer pain of the perforation,' the doctor said. 'Without anesthesia, no one would be strong enough to withstand that sort of pain.' She drew everyone's attention back to the body. 'Despite the tremendous pain and the viciousness of the attack, the wound to her jaw didn't kill her. What it did do was fill her mouth with blood . . . too much blood.'

Garcia uncomfortably shifted his weight from one foot to another.

'In any other position,' Dr. Hove added, 'sitting down . . . laying down . . . standing up . . . whatever, she would've been able to spit out some of the blood from her mouth, but strung out through her jaw . . .' To demonstrate, the doctor threw her head back as far as it could go. 'This position is severely problematic for two reasons. One . . .' She pointed to her own throat. 'It constricts the throat, making swallowing anything, even saliva, a difficult job. Two – it creates a gravitational pull, so all the blood that inundated her mouth had nowhere else to go but down.' She indicated with her index finger. 'If she still had her tongue, she could've maybe moved it up and down, pushing some of the blood out of her mouth.'

'But the tongue was gone,' Garcia said, his eyes going back to the deformed face on the autopsy table.

Dr. Hove nodded. 'Her tongue was gone. All the blood in her mouth had nowhere else to go but down to her already constricted throat. She swallowed some, of course, but it was too much blood. In time, it obstructed her respiratory system. Blood was found inside her lungs, just like water is found in the lungs of a drowning victim. Like I said, she partially drowned, partially suffocated. Her eyes were dotted with petechiae. Blood toxicology will still be a couple of days, but I suppose that she was sedated before being tied up.'

Silence ruled the room for a moment.

'How long do you think she would've lasted before she finally suffocated?' Hunter asked.

'Not very long,' Dr. Hove confirmed. 'Just a matter of minutes, really, but even seconds would've felt like an eternity for her. The pain ... the agony ... the desperation to take in oxygen.' She shook her head in disgust. 'This woman's last few minutes on this planet were undoubtedly the most painful minutes of her entire life.'

Another silent moment went by before Garcia spoke.

'Was she sexually assaulted?' he asked.

'Not in the way that you are thinking. She wasn't raped,' Dr. Hove explained, as she turned to direct their attention to a strip of paper on the instruments trolley. 'But this was left inside her vaginal canal.'

Hunter and Garcia approached the trolley.

The strip of paper contained a single, handwritten sentence:

'Through these eyes, no one will ever look as perfect as you did.'

Eleven

'"Through these eyes,"' Garcia quoted, as soon as he and Hunter got back into his car, '"no one will ever look as perfect as you did"? What the hell do you think that means?'

Hunter pressed his lips together as he shook his head. 'I'm not really sure. It could be a love poem ... or a line from a poem. It could be the lyrics to a song ... a line from a movie ... or something that the perp wrote himself.'

'So you never seen it before?' Garcia asked.

Hunter frowned at him. 'No. Why would I?'

'Because you read a hell of a lot ... a lot more than I do. Just gambling on the chance that you had come across it somewhere.'

'Not that I can remember, but I'll get Research on it.'

Once they got back at the Police Administration Building, Hunter and Garcia decided to split the afternoon workload. Garcia went to see Kelly-Ann Teller, Melissa Hawthorne's friend, whose party she was at on Saturday evening, while Hunter was once again tasked with trying to interview Melissa's stepsister, Janet, who shared a small one-bedroom flat with her boyfriend, Thomas Molina. The apartment was located less than five blocks away from Melissa's house.

Hunter parked on the street, directly in front of Janet's apartment block. It was a simple building, with a dirty yellow façade, white windows and a couple of small balconies showing at the front of it. The intercom at the entrance didn't work, but the lock mechanism at the front door was busted, which meant that the door never really locked. Hunter pushed it open and took the stairs up to the first floor.

Janet's apartment was number 102, the second door on the right down a narrow, windowless corridor, where one of the two fluorescent tubes along the ceiling flickered on and off like a strobe light. There was no doorbell. Hunter knocked three times and waited. He had called beforehand and spoken to Thomas, Janet's boyfriend, who had said that he wasn't sure how much help Janet could be. She was still in shock and since yesterday had barely done anything else but cry. Last night, after a hysterical episode, she'd had to be sedated to fall asleep.

Hunter had been in that same situation so many times that he had lost count. More often than not, interviewing someone who was still in shock resulted in either very unreliable information, or absolutely nothing at all, but Janet hadn't been an eyewitness to a crime. What Hunter wanted to ask her didn't rely on her immediate memory.

He was about to knock again when he heard heavy footsteps approaching from inside. The peephole darkened and Hunter held up his credentials. A couple of seconds later, the door unlocked and it was pulled open by a well-built, six-foot-one African-American man, wearing black jogging trousers and a purple and yellow LA Lakers jersey with the number eight across his chest. His exposed arms were covered in black-and-gray tattoos. His hair was cut short, military style, and his seven o'clock shadow had been expertly trimmed to accentuate his jaw. He looked to be around twenty-five years old.

'Thomas Molina?' Hunter asked, locking eyes with the man, who regarded Hunter and his credentials for another few seconds. 'I'm Detective Robert Hunter of the LAPD. We spoke on the phone earlier.'

'Call me Tom,' the man replied, his voice matching his strong frame. 'Only my mother calls me Thomas, and she only does it when she's angry.'

Hunter waited, but Tom said nothing else.

'Is it OK if I come in?'

Tom hesitated for a moment. 'I don't know, man. Like I said on the phone, since yesterday, Janet has done nothing else but cry, sometimes hysterically. She's finally calmed down for a little. Talking to her will just start things up again.'

'I understand, Tom, and if it were an option, I would not bother Miss Lang or you, but it really is important to our investigation that I talk to her. I'll be as brief as I possibly can.'

Tom's head angled to one side as he considered Hunter's words. 'Alright, come in,' he finally agreed, pulling the door fully open and taking a step to his left.

'Thank you.'

The front door opened directly into the apartment's living room, which was small and modestly furnished. Janet was sitting by the room's only window, which faced west, at a small circular table with four chairs. On the table next to her was a small plate with an uneaten ham and cheese sandwich and a glass of milk.

She didn't acknowledge Hunter.

'I told you, bro,' Tom whispered, as he gestured towards Janet. 'She ain't talking much. She ain't even eating.'

Janet Lang seemed to be a couple of inches taller and maybe twenty pounds heavier than her sister. Her black hair was cut low to the nape of her neck, framing an almond-shaped face. Her eyes were wide, but slightly tilted up at the corners. Her skin was also half a shade lighter than Melissa's. Her arms were slender and her hands small and delicate. Most of the red varnish on her fingernails was chipped.

'Has she taken any medication in the past two to three hours?' Hunter asked. 'Sedatives . . . anything?'

'No, bro, nothing,' Tom replied.

Hunter nodded his understanding before approaching the table and taking a seat across from Janet.

Her eyes didn't move from the world outside her window.

'Hello, Miss Lang,' he said in a steady, almost doctor-like voice. 'Remember me? I'm Detective Robert Hunter. We spoke yesterday.'

No movement from Janet, except for tears that started to well up in her eyes again.

'Miss Lang,' Hunter began. 'I know that this is terribly hard for you right now. I know that you don't feel like talking . . . not to me or anyone, but if I could ask you just a few more questions, it could really help our investigation.' He paused and waited.

Without looking back at Hunter, Janet squeezed her eyes and tears began running down her cheeks. She swallowed dry.

From his jacket pocket, Hunter retrieved a paper tissue and offered it to Janet.

She didn't take it.

From experience, Hunter knew that in general, the best approach in these situations was to simply ask the first question. That was exactly what he was about to do when Janet beat him to the punch.

'Why?' she asked, as a teardrop ran to the tip of her nose. 'Why would someone do something like that to Mel?'

Hunter understood that Janet wasn't really expecting a reply because no reply would ever make sense. She was just venting her anger . . . her anguish . . . her pain. He stayed silent, allowing her to carry on.

'Did you see what was done to my sister?' There was so much pain in Janet's voice that it squeaked at times. 'Did you see her face . . . her mouth? What kind of monster could do something like that to another human being? To someone like Mel?'

She broke down in sobs, as her entire body shook with emotion.

Hunter felt an odd sadness wrap itself around his heart and slowly begin to squeeze. Those sobs . . . that pain . . . that was just the beginning for what was to come for Janet Lang. Finding the tortured and mutilated body of a loved one had the power to do much more than just fracture a human mind on the spot. It could completely obliterate it. Only time would tell the sort of damage that Janet's psyche had sustained.

Hunter didn't push. Instead, he allowed his gaze to move on to a shelving unit on the corner, where several photographs were displayed in picture frames. Melissa appeared in most of them. Always smiling a smile that seemed bigger than her . . . bigger than the world. Janet's framed high school diploma split the photo frames into two groups.

'Mel was the sweetest person you'd ever meet,' Janet said, as if she had followed Hunter's stare to the photos. Her voice was still faltering. 'She was friendly, compassionate, understanding, forgiving . . .' She slightly shook her head. 'She never talked bad about anyone. Always saw the good in others . . . never the bad. She was one of those people who always had a smile ready, and her smile was contagious. Always with an uplifting comment, no matter how bad the situation was.' Janet finally broke eye contact with the window to look at Hunter. 'She was more than my big sister. She was my best friend. The one person that was always there for me, no matter what. The one person I could count on, no matter what. Never judging . . . never criticizing . . . always helping. I looked up to her so much.'

Hunter stayed quiet for two reasons: one, words would be the most meaningless things he could offer Janet right at that moment; and two, she was talking, which was exactly what Hunter needed. He just had to find the right moment for his questions.

He once again held out the tissue for her, and once again, she didn't take it, preferring to use her left hand to wipe the tears from her face before chuckling angrily.

'Typical,' she said almost derisively, as her stare returned to the window.

'What is?' Hunter asked.

'That a white cop would be assigned to investigate the murder of a black woman.' Janet turned her neck to lock eyes with Hunter. 'No offense, Detective . . . ?'

'Hunter.'

'No offense, Detective Hunter.' Despite all the sadness, an underlying anger punctuated by hopelessness made itself heard in Janet's voice. 'I'm sure that you are good at what you do, but this is still America, where so-called police officers will kneel on a black man's neck until he's dead and say that they were doing their duty.'

Through the corner of his eyes, Hunter saw Tom, who had taken a seat on the sofa, nod approvingly.

'Our system is broken and corrupt,' Janet said, as she sniffled and wiped some more tears from her face. 'Even more so when the subject is a black person.'

Hunter wasn't really expecting that sort of response, but he wasn't surprised, or offended. The events that had, not so long ago, taken place in the USA and led to the rise of the Black Lives Matter movement had become infamous all over the world. The footage that had gone viral had been indisputable. The brutality that had been used by the police had been inexcusable and shameful.

The air around them seemed to thicken with the pain in Janet's tone.

Hunter breathed it all in and held her stare.

'I understand how you feel, Miss Lang,' he said, being careful not to sound condescending. 'I also understand that there's nothing I can say that will change that feeling. All I can tell you . . . all I can give you . . . is my word that I will do everything I can to bring the person responsible for what happened to your sister to justice.'

'Your word?' Janet shot back with a sarcastic chuckle. 'You're giving me your word, are you?'

Hunter lifted his hands in surrender. 'I know that my word means absolutely nothing to you. To you, I'm just another white cop following protocol.' He paused and exhaled. 'But my word is the most important thing . . . the only valuable thing I have, Miss Lang. To me, it means everything. I have never once broken it.'

Through her tears, Janet regarded Hunter quite intensely. In his eyes, she recognized something she didn't see too often – sincerity. She sniffled again and Hunter, for the third time, offered her the paper tissue he was holding.

This time, she finally took it and dabbed it against her nose.

Hunter seized the opportunity.

'Yesterday you told me that your sister wasn't seeing anyone. Romantically, I mean. Is that correct?'

Janet sucked in a lumpy breath through her nose before nodding.

'And you're sure that she would've told you if she were?'

Another nod from Janet. 'We talked about everything. Mel would have no reason to hide something like that from anyone, least of all me. She was a very confident person.'

'OK,' Hunter accepted it. 'And you told me that the last time you spoke with your sister before the party on Saturday had been on Wednesday, is that right?'

This time Janet didn't actually nod. She simply allowed her head to drop forward.

'They met for dinner.' The comment came from Tom. 'Janet and Mel used to meet for either dinner or lunch at least twice a week. The last time was on Wednesday.'

'We also spoke briefly on the phone on Saturday,' Janet added. 'Before the party. I just asked her what she'd be wearing and what time she was thinking about getting there.'

Hunter acknowledged her reply. 'And your sister didn't mention anything about anyone that she might've met recently?'

It took Janet a few seconds to respond. 'No.'

'So as far as you are aware, the last person she dated, or had any sort of romantic connections with, was Kevin Garrison, her ex-boyfriend.'

Janet went silent again, her eyes wandering the room like lost souls.

'Miss Lang?' Hunter said, trying to bring her attention back to him.

Two more seconds went by before her gaze settled on his face and she nodded. 'Yes. Kevin.'

'How long were they together for, do you remember?'

Janet went quiet again, but Tom offered a response.

'They started dating roughly around the same time as Janet and I did,' he said. 'We've been together for just over two and a half years, so I'd say that they were together for about two; am I right, babe?'

Janet finally nodded. 'Yes, about two years.' Her voice wavered again.

'And you said that they split up around six or seven months ago, is that correct?'

'Yeah.'

Hunter stayed on the subject. 'Was he ever violent towards your sister?'

'Kevin was an asshole in many ways.' Tom again. 'No doubt about that, but he was never violent towards Mel, not even verbally. At least not that we know of.' His gaze moved to Janet, who shook her head.

'No,' she confirmed. 'He wasn't a violent person.'

'Do you know where I can find him? I'd like to ask him a few questions.'

Janet didn't answer. Instead, she looked down at her hands and at the crumpled-up tissue she was holding.

'Kevin is a gym buff,' Tom took over again. 'Trains five to six times a week. Early mornings.'

'Do you know which gym?'

'Yeah, he trains at SixPax in Culver City.'

'How about any admirers?' Hunter ventured. 'You know ... people who followed her on social media. Sometimes these people can become problematic. Did she ever mention anything about anyone who she thought was a little too insistent, or creepy, or maybe someone who made her feel uncomfortable in some way? Maybe sending her unsolicited pictures, or just ... romantic poems, or quotes, or something?'

Janet used the crumpled tissue against her nose one more time. 'Not really.'

Hunter offered her a new one.

'Not really isn't exactly "no",' he said.

'She would sometimes get the random dick pic sent to her,' Janet explained. 'It happens. Some idiots out there think that they can impress a woman with the size of their penises, or lack of it. Mel and I used to laugh about it every time she got one.'

'Did it happen often?'

'Not really. A handful times at the most.'

'Any of those times recently?'

'Umm ...' The head shake came before the vocal answer. 'No. I don't think so. I can't really remember.' Janet's chin dropped to her chest before coming back up. Her eyes widened at Hunter. 'Hold on ... Mel was chatting to someone at the bar on Saturday evening.'

'Chatting to someone?'

'Yeah,' Janet confirmed. 'When we left, we went to say bye to Mel. She was at the bar, chatting to this guy – tall, dark hair.'

'A guest at the party?'

'No, I don't think he was.' The reply came from Tom. 'Kelly-Ann had a section by the pool reserved for her party,' he explained, 'but the bar was open as normal. I think he was just there having a drink.'

'You said they were chatting – as in ...?'

'As in laughing together, flirting, getting on like a house on fire, you know?'

'Do you think that Melissa could've invited him back to her place for a nightcap, or something?'

Janet looked at him with sad eyes. 'I doubt it,' she said, her tone just a hairline away from sounding offended. 'My sister wasn't a one-night stand kind of girl.'

Sex could mean so many different things at different times. Hunter knew that. Maybe that night Melissa needed the sort of emotional and physical relief that sex could bring a person. Or maybe she believed that whatever happened that night would develop into something more meaningful than a simple one-night stand. There were so many scenarios that Hunter could use to counter-argue Janet's statement, but none of them would make a difference ... and all of them, no matter how diplomatically Hunter put them forward, could sound offensive. He decided to let it go and move on.

'When you went to say goodbye,' he said, 'did Melissa introduce the person that she was talking to? Do you remember his name?'

Tom squinted at nothing at all before looking at Janet.

'She did introduce him to us,' he said. 'But I can't remember his name. Can you, babe?'

Once again, all Janet could do was shake her head.

'And what time was that? What time did you leave the party?'

Tom looked at Janet, but she had gone back to staring at the window in an almost catatonic state.

'It was around half past midnight,' he finally said. 'Maybe a quarter to one ... no later than that.'

Hunter wrote it down. 'How about Melissa? Did she mention anything about how she would be getting home? Was she getting a ride with anyone from the party?'

'No.' Once again, the answer came from Tom. 'She didn't mention anything about a ride. Janet did ask her just before we left. Mel told us that she was getting a cab home.'

'That's good to know,' Hunter said, as he took note.

'Why?' Tom asked with concern. 'Back at her place, was there any indication that she had company that night? A second wine glass? An extra wet towel? Marks on the bed sheets? Anything like that?'

Hunter looked back at him curiously.

'I watch the Crime Channel,' Tom clarified, looking a little smug.

Hunter did his best not to roll his eyes. 'No, we haven't found a second wine glass, or an extra wet towel, or anything, but we also found no sign of forced entry anywhere – doors or windows. So there's a chance that Melissa willingly let her attacker into her house.'

Hunter's statement managed to regain Janet's attention. He breathed in through his nose and out through his mouth before he spoke again. 'We also found a note.'

'A note?' Janet asked. 'What sort of note?'

'A romantic one, it seems.' Hunter reached into his inside jacket pocket to retrieve his cellphone. From the photo gallery, he showed Janet the photo he had taken from the note back at the morgue.

Tom got closer to have a look.

Janet read the words on the note – 'Through these eyes, no one will ever look as perfect as you did.' – and they brought a fresh onslaught of tears to her eyes.

Hunter offered her a new paper tissue.

'Where was this found?' Tom asked.

'In the kitchen,' Hunter lied. He saw no reason to add to Janet's pain by revealing that the killer had also violated her sister by inserting a note into her body.

Janet looked back at Hunter with questioning eyes. She had found the body and obviously didn't remember seeing a note in her sister's kitchen.

'It was folded,' Hunter added, indicating the paper creases that could be seen on the photo. 'Left by the stove.'

Janet's stare returned to the photo on Hunter's phone and she began sobbing.

'Do you have any idea who could've written those words to your sister?' he asked. 'Could this have been Kevin . . . maybe?'

It took Janet several long seconds to control her tears. When she finally did, she dropped a bomb on Hunter.

'I don't know if those words are Mel's or not. I didn't know her to write poetry, or anything like that, but that . . .' She pointed at the photo. 'That's definitely Mel's handwriting.'

Twelve

Heavy clouds had been slowly gathering above Downtown Los Angeles for most of the afternoon. At around five o'clock, the same time that Hunter and Garcia met back at the UVC Unit's office, the first drops of rain finally began assaulting the city. The two detectives had barely gotten to their desks when Captain Blake sneaked up on them.

'OK, what is this note that was found in the victim's body?' she asked.

Garcia, who had his back to the door and hadn't seen the captain enter, jumped as the door closed behind her.

'Damn, Captain, where did you come from? And do you have a tracker on us, or something? We literarily just got in.'

The captain scowled back at him. 'This is my department. My floor. I've got eyes everywhere. So, the note. What's that all about?'

While Garcia quickly ran Captain Blake through all the autopsy findings, including the note, Hunter connected his cellphone to his computer and printed out the photo he had taken of it.

'"Through these eyes, no one will ever look as perfect as you did."' the captain read out loud before squinting at her detectives. 'And this was left inside her vagina?'

Garcia nodded. 'Inside a grip-seal plastic bag.'

'I take it that both the note and the bag have already been sent to forensics for analysis and graphology?'

'They have,' Garcia confirmed.

'There's no need to bother with graphology any more,' Hunter said, bringing everyone's attention to him.

'What do you mean?' Garcia asked. 'Why not?'

'It's Melissa Hawthorne's handwriting,' Hunter explained, approaching the picture board and pinning the photo printout onto it. 'I talked to Janet earlier today, Melissa's stepsister. I showed her the photo on my phone.'

'And she was one hundred percent sure it's her sister's hand-writing?' Captain Blake asked.

'She had no doubt.'

In silence, Captain Blake read the sentence one more time. 'Do we know what that is? I mean . . . are those lyrics to a song? Is that a poem by someone? Words from a film? Were those the victim's words or are they by the killer himself?'

'I did a basic internet search,' Hunter informed her. 'It came back with nothing – no lyrics . . . no poem . . . no nursery rhyme . . . no movie line . . . nothing. At least nothing that has been published on the Net with those words in that exact sequence. I've already passed it on to our research team for a more in-depth search. Janet Lang also told me that as far as she knew, her sister wasn't one to write poetry, or song lyrics, or anything similar to that . . .' Hunter pointed to the board before continuing. 'But I'm going to go back to Melissa's house to have a look around. It's not uncommon for people to have poetry, lyrics, even drawing as a secret hobby. Some people like to write down their innermost, personal thoughts . . . feelings . . . desires . . . whatever . . . but they do it for themselves, not for sharing.'

'Like a secret diary,' Captain Blake said.

'Something similar, yeah.'

Captain Blake studied the photo on the board for a moment longer.

'Regardless if these are the victim's words or not,' she said, 'what's the theory here? That the killer made her write this down before inserting it inside her and hanging her up by the mouth?'

Doubt danced in the curve of her words.

'Presumably, yes.' Hunter took a seat behind his desk.

Captain Blake coughed a breath. 'Well, I'm no expert here, but to me, this reads like some sort of love declaration from a disgruntled ex-boyfriend . . . or a lover . . . or maybe someone she turned down? Some idiot whose pride she hurt.'

'That's very possible,' Hunter accepted. 'And that's definitely one avenue that we're going to pursue. Like it was mentioned this morning, Melissa ended her relationship with Kevin Garrison around six or seven months ago.'

'Yeah, you said,' the captain remembered. 'He was cheating on her, right?'

'That's correct.'

'But why make *her* write it down?' Garcia asked, with a shrug. 'It would make more sense if the killer had written it himself, don't you think?' He lifted a hand to stop all the comebacks. 'Yes, I know that if the killer had handwritten the note himself, he would've been giving us his handwriting, but he could've printed it out, or something, don't you think?'

'Meaning,' Hunter said.

Garcia heard a question. 'Meaning exactly that,' he retorted, nodding at his partner. 'That he could've printed it out.'

Hunter shook his head. 'It wasn't a question. It was an answer. The killer made the victim write it down because it meant something to him. He wanted the note to be in her handwriting for a reason. There's meaning behind everything he does. Trust me. And that would also be why he made her write it down more than once.'

'More than once?' The captain found that strange. 'Why do you say that? Were earlier drafts found in her house?'

'No. None.' The answer came from Garcia, as he turned to Hunter. 'Were there?'

Hunter shook his head. 'No.'

Captain Blake looked more confused. 'So how do you know that the killer made her write that down more than once?'

'Have a look at the note again,' Hunter said, pointing at the board.

Both Garcia and Captain Blake walked over to it and restudied the note. Each of them looked for something different.

Captain Blake squinted at the photo, trying to identify pre-existing grooves on the piece of paper behind the writing. She saw none.

Initially, Garcia looked for the same telltale signs, but quickly realized what he had missed.

'The handwriting itself,' he said, turning to face Hunter, who smiled back at him.

'The handwriting?' the captain asked, moving her attention to it.

'It's perfect,' Garcia said.

It took another couple of seconds before the penny dropped for Captain Blake. 'If the killer really did force the victim to write those words down before killing her, she would've been terrified and under duress, her hand would've been too unsteady. The handwriting would've been all over the place.'

'No doubt,' Hunter confirmed. 'Which clearly isn't the case here, and that leaves us with a few alternatives, but the two most probable ones are – the killer made the victim write those words down until the unsteadiness was gone from her handwriting, or the killer's an expert forger.'

'Could this really have been her ex-boyfriend?' Captain Blake asked. 'What's his name again?'

'Kevin Garrison,' Garcia replied.

'I ask that because this . . .' The captain gestured at the whole board. 'This isn't a crime of passion. We've seen plenty of those and this isn't it. This is hate and anger and everything that's bad.'

'Right now, we know very little about Kevin Garrison,' Hunter said, consulting his notepad. 'But finding him won't be much of a problem. He trains at a gym in Culver City every morning. I'll be paying them a visit tomorrow, but apparently, we also have a mystery guest.'

'What do you mean, "mystery guest"?' Captain Blake asked.

'Janet also told me that Melissa was chatting to someone at the bar on Saturday night. Someone who didn't seem to be a guest at Kelly-Ann's birthday party.'

Captain Blake's question was asked with simple eyebrow movement.

'Kelly-Ann had a section of the Broken Shaker cocktail lounge reserved for her party,' Hunter clarified. 'But the bar was also open for regular customers. Janet and her boyfriend, Tom were just leaving when they saw Melissa and this mystery man at the bar. They went over to say goodbye . . . and they were introduced, but neither Janet nor Tom remember his name.'

'Mark,' Garcia said from his desk, as he flipped open his own pocket notepad. 'The mystery man Melissa was chatting to at the bar? His name was Mark.'

Hunter and Captain Blake turned to look at him.

'Kelly-Ann invited thirty-five people to her party,' Garcia informed them. 'The turnout was thirty-one. I talked to her and her boyfriend, plus eight other guests this afternoon – more to come. And you're right,' he said, addressing Hunter. 'Melissa was chatting to someone at the bar who wasn't a guest at the party. Kelly-Ann and her boyfriend saw them too, and so did three of the other eight guests I talked to.' Garcia flipped a page on his notepad. 'Kelly-Ann actually talked to him for a little while. Melissa introduced them. Kelly-Ann was one hundred percent sure that his name was Mark. She remembered it because it's the same as her father's.'

'No last name?' Captain Blake asked.

'No,' Garcia replied with a short laugh. 'They met in a bar, Captain. How many people do you meet in a bar that introduced themselves using their last name as well?'

'Most of them,' the captain volleyed back.

'This group is in their mid-twenties,' Garcia countered.

'OK, point taken. How about a facial composite? Or maybe even a photo? Nowadays everyone is snapping photos everywhere and all the time, aren't they? I'd expect that at a birthday party, a lot of photos were taken. Maybe someone snapped this "Mark" character at the bar by chance. Maybe in the background?'

'My thoughts exactly,' Garcia replied. 'I did ask Kelley-Ann, her boyfriend and all eight guests I talked to this afternoon if they had taken any photos at the party.'

'And . . .?'

'They all did. And obviously, Kelly-Ann and her boyfriend had loads, but the problem is that the bar was located right across the rooftop from the area that had been allocated for the party.' He shook his head. 'You couldn't even see the bar in any of the photos that I looked at today, and I looked at every single one of them.'

'CCTV cameras,' Hunter suggested. 'They probably have a couple at the bar area, but even if not, the Broken Shaker is the rooftop bar at the Freehand Hotel. To go up to the bar, everyone has to go through the lobby, and every hotel lobby has got CCTV.'

'Once again, my thoughts exactly,' Garcia agreed, 'and I've already called the hotel to check. They do have CCTV cameras over at the bar area in the Broken Shaker. I'm going to go pay them a visit . . .' He checked his watch. It was coming up to 5:30 p.m. 'Right about now. Want to come along? They're just a mile down the road.'

Before Garcia had even finished his sentence, Hunter had already reached for his jacket.

Thirteen

At the hotel pool rooftop, Hunter and Garcia lost no time explaining to Christina D'Angelo, the manager of the Broken Shaker, the reason for their visit. After checking their credentials, she took them straight to the office where the CCTV recordings were kept, which was located to the right of the bar.

The office was spacious but a little cluttered.

'Please excuse the mess,' Christina said, as she rounded the only desk in the room and hit the spacebar key to wake up the computer on it. 'We usually don't have visitors in here.' She indicated the pile of folded chairs on the corner. 'Feel free to grab a couple of those.'

As Hunter and Garcia picked up the chairs, Christina clicked away on the computer.

'Saturday was a very busy night for us,' she began. 'All in all, from opening to closing, we must've had around four hundred people come and go throughout the evening, maybe more. The two cameras we have are on the ceiling in the bar, just outside.'

'Yeah, I saw them,' Hunter said, bringing his chair to her right. Garcia took his to her left.

'And that could be a problem,' Christina said, as the images on the two monitors in front of them materialized. The ceiling cameras were aimed at the bar's serving counter. 'If the person you're looking for didn't come to the bar, meaning – if he or she

was at a table and ordering drinks from one of our waitresses –
then these recordings will be of no use to you. These are the only
two cameras we have up here and they don't cover the tables.'

'He was at the bar,' Garcia said, commanding her stare. 'I was
told that he was sitting at this end.' On one of the monitors, he
indicated the far left of the bar.

'OK,' Christina said with a nod. 'That helps a lot. Now, problem number two – do you have a time frame in mind? Because if
you don't, you could be looking at over ten hours of footage here.'

'Let's start at midnight,' Hunter said, remembering the conversation he'd had with Janet and Tom that afternoon. He moved his
chair a fraction closer to the desk. 'We can go back and forth from
there, but I know that he was seen at the bar sometime between
midnight and one in the morning.'

'Sure,' the manager said, typing the time into the timeframe
search box. She hit 'enter' and the image on the monitors jumped
to show a very busy bar, where two bartenders moved as quickly
as they could, taking orders from customers and waitresses alike.
One of the bartenders was the same tall, Hispanic man who was
working the bar just outside the office. Standing at the left end
of the bar were three women and two men. They didn't seem to
be together. None of the women was Melissa Hawthorne. The
clock on the top right of both monitors began counting up from
12:00 a.m.

'May I?' Hunter asked, indicating the keyboard.

'Of course. Sorry.' Christina stood up. 'Here, take my seat.'

The two of them swapped chairs.

The controls on the screen were pretty self-explanatory.
Hunter fast-forwarded the images, making the footage move at
eight times its normal speed.

Garcia leaned forward, placing his elbows on the desk. His eyes
squinted in concentration.

On the screen, as the bartenders prepared and handed out

drinks, customers and waitresses moved to and from the bar in a seemingly chaotic fashion.

00:05 a.m. – no sign of Melissa yet.

'Do you mind very much if I leave you to it?' Christina asked, once again getting to her feet. 'It's the beginning of the evening and I need to make sure that everything is running smoothly out there.'

'Please do,' Hunter said, pausing the images for a second. 'There's no reason for us to keep you here, especially as we might be at this for a while.'

'Take your time,' she said, crossing the office to reach the door. 'If you need me for anything else, I'll be either in the restaurant or the bar area.'

Christina closed the door behind her and Hunter and Garcia's attention returned to the monitors.

At high-speed, customers came and went, with some pausing at the bar for a lot longer than others, but it wasn't until 00:23 that Melissa finally appeared on the screen. Both detectives spotted her at the same time.

'There she is,' Garcia said, his index finger pointing at the monitor on the left.

Hunter quickly returned the footage back to normal speed. The images showed Melissa getting to the bar, leaning forward, placing both elbows on the counter and lacing her finger together. She wore an elegant shirtwaist flared tea swing dress in red. She didn't look to be exactly sober.

It took the bartender just a few seconds to notice her. He handed a customer who was standing at the other end of the bar a colorful cocktail in a tall glass and walked over to Melissa. They both smiled politely at each other before the bartender leaned over, moving his ear a little closer to her mouth to take her order.

The elevated, ceiling-height camera angle wasn't great. Hunter could only partially see Melissa's lip movement.

'Did you catch that?' Garcia asked, knowing that Hunter could lip-read, something he had learned when he was a young boy.

'No, not exactly.'

As the bartender turned away to start mixing Melissa's drink, a tall, well-built, dark-haired man came up to the bar and took the space directly to her left. He wore dark trousers and a white button-up shirt, under a blue blazer jacket.

'And here is our mysterious Mark,' Garcia said, instinctively moving a couple of inches closer to the screen. The time was 00:25.

Hunter did the same, but the man had positioned himself just behind the last pillar on the left. His face was around eighty percent obscured by the wooden pillar.

'Oh that's great,' Garcia commented, angling his head left then right, as if that would allow him a better view of the man's face.

Hunter watched in silence.

Within just a few seconds, the man looked at Melissa before pointing down at her shoes. She turned her neck to look back at him, looked down, smiled, looked down again, and then her lips moved. This time Hunter read them clearly: *Thank you. They are new.*

'Very smooth,' Hunter said with an approving nod. 'Mentioning her shoes instead of straight away paying her a beauty compliment is a great icebreaker. It also puts forward the idea that he's attentive to details, not only the obvious.'

'And women love that,' Garcia agreed.

'And most also love shoes.'

The smile stayed on Melissa's lips for a few more seconds before it turned into an animated laugh.

'A shoe compliment followed by some quick joke to make her laugh,' Hunter commented. 'He knows what he's doing.'

'C'mon, Mark,' Garcia urged the man. 'Lean forward just a little so we can see your face.'

But even though Mark had by then turned his whole body to

properly face Melissa, he stayed securely behind the pillar – his mouth one hundred percent covered by it.

On the screen, Melissa smiled again and then it was her turn to angle her body to fully face Mark. If he knew how to read body language, and Hunter was pretty sure he did, she'd just fully agreed to his company.

The bartender returned with Melissa's drink – a classic mojito by the looks of it. As he approached Melissa, something caught Hunter's attention. He waited to see if Garcia saw it too, but Garcia didn't mention anything. Hunter made a mental note of the frame time and allowed the footage to play on. They watched, as Mark ordered his drink. He also insisted on paying for Melissa's.

She accepted it.

Soon after that, Mark ordered a couple of Jägerbombs.

They talked and laughed for another four minutes until Janet and Tom joined them at the bar.

00:34.

'Is that her stepsister and her boyfriend?' Garcia asked.

'Yes, that's them,' Hunter confirmed.

They stayed for less than two minutes before they bid Melissa and Mark goodbye. Janet also appeared to be quite inebriated.

Another five minutes went by before another couple came up to Melissa and Mark. This time, it was a short-haired blonde woman with a contagious smile, accompanied by a skinny man with his hair tied back into a man bun.

'That's Kelly-Ann and her boyfriend, Justin,' Garcia informed Hunter.

00:42.

On the screen, they all shook hands and Mark ordered four more shots of Jägerbombs.

Garcia pinched his bottom lip as he studied the images. 'This doesn't seem right.'

'What?' Hunter asked. 'The fact that we've been watching them at the bar for over fifteen minutes now and Mark has not once moved from behind that pillar?'

'Exactly,' Garcia agreed, nodding a few times in quick succession. 'It looks like he knows where the bar CCTV cameras are. His position behind that pillar seems strategic, not by chance.'

Kelly-Ann and her boyfriend left just after the round of shots.

Mark and Melissa stayed at the bar. They talked for another eight minutes before Mark reached inside his jacket pocket for his cellphone and handed it to Melissa. She typed something into it and handed it back to Mark.

'Well, he's definitely got her number,' Garcia said.

Hunter was hoping that Mark would, right there and then, place a call to Melissa. That would confirm that she had given him the right number and it would automatically give her his number, but Mark simply returned his cellphone to his pocket.

'No confirming callback,' Garcia said. He had clearly been expecting the same as Hunter.

Melissa and Mark stayed at the bar for another fifteen minutes, during which time they had another drink each and two new rounds of shots, this time, tequila. Every time the bartender brought them their order, Hunter would slow the footage down to check if Mark had maybe slipped something into Melissa's drink.

If he had, they never saw it.

During that whole period, not once did Mark's face become fully visible.

As Melissa finished her drink, she finally checked her watch before telling Mark that she needed to go. She then fetched her cellphone to use an app. A few screen taps later and Hunter was able to read her lips again.

Three minutes, she told Mark.

On the screen, after telling Mark that her cab was on its way, Melissa got to her feet. Mark said something in return that prompted a shy, perhaps even embarrassed smile. Hunter read her lips for her reply.

Maybe next time. The embarrassed smile became a disarming one. *I have to meet my sister tomorrow, but ... message me. We can meet up later in the week if you like.*

Holding on to her hand, Mark said something that brought the embarrassed smile back to Melissa's lips.

I'm sure, she replied, her head tilting to one side. *But tonight I really can't. But call me, OK? We'll meet up.* She finally turned and walked away.

Less than a minute later, Mark was gone.

Hunter pressed 'stop'.

'We just watched a little over half an hour of footage here,' Garcia said, his eyes widening at Hunter. 'And this Mark character managed to stay behind that pillar throughout all of it. What are the chances of that?'

'Statistically, very slim.'

'Unless it was done on purpose,' Garcia shot back.

'There's something else too,' Hunter added. 'Did you notice that Mark paid for all of his rounds – drinks and shots – with cash. Every single time. No electronic trail.'

'Sonofabitch!'

Hunter rewound the footage to the counter time he had memorized earlier and quickly searched for the best frame before pressing 'print screen' on the keyboard.

'Why do you need that for?' Garcia frowned. 'His face doesn't appear on any of it.'

'I know,' Hunter admitted it. 'But there's something that I need to ask the bartender outside.'

'What? If he remembers this Mark character?'

'He does.' Hunter's tone was confident.

Garcia got to his feet. 'How do you know that he does?'

'You'll see.'

Fourteen

Hunter and Garcia exited the office to find the tall bartender mixing the last of four cocktails. At that time, there were only two customers sitting at the bar – a young couple, who were standing a little to the right, sipping on frozen margaritas. Hunter and Garcia positioned themselves on the left, at the exact location where Mark had stood.

'I'll be with you gentlemen in just a sec,' the bartender said, as he used a strainer to pour the drink he had just mixed into a tall glass before garnishing it with a triangular slice of pineapple. He placed the drink on the tray, where three other cocktails were waiting.

'What can I get you gentlemen?' he asked, approaching both detectives and placing two round coasters in front of them.

Hunter and Garcia quickly displayed their credentials and introduced themselves.

'I'm Roger,' the bartender said before nodding. 'Yeah, I saw you go into the office with Chris. She told me that you're trying to identify someone who was here, at the Shaker, on Saturday evening, right?'

'That's right,' Hunter confirmed, pointing to his feet. 'Someone who was standing exactly here.'

Roger gave Hunter a sad smile. 'Saturday night was a busy night. A lot of people stood at that spot throughout the evening.'

'I have no doubt,' Hunter agreed. 'But I'm sure that you'll remember this one.' He placed the printout he had with him on the bar counter. It showed Mark standing where Hunter was – his face almost completely obscured by the leftmost bar pillar. Melissa was standing where Garcia stood, her smiling face clearly visible, but the main reason why Hunter had chosen that particular frame to printout was because the bartender was also in it. He had just brought Melissa the first mojito she'd ordered at the bar, but his gaze wasn't on her, it was on Mark, and the look on his face was what had caught Hunter's attention. His eyebrows were arched down slightly, while the corners of his mouth had been stretched out, pressing his lips tightly against each other – clearly a disapproving look.

Sure, the bartender's facial expression could've been simple jealousy. Maybe he'd been hoping to flirt with Melissa, but while he was busy preparing her cocktail, Mark had beaten him to the punch . . . maybe . . . but Hunter had always been a few levels above most when it came to analyzing people's behavior . . . their mannerisms . . . their facial expressions . . . their attitudes . . . all of it. Roger's disapproving look hadn't been fueled only by jealousy. Hunter was very sure of that.

The bartender looked down at the printout and in one second flat his lips drew the exact same thin line from the image.

'Oh,' he said, using his right index finger to tap the image. 'Him?'

'Do you know him?' Garcia asked, his tone skeptical.

A firm shake of the head. 'No. Not really.'

Garcia peeked at Hunter before his gaze landed on the bartender again. 'And what does "not really" actually mean?'

Roger shrugged. 'I don't know who he is.'

There clearly was a 'but' hidden at the end of that sentence. Hunter pushed for it.

'But you've seen him here before.'

'Yes,' Roger admitted. 'At least once before.'

'And you don't like him very much,' Hunter again.

Roger shifted his weight from one foot to the other as he pondered the best way to reply.

'It's not my job to be judgemental,' he began. 'He's a customer. He comes to the bar . . . I serve him . . . he pays . . . it's that simple.'

'Still,' Hunter insisted. 'There's something about him that bothers you.'

Roger gave both detectives a sideways look. 'It's just . . . his attitude towards women.'

Hunter and Garcia could guess what he meant, but they needed to hear it from him. Garcia pushed.

'What about his attitude towards women? What's wrong with it?'

The bartender scratched the back of his neck. 'It's a little . . . slimy.' He lifted his hands in an apologetic gesture. 'What I mean is that he's a Casanova. He's a good-looking guy and he knows it. He uses that to his advantage – he spots an attractive woman, approaches her and sweet-talks her. What happens from there, I don't know, but I've been a bartender for almost ten years now. I've seen and heard plenty of guys like him before – the Casanovas . . . the sweet-talkers . . . the smooth operators. They lurk around in every bar, every cocktail lounge, especially the upper class ones. Some are after just easy, one-night sex . . . some are proper conmen.'

'And this guy?' Garcia's turn to use his index finger to tap the image on the counter. 'What do you think he is? A charmer or a conman?'

Roger shook his head at Garcia. 'Like I've said before – it's not my job, or my place to judge.'

'But you mentioned that his attitude was a little slimy.' Hunter took over again. 'I'm assuming you overheard some of his conversation.'

Though Hunter had used the word 'assuming', from the

footage he'd just watched, he knew for certain that the bartender had overheard at least some of what Mark and Melissa had been saying.

Roger didn't look embarrassed.

'Unfortunately that's something that we can't really help,' he explained. 'It's not a very large working floor area in here.' He indicated the other side of the counter, where he stood. 'On a busy night, like this past Saturday, the bar gets jammed. With the loud music . . .' He indicated the DJ booth to their right. 'People at the bar raise their voices. We always end up overhearing conversations. It's a fact.'

'And in this case,' Garcia asked, 'what did you overhear?'

Another shrug from the bartender. 'Nothing out of the ordinary, really. Just . . .' He made a silly face. 'Cheesy pickup lines, and loads of compliments, not only to how attractive this lady really was,' he pointed to Melissa on the printout, 'but also to her taste in clothes and shoes and perfume and whathaveyou. Like I said – he's a very smooth operator. He knows how to charm a lady.'

They were interrupted by a waitress with a restaurant table order. It took Roger less than a minute to prepare the drinks.

Once the bartender came back to them, Hunter indicated Mark on the printout. 'In the CCTV footage, he paid for a few rounds of drinks, but always in cash. The previous time you said you remember seeing him here, can you remember if he did the same or did he ever use plastic?'

Roger didn't even try to think about it.

'I'm sorry, but there's no way I'll be able to remember that. He's not a regular, you see? It's not like I see him here every weekend.' He shrugged again. 'To be honest, I remember him by default because he's always chatting to attractive women . . . women that catch the eye, do you know what I mean?' His gaze returned to the printout. 'May I ask what this is all about? Did something happen to this lady? Did she get conned? Did he take her purse or something?'

Garcia collected the printout from the counter. 'She was murdered that night. After she left here.'

The look on Roger's face exploded into a mixture of legitimate shock and surprise. 'Murdered?'

'These women you've mentioned?' Garcia was quick to question. 'The ones that catch the eye ... the ones that you saw him chatting to the previous time ... are *they* regulars? Have you seen them here since? Any of them here tonight?'

The look on Roger's face changed again, this time into a serious, thoughtful one. 'I don't think so,' he said after several pensive seconds. 'I can't really remember.'

'I thought you said that these were eye-catching women,' Garcia challenged.

'They were.' His demeanor turned a little defensive. 'But a large number of our customers are actually guests here at the hotel. Many come up here out of pure convenience – if you had a little too much to drink, it's a lot easier to stumble back to your room than to try to jump in a cab when you are somewhere else in town, you see? That's also why a lot of these 'charmer' types prefer hotel bars. We get a lot of executive women travelling alone on business trips.' He shrugged. 'Men aren't the only ones who like to have a little extra-marital fun when they're away from home, do you catch my drift? These women get charmed up here in the bar and if they feel like it, their room is just a few floors down. Like I said – convenience – it plays a big part for both sides – the women and the charmers.'

Hunter nodded his understanding before placing his card on the bar counter.

'This Casanova, as you called him, was one of the last people to see the woman he was talking to alive. We need to track him down. If you see him again, please call us straight away. No hesitation, you understand?'

'Yes, of course.' Roger picked up the card.

'If needed,' Hunter asked, zipping up his jacket, 'do you think you could describe what this Casanova looked like to a sketch artist?'

Roger nodded, but there was no certainty in the gesture. 'Sure . . . I mean . . . I can try.'

Fifteen

From the cocktail bar, Hunter and Garcia took the lift down to the ground floor to talk to the hotel's head of security.

To get to the Broken Shaker, located all the way on the rooftop, Mark would've had to walk through the reception lobby. There was no other alternative. Hunter had spotted three CCTV cameras in the lobby area when they came in. Also, unless Mark had decided to climb up fifteen floors on foot, he had to have taken one of the lifts up. There were three lifts at the Freehand Hotel. All three were equipped with a ceiling CCTV camera.

Hunter and Garcia didn't know what Mark looked like, but thanks to the footage from the Broken Shaker bar cameras, they knew what he was wearing on Saturday night. All they had to do was pick him out in the footage from either the lobby cameras, or the lift ones.

They knew that Melissa Hawthorne had left the Broken Shaker at around 1:25 am. Mark had left just a minute or two after her, so it made sense for Hunter and Garcia to start with the lift cameras footage: cue time – 1:24 a.m.

'There she is,' Garcia said, indicating on the screen.

Melissa had taken the first elevator on the left at 1:25:42 a.m. She was alone. Exactly one minute and twenty seconds after her, Mark took the middle lift, heading down to the hotel lobby.

'Hold on,' Garcia said, pointing at the screen. 'Is that him? The guy in the hat?'

'Yes, that's him,' Hunter confirmed, nodding slowly.

On the screen, Mark had entered the elevator wearing a black Panama hat. He was looking down at his cellphone, which he held in his right hand. Not once throughout the entire ride did he divert his eyes from his phone.

'Oh that's just great,' Garcia commented, as Mark stepped out of the elevator.

'Lobby cameras,' Hunter said, noting down the time.

It took him just a few seconds to switch the footage, but their luck didn't change. At 1:28:10 a.m. Mark exited the lift, crossed the lobby floor and exited the hotel, all the while with his head down, staring at his phone. No clear shot of his face.

Garcia chuckled, sarcastically. 'Surprise, surprise – he doesn't look up. Not even for a millisecond.'

They rewound the footage back just a couple of minutes, until the lobby cameras had picked up Melissa Hawthorne exiting the lift. She had paused by the front door and checked her phone before finally leaving the hotel.

'He was right behind her,' Garcia said, filling the silence that had come between them.

Hunter took note of the time on the screen – 1:26:45 a.m. That would help track down the cab driver who had picked Melissa up that morning.

'Get comfortable,' he said, puffing out a breath. 'We're going to need to search for when he arrived.'

They spent just a little over forty-five minutes speeding through almost four hours of footage, until they finally spotted Mark again. He had entered the hotel lobby, alone, at 9:27 p.m. – Panama hat on, phone out, head down.

'And here we go again,' Garcia commented.

Hunter and Garcia watched as Mark crossed the lobby floor and, together with a hotel guest, took the lift on the left going up.

Back to the lift footage.

The hotel guest — an overweight man with a receding hair-line — travelled up to floor six, while Mark went all the way to the rooftop. And that was when Hunter and Garcia finally caught a brink of a break.

As the lift doors open, a guest who looked to be a little past his legal limit stumbled into the lift, and he and Mark almost collided, which forced Mark to look up for just an instant.

Hunter immediately reached for the pause button before rewinding the footage frame by frame, but though Mark had lifted his head to look at the guest, the Panama hat, together with the awkward camera angle, still kept most of his face hidden.

'That's it?' Garcia asked, squinting at the screen. 'That's the best we can get?'

'Pretty much,' Hunter confirmed.

The camera had caught Mark's right profile, showing a squared chin and a strong jawline, but that was about it — no nose, no lips, no eyes.

Despite choosing the best frame before hitting the 'print screen' button on the keyboard, Hunter's disappointment was obvious.

'I don't think that even Forensics IT, with one of their "wonder apps", would be able to hypothesize the rest of his face. There isn't much here to go on, but I'll ask them anyway.'

'His whole attitude is just wrong, Robert,' Garcia complained, as Hunter picked up the printout. 'The hat, the way he's always looking down at his phone, the strategic position at the bar upstairs . . . all of it. It's wrong.'

Hunter showed the printout to Garcia.

'Seriously?' Garcia chuckled. 'This is the best we have? He could be anyone.'

'That's the best we have,' Hunter confirmed.

Garcia laughed. 'Which means that we've got diddly shit.'

Sixteen

After finishing her third twelve-hour shift in just as many days, an exhausted Kirsten Hansen sat in the nurses' room on the second floor of the Los Angeles Surge Hospital in Westlake. Her hands were shaky, her eyes were tired and gritty, and her brain felt numb and fatigued. The time was 9:24 p.m.

Kirsten had been a nurse with the Surgical Emergency Unit at the LASH for four years and in that time she'd assisted in hundreds of operations, but this had been her first septal myectomy surgery — a very complex procedure performed to reduce the thickness of the heart muscles, a symptom of patients diagnosed with advanced stages of hypertrophic cardiomyopathy (HCM). Originally, the surgery was supposed to have taken around six hours, but due to a minor problem with the bypass machine, their total time inside the operation theater neared nine and a half hours. In the end, the surgery was a success, but the team did come a hair away from losing the patient.

Though Kirsten wasn't a surgeon, she had played a very important part in the entire procedure and in keeping the patient alive.

In the hospital parking lot, she sat at the steering wheel of her Hyundai Accent and looked at herself in the rear-view mirror. There was no denying that she looked drained, but behind the mask of exhaustion was a very proud Kirsten Hansen.

'You did good today, girl,' she said, as she smiled at herself.
'You did good.'

Her hands were still a little shaky so she reached inside the
glove compartment for her cigarettes.

Yes, sure, smoking was bad for you, everyone knew that, especially a health professional like Kirsten, but she wasn't a heavy
smoker. In fact, she was barely a smoker at all. It wasn't the taste
of cigarettes that she craved. It was their almost magical, calming
effect and she wasn't ashamed to admit it.

Kirsten brought a cigarette to her lips, lit it up and took a
long drag. She sat back on the driver's seat, closed her eyes and
allowed the nicotine to do its job. Four drags in and she felt ten
times better – no shaky hands ... no racy heart. She had one
last drag before stubbing the cigarette out and checking the
time – 9:58 p.m.

Kirsten hadn't counting on leaving the hospital so late that
night, but as she turned on her engine, she shrugged at the time,
because the truth was – it didn't actually matter.

She was off for the next two days, and her fiancé, Troy Foster,
with whom she shared a two-bedroom house in Alhambra, was
out of town until tomorrow evening.

Troy, who was a sales manager at a guns store, had travelled
to San Francisco on Friday to attend a three-day Ammo and
Weapons Expo. Not only did Kirsten have the house all to herself
for one last night, but she also didn't have to wake up early in the
morning. Despite the late hour, she could still get home, pour
herself a large glass of wine, order some pizza and quietly binge
on some pointless TV series until the early hours of the morning.

That thought put a smile on Kirsten's lips.

Not that she didn't miss Troy. She did. Very much. They'd
been dating for three years and they were engaged to get married
in seven months' time, but they had also been living together
for nearly two years now. Due to Kirsten's night shift work

schedule, Troy did get the house all to himself at least a couple of nights a week, but not Kirsten. If lucky, she would get a night in, all by herself, once every six weeks, when Troy would have a testosterone-filled boys' night out with his friends.

The drive from the hospital to her house in Alhambra took only twenty minutes, and the first thing she did as she got in was to call for a pizza – extra hot pepperoni with double cheese.

Measuring five-foot seven, with dirty-blonde hair that was always cut into a classic bob style, light-blue eyes, a heart-shaped face, and a smile that could warm a cold room, Kirsten had always tried to take care of her health and her appearance. Food-wise, she usually steered herself toward the healthier option, but sometimes, all she really needed was comfort food, and for her, very few things were more comforting than extra hot pepperoni pizza with double cheese.

According to the app on her phone, the pizza would be about twenty-five minutes.

Kirsten didn't like opening a bottle of wine without Troy, but just like everything in life, there were exceptions, and right then, she needed a glass of wine.

She chose something that she knew she would love – a bottle of Zinfandel from Napa Valley. While the wine breathed in a glass, Kirsten took a quick shower, which helped her relax.

With her hair wrapped into a fluffy towel and comfortably in her leopard-print bathrobe, Kirsten returned to the kitchen and reached for her wine glass.

Who knew that heaven could be red and in liquid form, she thought, as she closed her eyes and took a moment to appreciate the soft flavors that developed in her mouth – cherries, raspberries, and light spice, with notes of wood herbs.

Ding, ding.

New text message – her pizza was on its way.

In the living room, Kirsten switched on the TV and cued up the second episode of a series she had started watching the previous week – a love triangle involving a nun, in some fictitious city in rural America. Just before she pressed the 'play' button, her phone rang. It was her fiancé.

Troy and Kirsten didn't chat for long. She told him about her long day at the hospital and he told her about some new machine gun he had seen at the Expo.

'*OK, baby, I gotta go*,' Troy said, sounding tired. '*I wanna try to get an early night. I'm meeting a supplier for breakfast tomorrow morning and I'll hit the road straight after.*'

'Sounds great, honey. Do you know what time you'll be getting home?'

'*I'm aiming for about seven or eight in the evening, but I'll keep you posted.*'

'OK, baby, sleep well. I'm just about to go binge on some brain-numbing TV for a while. Just waiting for my pizza first.'

'*Oh, it's pizza night, is it?*'

'And wine ... lots of it. I'm off for the next two days, remember?'

'*Don't finish all the wine. Wait for me. We can have our own private party tomorrow night.*'

'You got yourself a deal.'

'*I'll see you tomorrow, beautiful. Miss you and love you.*'

'Miss you and love you more.'

Less than a minute after Kirsten put the phone down, her doorbell rang. Pizza time.

She gave the delivery guy a ten-dollar-tip, brought the pizza to the living room, placed the box on the coffee table and returned to the kitchen to grab some paper towels. No plates. Pizza, she believed, tasted better when you held the slice in your hand.

As she tore a couple of sheets from the paper towel dispenser, Kirsten felt a light draft of cold air kiss her right cheek. She turned to find that a strong gust of wind had pushed the window opened just a touch.

'Again?' she asked out loud, half annoyed, shaking her head. 'Goddamn it, Troy.'

Troy had a habit of opening the kitchen window when cooking, instead of switching on the extraction unit above the stove. More often than not, he would forget to lock it back, but tonight that really annoyed Kirsten because it meant that the window had been left unlocked since Friday, the day Troy left for San Francisco. It was Monday night. With Kirsten being at the hospital for most of the past three days, anyone could've climbed in and stolen whatever they liked.

Troy would be getting an earful next time he called.

Kirsten locked the window and returned to the living room, where she got comfortable on the sofa, but her binge-watch session didn't quite go as planned. She only managed to watch a single episode, in which time she finished half of her bottle of wine and ate three-quarters of her pizza. She did think about starting episode three, but after all that wine and such a hard day at the hospital, she was feeling a little woozy and exhausted. She switched off the TV and put the rest of the pizza in the fridge. She loved cold pizza for breakfast.

Being in between the sheets without Troy did feel awfully lonely, and since she was unable to hug him, she threw her arm over his pillow and brought it to her face.

At that exact moment, her cellphone beeped and vibrated on her bedside table, announcing a new text message. The unexpected sound startled her. The digital clock on her bedside table read: 00:29.

Kirsten let go of Troy's pillow and reached for her phone, fully expecting it to be him, sending her another 'I love you' message. He was that kind of guy – romantic and attentive.

Absentmindedly, Kirsten opened the message without checking the sender's number.

Rough day at the hospital today, Kirsten? How was the pizza?

Surprised, she blinked a couple of times to unblur her vision. This couldn't be Troy. He very rarely called her by her name. It was always 'baby', or 'my love', or some permutation of it, especially on text messages. He also preferred using WhatsApp instead of regular SMS.

Kirsten, at last, checked for the sender.

'Unknown Number.'

Who is this? she typed back.

The reply came back in just a few seconds. *I'm am an educator, Kirsten . . . a mentor, if you will.*

'What?' Kirsten asked out loud, frowning at her phone, before typing exactly that back.

I am a mentor. You know what that means, don't you? And this . . . this will be a lesson.

Kirsten switched on her bedside lamp and sat up against the headboard.

Seriously, who is this? she texted back. *I had a long day at the hosp tdy and I'm already in bed. In fact, ur message woke me up. Not really in the mood for jks.*

She stared at her screen for the next thirteen seconds before a reply appeared.

Jokes? Who said that this was a joke?

Kirsten truly wasn't in the mood for any of this.

Look, I'm really not doing this with u. U either tell me who this is in your nxt txt, or I'm blocking ur ass, got it?

Once again, she waited, during which time she searched her brain for who could be messaging her anytime past midnight on a Tuesday morning. Yes, there was a very slight possibility that this could be Troy pranking her, but if it were him, he knew that when Kirsten started using words like 'ass' in her sentences, it meant that her patience was wearing thin. If this were Troy, the joke would end now. He would not push any further.

Her phone finally vibrated again in her hand.

I've already told you who this is. I'm a mentor. And this isn't a prank, Kirsten. What this is, like I said, is a lesson.

Kirsten chuckled humorlessly at the message, but though her intention really was to block the sender, her curiosity was engaged.

A lesson? She typed. *A lesson in what? How to be annoying?*

The reply came back in exactly twenty seconds.

Actually, this will be a lesson in three subjects.

'OK,' Kirsten laughed. 'Good to know.' She really had had enough of this, but though blocking calls and messages from unknown numbers was very possible, it wasn't quite as straight forward as blocking a call from unhidden numbers, and Kirsten was no phone expert

She tapped the ellipses at the top right hand corner of her screen to call the drop-down menu. As the menu popped up, it showed no option to 'block'.

Ding, ding.

A new text message from 'The Mentor'.

Kirsten opened it.

But before we start our lesson, Kirsten, I've got a question for you. . .

There was a deliberate break.

Ding, ding.

Does it scare you?

'Does what scare me?' Kirsten asked herself, with a chuckle. 'Getting stupid text mess—'

Ding, ding.

Knowing that you will die tonight?

Seventeen

Outside, the night had grown cold and ominous. The moon and the stars had given way to a long, dense and menacing dark sheet of clouds. Unsteady gusts of wind came and went like lost ghosts, haunting the streets. The scent of oncoming rain had been slowly filling the air like burning incense for the last hour, and just as Kirsten read that last message, the first heavy drops began drumming against her rooftop.

Kirsten wasn't one to scare easily, but right then, sitting alone in her bed, with the rest of the house in total darkness and the rain rattling against her windows, she felt unsettled.

She read the two last messages again.

Does it scare you?

Knowing that you will die tonight?

She, once more, tapped the ellipses on the top right hand corner of her screen and searched for the 'block' option on the drop down menu. It must be there somewhere.

It wasn't.

Ding, ding.

A new message.

Shall we make a start with the first lesson, Kirsten? FEAR.

Kirsten hesitated for a second, unsure of what to do. Yes, she could simply turn her phone off and put it away, but that just meant that when she turned it back on, in the morning, it would go crazy with all the unread messages. Plus, Kirsten had always been a curious soul. There was no way that she would be able to fall asleep knowing that some idiot was sending her stupid messages, trying to prank her, because this had to be a prank ... right? There really was no other explanation for it.

Instead of putting her phone away, she decided to type one last message.

Look, this has now gone way too far. It wasn't funny to begin with and now, it's just plain stupid. I'm tired ... it's late ... and I had a very difficult day at the hosp. Don't message me ag—

Ding, ding. A new message arrived before Kirsten had finished typing hers.

I'm not sure if you noticed it, Kirsten, but the window in your kitchen was left unlocked.

Kirsten's fingers trembled against her cellphone screen. How the hell could this freak know about the unlocked window?

She quickly deleted what she had just typed and started a brand new message.

This really isn't funny.

The reply came moments later.

The reason I know that the window was left unlocked, Kirsten, is because I was the one who unlocked it.

Kirsten's instinctive reaction was to look in the direction of the door to her bedroom. As she did, a horrible shiver shot down her spine. She immediately began doubting her own thoughts.

Could this actually be Troy? Who else would've known about the kitchen window?

Troy, is this u? If it is, I swear to God.

No, this isn't Troy, came the reply. *This is the person who left your kitchen window unlocked...*

Another deliberate break.

New message.

After I climbed through into your house and hid some-where inside.

Kirsten's breath caught on her throat. She had to read the message a couple of times just to be sure.

Ding, ding.

That's right, Kirsten. I'm in here with you. Just the two of us. So how would you like to play a game of hide and seek? I'm hiding ... now you seek.

That was it. Enough was enough.

OK, u fucking freak, she typed back. It was better to sound angry than scared. *That's it. I'm calling the cops on ur ass.*

Ding, ding.

A pop-up displaying just part of the new message appeared at the top of Kirsten's screen. She tried to dismiss it, but her unsteady fingers tapped it instead and the full message was displayed.

What if I told you that I was already inside your bedroom?

Kirsten's heart did a triple somersault inside her chest and she shifted in bed, her eyes sweeping the room, the corners, the shadows ... but even with the bedside lamp on, there were too many of them.

Ding, ding.

There aren't that many places to hide in here, Kirsten. In fact, there are only two places where I could be.

Kirsten's breathing became heavy. She was about to reach over to the bedside lamp on Troy's side of the bed when a new message arrived.

Would it scare you if all of a sudden, you felt something move from under your bed?

'What?' Kirsten yelped. Reflexively, she brought her knees to her chest to make herself into a human ball.

Prank or not ... lesson or not ... 'fear' had definitely been achieved.

Ding, ding.

Would you look, Kirsten? Would you stretch your body and look under your bed . . . right now?

Kirsten didn't look under the bed, but she did angle her body slightly so she could see past the edge of it on the side that she was on – the left side. Her gaze stayed on the floor for several seconds – nothing there but her slippers. She took a deep breath, readying herself to scoot over and have a look on the other side, when she received a new message.

How about your wardrobe, Kirsten? I could be hiding in there.
Ding, ding.
Have you noticed anything different about your wardrobe?

Kirsten's eyes immediately moved from her cellphone screen to her wardrobe, which was built into the wall across the room from where the bed was, and she froze in place.

The doors were just a little ajar, and she was pretty certain that after her shower, once she'd collected her slippers from the wardrobe and gone back to the living room to wait for her pizza, she had closed them both.

Fear was starting to turn into panic.

Outside, the rain was getting heavier and heavier . . . the drumming against her window and rooftop, louder and louder.

Kirsten's attention returned to her cellphone. She was done playing this stupid game.

Yes, she was scared, and no, she was not about to get out of bed and go check under it or inside her wardrobe. What she was about to do was dial 911.

New message.
Did you notice the doors?

'Fuck this bullshit,' Kirsten whispered to herself. As she tapped the phone app, her frightened gaze returned to the wardrobe. The doors were still ajar, but she could swear that there was something else different about it now . . . Kirsten couldn't quite tell what it was and instinctively, her eyes squinted at it to gain better focus.

With her full attention fixed on the wardrobe, she never noticed the figure, dressed all in black, that began slowly slithering from under her bed.

Eighteen

The morning was damp and cold. Puddles on the ground reflected the scale of the night's downpour, which lasted until around 4:30 a.m.

Hunter had managed just a little over four non-consecutive hours of sleep, which, for someone who suffered from chronic insomnia, wasn't at all bad going.

After dropping by the SixPax gym in Culver City, he arrived at the Police Administration Building at 07:26 – twenty-six minutes after Garcia.

'How did it go with Kevin Garrison?' Garcia asked, as Hunter entered the office and closed the door behind him.

'No Bill,' Hunter replied, getting to his desk. 'He's not our guy.'

'Really?' Garcia sat back on his chair. He sounded truly disappointed. 'How come? What did he say?'

'I didn't talk to him. He wasn't there.' Hunter said. 'But I did speak to one of the trainers in the gym. Kevin has been in Sacramento since Friday. He and two other gym members competed at the IFBB Pro-League, which took place over the weekend. He placed fourth.' He shook his head. 'He wasn't in LA the night Melissa was murdered and his alibi is watertight. He's not our guy.'

Garcia rested his elbow on his desk and scratched his chin. 'So now our only person of interest is "Sleazy Mark", if Mark even is his real name.'

'So far, yes,' Hunter agreed, as he took a seat behind his desk. 'Any news from Forensics?'

'Nothing yet, but we got a report back from Research on the cross reference I asked them to do for any similar murders.'

'Any luck?'

Garcia breathed out disappointment. 'I'm still just scamming through the list, trying to see if anything sticks out, but I guess that would depend on what you'd call "similar".' He used his mouse to scroll down on his screen. 'Be warned, Research was kind enough to include crime scene photos with all of these, and they've sent us violent murders coming from all over the map – New York, Chicago, Miami, Seattle, LA, you name it – but I still haven't come across anything in the vein of what we've got. For example, there are plenty of crime scenes where the victim was left hanging, but not a single one was hooked or lifted by the mouth. Other than the expected "rope", we've got cases where the perpetrator has used a variety of different props – electric cables, chains, pantyhose, dog collars, work ties ... even a cincture. We also have plenty of cases where the victim was left hanging by the feet, or arms.' Another scroll down. 'There are a handful of cases here where a meat or bale hook was used, but the victim was only lifted from the ground and left hanging in three of those crime scenes, and in all three of them, the victims were found inside a meat locker, and the hook perforated the victims' back, not their mouth, face or skull.'

Hunter nodded, his eyes on his computer screen.

'We also have several cases showing severe facial disfiguration,' Garcia continued. 'Cuts ... mutilation ... beaten to a pulp ... acid burns ... fire burns ... throat sliced from ear to ear ... skull crushed.' He threw his hands up in the air in a 'go figure' gesture. 'Research did come across one case where the perpetrator practically ripped his victim's mandible off her face, but this is going back fifteen years, there was no hanging and the perp was her own husband, who was caught and convicted.' He lifted a hand to pause Hunter before he spoke. 'I understand that we are not looking for an identical crime scene to the one we have. What we're looking for is some sort of preceding escalation, right? Something not as severe, but with hints that it could escalate to the level of brutality that we got.'

'Yes, that's the theory,' Hunter agreed, also scrolling down on his screen.

'But how do we know what it can escalate from?' Garcia asked. 'I mean, are we looking for something . . . let's say, just a little less violent than what we've got? Or a lot less violent? Can this have escalated from something that would've looked a lot different? No hanging? No facial disfiguration? What? Because I'm a little lost here.'

Hunter sat back on his chair and rubbed his eyes. 'That *is* the problem, Carlos. Human behavior is not an exact science. Patterns change and they can change drastically from person to person.' His turn to lift a hand at Garcia. 'With that said, it would be very unnatural for our perp to go from no, little and even moderate violence, to the level of brutality displayed in our crime scene.'

'And that's my point,' Garcia said, both of his index fingers pointing at Hunter.

Garcia understood the escalation theory well – if this killer was killing because of an urge that he couldn't control, some kind of compulsion that came from within – nine times out of ten, that compulsion started small, probably not even as a homicide. Whatever that compulsion was, the perp would somehow feed it to curb the urge. That feeding, whatever it was, would initiate the cycle. Soon enough, the urge would come back . . . stronger . . . hungrier . . . but not by much, demanding just a little bit more. Unable to deny it, the perp would feed the monster again, giving it that little bit more than it had asked for. The pattern would then repeat itself, always escalating . . . always demanding more with every cycle.

'If what we saw at the crime scene really was the result of escalation,' Garcia carried on, 'then this killer has reached "boss level", which means that he's been active for a long time . . . probably years. Since he's now active in LA, it stands to reason that he's committed other crimes in this city, probably homicides.'

'So how come none of his previous crimes ever came to our attention, right?' Hunter said, anticipating what Garcia was about to ask.

'Exactly,' Garcia confirmed. 'We're the UVC Unit. Something would've come to us.'

'Maybe, but remember that the escalation theory isn't infallible. Cases of cognitive escalation do exist, where the majority of the escalation happens inside a person's mind. When the monster inside becomes too big, too hungry for the cognitive process, the perp finally acts on it. In those cases, their first murder tends to show severe violence.'

'You think that that could be the case here?' Garcia's chin tipped toward his chest as he asked the question.

'I don't know, Carlos. Yes, it could be, because nothing in human behavior is set in stone. But we still know very little about this case. This killer might not be serial . . . this could've been an isolated racial crime . . . there are lots of possibilities. All we're doing by checking older cases is examining one of the possibilities, that's all.'

Garcia slumped back on his chair at the exact same time that a bell-like sound came from his and Hunter's computer, announcing a new email.

Garcia checked the title.

'Oh wow! I wasn't expecting this until later in the week, if we were lucky.'

'What is that?' Hunter asked.

'Melissa Hawthorne's phone calls and texts transcripts,' Garcia said, nodding at Hunter's monitor on his desk. 'Check your email.'

Hunter did. The email came with two attached files – 'Phone Calls' and 'SMS Text Messages'.

Nineteen

While Hunter was still scanning through the list that they had received from Research, Garcia opened the first of the two attached files – 'Phone Calls' – and quickly skimmed through the last phone call Melissa Hawthorne had received.

'Crap!' he said after just a few seconds.

'What's wrong? Hunter asked.

Garcia kept his eyes on his computer screen. 'I was hoping that maybe "Sleazy Mark" would've called the victim after they left the Broken Shaker. You know? Just to check that she hadn't given him the wrong number.'

'Nothing?' Hunter minimized the list and moved on to the email.

'Nope. Not from him. The last ever call Melissa Hawthorne received was at 18:33 on Saturday evening, the night of the party. That was probably the call she got from Janet.'

'Maybe he sent her a text, instead,' Hunter suggested, quickly double-clicking the second attachment to the email – the list of SMS text messages.

'Maybe,' Garcia agreed, but he stayed with the phone call transcripts for the moment.

As the file opened on Hunter's screen, his eyes settled on the first conversation and he went eerily silent.

Garcia was too engrossed in the phone call transcripts to notice the look on Hunter's face.

'Forget about the phone calls, Carlos,' Hunter said, a disbelieving edge to his voice. 'Have a look at the text messages file.'

'Did he message her?' Garcia's tone, on the other hand, carried a full measure of excitement.

'I'm not sure, but the killer certainly did.'

'What?' Garcia's eyes lifted from his screen to look back at Hunter.

'First conversation in the file. But her last ever one. First message arrived at 02:32 on Sunday morning.'

Garcia opened the file. As he read through the conversation that Hunter had flagged, the expression on his face changed – from curious to intrigued, to doubtful, to confused, and finally to shocked.

'You've got to be shitting me,' he said, quickly minimizing the text messages transcript and rechecking the email he had received. There really were only two attached files. 'What the hell?' He shook his head at his screen before looking at Hunter. 'There's no video file. The transcript says that the message came with a video attachment. Where's the video? Why wasn't it included in the email?'

'Probably because it wasn't requested,' Hunter informed him.

'It wasn't requested because we didn't know that there could or would be a video file,' Garcia replied, with annoyance. 'But since there was one, it should've gone without saying, right?'

'Nothing ever goes without saying when it comes to cellphone providers surrendering private videos and photos, Carlos. You know that. We'll need a warrant.'

Garcia did know that. In the USA, the law concerning what cellphone providers could store from their customers was very broad. In a nutshell, it was mainly up to the providers themselves to decide what they would archive from calls and messages other than normal audio and text files. It was true that most providers chose to archive just about everything, but to protect themselves against privacy lawsuits, they put up a world of walls when asked to disclose private images and video.

'I thought this had moved way too fast for a cellphone provider,' Garcia said. 'Something just had to be missing. I'll put in a request for the warrant as soon as Captain Blake gets in.'

Hunter's attention went back to his computer. He reread the messages that the killer had sent Melissa twice over before sitting back on his chair, resting his elbows on the armrests and interlacing his fingers in front of his chin.

'There's a hell of a lot that we can interpret from all this,' Garcia said, breaking the silence that had taken over the room.

'OK.' Hunter nodded. 'What's your take?'

'Well ...' Garcia leaned forward. 'Right from the start we have – "Did you have fun at the party?" – which shows that the killer knew that Melissa had been to a party that night.'

Hunter nodded.

'That strengthens the case for "Sleazy Mark",' Garcia continued. 'He met her at the party ... he knew her name ... he *had* her phone number, and he could've followed her home without her noticing it. As we found out through the CCTV footage, he did leave the hotel pretty much on her heels, remember? He could've jumped in a car, or a cab, and easily followed her back to her place.'

'True,' Hunter agreed. 'But if that's the case, then "Sleazy Mark" was posing.'

'Posing?' Garcia frowned. 'What do you mean?'

'We've already accepted that this couldn't have been a spur-of-the-moment attack, right? It was too well planned ... too elaborate ... and this text conversation solidifies that assumption. So sure, "Sleazy Mark" could've made himself known to Melissa that night, at the Broken Shaker, but if he really is her killer, than he clearly had the whole thing planned beforehand. Melissa might've only met him on Saturday night, but from his side, that meeting wasn't by chance. He was there for her.'

Garcia pointed an index finger at Hunter. 'Very true. Sorry, I'd forgotten about that for a moment, and from the CCTV camera footage . . . from the way we saw "Sleazy Mark" acting at the bar . . .' Garcia shook his head. 'I wouldn't put it past him. He knew exactly what he was doing.'

'I agree. "Sleazy Mark" is still very much our prime suspect.'

Garcia returned to the text message.

'Now this is the bit that really bothers me – "*Who am I? Well . . . to you, I'll be a mentor, Melissa*".' His eyebrows lifted at Hunter. 'He gives himself an alias, Robert – Mentor – and that freaks me out because we both know that killers who do that, do it for a reason – they want the notoriety . . . they want the world to know what they've done . . . what they've accomplished – BTK, Son of Sam, The Grim Sleeper . . . history is full of them. And we also know that that means that there's more to come. Melissa is only the beginning.'

'That's a possibility,' Hunter agreed. 'But I'm not one hundred percent sure here.'

'Really? Why not?'

Hunter angled his head slightly to one side. 'To me, there's something in the way that the killer phrased his reply that comes across too unconcerned – "Who am I? Well . . . to you, I'll be a mentor, Melissa." I can practically hear the shrug in those words, can't you? As if he doesn't really care for the name he'd just given himself.'

Garcia's attention returned to that specific line on the transcript.

'You're right,' Hunter confirmed. 'Killers like BTK, Son of Sam, or the Grim Sleeper, they want the notoriety . . . they want to be known . . . and that notoriety comes via their aliases, even after they've been caught. It's an extremely important part to who they are . . . who they want to be.' He pointed to his monitor. 'In his reply, the killer didn't even capitalize the word "mentor", as if it doesn't really matter to him. He also used the words "to you", almost as if with a different victim, he would've picked a different alias.'

Garcia thought about that for a second.

'I might be wrong,' Hunter accepted. 'But reading this entire exchange of messages again, I don't get the impression that this killer cares too much about the alias he gave himself. He's not doing this for notoriety.'

'Alright,' Garcia nodded. 'So what's your take on this then?'

Hunter breathed out. 'That this whole exchange was, in fact, what the killer called his first lesson – fear. He wanted Melissa to be scared, and he brought that fear to her gradually and expertly. First, the mysterious messenger who introduces himself as the Mentor – then . . .' as he spoke, Hunter moved his hand up in steps to show 'escalation'. 'He tells her that he's going to teach her about fear . . . pain . . . and death. Sure, that could be a little scary, but just like you see from Melissa's replies, her first thought is – "this has got to be a joke, right?" She even tries calling Mark's bluff because for some reason, she thought that this could've been him.'

'Which again,' Garcia reiterated, 'strengthens the case for "Sleazy Mark".'

Hunter agreed before moving his hand up another step. 'After that, it gets serious.' He read from the transcript. '"It means that tonight, Melissa, after you got back from your little soirée and stumbled out of the cab . . . about half an hour ago . . . you forgot to lock your front door." He knew that she had stumbled out her cab . . . and he knew the timeframe.'

Garcia nodded. 'Now Melissa knows that this isn't a joke. There was no way that this "Mentor" could've known about any of that, unless he had followed her home from the party, was already in her house when she got there, or he was hiding somewhere outside, waiting for her to arrive.'

'Exactly,' Hunter agreed. 'And he finishes it all off with

victim-blaming – you forgot to lock your front door – this is really all your fault, not mine.'

'I picked that up too,' Garcia agreed. 'And you're right – alone, at home, at that time? There's no way that Melissa wasn't terrified by the end of those text messages.'

'Like I said – expert gradual escalation.'

'And I bet that the missing video here is the icing on the cake, right? What truly petrified her.'

Hunter nodded. 'We need to get that warrant.'

Twenty

Janet Lang woke up in fright from another soul-disturbing nightmare. This time, she saw her sister, Melissa, begging her for help, but Janet could hardly understand what she was saying. Melissa wasn't hanging from a cable, but she did have a giant hook through her lower jaw and every time she spoke, blood splattered from her mouth, coloring the air with a crimson mist. The mist would turn into clouds and blood would rain in the living room.

Since Sunday morning, the morning Janet had found Melissa's body, her days and nights consisted mainly of her dozing off – sometimes due to medication, sometimes due to pure exhaustion – and then being brutally awaken by nightmares so unsettling and vivid her whole body would shake. Twice her dreams had been so terrifying that Janet had lost control and wet herself.

This time, Janet had fallen asleep in her bedroom, while Tom was in the kitchen, preparing himself a sandwich. The one he had made for Janet at 6 a.m. was still untouched, sitting on a plate on her bedside table.

Tom had taken a week off work to stay by her side and he would have been lying if he hadn't admitted that he was very concerned.

He knew that mentally, Janet had always been a very strong person, but even the strongest of minds could break if pushed far enough. It was true that there weren't many life events that could, with a single blow, fracture a mind way beyond the point of no return. Unfortunately, finding a loved one brutally murdered was right at the top of the list of such events and Melissa had been much more than just a beloved sister to Janet. She had been Janet's best friend and the rock she could always lean against no matter what. Without Melissa, Janet could easily become a lost soul. Tom knew that too.

He had just taken a bite of his peanut butter and jelly sandwich when he heard Janet's muffled scream. He dropped the sandwich on the kitchen counter and hurried into their bedroom. Janet was sitting on their bed, knees against her chest, sobbing, with her face buried into her hands.

'It's OK, baby,' Tom said, as he reached her. 'It was just a dream . . . just a dream.' He placed his arms around her and brought her towards him.

Janet allowed herself to be hugged, but she didn't hug back, keeping her face hidden in her hands.

'I'm here, Jen . . . I'm here.' Tom reached for her hands. 'Look at me, baby. It was only a dream.' He kissed both of her hands and caressed her hair. 'Please, look at me, Jen.'

Still sobbing, Janet finally allowed her hands to drop and locked eyes with him.

He kissed her cheeks and tried wiping away her tears, but Janet couldn't stop crying.

'It's alright, baby,' Tom tried again. 'It's gone. It was a dream . . . nothing but a bad dream . . . that's all. It's not real.'

'That's where you're wrong, Tom,' Janet hit back, her tone full of pain. 'Because *it is* real . . . Mel is gone, Tom . . .' Her voice thinned. 'She's gone. Mel is dead. She's dead. My sister is not here anymore.' Her hands returned to her face.

Tom couldn't believe that he had chosen his words so poorly. He hugged her tighter, his heart broken inside of him. 'I'm so sorry, baby.' It was his turn to fight back tears. 'I'm so, so sorry.'

In his arms, he could feel Janet shaking. Not knowing what else to say, he simply held her tight, until the sobbing had turned to sniffles.

'Why don't you come sit in the living room with me, Jen?' Tom asked, once again wiping away tears from Janet's face. 'We can watch some old show re-run. Something light . . . something easy to watch. What do you think?'

Janet stayed silent.

Tom kissed her forehead and then her cheeks. 'C'mon.' He got up, but kept her hands in his. 'Come with me. Let's sit on the sofa for a little. I'll make popcorn.'

Janet looked away, trying to decide what to do. She really didn't want to face reality. At least not at the moment. Every second she spent awake, she knew that she would spend thinking of her sister, who she would never, ever see again . . . but despite how exhausted she felt, she was also terrified of falling back asleep. Actually, she was terrified of even closing her eyes because every time she did, the images that she saw that Sunday morning were there, waiting for her, as if they had been forever etched on the inside of her eyelids.

Tom read the indecision in Janet's face – stay awake, or try to fall back asleep. She needed rest, he knew that, but sleep wasn't bringing her any. If she came to the living room with him, he could at least be by her side. He tried again.

'C'mon, baby. Sit with me just for an hour or so.' His tone was pleading and tender.

Still sniffling, Janet finally nodded and slowly got to her feet. Tom let go of her hands and she used a paper tissue to dry her face. As they got to the bedroom door, Janet paused.

'My phone,' she said, pointing at her bedside table. 'Let me get my phone. I haven't checked it since last night.'

Janet had put her cellphone on silent – no ring and no vibration. Tom waited.

She grabbed her phone and checked its screen – ten missed calls and over twenty messages. She breathed out and rejoined her boyfriend.

In the living room, while Tom searched through seemingly hundreds of satellite channels for something watchable, Janet scrolled through the missing calls – one from her doctor, eight from friends and one from her boss at work. She decided that she would call them all back later. She just didn't have the strength for a phone conversation with anyone right then. Instead, she moved on to the messages. Most of them were from friends – twenty-four WhatsApp messages and one SMS text. The SMS had come from an unknown number. Janet thumbed down on her screen to check the message preview and was instantly surprised. The preview read 'Melissa'. The body of the message contained just a video, no text.

Janet's response was automatic. She simply tapped the preview to open the message. As it did, the sent video filled her screen and her heart immediately shot up to her throat, almost choking her. Her body lost all of its strength, her arms went limp and she dropped her phone onto the floor.

The shriek that came out of her vocal cords was a sound that Tom had never heard before . . . and it frightened him stiff.

Twenty-one

At the Police Administration Building, Hunter and Garcia were standing inside Captain Blake's office. She had just read through the transcript of the text conversation between the killer and Melissa Hawthorne.

'The video?' she asked, lifting the transcript in her hand. 'Where's the video that was sent?'

'Exactly,' Garcia replied with a single nod. 'You would've thought that they would've included it with our request, wouldn't you?'

'They didn't?' The surprise in her tone was genuine.

'We need a warrant, Captain,' Hunter jumped in. 'You know how heavily cellphone providers shield themselves from privacy lawsuits. It's a private video.'

'Unbelievable,' Captain Blake said, as she pressed the intercom button on the phone on her desk.

'*Yes, Captain?*' Officer Teresa Broody's voice came through the tiny speaker. She partially took care of Captain Blake's daily agenda.

'Teresa, can you please get Judge Peterson at the Metropolitan Courthouse on the line?'

'*Right away, Captain.*'

'Do you think there's a chance that this killer showed his face on this video?' the captain asked Hunter and Garcia, as she let go of the intercom button.

Both detectives shrugged back at her.

'That's what he says, isn't it?' Captain Blake checked the transcript again. 'Right here – "Don't worry. I've locked your door for you. Here, have a look."'

'The video could've shown just about anything, Captain,' Hunter speculated. 'A shot of the door being closed ... a shot of a hand turning the lock ... a shot of the door ajar ... whatever. Right now there's no telling.'

'Or even a shot of someone in a mask locking the door,' Garcia added. 'The main intention of that entire text conversation was to scare Melissa. This is the "fear" lesson, Captain. What could be scarier than you knowing that you're locked inside your own house with an intruder?'

'Maybe,' the captain agreed. 'But don't ever underestimate the stupidity of some people. Maybe this killer believed that by taking the victim's phone away with him, he would be in the clear.'

'We can but hope,' Garcia said.

'*Judge Peterson is on line one, Captain,*' Officer Broody's voice announced through the intercom.

Captain Blake took the call and Hunter and Garcia waited while she gave Judge Peterson a quick run through the situation before giving him Melissa's name and number and asking him to issue the warrant.

The Judge and Captain Blake went back a long way. He had always trusted her judgement. Eight out of ten times, when she needed a warrant for anything, she would go to him.

'*Send an officer over, Barbara,*' he told her. '*The warrant will be ready by the time they get here.*'

Captain Blake put down her phone and immediately used the intercom to ask Officer Broody to send a uniformed officer to the Metropolitan Courthouse to pick up the warrant.

As soon as she let go of the 'talk' button, Hunter's cellphone vibrated inside his jacket pocket. He checked the display screen.

The number displayed wasn't on his contact list. He lifted a hand at the captain, as he took the call.

'Detective Hunter, UVC Unit.'

He listened for about five seconds, after which Garcia and Captain Blake watched his facial expression change, as if Hunter hadn't quite understood what was said.

'Hold on, Tom,' he said into his phone, his voice steady. 'Take a breath and tell me that again from the beginning.' He walked over to the north-west corner of the office.

'Who's Tom?' Captain Blake whispered the question to Garcia, who, with a pensive look, shrugged at her.

'Janet has received what?' Hunter said.

That refreshed Garcia's memory. 'He's Janet Lang's boyfriend,' he whispered back to the captain. 'The victim's sister.'

'When?' Hunter asked Tom.

. . .

'I'm guessing it came from an unknown number,' Hunter said.

Garcia's eyes widened at his partner. 'What happened?'

Hunter gestured him to give him a moment.

'Tom . . . Tom . . . listen . . . it's a lot easier if you forward it to me, and I mean right now. Can you do that?'

Hunter nodded sadly as he listened to Tom's reply.

'I'm so sorry that this has happened, Tom, and yes, I can imagine how distraught Janet must be.'

. . .

'There's really nothing that we could've done that would've prevented that from happening, Tom, but we might be able to get a location.'

. . .

'Yes, I can try to run a trace from here. If you forward the message to me from her phone, I'll have her number. I'll take it from there. Can you do that?'

. . .

'Yes, right now.'

. . .

'Thank you. I'll get back to you.' Hunter disconnected.

'What was that all about?' Garcia asked. 'What message?'

'Janet, Melissa's sister, received a message earlier this morn-ing,' Hunter explained. 'No words. Just a video.'

'From who?' Captain Blake, this time. 'The killer?'

'I can't be sure, but apparently so.'

Hunter's phone vibrated again, this time two quick bursts announcing a new text message. Hunter immediately opened the message and as the video clip began playing on his screen, his eyes narrowed for a moment before he exhaled a heavy breath.

'Fuck!'

Twenty-two

Barbara Blake had been the Captain of the LAPD Robbery and Homicide Division for almost thirteen years. In that period, she could count on one hand the number of times she'd ever heard Hunter curse.

Garcia immediately shot to his partner's side. Captain Blake was hot on his heels.

Hunter rewound the video back to the beginning and angled the phone on his hand so that both of them could see its screen. There were three heartbeats worth of anxious silence before Hunter hit the 'play' button again.

'What . . . the ass-ripping fuck?' Garcia whispered. The look on his face was pure disbelief.

While in thirteen years Captain Blake had only heard Hunter curse a handful of times, Garcia, on the other hand, was a whole different proposition. This time, she had to admit that he had a point.

The video that Hunter had shown them had been shot inside Melissa Hawthorne's kitchen, on the night of her murder . . . and it was simply grotesque.

It began with a shot of Melissa in a standing position. She had been stripped naked, her hands had been bound behind her back and her feet were tied together at the ankles. The large fishing hook that the killer had used had also already crudely perforated her lower jaw, with the rope attached to the hook strung out over the beam. The images showed blood cascading from her wound and her open mouth in sheets, covering her body in a thin red, horrific blanket, but Melissa was still alive.

As the video played on, she convulsed and gagged, vomiting blood up in the air and onto her face. That was when the camera zoomed in on her eyes. They were wide open and one didn't have to be an expert to see that they were full of pain, fear and unimaginable terror. A second later, the shot zoomed back out to show that her feet, despite being bound together, were flat against the floor and her jaw was still in place, but not for long.

The next shot made everyone sick to their stomachs. It showed the exact moment that the climbing rope was pulled tight to hoist Melissa up in the air by her mouth. Hunter, Garcia and Captain Blake watched as Melissa's body jerked awkwardly, her legs desperately kicking out while her feet angled downwards, tiptoeing, trying in vain to find the floor. The scream that came out of her lips was drowned by the sheer amount of blood in her mouth, which gurgled as if it had boiled.

Melissa's frantic fight for life actually acted against her, as her hysterical body twists added considerable strain to her neck and jaw. It was during her chaotic struggle that they all heard a disturbing bone shattering noise come from Hunter's tiny cellphone speakers. Her mandible had finally dislocated and fractured.

The final shot showed Melissa convulsing just one more time before her entire body went still – her eyes finally closing for the last time, but the killer wasn't done yet. Just before a final fade out, the killer had added a line of text across the bottom of the video:

'JUST LIKE A FISH.'

'Jesus H Christ!' Captain Blake's words tumbled out of her lips in a monotone. 'This was sent to her sister?'

Hunter nodded. 'I'll see if Research can trace it.' He quickly placed a call to his research team.

'Why?' the captain asked, once Hunter was done with the call. She shook her head as he shrugged.

'This is so completely messed up,' Garcia said. 'This killer is a fucking freak.'

'It wasn't a rhetorical question, Robert,' Captain Blake insisted. 'Why would this killer send something like this to the victim's sister? What's the point? What could he possibly get from this? Unless this really is a racial crime.'

'Are you asking us if she's at risk, Captain?' The question came from Garcia.

Captain Blake faced him. 'Do you think she is? Is this why this killer is taunting her? Is he going after her too?'

After watching that video, Hunter had also considered that same possibility.

'She could be,' he acknowledged. 'But . . .' He shook his head.

'But . . .?' Captain Blake prodded.

Before Hunter could answer, his cellphone rang. He took the call, listened for several seconds and then disconnected.

'Research?' Garcia asked.

Hunter nodded. 'No trace. No GPS on the sender's phone.'

Garcia didn't look surprised.

Hunter took a moment, trying to choose the correct words. 'If Janet Lang really is at risk from the same killer who murdered her sister, then this is a lot more personal than what we initially thought, and this killer is a lot bolder than we're giving him credit for.'

As she thought about it, Captain Blake rubbed her thumb over the knuckles of one hand, back and forth over the knobs of bone.

'It would mean that this killer has some sort of personal beef with the Hawthornes,' she finally concluded. 'Or at least the two sisters.'

'Possibly,' Hunter agreed.

'But he would've anticipated that we would be in contact with the younger sister,' Captain Blake continued. 'The logical move for her, once she got that message, would be to contact us straight away . . . like she did. That means that he would also expect us to know about the message . . . like we do. And if he has more than half a brain cell, he'd once again anticipate that we would come to the conclusion we just did – that this could be interpreted as a threat on her life. And if the LAPD comes to that conclusion, it stands to reason that we might consider putting her under protection.' The Captain returned to the seat behind her desk before pointing at Hunter. 'That's what you meant when you said that this killer could be a lot bolder than we're giving him credit for, right?'

Once again, Hunter nodded. 'If he really is after Janet Lang, he just made his job a lot harder. The video acts as a warning.'

There was a long pause, where Captain Blake weighed her options. It was only February, still early in the year, but she was experienced enough to know that she had to tread on eggshells when it came to the budget, especially with all the cuts that had been announced by the Governor.

'Maybe he hasn't made his job a lot harder,' she said at last, shaking her head at her detectives. 'Because I can't justify putting Miss Lang under any kind of police protection. Not if all we have is just that video clip.'

Garcia looked at Hunter with eyes that spoke volumes, but neither of them tried arguing. They too were experienced enough to know that Captain Blake was right. In the end, it wasn't one hundred percent her call. She would still need to justify her decision to the Chief of Police. Despite being shocking and psychologically destructive, the video that Janet Lang had received wasn't a direct threat on her life. It could perhaps be interpreted that way, but interpretation, no matter how plausible, always left margin for doubt, and doubt wouldn't cut it with the Chief of Police.

The second problem the captain would have if she assigned a

protection team to Janet was the question of how long she would do it for? If this killer really was after Janet, there was no telling when he would strike. It could be today, tomorrow, next week, next year ... no one knew. Assigning a police protection team to anyone indefinitely was just unrealistic. Everyone in the room knew that.

As Hunter returned his cellphone to his pocket, a knock came at the captain's door.

'What is it?' she called from her desk, angling her body a little to the right so she could see past her detectives.

Hunter and Garcia glanced over at the door, which was pushed open by a young uniformed police officer. His police cap was securely held under his left arm. In his right hand, he had a large envelope.

'Excuse me, Captain Blake,' the officer said in a soft but firm voice, lifting the envelope. 'I was sent to pick up a warrant from the Metropolitan Courthouse?'

With her right hand, the captain motioned him inside before pointing at Hunter and Garcia. 'Just give it straight to them.'

The officer handed the envelope to Hunter and Captain Blake waited until he'd left her office.

'Go get this video from the cellphone provider,' she said, pointing at the door. 'Now.'

Twenty-three

Five minutes and one internal phone call after Hunter and Garcia had arrived at the headquarters of AT&T Entertainment Group, which was located just across the road from the famous LA Times building, they found themselves inside a conference room on the third floor of 'Building Two', sitting across the table from one of the phone provider's corporate lawyers. He was a tall and skinny man in his early forties, whose dark, pinstriped suit seemed to have come out of the dry cleaners just minutes before he entered the room, and he introduced himself as Martin Carr.

Not much was said. The warrant did all the talking. The lawyer was just corporate precaution.

'I'll get this sorted out for you as fast as I can, Detectives,' Martin said, giving Hunter and Garcia an unconcerned smile that seemed to indicate that he had seen just about everything up to this point in his life worth seeing. 'Shall I get this emailed straight to you?'

'We'd appreciate that,' Hunter said, writing down his and Garcia's email onto a piece of paper and handing it to the lawyer. 'But if possible, we'd also like a hard copy.'

'Of course,' Martin replied, as his gaze moved to the piece of paper that Hunter had just handed him. 'I can arrange that, no problem. You're welcome to wait in here or downstairs in the lobby. Your choice.'

'I guess here will be just fine, thank you,' Garcia replied, looking at Hunter for confirmation.

Hunter nodded back at him.

'Sure, make yourselves comfortable. There's a coffee machine just at the end of the corridor. It's free. No money needed.'

'That's quite handy,' Garcia said. 'Thank you.'

As Martin reached the door, he turned and indicated the three laptops at one end of the twelve-seater conference table. 'I'm not sure how long this might take. Hopefully not too long, but feel free to use any of those to browse the web, check emails, or whatever you like.' The unconcerned smile returned to his lips. 'Of course triple-X sites are blocked.'

Hunter and Garcia looked back at him in silence, eyes fierce, a blank expression over both of their faces.

'Umm . . . that was a joke,' Martin said, the smile dropping to the floor.

'A joke?' Garcia asked, his tone serious. 'So triple-X sites aren't blocked?'

'No,' Martin replied, awkwardly. 'They are blocked.'

'So . . . what was the joke?' Garcia asked, the blank expression on his face turning solemn.

'Umm . . .' The lawyer shifted his weight from foot to foot and quickly decided that his best move would be to just let it go. He lifted the warrant in his hand and nodded, uneasily. 'Let me go get this done,' he said before swiftly exiting the room. As the door closed behind him, Garcia finally smiled.

'Of course triple-X sites are blocked,' he said, putting on a sarcastic voice and shaking his head from side to side.

'I don't think he'll be making that joke again anytime soon,' Hunter said.

Nearly half an hour went by before the lawyer finally returned to the room.

'Sorry it took me so long,' he said, retrieving a pen drive from his right suit pocket. 'It can take a while to find the right person for such a specific job in here, but here you go.'

Hunter stood up and met him halfway between the door and the conference table.

'The same file has also been sent to both of your emails, as discussed,' Martin informed them.

Garcia fetched his cellphone from his pocket and quickly checked his email.

'Yeah, we've got it,' he announced, nodding at Hunter as he got to his feet.

Down in the parking lot, neither detective wanted to wait until they were back at the PAB to have a look at the video that the killer had sent Melissa. As they got back into Garcia's Honda Civic, Hunter used his cellphone to go into his inbox, found the email from AT&T and tapped the attached file. As the video loaded, he tipped his phone just enough so that Garcia could also see its screen.

They watched as the leather-gloved hand turned the key to lock Melissa's front door before removing them from the lock itself. Then they saw the camera pan right to show the time – 2:24 a.m.

'What time did she get this?' Garcia asked. 'Do you remember?'

Hunter paused the video. 'Around 2:38 a.m.'

'So the killer was inside her house all that time?' Garcia's tone was a mixture of surprise and doubt. 'Why? What was he doing? What was he waiting for?'

'Maybe he was waiting for her to go to bed,' Hunter speculated, trying to visualize the scene in his head. 'Remember that the reason for the text messages and this video clip was to induce fear. The killer wanted her to be scared. It was part of his plan. Waiting until all the lights were turned off and she was comfortably in bed would, no doubt, add to the "fear factor".'

Garcia agreed, but he still had questions. 'So we know that Melissa got a cab from the party at the hotel just before one thirty in the morning, right?'

Hunter nodded. '1:28 a.m.'

'At that time, a cab from the Freehand Hotel downtown to her house in Leimert Park wouldn't take longer than twenty ... twenty-five minutes max. She would've been home by 2 a.m., easy. But she only got the text with this video at 2:38, 2:39 a.m. That's over half hour after she got home. Even the first of the texts sent to her by the killer – that was at 2:32 a.m., if I remember correctly.'

'That's right,' Hunter confirmed.

'So the killer's first text to her that night was sent eight minutes after he shot this video,' Garcia said. 'Why did he wait so long? Where was she?'

'Probably taking a shower,' Hunter suggested.

'So the killer hid somewhere inside her house, waited for her to go have a shower, shot the video, waited for her to go to bed and *then* started with the texts.'

'It would seem so,' Hunter confirmed.

Garcia shook his head as he mentally ran through the scene. 'That shows patience and a lot of self-discipline.'

'It also shows that he's calm and collected,' Hunter added. 'No rush ... no panic.'

'If he wanted her scared,' Garcia said, 'this would've done it, alright. No way she watched this video alone at home and didn't freak the fuck out.'

'The video isn't over yet,' Hunter said, checking his cellphone screen. 'There are four seconds left.'

Garcia repositioned himself so that he could once again see the screen.

Hunter re-started the video.

No much happened in the remaining four seconds. The camera stayed on the kitchen clock, but in the last two seconds, a sound came through the tiny speakers on Hunter's phone that made their hearts skip a collective beat.

'What was that?' Garcia asked, his eyebrows knit.

'It sounded like a whisper,' Hunter replied, immediately rewinding the video just a few seconds. He thumbed the volume button, taking it to as loud as it would go. As he once again tapped on his screen to re-start the video, he and Garcia moved their right ear to just an inch from the cellphone.

Hunter had been right. The killer had said something into the microphone. Three barely audible words, but powerful enough to petrify anyone.

As if the words weren't already terrifying enough, the killer whispered them in a lover's caress that ratcheted them up to horrifying:

'*I'm already inside.*'

Twenty-four

The sky above San Francisco was a patchwork of blue and white. Thin clouds paled the morning sun, but enough light shone through to warm the day into a comfortable enough temperature to allow Troy Foster to wear his favorite camouflage T-shirt.

Just like he had told Kirsten he would, after his meeting that morning, Troy jumped straight into his pickup truck and promptly hit the road. By 10:40 he was crossing Oakland Bay Bridge, and by 11:30, he'd already joined Interstate 5, heading toward Los Angeles.

In a perfect world, the 390-mile trip between San Francisco and LA would've taken Troy five to six hours to complete, but the Interstates in California very rarely played by the rules, and the I-5 was one of the busiest in the entire state. That day, too many heavy-duty vehicles and a mile long stretch of roadworks served to add an extra two and half hours to the trip, with traffic slowing down to a snail's pace just as Troy reached Fresno County. His solution, since there was nothing else he could do, was to simply turn up the music.

That morning, as he was leaving San Francisco, Troy had called Kirsten, just to let her know that he was indeed on his way. He got no reply. Instead, after the fifth unanswered ring, the call went into her voicemail. He'd left her a quick message, telling her that he was on the road. He'd also told her that he would call again later and that he would keep her informed of any delays.

Troy called again at around 1:30 p.m., during his lunch stop. Once again, no reply – five rings later, he got Kirsten's voicemail.

'Hey baby, it's me. Did you get my first message? Where are you? Anyway, just to let you know that traffic so far has been OK. If it carries on like this, I really should be home sometime between six and seven. Miss you. Call me back, or text me just so I know that you've got my messages. Gotta run. Love you.'

Just in case there was something wrong with Kirsten's voicemail, Troy also sent her a WhatsApp message. Two hours later and he still hadn't heard from her. He wasn't necessarily worried. Not yet. At work, Kirsten never kept her phone on her. She couldn't have it ringing inside an operation theater, so it stayed in her locker. That created a habit in which most days, she would completely forget about her phone and only check it at the end of her shift, but today was Kirsten's day off. Sure, she tended to always leave her phone on silent and sometimes, on days off, she would go for a run and leave it at home – but even if that had been the case, Troy's first message to her had been left before eleven that morning, as he was leaving his hotel. It was now almost four in the afternoon. She should've checked her phone by now.

There was the chance that his fiancée had managed to lose or somehow damage her phone. She'd done it before.

By 07:30 p.m., when Troy made his final stop – about one and a half hours outside LA – he still hadn't heard a peep from Kirsten.

And he was starting to worry.

Naturally, he tried to imagine why she hadn't called him back or even sent him a message. Was she angry with him for some reason? If she were, he couldn't figure out why. The only plausible explanation he managed to come up with for Kirsten's total radio silence was if she had been called into the hospital.

Maybe one of the nurses called in sick and they had to drag her in last minute, he thought. It'd happened several times before.

If Kirsten had to cover an entire afternoon shift, it would explain why she hadn't called or messaged him yet.

That must be it, Troy decided. *They must've called her in.*

Still, as he pulled up to the gas station, he reached for his phone to place one more call to Kirsten.

Voicemail.

'Hey, baby, it's me again. Are you alright? You're not pissed at me, are you? No of course not. I'm perfect.' He chuckled. 'Well, I'm guessing that someone called in sick and you had to drag your ass into work on your day off, am I right? That sucks balls, baby. I know that you can't say "no", but still . . . it sucks. Anyway . . . quick update. Since my last message, traffic went to hell and things got really delayed. It's already seven-thirty and I'm still about one and a half hours away. If nothing else goes wrong, I should be home sometime between nine and ten, but please either call or message me back once you get this. Love you and can't wait to see you.'

It was getting late and Troy was starting to get hungry again. Now that he knew that he wouldn't make it home by dinnertime, he decided to grab another burger with a large side of fries, but this time he took everything back to his truck. To try to make up some more time, he decided to eat while he drove.

Traffic did ease up a little and he made it into Greater LA by 8:30 p.m. By nine o'clock, Troy was on the south side of the Hills, where he decided to take the Foothill Freeway instead of the Golden Gate one. The Golden Gate Freeway would take him through Downtown Los Angeles, where traffic, no matter the time or the day, was usually a problem. It turned out to be a good decision. Traffic on Foothill Freeway was as normal as normal could be.

As Troy crossed through Glendale, he checked the clock on his dashboard – 09:15 p.m. and still no word from Kirsten. Not even a text message.

Had they slapped her with a double shift on her day off? If they had, she would be on duty for sixteen, maybe eighteen hours straight. That would really suck, but it wouldn't surprise him. Kirsten had told him countless times about how understaffed the hospital was and how overworked they all were – doctors and nurses.

Troy was still wondering if that was why Kirsten hadn't been in contact yet when he finally turned left into his street. The time was 09:35 p.m.

The house they rented together was the last one on the right – just a small, single-story, two-bedroom, white-fronted house with a small front garden. As he pulled up in front of it, he frowned. Kirsten's car was parked on their driveway.

'What the hell?' Troy whispered to himself, parking directly behind her car before reaching in the back for his army bag. He preferred those to suitcases. 'She's home? Then why hasn't she called me?'

His eyes moved to their two front windows. The lights were off.

In a surge of optimism, his brain threw one more possible answer at him.

Maybe she was covering for someone at the hospital and she just got home. Maybe just a minute before she did. Maybe she was hoping that he'd be home already.

Still. She could've at least texted me just to tell me that she was OK.

And just like that, worry became annoyance.

Troy walked up to their dark blue front door and used his key to unlock it.

The key didn't turn.

The door was already unlocked.

That was unusual. Kirsten was always very attentive about locking the door and the windows. Troy was the one who would sometimes forget to shut or lock a window – and sometimes even their front door.

'Baby, I'm home,' Troy called out, as he stepped into their living room, closed the door behind him and switched on the lights. Kirsten's house keys were dangling from the lock, on the inside of the door. 'You forgot to lock the front door. That's usually me.'

Absentmindedly, Troy's gaze scanned the room and his eyes narrowed in a doubtful look. Something didn't feel quite right, but he couldn't tell exactly what it was. The furniture all seemed to be in the right place and there was no mess anywhere ... so what the hell was it that was bothering him?

Maybe it was how quiet and still the house was, and that was when it dawned on Troy. He had probably been right about Kirsten having been called in to sub for someone earlier in the day. She, no doubt, finished her shift late and came straight home. She was probably exhausted and had collapsed in bed, which had been known to happen after a heavy and stressful shift.

Troy angled his body a little to his right, so he could look down the corridor that led deeper into the house and to their bedroom, at the far end of it. Though the lights in the corridor were off, he could still see that the door to their room was ajar. That was how Kirsten always left it when they went to bed.

Troy carefully put down his bag, so as not to make too much noise.

In a minute he would go check on her and give her a kiss. He'd missed her, but first he needed a beer. He'd been driving for over ten hours and he too felt a little stressed and exhausted. A beer would smooth him out.

He walked over to the kitchen, pulled open the fridge door and reached for a cold one. As he took his first swig, he paused and smelled the bottle. No, it wasn't that, but something did smell a little odd ... the kind of odd that was hard to explain – not exactly sour, not exactly bitter, not exactly out-of-date, not exactly sweet, and not exactly moldy, but a combination of all of those.

Something subtle that didn't immediately insult the nostrils, but with time, it became noticeable.

He reopened the fridge and smelled the inside of the door and each of the four shelves. Nothing there. He tried the drawer at the bottom where they kept vegetables. It was almost empty, just a couple of carrots that didn't seem to be past their best. They weren't the source of the smell either.

Troy closed the fridge and began smelling the air around him, like a dog trying to pick up a scent. Yes, the odd smell was there, no doubt about it, faintly lingering in the air. Troy smelled around in the kitchen, then in the living room, but still he couldn't identify its source. As he walked past the entrance to the hallway he paused. There, the smell became just a little more pronounced. Whatever it was, it was coming from deeper inside the house.

Stepping as lightly as he could, he entered the hallway without reaching for the light switch. He didn't want to wake up Kirsten. As Troy walked past the guest room, he stuck his face passed the door and sniffed the air.

It wasn't coming from in there.

He did the same as he walked past the bathroom.

Not from there either, but the scent was clearly gaining a little more strength.

Only place left was their bedroom.

Had Kirsten brought some food into the room with her? If she had, that was very unlike her. Wine, yes. Food, no.

At the door to their room, Troy paused and once again sniffed the air. The smell was definitely coming from in there. Troy's gaze moved to their bed and his eyes tried to refocus. The light that seeped through from the living room and travelled down their short hallway was faint and weak, allowing him to make out only rough outlines – nevertheless, the shapes he saw on the bed seemed wrong . . . completely wrong.

'Baby?' he called, his tone doubtful, his voice loud enough to be heard.

No movement. No reply.

'Kirsten?' Troy called again, as his fingers found the light switch.

Bright light exploded out of the chandelier fixture on the room's ceiling, bathing the space in brightness.

What Troy saw hit him like a meteor.

In a blink of an eye, the world lost all its purpose.

Nothing made sense.

Troy felt his stomach drop to the floor in total and utter desperation.

'Kirsten?' he yelled at the top of his voice, but her name came out sounding like the bone-chilling shriek a feral beast makes when injured.

Troy ran to the bed, his whole body trembling with a chill that sank into his bones.

'Baby? Baby?' He kneeled by the bed, his terrified eyes blurred by an explosion of tears.

He wanted to reach for her . . . to hug her . . . to kiss her . . . but he didn't. The room spun around him in doubt, because the truth was, Troy couldn't be sure if the body on their bed belonged to Kirsten or not.

Twenty-five

It was past eleven thirty at night when Hunter got the call. Though he'd been in bed for a little over half an hour, he wasn't asleep.

Hunter had lived with insomnia for most of his life and gone were the days when he would waste time fighting it, because he couldn't win. He knew that. Nowadays, he simply rolled with it the best way he knew how, and that was exactly what he was doing – laying on his back, immobile, eyes closed, breathing steadily. In doing that, despite being awake, despite his brain not letting go, his muscles were getting as much rest as they could outside the benefit of sleep, and so were his eyes.

In his head, Hunter had been going over and over the text conversation between the killer and Melissa when his cellphone vibrated on his bedside table. Without opening his eyes, he reached for it and brought it to his ear.

The call came from Detective Pedro Lopez from the Alhambra Police Department, and the conversation was punctuated by very similar tones to the one Hunter had had with Detective William Barnes on Sunday morning – a homicide in a residential street in Alhambra, which, without a shadow of a doubt, would eventually be escalated up to the LAPD Ultra Violent Crimes Unit, due to the brutality of the assault. All that Detective Lopez was trying to do was save everyone some time and paperwork.

Ten minutes after disconnecting from the call, Hunter was

heading north on Santa Fe Avenue, in the direction of Alhambra. Half an hour after that, he was parking by a white forensics-unit van, on a street that had already been largely cordoned off by Alhambra PD. A small crowd stood at the edge of the perimeter – most of them looked to be street neighbors.

It was a clear but cold night, with a beautiful full moon and plenty of stars. The wind that came in from the west was just strong enough to knock a couple of degrees off the already low night temperature.

Hunter stepped out of his car, zipped up his jacket and looked around. There were four black-and-white cruisers parked on the street, right in front of the last house on the right. A second perimeter, delimited by black and yellow crime-scene tape, had been established around the small, white-fronted house. Parked on its driveway was a white Chevrolet Malibu and a Ford pickup truck. There looked to be at least a couple of people sitting inside the pickup truck, but Hunter couldn't really tell from where he was standing.

He checked his watch – 12:36 a.m.

He looked around for his partner's car and as if on cue, it cleared the outer perimeter at the top of the street.

Hunter waited while Garcia parked on the road, partially blocking one of the neighbor's driveways.

'Have you been inside yet?' he asked as he joined Hunter, his head tipping in the direction of the house.

'Got here about thirty seconds before you,' Hunter replied with a jolt of the shoulders. 'Haven't even talked to anyone yet.'

Garcia's eyebrows lifted. 'I guess that's going to be dealt with right about now.'

'What?'

Garcia cocked his head back ever so slightly, his chin indicating that someone was approaching.

Hunter turned around to find a short and stocky man walking

toward them. He wore a dark, ill-fitting suit that had certainly seen better days.

'LAPD UVC Unit, right?' he asked, as he reached both detectives.

'That's us,' Garcia replied, credentials in hand. 'I'm Detective Garcia and this is Detective Hunter.'

'I'm Detective Pedro Lopez, Alhambra PD Homicide,' the man said in return. 'We spoke on the phone.' He nodded at Hunter.

Detective Lopez's black hair was combed back from a broad forehead. His beard was short, with spots of gray showing, but only around his chin. Small eyes looked at Hunter and Garcia from behind round glasses that sat under thick eyebrows. His round face looked like the type that didn't smile much.

'So what do we have here?' Garcia asked.

Lopez gestured with his head for them to follow him.

'Single victim,' he began. 'Female. Possible identity – Kirsten Hansen.'

'Possible?' Garcia interrupted.

Lopez paused and turned to face the UVC detectives. There was a quiet, indrawn breath, the kind that came before bad news.

'Whoever did this went to work on her big time. The disfigurement is like nothing I've ever seen ... and I've seen more than my share. I'm not really sure what you guys from Ultra Violent Crimes are used to, but I'm willing to bet it isn't something this.'

Garcia's gaze bounced to Hunter for a blink of an eye.

Lopez read the look. 'You'll see.' He carried on walking.

Hunter and Garcia followed.

'Hansen?' Hunter asked. 'Is she Danish?'

Lopez looked back at him quizzically.

'Hansen is a very typical Scandinavian family name,' Hunter explained. 'Mainly Danish.'

Lopez nodded once. 'If you say so, but I can't confirm that for you. The information we have at the moment is very limited and since I'm bumping this case up to UVC, I'll leave the discovery phase to you guys.'

'OK,' Garcia said, stifling a smile. 'So what's this limited information you have so far?'

'If the victim really is this Kirsten Hansen,' Lopez continued, 'she was twenty-nine years old. A surgical nurse for the Los Angeles Surge Hospital in Westlake.'

'Did she live alone?' Hunter asked. 'Who found the body?'

'No she didn't. She shared the house with her fiancé, Troy Foster. He was away, attending a weapons expo in San Francisco.' He lifted a hand and explained himself before the question came. 'He's the general manager for a guns and ammo store called Gun Gallery, in Glendale. The expo was a business trip. He got back earlier tonight and found the body.'

They neared the black pickup truck and Hunter could now tell that there were three people sitting inside it – two males and one female. One of the males had his face buried into his palms, clearly sobbing. The female also seemed to be crying.

'That's him in the pickup truck,' Lopez announced. 'We haven't managed to get much out of him. He's in shock and it's not surprising, but from what I understand, he drove up to San Francisco on Friday morning. The expo went from Saturday to Monday. On Tuesday morning, yesterday, Mr. Foster left his hotel and hit the road, leaving Frisco just before eleven in the morning. Traffic wasn't great on the interstate.' The shrug was evident on Lopez's next sentence. 'Well, it never is, really, but a six-hour journey took a little over nine. He arrived home last night, just before ten in the evening.' He nodded at the pickup truck. 'The two people with him are close friends. His brother and his mother are on their way. They should be here in an hour or so.'

'When was the last time he heard from his fiancée?' Garcia asked.

'From what I understand,' Lopez replied, his voice threaded

with uncertainty, 'and you guys can reconfirm all that at your leisure – they last spoke on the phone on Monday evening. Apparently, Mr. Foster tried calling his fiancée several times yesterday, prior to leaving San Francisco and then again throughout his journey back to LA. He never got a reply. He also sent her several text messages. They too went unanswered.'

They got to the white-fronted house and stooped under the crime-scene tape that surrounded the whole front yard.

'Forensics got here about forty-five minutes ago,' Lopez said. 'Maybe an hour ...' His eyebrows lifted like a drawbridge. 'And even they held their breaths for a moment once they got to the bedroom.'

'She was murdered in her bedroom?' Hunter asked.

Lopez looked down at his scuffed shoes before shaking his head in a doubtful and sad manner. 'I don't think so.'

Though the question was right at the tip of their tongues, neither Hunter nor Garcia voiced it. Instead, they signed the crime-scene manifest and were handed an individually wrapped, white Tyvek coverall each.

'This is where I say "nice to meet you and good luck". My work here is done,' Lopez said, scratching his raggedy beard. He paused as he got back to the crime-scene tape. 'Detectives ...'

Hunter and Garcia's attention moved back to him.

'I truly hope you catch whoever did this. What's in there is ...' He searched the air for the right word. 'Inhuman.'

Twenty-six

The wind seemed to be picking up, dropping the night temperature another degree or so. Hunter and Garcia finished suiting up, grabbed a pair of latex gloves each and entered the house.

The living room, right off the entryway, was small, but furnished with style. Two forensics agents were busy dusting surfaces and the windows for latent prints. The inside of the front door had clearly already been dusted.

In that first room, nothing seemed out of place. No clear signs of a struggle, but Hunter did notice a few drops of blood on the floor. They were drops, not splatters.

Hunter and Garcia greeted the agents with a simple nod before moving deeper into the house.

The corridor that led off the living room was wide but short. The walls were white and bare of any paintings or ornaments. There were two doors on the right, one on the left, and one at the end of it. They were all open. Bright forensics light spilled from the door at the end, causing shadows – presumably cast by the agents working the room – to dance against the corridor walls. On the floor, a few more sparse drops of blood could be seen.

As Hunter and Garcia walked past the first door on the right, they looked inside – a second bedroom, which looked to double as an office. No signs of a struggle in there either.

The door on the left was a bathroom, tiled in blue and white with a walk-in shower – no mess, nothing out of place. The next door on the right was a small storage room with towels, beddings, a vacuum cleaner, and various other household items. Three steps from there and they were at the last door – the main bedroom.

Three forensics agents were gathered around a double-sized bed that had its headboard against the east wall, directly opposite the bedroom door – one agent on each side of the bed and the third one at its foot. The two agents flanking the bed were down in a crouching position. Neither Hunter nor Garcia could quite see what the two agents were doing because their line of vision was obstructed by the agent at the foot of the bed, who was standing up.

The standing agent had heard the detectives' footsteps and turned to face them as soon as they got to the bedroom door. It was, once again, Dr Susan Slater.

Hunter met her stare and even from that distance, he saw a look in her light blue eyes that he had never seen before – not disgust, or outrage, but sadness, as if she'd given up hope in humanity.

'Robert ... Carlos ...' As Dr. Slater greeted them, she took a step to her right, clearing Hunter and Garcia's line of view. Their collective gaze moved to the metal-framed bed and to the body on it.

Detective Lopez was right, he thought. *This wasn't human.*

Twenty-seven

Outside, the wind was blowing in gusts and at different strengths, like waves breaking on a beach, but there was no rain. Every now and then, the wind would whistle eerily, as it hit one of the windowsills and then die down slowly, creating an unnerving whispering effect.

If Hunter had seen sadness in Dr. Slater's eyes a moment ago, she, in turn, also saw something that she had never seen before inside his – sadness, maybe . . . confusion and disbelief, for sure.

On the bed, resting against blood-soaked bed sheets, was the naked body of a woman. Her arms had been lifted above her head, with her hands tied together at the wrists by a piece of rope. Clipped onto that piece of rope, by means of a climbing sling hook, was a metal chain that looked to be around three to four feet long. At the other end of the chain was a new metal hook. This one was the shackle type – larger and much heavier than the one at her wrists, but it wasn't attached to anything. The odd rope-chain-hook set up was just there, carelessly thrown over the bed headboard.

Garcia was the first to break the solemn silence that sat between them all, his voice hesitant, his stare semi-lost, his mind struggling to comprehend the atrocities that had been done to the victim. 'What . . . happened to her?'

Most of the skin on her feet, legs, abdomen, arms, hands,

head, forehead, and face, were gone, exposing sore, inflamed flesh that was already turning brown from oxidation. Her breasts seemed to have been savagely hacked off her torso by some blunt instrument. Her nose had been completely shaved off, with only a small amount of cartilage left behind. In certain places, like her shoulders, hands, knees, elbows, head and face, some of her flesh and muscle seemed to have wasted away, displaying the raw bone beneath. Of those, some had clearly fractured multiple times. Most of her once-blonde hair looked to have been brutally scalped off her head, where parts of her skull were now visible, but what really seemed to have sickened everyone in that room was that her skin . . . her flesh . . . her muscle . . . didn't look to have been surgically removed. She hadn't been skinned, not in the medical sense of the word. What it did look like was that her skin, together with chunks of flesh and muscle, had somehow been violently scraped off her body. That crude scraping had also reached some of the exposed bone, where in parts, fragments were clearly missing. The result was uniquely grotesque – part raw flesh, part exposed skeleton, part deformed and disfigured body, all of it covered in a layer of blood that had already dried up.

Garcia's question was met with a long pause, where everyone's heartbeats seemed to stutter together with anxiety. Dr. Slater's stare drifted toward the body for an instant, before re-engaging with both detectives.

'To be one hundred percent certain,' she finally replied, the sadness in her eyes seeping through to her voice, 'we'll have to wait for the autopsy report.'

Hunter and Garcia stepped closer, flanking the bed like the other two forensics agents – Hunter on the right, Garcia on the left.

'But you do have a theory,' Hunter said, reading the doctor's facial expression.

She took a step back from the bed and Hunter could swear that he saw her shiver. 'We've only been here for about an hour,' she came back. 'And I would call it a guess rather than a theory, but yes, based on the state of the body and the few things we found . . . I could venture a guess as to what happened to her.'

Hunter's gaze shifted to the forensics agent on his side of the bed and he watched as the agent used a pair of surgical pincers to collect something from a piece of exposed flesh on the body's thigh, posterior side, just below the buttocks. He observed as the agent placed what he had collected into a transparent plastic evidence bag – a small rock pebble. The evidence bag already had several of them in it.

Garcia waited for Dr. Slater to elaborate further, but she had gone quiet again.

'Is it like a secret guess, Doc?' he asked. 'Or can you share it with us?'

'She was dragged.' The reply came from Hunter, not Dr. Slater.

'Dragged?' Garcia's eyes tracked over to his partner.

'That's our initial perception as well,' Dr. Slater said, giving both detectives a new head nod.

'Dragged, as in . . .?' Garcia's question danced in the air, unanswered, before Hunter finally took it on.

'As in towed by her hands behind a car or a motorbike,' he said. 'Dragged against some rough terrain by her wrists.' He indicated the heavy shackle hook at the far end of the metal chain. 'That's a pretty common tow hook. Also known as a shackle anchor. That's the clue.'

Garcia greeted Hunter's revelation with absolute silence, but the negative charge in the air that the implication had created lifted the hairs along his forearms.

Hunter then indicated the plastic evidence bag by the forensics agent next to him. 'The other clues are the gravel pebbles that seem to be embedded just about everywhere on her body.'

Garcia stretched his neck to look across the bed.

The forensics agent on Hunter's side lifted the evidence bag so the detective could see it. Once again, Garcia greeted Hunter's revelation with silence. His gaze skittered to the shackle hook, darted away to the evidence bag, then darted back to the hook.

'This whole "rope-chain-hook" set up at her wrists,' Hunter explained, his voice threaded with disgust. 'There's no reason for it to be here . . . in her bedroom. She wasn't murdered here. She didn't die here.'

'She was brought here after death,' Dr. Slater said, her voice gentle and respectful, her head nodding a couple of times.

'The killer,' Hunter continued, 'could've very easily freed her hands either before bringing her here, or once he placed her on the bed. But he didn't. He not only left the whole set-up in place, but he also positioned her like this.' He nodded at the victim. 'Arms above her head, as if she was being dragged. Why?'

Garcia's eyes went back to the arrangement at the victim's wrists, his line of thought catching up with Hunter's. 'Because he wanted us to know how he did this.'

'All the injuries you see here,' Dr. Slater took over again, her attention back on the body, 'would be consistent with that particular scenario.'

'But there's very little swelling,' Hunter said, his attention on the body's mutilated face.

'Good eye, Robert,' the doctor said, her head moving in agreement. 'Which indicates that she carried on being dragged way after she had lost her life.'

'Yeah, but why?' one of the forensics agents asked, allowing his curiosity to get the best of him. 'What's the point in carrying on hurting her after she was already gone?'

Dr. Slater looked at Hunter.

'Because the killer wasn't doing it just to hurt her,' he replied, stepping back from the bed. 'He was doing it for himself . . . for his own pleasure.' Hunter shook his head as soon as he said the word 'pleasure'. It just didn't sit right with the context of everything. 'Sadism is a compulsion. It satisfies something inside them.'

'Like scratching an itch,' Garcia added, instinctively miming it at the back of his left hand. 'Have you ever scratched an itch and it felt so good that you simply carried on scratching, even after the itch was gone? That's what a sadistic compulsion feels like.'

The agent chewed on that for a second before shaking his head at the thought.

Hunter tracked back to the bedroom door, his eyes studying the laminated-wood flooring. It was clean. No marks. No smudges.

'No drag marks,' the doctor said, figuring out what Hunter was looking for. 'A few blood drops along the corridor and in the living room, but that's all. That means that she wasn't dragged here. She was carried.'

Hunter nodded. 'Yes, I noticed the drops too.'

Garcia rounded the bed to the other side. 'But carrying her in here wouldn't be such a hard thing to do.' His chin jerked in the direction of the body. 'She's what . . . five-six . . . five-seven? And she looks to have been quite a slim woman – no more than 130, 140 pounds, I would say.'

'If that?' one of the forensics agents commented.

'Plus,' Garcia continued. 'I'm sure she was already dead. No fight . . . no struggle.'

'But there are too few drops of blood leading from the front door into this room,' Hunter said, still studying the floor. 'She must've been wrapped in something.'

'She was.' The confirmation came from the forensics agent to the left of the bed. 'Other than little pebbles, we've also collected several fibers from her body, which look synthetic. I'd say she was wrapped in a cheap rug or something similar. The lab will confirm it.'

'I understand that at this point, you won't know for sure,' Hunter addressed Dr. Slater. 'But as a ballpark figure, would you say that time of death was maybe fifteen ... sixteen hours ago, give or take an hour or two?'

The doctor pursed her lips as she thought about it. 'The body is in full rigor mortis.'

Both forensics agents nodded their agreement.

'So yeah,' Dr. Slater confirmed. 'As a ballpark figure, I'd say that that's a pretty good guess. How did you know?'

Hunter was yet to properly examine the body. From looks alone and considering the state that the body was in, Dr. Slater doubted that he could have known that *full* rigor mortis had already been achieved.

'Because she clearly wasn't murdered in this room,' Hunter replied, walking back to the bed. 'And like you've said, someone have to have carried her in here.' He indicated the window. 'It doesn't look like a busy street, but it's a residential one. Loads of neighbors. To get her into this room and onto that bed, the killer would've had to have brought her here in a vehicle, parked somewhere outside, maybe even in the driveway, and carried her inside. The safest time to do that, if you're trying to avoid being spotted by a neighbor, would be the really early hours of the morning – 3, 4 a.m., maybe?'

Everyone's agreement came in the form of a heavy, almost leaden silence.

'Still,' Hunter continued, this time addressing his partner, 'the killer would've had to have driven in and out of this street, parked, picked her up, carried her inside and posed her on the bed. Maybe one of the neighbors is a night owl.'

Garcia got the hint. 'I'll get a team to start the door-to-door as soon as possible.' He checked his watch. 'The neighbors all seem to be up anyway.'

Hunter walked over to the wooden dresser that was pushed up by the wall to the right of the bed. A tall, oval mirror centered the dresser. To its left there were three perfume bottles, a jewelry box decorated with roses, and a couple of hairbrushes. To the right of the mirror was a lidless metal box filled with several pots, bottles and tubes of different types of moisturizing cream – hands, face, feet, body and eyes.

Hunter pulled open the first of the three drawers on the dresser – it was filled with makeup brushes of all different thickness and sizes. Second drawer – eyeshadow pallets, about five of them. Last drawer – a diverse rainbow of lipsticks, eyeliners and eyebrow pencils.

Also on the dresser, just behind the perfume bottles, was a small, four-by-six-inch picture frame.

Hunter reached for it.

The photo showed a couple at the beach, smiling at the camera. The ocean behind them seemed calm, with the waves reflecting the sun high up on the sky. The woman in the photo was hugging the man from behind, her arms thrown over his shoulders, her right cheek softly touching his left one.

'That's her,' Dr. Slater said. 'Very pretty . . . stunning smile.'

Hunter's eyes studied the woman on the picture for a moment longer. Dr. Slater wasn't just being nice. The woman's attractiveness was unmistakable. She was pale, with nearly translucent white gold hair, porcelain skin, and lips that only hinted at pink. Her smile wasn't only stunning . . . it was perfect, showing beautifully aligned, flawless white teeth. Her round eyes were of a deep blue color that rivaled the clear sky behind them.

'To be absolutely sure that this is her,' the forensics agent on the right side of the bed commented, 'we will need a DNA test.'

Hunter put down the photo and allowed his stare to track back to the victim's body on the bed. The reason for the comment was obvious. The disfigurement had been absolute.

Hunter didn't voice a reply, but he had no doubt that the body on the bed belonged to Kirsten Hansen. Why else would the killer have placed her in her room and on her bed? It followed the same logic as to why the killer had left the rope-chain-hook set up still attached to her wrists – he wanted everyone to know how he did this. He also wanted everyone to know who he had done this to.

Twenty-eight

Finally, the wind outside began easing down. The windowsill whistles had gone quiet, but the whispers still came and went at odd intervals, like hushed voices exchanging secrets.

'Now that both of you have seen the body in situ,' Dr. Slater addressed the two detectives, 'I'm going to free her hands. I want to have a look at the marks on her wrists, plus we need to bag all this and send it for analysis.'

Hunter and Garcia nodded in unison.

'The ligature has already been photographed from all different angles,' the doctor clarified. 'The knot used looks to be a regular double knot, a wrap around, then another double knot. Nothing extraordinary about it.'

Hunter and Garcia had both already noticed that too. They watched as Dr. Slater reached for the sling hook attached to the rope around the victim's wrists and unclipped it. She then unclipped the hook from the chain before unclipping the chain from the larger tow hook at the other end.

As she disassembled the hooks from the chain, she passed the individual parts to the forensics agent to the left of the bed, who placed each of them inside a different evidence bag. That done, Dr. Slater carefully began undoing the knots at the victim's wrists. It took her less than a minute to completely free the hands. The fingers on both of them were clenched into tight fists.

As the doctor removed the rope and passed it to the agent for bagging and tagging, the victim's arms, due to the stiffness caused by rigor mortis, stayed exactly where they were. Dr. Slater moved closer, bringing her face to just a couple of inches from the victim's wrists to study the ligature marks. Despite the rope having cut deep into the victim's skin and flesh, the wounds on her wrists were the least gruesome of all.

'Poor girl,' Dr. Slater said, her words heavy. 'This is just . . .' As she shook her head, the light that came from behind her reflected on something that caught her eye and made her pause.

Hunter was quick to notice the change in the doctor's attitude. Her head tilted left, then right, as she searched for a better line of vision. Her eyes were locked onto the victim's clenched right fist.

'Can you pass me a pair of forceps, please,' she asked one of the agents by the bed.

'Something wrong?' Hunter asked with renewed interest.

Garcia also perked up like a predator that had just spotted a new prey.

'I'm not exactly sure,' Dr. Slater replied, as the agent handed her the forceps she requested. 'But she seems to be clinging on to something.'

'Clinging?' Garcia asked, he and Hunter quickly returning to the side of the bed.

'Yes, there seems to be something in her right hand.' The doctor indicated with the forceps. 'Hard to see it, but the light got through the gaps between her finger and I saw something reflect.'

Both detectives angled their bodies, trying to get a better look, but they kept their distance, allowing the doctor to do her job unperturbed.

'It looks like . . . a small plastic bag,' she announced. 'Or something similar.' She gently used the forceps to grab hold of the tiny edge that she could see.

Hunter repositioned himself closer to the head of the bed.

The two forensics agents also stopped what they were doing, anticipation masking their faces.

Dr. Slater began to slowly retrieve whatever it was that had been locked in the victim's grip. 'It's definitely some sort of plastic bag,' she confirmed, readjusting the forceps so not to rip it. 'And . . . it looks to contain something.'

'Something like what?' Garcia asked.

'I'm not sure yet, but it looks like . . .' The doctor paused and the room went still, as if holding its breath. 'A piece of paper . . . a rolled-up piece of paper.'

Both detectives exchanged a half concerned, half expectant look.

'Can I have a second pair of forceps, please?' Dr. Slater asked, extending her left arm out but keeping her eyes on the small plastic bag. 'The dried-up blood on her hand is acting like glue in places. I don't want to rip the bag.'

The agent handed her the second pair of forceps and she went back to work, carefully pinching, pulling, swiveling . . . little by little extracting the small bag from the victim's grip.

All everyone else could do was watch.

It took Dr. Slater just over two minutes to finally pull the bag free.

'Interesting,' she said, straightening herself up – a grip-seal plastic bag of about two square inches dangled from the tip of the forceps in her right hand. Inside it, there was a piece of paper that had been rolled up into a small tube. 'Can I get this photographed, please?'

The agent to her right reached for the digital camera in his briefcase and quickly snapped a few shots.

'What exactly is that?' he asked. 'A note?'

Dr. Slater turned to face Hunter and Garcia. 'It's your case – your call. Want to find out here, or wait for me to send this to the lab for analysis?'

Garcia peeked at Hunter for confirmation, but he didn't really have to. He knew what the answer would be. Neither of them was prepared to wait until mid-morning to find out what that piece of paper really was.

'We'll take option one, please,' Garcia replied, giving the doctor a firm nod.

'Alright.'

Though her mouth was covered by her standard issue forensics mask, the doctor's smile came through in the corners of her eyes. She too couldn't wait to find out what they were looking at.

'Over there,' she said, her head angling in the direction of the dresser. If she was to open that grip-seal plastic bag right then, at the crime scene, she wanted to do it over a flat surface in case something they couldn't yet see fell out of it.

Hunter and Garcia followed behind her, and so did the two forensics agents.

Dr. Slater put down the forceps and used her gloved fingers to pull open the grip seal on the plastic bag. That done, she tipped the rolled-up piece of paper onto the palm of her left hand.

Everyone's gaze followed her every move.

Next, the doctor used her right thumb and index finger to very gently squeeze the tiny paper tube.

'It doesn't seem to contain any objects inside,' she informed everyone. She then proceeded to pick the tiny paper tube up and lightly tap both of its ends against her palm, checking for possible powder content.

Nothing.

Only one thing left to do.

Under everyone's watchful eyes, Dr. Slater slowly and very carefully unrolled it.

If the room had a heartbeat, it stood steady.

Being much taller than the doctor's five-foot-seven, Hunter and Garcia simply stood behind her, looking over her shoulders.

The tube unrolled to show a piece of paper measuring about five-and-a-half inches long by one-and-a-half wide. Nothing else inside it, except for a single, handwritten sentence.

Garcia's eyes stayed on the note in Dr. Slater's hands for just a breath before snapping to Hunter. Two seconds later, he turned to look at the body on the bed. Confusion and surprise made his mouth drop half open.

'No ... goddamn ... way! *How is that even possible?*'

Twenty-nine

Hunter and Garcia stayed behind for another hour or so after Kirsten Hansen's body was finally placed in a coroner's van and transported back to the Los Angeles Department of Medical Examiner-Coroner on North Mission Road. While Dr. Slater and her team worked the scene and Garcia looked through the house searching for clues, Hunter went outside to try to talk to Troy Foster, who was still sitting inside his pickup truck, forehead resting on the palms of his hands, elbows resting on his knees, shock making his entire body convulse involuntarily every now and then.

His two friends were still sitting with him.

Troy was just as tall and as well built as Hunter, with the broad shoulders of a linebacker and the arms of a professional gymnast, but when he stepped out of his truck to meet the detective, he looked small and defeated, his head drooped, his body sagging beneath the devastating weight of grief.

Just like when Hunter tried talking to Janet Lang outside Melissa's house on Sunday evening, it took him almost an hour to get the most basic information out of Troy. Most of the time, once Hunter had asked him a question, his damp, bloodshot eyes would go a little distant. When they finally snapped back to Hunter, they were lost and unfocused ... his voice shaky and weak ... his pain visible ... palpable ... contagious. When he spoke, his breathing would sometimes catch in his throat, forcing his ribcage to lift and fall in an odd rhythm, as if oxygen around him was scarce. Words and sentences would form slowly, as if putting them together required the kind of strength that Troy simply didn't possess at the time.

Hunter didn't want to push it. Troy's pain was intoxicating. His brain was struggling to comprehend reality because right then, reality simply seemed unreal, but there was something that Hunter really needed to ask Troy.

'Mr. Foster?' he said, his tone tender, his voice quiet. 'I understand how difficult this is for you, but if I could ask you just one final question? It truly is very important.'

At first it seemed like Troy hadn't even heard Hunter, but then he finally nodded – his weathered cheeks red, his eyes damp, his arms hugging his chest like a protective shield, bracing himself for what was to come.

'We found a note inside your bedroom,' Hunter began, as he reached for his cellphone. 'I was wondering if you could have a look at it.'

The gentleness with which Hunter said those words seemed to do nothing to actually soften the blow for Troy, who blinked, trying to clear the blurriness in his eyes before facing Hunter. His arm-shield became a little tighter and his shoulders hunched up. 'You found a note? Where?'

'Under the bed,' Hunter lied. He hated doing it, but he also saw no reason in making this any harder than it already was.

'What note? What did it say?' The stress level in Troy's voice made it croak.

Hunter loaded up the photo he had taken of the note onto his cellphone screen and showed it to Troy, who blinked again, this time a little faster and a little harder than before. His lips moved as he read the words, but no sound came out.

Hunter waited.

Troy finally dragged his eyes from Hunter's cellphone screen to look back at the detective. He was starting to shake again.

'I . . . don't understand.'

'Have you ever seen this sentence before?' Hunter asked.

Troy read it again for good measure. 'No . . . never. Did . . .?' His voice caught against the wind before wrapping itself around Hunter. 'Did she write this for me?'

Hunter's breathing stuttered, his blood rushing past his eardrums as if it were being pumped by a high-pressure washer. That was exactly what he needed to confirm.

'Do you recognize the handwriting?' he asked, being careful to keep his tone steady. 'Is it Miss Hansen's?'

This time Troy's tears were too many for him to hold them back. They ran down his cheeks undisturbed, until they dropped off his chin.

'Yes,' he finally replied, his voice rough against his throat. In his eyes, Hunter could see that for Troy, the world made no sense anymore. 'That's her handwriting. Did she write this for me?' he asked again, his arms at last uncrossing from his chest to grab Hunter by the shoulders. 'Did she? Please tell me. Is this for me?'

Hunter could feel his whole body shaking.

'Tell me . . . did she?'

Their eyes locked, but Hunter stayed quiet. There was nothing he could say.

Thirty

Hunter stayed with Troy until his mother and brother arrived. He gave both of them his card and told them to not hesitate in contacting him if they needed anything.

Troy would be staying with his mother in Sylmar for the time being.

Garcia met Hunter outside the house, once Troy had finally left.

'How's he doing?' he asked, his voice raspy, his eyes tired.

Hunter shook his head without meeting his partner's gaze. 'In shock ... broken. It will take him years to recover from this ... if he ever does.'

Garcia wasn't surprised. How could anyone walk in on the person they loved, the person that they were supposed to marry, find them in that state and not be wounded for life?

Garcia used his thumb and forefinger to gently massage his closed eyelids. 'Did you manage to get anything at all out of him? The note? The handwriting? Is it his fiancée's? Did he recognize it?'

Hunter nodded. 'It's hers. He had no doubt about it.'

'Motherfucker!' Garcia said, turning to look back at the house. 'This makes no sense, Robert. You know that, right? The MO ... the signature ... none of it matches.'

This time their eyes met.

'Have they found her phone?' Hunter asked.

Garcia shook his head. 'No. Not yet. And if we're really talking about the same killer here … we won't. It's probably been destroyed.'

'We need to check her text messages.'

Garcia's focus sharpened. 'Do you think that …' He didn't finish his sentence. He simply allowed his abandoned words to float away. 'Of course.' He answered his own unasked question: 'If this is the same killer, then we know that the first thing he's after is fear. He thrives on it. It's a compulsion.'

Hunter agreed again. 'I didn't manage to get much else out of Troy,' he explained. 'With the exception of one thing.'

'And what was that?'

'Troy told me that he'd spoken to Kirsten on Monday night at around ten forty-five … eleven o'clock. She was home. She had come in late from her hospital shift and had ordered a pizza that night. She wanted to watch some TV.'

The dots connected quickly.

'So the killer took her from here?' Garcia's attention jumped back to the house.

'It seems so,' Hunter confirmed.

There was a pregnant, pensive pause, in which Garcia's gaze shifted from the house to Kirsten's Malibu parked on the driveway.

'Can you imagine the killer's determination here?' he asked, his head shaking ever so slightly. 'He broke into her house, subdued her, took her away, and then hooked her onto the back of a vehicle before dragging her against the ground until she was dead … until half of her body had been scrapped off.' He paused for breath. 'He then collected her, placed her back in the car, brought her back to her house and posed her on the bed like that. Who the fuck is this killer, Robert? An army of demons?'

Despite sharing his partner's anger and frustration, Hunter's voice stayed placid, his tone analytical.

'Not only determination, Carlos, but also a lot of planning. The location where he took her . . . where she died. It wasn't just a random spot somewhere. It was expertly chosen – an open stretch of road, a disused parking lot, or maybe even some sort of large building . . . a hangar, a storage ground . . . abandoned for sure . . . somewhere secluded enough that no one would witness the carnage that he wanted to inflict on her. A place where he'd be able to drive around with her hanging from the back of his vehicle for what? Ten . . . twenty . . . thirty minutes? More?'

Garcia didn't reply. All he did was press his lips together until he felt the sharpness of his teeth against the flesh.

'However long it took,' Hunter continued, 'he didn't care; because I'm sure that he was certain that there would be no prying eyes.'

Both detectives went silent for a moment.

'If this really is the same killer,' Hunter said, bringing Garcia's attention back to him, 'then I'm positive that he'll stick to the same MO. That means that he will have messaged Kirsten before taking her. Like you said – he wants their fear. It's a compulsion.'

Garcia nodded. 'I'll get in touch with her cellphone provider first thing in the morning. This time, I'll make sure they understand that if there is a video attached to any message, we need it.'

Hunter had once again turned to face the house. 'Go home, Carlos. It's late. Get some rest and I'll see you in the morning.'

'Are you staying?' Garcia checked his watch. It was getting close to 3 a.m.

'Not for much longer. I'll go talk to the forensics team, have one more look around then I'll go. Not much else we can do here anyway.'

Thirty-one

Back in his apartment, Hunter spent the rest of the night awake. Once again, he lay in bed as still as he could, allowing his body to rest, but his brain was knocking balls out of the park, playing a puzzle game where not a single piece fitted the frame.

Maybe Garcia was right. Maybe this killer *was* an army of demons . . . internal demons who wouldn't allow him to rest, always pushing for more – more pain . . . more suffering . . . more cruelty . . . more fear . . . more sadism. Or maybe this killer was simply psychotic. Maybe he heard voices in his head, which tormented his soul way beyond what he could control. How else could anyone explain the absurd way in which this killer operated? His MO was like nothing Hunter had even heard of before. From what he had seen so far, the killer's MO was divided into six distinct stages.

One – fear: this killer was hungry for his victims' fear, and the way that he'd decided to feed that hunger was by hiding inside his victims' houses before sending them text messages, telling them that he was there and that they would die that night, toying with them, pushing their fear to the limit.

Two – capture: the exact method or methods were yet unknown, but since he was already hiding inside the victims' houses, capturing them wouldn't pose that much of a problem.

Three – handwritten note: for some reason, this killer would force his victims to write down something that looked like a line from a poem, or the lyrics to some romantic song. Its significance was yet unknown.

Four – torture: this killer didn't just feed on his victims' fear. He was also after their pain ... their last breath of agony. To satisfy his hunger, every death so far had been prefaced by some cruel and sordid torture method.

Five – murder: stages four and five could arguably be grouped into a single stage, as the torture process inevitably morphed into the kill method – but what was interesting and immensely unusual was that the murders differed greatly from each other – the MOs ... the signature ... everything seemed to be different. Hunter was positive that this, too, had to have a meaning.

Six – staging: this killer seemed to also enjoy staging the bodies. Maybe he did it for himself ... maybe he did it because he wanted the victims to be found in that way. Maybe it was both. Hunter wasn't sure.

With so many stages to this killer's 'obsession' with his victims, there was no wonder that he was so organized and methodical – each stage, in both murders, had been executed with tremendous precision. No mistakes; or at least, if there had been any, Hunter and Garcia hadn't found them yet.

By 5:30 a.m. Hunter had showered and was all ready to go. By 6:00, he was sitting at his desk inside the UVC Unit's office, and by 6:45, he had already dropped the official paperwork for the new investigation on Captain Blake's desk. By 7:30 a.m., he was back in Alhambra.

Forensics had finally wrapped up the scene, so Hunter had the house all to himself. He spent almost an hour walking from room to room ... trying to visualize what had happened. How did the killer get in? Why did it look like there had been no struggle? Why murder someone in the way Kirsten Hansen had been murdered? Why leave a note in her hand? What was this killer really trying to tell them?

Hunter finally exited the house through the kitchen door and joined the uniformed officers outside, on what was still left of the door-to-door enquiry.

Two of the neighboring houses did have security cameras outside, like Hunter had guessed, but once again, Lady Luck wasn't kind. With one of them, the camera had been busted for almost a year – with the other, the house was set quite a way back from the street and the camera was trained mainly on the house's front porch. Its range didn't reach as far as the street in front of their driveway.

The door-to-door had also given them nothing. None of the neighbors had seen or heard anything suspicious late on Monday night or early on Tuesday morning, but as Hunter read through what the officers had so far, he noticed something interesting. One of the neighbors – a Mr. Mike Hennessey, sixty-nine years old, who lived across the road and one house to the right from Kirsten and Troy – hadn't reported seeing anything suspicious, but he had reported seeing both cars – Kirsten's white Chevrolet Malibu and Troy's black Ford pickup truck – parked on their driveway in the very early hours of Tuesday morning.

'How could that be?' Hunter asked himself. According to Troy, he didn't get to his house until around 9:30 p.m. that evening, so how was his car on their driveway in the early hours of the morning?

Mr. Hennessey's property was a white-fronted, split-level house, with wide windows on both levels that faced the street. Parked on his driveway was a blue Honda Accord, one of the older models. His front garden was very well-cared for.

Before ringing the doorbell, Hunter paused by the front door and turned to look back at Kirsten and Troy's house. He then crossed the front garden and repeated the movement, this time standing by the window on the bottom level. The window on the top level was directly above it. From both positions, he had a clear line of sight to Kirsten and Troy's driveway.

Back at the front door, Hunter rang the bell, took two steps
back and waited. A few seconds later, he saw the peephole darken.
A second after that, the door was unlocked and pulled open.

Mr. Hennessey was a tiny man – about five-foot five, with a
receding hairline, red cheeks, and deep brown eyes that sat behind
a pair of thick glasses perched on a thin nose. His clothes hung
awkwardly on his skinny body.

'How can I help you, young man?' he asked, as his eyes settled
on Hunter. His voice was gentle, but not fragile, his demeanor
welcoming.

Hunter quickly introduced himself before explaining that he
just wanted to confirm the information that he had given the
officer who had spoken with him a little earlier that morning.

'Of course,' Mr. Hennessey said politely, his expression calm.
'What would you like me to confirm?'

'Could I first ask you,' Hunter began, slightly turning his body
to indicate Kirsten and Troy's house, 'how well do you know the
couple on house 802 – Troy Foster and Kirsten Hansen?'

'Oh, not well at all,' Mr. Hennessey replied, his gaze skipping
to their house for just a second before returning to Hunter. 'To
be honest, I didn't even really know their names until now, but
I know who they are … I mean, sometimes when I'm by the
window, or I'm attending to my front garden or something, I see
them getting in or out of their cars, or taking the trash out … you
know, things like that.' There was a shrug in Mr. Hennessey's
tone. 'Sometimes I also see him out on his driveway washing his
truck, but I've never engaged any of them in conversation, if that's
what you're asking.'

'But you know what cars they drive?' Hunter asked, throwing
his right thumb over his shoulder.

'Yes, sure.' Mr. Hennessey's stare skipped back to Kirsten
and Troy's driveway for a moment. Kirsten's Ford Malibu was
still there, but Troy's truck was gone. His brother had driven

it back to their mother's house in Sylmar in the early hours of the morning.

'She drives the white car, right over there.' Mr. Hennessey pointed to it. 'And he, the black pickup truck.'

Hunter needed to dig a little deeper. It helped that the truck was gone. 'Do you happen to know what kind of truck he drives? Maybe the make or model?'

Mr. Hennessey's head angled right as he apologized. 'I'm so sorry, but I know nothing about cars.' He nodded at the Honda Accord on his driveway. 'I've had this old thing for years, and I can barely tell you any of the specifics. To me all that a car has to do is get you from A to B, the rest . . .' He allowed the sentence to hang with a shrug.

Hunter nodded his understanding before continuing. 'But you told the officer this morning that you saw both cars on the driveway of house 802 in the early hours of Tuesday morning, is that correct?'

'That is indeed,' the old man confirmed.

'What sort of time was that, can you remember?'

'Sure,' Mr. Hennessey replied. No hesitation. No need to think about it. 'It was around a quarter past four in the morning.'

Either Hunter's expression gave it away, or Mr. Hennessey felt like he'd better clarify, because he immediately followed it up with an explanation.

'Since my wife passed, just over a year and a half ago, I never seem to get that much sleep.' At the mention of his wife's passing, Mr. Hennessey's eyes seemed to lose most of the sparkle they had in them. 'Most mornings I'm up by four . . . five if I'm lucky. The bed . . . the room . . . the whole house has become too big for me, if you know what I mean, but at the same time, I wouldn't be able to get rid of it. Memories are all I really have now, you see?' His gentle voice became even more tender. His eyes skittered to a point somewhere in the distance, where they stayed for a couple of seconds before he blinked and looked at the floor. 'Anyway . . . yesterday I was up by four. Like I do every day, as soon as I wake up, I make the bed, then I pull open the curtains, then I go downstairs to have some coffee.'

'And you saw both cars on the driveway from your bedroom window?' Hunter asked.

'That's correct,' Mr. Hennessey confirmed, as his index finger pointed up. 'My bedroom faces the street.'

'Do you remember the position of the cars? How they were parked?'

'Yes, of course.' The old man extended his right arm to indicate: 'The white car was where it is right now – first into the driveway, closer to the house. The black pickup truck was parked right behind it.'

'And you're sure the truck was there?'

'I'm positive, yes.'

Hunter once again turned to look back at Kirsten and Troy's house. It would've been dark at around 4 a.m., but on the street, just off to the right of their driveway, there was a lamp post. It wouldn't have lit up the entire driveway, but it would've been more than enough to allow Mr. Hennessey to see Troy's truck, especially as it was parked closer to the street.

'And how certain are you,' Hunter asked, 'that the truck you saw was Mr. Foster's truck – the exact same black pickup truck you always see on their driveway?'

Mr. Hennessey's chin angled left as he looked back at Hunter a little sideways. 'Oh . . . I see,' he said, as his brain quickly caught up with what Hunter meant. He looked away again. When his eyes snapped back to Hunter, they were full of uncertainty.

'If I'm completely honest,' he said, almost as if apologizing, 'I'm not certain of that at all. It was a similar-looking pickup truck . . . same color . . . parked on *their* driveway. It was nighttime and I had just woken up. When I looked out the window, I registered both cars because their house is practically directly in front of mine, but I wasn't exactly looking at their house or their driveway. My eyes took the image of the street as a whole. No real thought given to any of it.' He paused to adjust his glasses on his nose. 'The problem, you see, is that if the brain isn't specifically looking for details . . . if it isn't trying to identify any differences, chances are, it won't spot them if they do exist.'

Hunter's eyebrows arched in surprise. He wasn't expecting a psychological explanation.

'Because everything was as it usually is,' Mr. Hennessey continued. 'A black pickup truck parked on the same driveway as always, my brain accepted the image as normal . . . nothing odd . . . nothing out of the ordinary.' He coughed to clear his throat. 'So if you're are asking me if it could've been a different pickup truck, the answer is – yes, it could've been a different pickup truck . . . different model . . . even a different make, but because the color and shape were similar and the parking position was as it always is, my brain just assumed it was the same. It's a common function of the human brain . . .'

'Subconscious perceptual recognition,' Hunter said, giving the old man a nod.

This time, it was Mr. Hennessy's eyes that showed surprise.

'Are you a psychologist, sir?' Hunter asked.

'I *was* a psychiatrist,' Mr. Hennessy replied. 'Retired now.' The surprise was still there, in the anatomy of his words. 'Are you? How did you know about . . .?'

'I read a lot,' Hunter said, choosing not to go into any details.

'Oh, alright.' Mr. Hennessy accepted it, but Hunter could tell that he hadn't bought it.

'I'm assuming you never saw the pickup truck leaving, right?' Hunter asked.

'Unfortunately no.' The old man looked down at his shoes. 'But I'm sure that it wasn't there anymore by about six-thirty in the morning.' He paused as his gaze came back up. 'I come out to water some of my flowers at around six-thirty every morning.' He pointed at them in his garden. 'The pickup truck wasn't there anymore. I'm certain.'

Hunter didn't doubt that at all.

He thanked the old man for his time, but as he turned to leave, Mr. Hennessey stopped him.

'Detective,' he called, apprehension coating his words. 'The truck that I saw yesterday morning; it didn't really belong to house 802, did it?'

Hunter knew why he asked the question. He understood why there was apprehension in his tone. Mr. Hennessey was clearly an educated and intelligent man, and from Hunter's line of questioning he had figured out that the truck that he'd seen on the early hours of Tuesday morning must've belonged to the person who had murdered his neighbor. If so, then the killer was there, just across the road from him. That knowledge alone was more than enough to trigger a rollercoaster of questions inside the human mind. *What if the killer had come into this house instead of the one across the street? What if he had stayed by his window for another minute, or two, or five, would he have witnessed the killer leaving house 802?*

The questions were many.

Hunter had to play politician.

'I'm just trying to confirm details, that's all,' he replied, matter-of-factly. 'Just following up some of the accounts with a few more questions.'

He knew full well that his answer didn't match Mr. Hennessey's question, but right then, that was the best he could do.

Thirty-two

After speaking with Mr. Hennessey, Hunter drove straight back to the Police Administration Building. During the drive, he thought about a detail he had noticed when he exited Kirsten and Troy's house via the kitchen door and how that would've worked with the information he had obtained from the retired psychiatrist. One word came to mind: 'clever'.

Back at the UVC Unit office, Garcia had just finished pinning the last two crime-scene photos they had received from Dr. Slater's team to their picture board. He'd been staring at everything for several minutes, his attention jumping from photo to photo. On the left – Melissa Hawthorne's crime scene. On the right – Kirsten Hansen's.

Garcia's stare tracked back to the photo of the note that was found inside Melissa Hawthorne before moving over to the one that was found in Kirsten Hansen's grip.

'What does this mean?' he whispered to himself, taking a step back from the board, just as Hunter pulled open the door to their office. Garcia knew that his partner had returned to the crime scene earlier in the morning.

'Anything?' he asked, tentatively.

'Maybe,' Hunter replied, unzipping his jacket and placing it on the back of his chair before switching on his computer. 'One of the neighbors saw Troy Foster's pickup truck parked on their driveway, just behind Kirsten's car, at around 4 a.m. yester-day morning.'

'What?' The tension in Garcia's forehead pushed his eyebrows close together, creating two creases that almost perfectly followed the vertical lines of his nose. 'How's that possible?'

'That's just it,' Hunter replied. 'It isn't. Troy Foster was in San Francisco at that time.'

Garcia turned to face his partner. 'So the neighbor was lying? Why?'

'That's just it again,' Hunter said, as he joined Garcia by the board. 'I don't think he was lying.'

Garcia's thought process caught up in just a split second. 'He saw the killer's vehicle,' he said, his eyes widening.

Hunter nodded.

'License plate?' Garcia asked with renewed excitement. 'Bumper sticker ... a dent ... a scratch ... anything that can help us identify it?'

Hunter shook his head. 'Nothing other than it was a black pickup truck. It could've been the same make and model as the one that belongs to Troy Foster, or a different one, similar in shape.'

Garcia paused, frowned, then huffed a breath. 'What? So what this neighbor saw was a black pickup truck? That's it?'

'Yes.'

'No details ... no anything ... just a black pickup truck.'

'Yes.' Hunter quickly proceeded to tell Garcia about his con-versation with Mr. Hennessey.

'So, in truth,' Garcia commented, 'it could've been any pickup truck, as long as it was black.'

'It could have, yes,' Hunter agreed, his attention on the pic-ture board, not on his partner. 'But I don't think it was just any pickup truck.'

Hunter's comment earned him an intrigued look from Garcia, which quickly turned into an understanding one.

'Risk minimizing,' Garcia said. 'The killer either used an identical or very similar pickup truck to Troy's.'

Hunter's agreement came as a subtle eyebrow lift.

'That way,' Garcia continued, 'the killer could've parked right on the victim's driveway, which would've made the task of bringing a subdued Kirsten out to the car and then later her body from the car back into the house, much easier. But best of all, like you said, even if seen, it wouldn't have raised any eyebrows from any of the neighbors.' He chuckled. 'Clever.'

'Very,' Hunter said in return. 'The killer knew that he would need time to get Kirsten out of the house and then bring her body back in. In the second instance, it could've taken him a while because he wanted to pose her body on the bed. The car could've been parked out on the driveway for some time.'

'And the longer it was there, the higher the chances of someone noticing it.'

'Risk-minimizing strategy at its absolute best,' Hunter confirmed. 'Even more so because the pickup truck provided the killer with great cover from prying eyes.' He once again pointed to the photo showing both cars on the driveway before explaining: 'This morning, as I was leaving the house, I exited via their kitchen door, which is located on this side of the building.' He indicated on the picture, even though the door couldn't be seen. 'Their house is the last on the street. There's nothing to the left of it. With both cars parked on the driveway, the killer could've exited through the driver's side and used the kitchen door. That way, no neighbor, from whatever position ... from whatever window ... would've been able to properly spot him entering or exiting the house. He could've taken his time dragging the victim into and out of the truck.'

Garcia stepped closer to the board again, his attention on the photo that Hunter had indicated. 'So the killer either hires, buys or steals a similar-looking pickup truck to Troy's.'

'Yes.' Hunter agreed.

'I'll ask Research to—'

'I already did,' Hunter informed him. 'I called them from the car on my way back here.'

Garcia's breath rattled on the way in and whistled on the way out. 'If we're right about all this, that's one hell of a lot of effort for one victim. Why?'

As Hunter's lips parted for a possible reply, the door to their office was pulled open so fast that a couple of pieces of paper flew off Garcia's desk, landing by Captain Blake's feet, who had just entered the room. In her right hand, she had the report that Hunter had dropped on her desk earlier that morning. As she waved the report at them, her chin angled down so she could look at her detectives over the rim of her reading glasses, her eyes wide, her demeanor challenging.

'Show me.'

Thirty-three

The UVC Unit's office was small and cramped. 'Shoebox' was the term most commonly used by both Hunter and Garcia, but despite its size, everything had its own place. The picture board, for example, sat across the room and a little to the left from the entry door, just past the detectives' desks. From where the captain was standing, she would've had a clear view of it, if not for Hunter and Garcia standing in the way.

Garcia took a step to his left while Hunter took one to his right.

'Which part exactly would you like us to show you, Captain?' Garcia asked, broadly indicating the entire board in front of him. 'Because we do have a Vegas-style buffet of surprises right here.'

Captain Blake didn't reply. Instead, she allowed the door to close behind her, pulled her reading glasses from her face and in silence, approached both detectives and the picture board, her gaze transfixed on the photos pinned to its right half. She blinked a couple of times as her attention settled on the first of a series of photos showing Kirsten Hansen's body on her bed, her arms lifted above her head, her hands tied at the wrists, the entire rope-chain-hook set-up still in place. Insanity clearly colliding with reality.

Hunter and Garcia stayed quiet, allowing her to take in all the horror in those pictures at her own pace.

She opened her mouth, then closed it again. She'd been about to say something, but in the end, all she did was let go of a breath that seemed to have depleted her of hope. In her eyes was a mixture of anger and sadness.

Another thirty seconds went by, where her attention slowly moved from one photo to another.

'In here,' she lifted the report in her hands, her voice placid, 'it says that the assumption is that she was hooked to the back of a vehicle and dragged against the ground until she was dead. Has this been confirmed?'

'Not yet,' Garcia replied. 'We're waiting on the autopsy results.'

There was a 'but' riding in the wake of those words. Captain Blake waited for it. When it didn't materialize, she filled in the blanks. 'Not confirmed yet, but it will be.'

'We're all sure of it,' the reply came from Hunter.

The captain's stare dropped to the report in her hand for a moment before returning to the photos. She impatiently searched the board, but with so many images on it, she didn't find the one that she was looking for. Instead, she pinned Hunter down.

'You also said in the report that we are dealing with the same perp here.' Instinctively, she indicated the photos relating to Melissa Hawthorne's murder. 'How is this possible? Where is this note that was found in her hand?' She pointed to Kirsten Hansen's half of the board.

Garcia had placed the photos of both notes, the one found inside Melissa's body and the one found in Kirsten's hand, side by side right at the bottom of the board. He pointed to them.

Captain Blake reread Melissa's note first before reading Kirsten's.

Melissa's note read: 'Through these eyes, no one will ever look as perfect as you did.'

Kirsten's note read: 'Through this heart, no love will ever surpass my love for you.'

Though the notes weren't identical, it was clear to see that they carried the same tone, the same rhythm, and the same theme.

Captain Blake pinched her lower lip for a quick second. 'Sounds like a love poem.'

'It does,' Hunter agreed. 'Or maybe a song, right?' He lifted his hand to indicate that he didn't really need a reply. 'What I'm trying to get to here, Captain, is that they seem to go together, as if both lines come from the same composition, but they've been split up.'

In silence, Captain Blake reread both notes.

'I ran a basic Internet search on both lines again,' Hunter said. 'I tried them one by one. I tried them together. I inverted them. I mixed them up.' He shook his head. 'Nothing. Whatever this is, it doesn't seem to be out there.'

'Which probably means that our killer writes them himself,' Garcia said, but quickly corrected his mistake. 'I mean, he creates them himself, or so we believe, but he makes his victim's write them down before murdering them.'

'Her fiancé confirmed it,' Hunter said, clarifying Captain Blake's unasked question. 'It's Kirsten Hansen's handwriting on the note.'

Captain Blake exhaled a heavy breath and put down the file she'd been holding.

'Also,' Garcia added, 'just like with Melissa Hawthorne, Miss Hansen's cellphone is missing.'

The captain took a moment to process that information.

'Text messages,' she said, her stare moving back to the board and to the transcript of the messages that the killer had sent Melissa on the night she was murdered.

'We think so, yes,' Garcia confirmed. 'I've already got in touch with her cellphone provider just before you got here.' He nodded at Hunter. 'Which, luckily enough, was once again AT&T. This time I took no chances. I called Martin Carr directly.'

'Who?' Captain Blake asked.

'The lawyer we spoke to when we visited AT&T headquarters yesterday,' Hunter explained.

Garcia nodded. 'He promised me that this time they'll include any videos, or images attached to any of her recent messages.'

'Recent, as in . . .?' the captain asked.

'Same as Miss Hawthorne's – the past three months. I also made it clear that this was as urgent as it got, so we might get something by the end of today.'

'Great.' Hunter nodded back at his partner.

'So who is *this* girl,' the captain asked, stepping back from the board to lean against the edge of Hunter's desk. 'What do we know about her?'

'Got the file from Research about half an hour ago,' Garcia said, walking back to his computer and opening the attachment on the email he had received from his team. 'Kirsten Hansen – twenty-nine years old. She worked as a surgical nurse for the Los Angeles Surge Hospital in Westlake. She was born in . . .' He paused and once again nodded at Hunter. 'You were right on the money there – Denmark. A city called Odense. Came to the US eight years ago, on her own, to study nursing at UCLA. Graduated three and a half years ago with a Masters of Science in Nursing. Did her residency at . . .' Garcia scrolled down on his screen. 'The same hospital she works now – LA Surge. Lived with her fiancé, Troy Foster, in Alhambra.'

'They'd been together for three years,' Hunter told Captain Blake. 'He found the body.'

'Like most people nowadays,' Garcia continued, 'she has a few social media accounts. The usual suspects – Facebook, Instagram and Twitter. We'll be looking into all of it.' Garcia scrolled down some more. 'Her record is squeaky clean. Not even a parking ticket. Her credit card was last used on the night she was murdered. She ordered a pizza from Angelo's Pizzeria on West Valley Boulevard, just over a mile from her place.'

'Did the pizza get delivered?' the captain asked.

'It did, yes,' Hunter said. 'They open at 11 a.m. I'll drop by later on today to see if I can talk to the deliveryman. Maybe he saw the killer's pickup truck parked somewhere on the street, or something.'

The captain's eyebrows knitted. 'How do you know the killer was driving a pickup truck?'

Hunter quickly ran Captain Blake through their theory. He also explained why they thought that there was a big possibility that the killer was already hiding inside the victim's house when the pizza was delivered.

'If this really is the same guy,' Garcia came back, once again indicating the photos of the two notes on the board, 'then chances are that some of his MO repeats itself.'

'Whoever this killer is,' Hunter said, 'he seems to be very fluent in both physical and psychological torture.'

'The text messages,' Captain Blake concluded.

Hunter nodded, as he returned to the board and indicated the transcript from the text message conversation between Melissa and the killer. 'We know what his MO is because he wrote it down. He wants to teach his victims about fear, pain, and death. That's his compulsion. And he loves all of it.'

The moment that followed was silent and anxious.

Captain Blake closed her eyes and used the tips of her fingers to massage her temples. She wasn't looking forward to the headache that she knew was coming.

'OK, let me backtrack just a little here,' she finally said. 'I know that when the first note was found, we discussed the possibility of it being some sort of declaration of love or not. We never got to a conclusion. Now with the second note, we are considering the possibility of this being one single composition – a poem ... a song ... whatever.' The captain raised her hands and shrugged at the same time. 'Let's call it a poem for ease of reference here. Anyway, it seems to me that this second note strengthens that initial suggestion, doesn't it? He's even used the word "love" in it.

Twice. Could this killer have dated both victims at some point in his life? Maybe he fell in love with both of them and got dumped by both of them. Maybe this is his psychotic revenge.'

'Yes,' Garcia replied. 'That's a very distinct possibility, Captain, and we'll be looking into every ex-boyfriend, fling, hook-up, whatever we can find.'

Hunter paused by the window. On the street below, he observed a woman pushing a baby in a stroller across the road on a red light.

'The more I think about the lines on those notes,' he said, his eyes on the street. 'The more it takes me back to Miss Peterson.'

'Excuse me?' Captain Blake coughed the first word. 'Who the hell is Miss Peterson?'

'My seventh grade English teacher,' Hunter replied. 'For the entire year, the last twenty minutes of her classes were always on poetry. There's something that she taught us about it, that I'll never forget.'

'And that is?'

'That poetry is totally open to interpretation, Captain. In the sense that, if you give the same poem to "X" number of people and ask them to explain in their words what they just read, or what they think it means, you'll get "X" number of interpretations. And truthfully, none of them are really wrong. What I'm trying to get to here is that we could easily interpret these two lines as being from a love poem, but that would be *our* interpretation, not the killer's. This could be a nursery rhyme that his mother used to sing to him, for all we know, and he hated it.'

Captain Blake wouldn't let that go so easily. 'OK, so allow me to rephrase my question – what do *you* think it means?'

Hunter's stare returned to the window to his right. 'I'm not sure that my view on this matters right at this point.'

'You see, that's where you're wrong, Robert. The two of you are the lead detectives in this investigation. What you think, about any of it, steers it in one direction or another. This killer isn't leaving notes behind for sport. He knows they'll be found and he knows that they'll be found by us. They're a challenge . . . a taunt.' Her index finger stabbed in Hunter's direction. 'You told me that, more than once. In fact, you tell me that every time a killer leaves a note, a drawing, an object, or whatever behind for us to find, they are clues that we need to interpret. Just like a poem. And you're the expert when it comes to thinking like a killer . . . when it comes to seeing things through the eyes of a completely deranged psychopath. Hence the purpose of this whole department.' She gestured broadly at the office. 'If anyone can have a stab at what these words really mean to this killer – you're it, Robert. So please spare me the bullshit about "it doesn't matter what I think" because we all know it does.'

Garcia used his thumb to rub between his eyebrows. 'The captain's got a point, Robert. I flunked poetry.'

Hunter turned to face the room. 'That's not exactly what I said, Captain. I didn't say that it doesn't matter what I think. I said that I'm not sure that my view on this matters *right at this point*.'

The captain once again crossed her arms in front of her. 'And what does that mean?'

'It means that – I don't think it's done.'

Captain Blake waited, but Hunter offered nothing more.

'What don't you think is done, Robert?' she asked.

'The poem. It seems . . . unfinished, Captain. I think that there's more to come.'

Thirty-four

'What *the hell* are you doing?' Josie Griffith asked, as the edges of her mouth angled up in an amused smile.

She had just stepped out of the bathroom and into their bedroom. Her husband, Oliver, was standing in front of the full-length mirror that doubled as a wardrobe door, seemingly struggling with his tie.

'What does it look like I'm doing, my love?' Oliver had learnt the habit of answering a question with a question from Josie. As a psychotherapist, it was something that she did professionally.

'It looks like you're trying to hang yourself, honey,' Josie replied. 'Are you subconsciously trying to tell me something?'

'I certainly am, Doctor.' Oliver turned to face her. 'I'm trying to tell you that I could do with some help here.'

Josie was wearing her favorite dark-purple shower robe, with a towel cozily wrapped around her head. Despite her out-of-the-shower attire, hidden hair and no make-up, she still looked far better than any human had a right to at that time in the morning.

Oliver allowed his arms to drop by his sides, as if he'd given up. 'Can you please help me, my love? I'm ten years old, all of a sudden. Do you know how to tie a tie?'

Oliver and Josie had met each other seventeen months ago, at a private party in Sherman Oaks, an upper class neighborhood in the San Fernando Valley region of Los Angeles. The attraction on both sides had been immediate and undeniable, but Josie was the one who made the first move.

'Are you scared of talking to me?' she had asked Oliver, as he was about to order a drink at the bar.

He hadn't seen her approaching and was completely caught by surprise.

'Umm . . .' He blinked twice, looked at the barman, then down at his shoes, then finally back at Josie. 'No, not real—' He hesitated. 'What do you mean?'

Oliver's awkwardness made Josie smile.

'Well, you've been checking me out since I walked in here about forty-five minutes ago,' she said before pausing long enough for Oliver to look a little embarrassed. 'But it's OK, because I've also been checking you out, and I know that you've noticed me doing so.'

Oliver shifted on his feet. 'A little bit, yeah!'

'So,' Josie continued, 'since I've noticed that you've noticed, I gave you plenty of opportunities to come and say "hi", but you passed on them all, which means that you're either very shy or completely clueless. Which one is it?'

Oliver gave her a timid smile. 'A bit of both, I guess.'

Josie smiled back.

They slept together on that first night. Eleven months later, they were married.

Josie walked up to her husband. 'It'll be my pleasure to help you, Mr. Griffith.' She kissed his lips before reaching for his tie. 'And yes, I do know how to tie a tie.'

There was no denying that Oliver Griffith was an attractive man. Tall, lean, elegant and unmistakably strong, he had the arms, shoulders and abs of a professional boxer, and the lips, smile, and jawline of a male model. He liked to keep his dark hair cut short and neat, but it didn't fall into any particular fashion style, which added an odd quirkiness to his charm. His eyes, which were a shade lighter than his hair, didn't give much away, except for a hint into his calm watchfulness and his keen intellect.

'Why are you wearing a suit and tie today, anyway?' Josie asked. 'What's the occasion?'

Oliver worked for a world-renowned advertising agency. He was what was known in the business as an 'Ideas Man', and he was brilliant at it. In the past three months alone, his creations had secured three new accounts for the agency. Two of those were multi-million dollar accounts from European companies.

'Meeting a possible new client this morning,' Oliver replied. 'And this could be mega – it's a Japanese electronics company. Very blue-collar, apparently, so Brendan told me to look the part.'

'You always look the part, honey.' Josie said, as she ran her fingers down his silky, steel-gray tie. 'So, which type of knot would you like?'

Oliver's eyes practically sparkled with surprise. 'How many do you know?'

She kissed him again. 'Four . . . I think.' As she replied, her head tilted a little to the right while she thought about it for a couple of seconds. 'Yes. Four – Windsor, Half-Windsor, Four-in-Hand and Simple.'

Oliver's head jerked back. 'And you never told me that before? How long have we been together?'

Josie gave Oliver her special 'you'd better be kidding' look – chin down, eyebrows arched, head angled left, eyes looking back at him like laser beams.

'It was a rhetorical question, my love.' Oliver paddled back, his tone unconvincing.

'Really?' Josie replied, letting go of his tie. 'So tell me, Mr. Griffith – how long *have* we been together?'

'Are you testing me?' Oliver asked, before mimicking his

wife's 'you'd better be kidding' look, though his lacked the ferocity of hers.

Josie didn't look amused.

'A year and a half,' he said, his tone calm, his demeanor relaxed. 'We dated for a year and we got married six months ago – on August 7th. Satisfied?'

'Seventeen months. Not a year and a half,' Josie corrected him, as she once again grabbed hold of his tie. 'But yes.' She smiled. 'At least you got the wedding date right, so you've passed.'

Oliver chuckled. 'You were testing me?'

'Life *is* a test in itself, honey.' She ran the tip of her right index finger down the contour of his jawline. 'So, which knot would you like?'

'Umm . . .' He shrugged. He didn't really know the difference between them. 'Surprise me.'

Josie bit her bottom lip, as her eyes refocused on Oliver's. 'Really?' Her hand dropped and with a single, smooth movement, she pulled open her robe. 'Like this sort of surprise?'

If Oliver had the body and muscles of a professional boxer, Josie had the sexy figure of a playboy model, coupled with the mind and the skills of a porn star.

She sensed his whole body tense.

Oliver breathed out slowly. He had to use every ounce of his willpower to keep his eyes still, and fixed on Josie's.

'Despite knowing every inch of your body, my love,' he said, his voice as steady as he could keep it, 'I'm not going to look down, because if I do, I'll be in trouble. I really need to get to this meeting. I can't be late. So please, please, please, can you hold on to that thought until tonight and just help me with my tie right now?'

'Are you sure?' Josie stepped closer, placing her leg between his and softly brushing the inside of her naked thigh against the inside of his clothed one. She didn't need to look down to know that the tease had had its desired effect. She felt it.

Oliver closed his eyes and tried his best to keep the pleasure moan that had lodged itself in his throat from escaping.

He failed . . . miserably.

'I . . .' He shook his head before reopening his eyes.

Josie held his stare for a couple more seconds.

'Alright,' she said, finally taking a step back, though the devilish smile on her lips became even more inviting. 'But promise me that we'll play tonight.'

'Oh, you better believe it.'

'And will you punish me for being such a bad girl and teasing you when I knew I shouldn't?'

Oliver took another deep breath to collect himself before using Josie's technique one more time. 'Do you want to be punished?'

Josie moved closer, yet again, angling her head to get to Oliver's right ear. The whisper that came out of her lips was softer than a plume.

'So, so, so much.'

She gently nibbled the tip of his earlobe, making Oliver's whole body shiver.

'You might have to tie me to the bed and spank me too,' she said in the same soft tone.

'Oh, I will most *definitely* do that, Mrs. Griffith.'

'I can't wait,' Josie whispered. As she stepped back again, she was careful to allow one of her nipples to gently brush against his right arm before slowly redoing her bathrobe. 'OK, honey, now hold your head still while I do your tie.'

'You are impossible,' he said before kissing her lips. 'Do you know that?'

'Of course I do,' she replied, her tone just as proud as the look in her eyes. 'Now hold still.'

Oliver did and less than a minute later, Josie was done.

'There you go,' she said, indicating the mirror. 'Have a look. Tell me what you think.'

Oliver turned to face the mirror and the surprise on his face was a picture. 'Oh my God. This is . . . perfect,' he said, addressing her reflection.

She shrugged, as if it were nothing. 'I *am* perfect, honey. Don't you know that?'

'Wow. Amazing.' Oliver's attention went back to his tie. 'So which knot is this one?'

'Oxford,' Josie answered, but paused immediately to think about it. 'At least I think it is. I get confused sometimes. It's been a while.' She undid the turban around her head and allowed her long blonde hair to fall down naturally before using her fingers to ruffle it a little.

'Whichever this one is, I love it.' He turned and kissed her again. 'And I love you. I'm seriously impressed here, though.' He reached for his charcoal suit blazer, which had been neatly laid on their king-sized bed. 'I really do need to get going now. What are your plans for today? Anything interesting?'

Josie walked over to her side of the wardrobe, opened one of the drawers and selected a purple pair of lacey panties and a matching bra.

'Same as every day, honey,' she replied, once again undoing her robe, but this time, she allowed it to fall to the floor. 'Seeing patients all day. This evening I'm meeting Sylvia for a quick drink in the Arts District, but I won't stay long. I need to be punished tonight, remember?'

'Yes, you do.' Oliver agreed, nodding vigorously.

'I also want to pack for the trip tonight because tomorrow it'll be a crazy rush. I'm booked solid at the practice all day and in the evening, I've got manicure, pedicure, and wax at the salon.'

Oliver turned to check his profile on the mirror. His tailor-made, business suit was cut in a classic style and it fitted him perfectly.

'Trip?' he asked, without breaking eye contact with his reflection.

Standing to his right, completely naked, Josie gave him a new *you'd better be kidding* look. This one seemed a lot more serious than the one from moments ago.

Oliver caught a glimpse of her stare in the mirror.

'Oh, of course,' he said, his hands coming up in an apologetic gesture. 'Stacey's hen night in Vegas. Is that this weekend already? Wow, that came around fast, didn't it?'

The question and the comment sounded genuine, even more so because Josie did agree with him.

'I know,' she replied, the 'you'd better be kidding' look all but gone. 'It feels like we booked everything last week instead of over a month and a half ago.'

Oliver adjusted his cuffs and turned to leave, but Josie stepped left to block his path.

'Are you gonna miss me while I'm in Vegas?' she asked, and as she did, she softly ran the tips of her fingernails down between her breasts. Her nipples were so hard they looked like they could cut glass.

Oliver paused. This time he couldn't stop his eyes from taking all of her in. 'Gosh, baby, you *are* beautiful and if I didn't have this meeting this morning . . .' He didn't finish his sentence. Instead, he shook his head while his eyes devoured Josie's body.

'So you *will* miss me?' she asked again.

'Of course I will miss you. You know that.'

Josie smiled, as she put on her panties. 'I do. I just wanted to hear you say it.'

'I really have to go, baby.' Oliver stepped forward and kissed her lips again. 'I'll see you tonight. I love you.'

'I love you more. Have a good day.'

Outside their house in Valencia, an upper-middle class neighborhood in Santa Clarita, Oliver checked his watch as he opened the door to his black Mercedes. If he rushed, he could still get to the agency in Hollywood in time.

As he backed up from his driveway and accelerated down the road, he never noticed the black pickup truck parked in front of his neighbor's house. The person behind the wheel had watched as Oliver got into his car and drove away.

Josie was now alone in the house.

The pickup truck driver smiled.

Thirty-five

Hunter's trip to Angelo's Pizzeria on West Valley Boulevard yielded no results. The pizza deliveryman did remember Monday night's delivery to Kirsten Hansen, mainly because the lady had given him a nice tip, but that was about it. If there had been a black pickup truck parked anywhere on her street at that time, he hadn't noticed it, just like he hadn't noticed anything else that might've been construed as suspicious.

It had been a long shot. Hunter knew that, but every now and then, some long shots paid off big time.

From the pizza parlor, Hunter drove straight to the Los Angeles Surge Hospital in Westlake, where he spent almost three hours talking to just about everyone he could – doctors, nurses, orderlies, the administration, the staff at the canteen, the security guards ... everyone – and not a single person had anything remotely derogatory to say about Kirsten Hansen. On the contrary, she was praised by everyone for her work ethic, for how friendly and caring she was, for how competent she was ... the compliments went on and on. It sounded like she was loved by everyone, but the real reason why Hunter wanted to visit the hospital was two-fold:

First – he wanted to ask some of the people who worked with Kirsten if any of them recognized either of the two lines that the killer had left at both crime scenes. Maybe it was something that had come in a 'Get Well' card ... maybe they had been written by a recovering patient ... Hunter was willing to try anything. The more people who saw those lines, the more chances he had of someone recognizing them.

Nobody did.

Second – Hunter had brought with him a copy of the printout that he and Garcia had obtained at the Freehand Hotel – the image of 'Sleazy Mark'. Like he had predicted, the LAPD Digital and Technical Support Unit hadn't managed to hypothesize the rest of Mark's face. A program did exist that could do just that, but it needed at least forty-five percent of the subject's face to start with. The hat that Mark had worn as he left the hotel, together with the poor CCTV camera angle, had managed to hide almost eighty percent of his face. They had still tried the program, but it failed every time. What they were left with was the facial composite that Roger, the bartender at the Broken Shaker, had given the LAPD sketch artist. It wasn't great, but it was all they had.

Hunter showed the printout, together with the facial composite, to everyone he spoke to, for one simple reason – he knew that this killer had to have tailed Kirsten for a while. Before he took her, he needed to have learnt her schedule and habits, and he needed to have had an itinerary and a plan of action in place. Kirsten, just like Melissa, had been pre-selected. They were not victims of chance, and as such, this killer had to have observed Kirsten for days ... weeks, maybe. And he would've been thorough. Of that, Hunter had no doubt. That meant that he probably observed her for hours on end with barely any breaks, and that was a risk. A small one, but a risk nonetheless. Maybe someone else from the hospital had noticed something – the same person hanging around the parking lot for hours, day after day, sitting inside his car, or parked across the street. Maybe the killer even risked walking into the hospital reception, or the canteen. Certain killers, especially the ones who pre-selected their victims, sometimes got a kick out of getting physically close to their subjects prior to the 'attack day'. Some even befriended them.

If 'Sleazy Mark' and the killer were one and the same, there was also a chance that he could've worn the same Panama hat to partially hide his face, as he stalked Kirsten. Maybe someone remembered it. Maybe someone remembered him.

However, just like before, no one did. The long shots simply weren't working for Hunter.

Once he left the hospital, he headed toward San Fernando Valley and the district of Sylmar, the northernmost neighborhood within the city of Los Angeles. That was where Troy was staying, at his mother's house.

Hunter understood that Troy would still be in shock. It had been less than twenty-four hours since he had walked into his bedroom and found the totally mutilated body of his fiancée on their bed – an image that would torment him for the rest of his days – but Hunter also knew that he needed to try to talk to Troy again before post-traumatic stress completely settled in.

The problem with post-traumatic stress for any investigating officer, in such cases as Troy's, was that the human mind demanded answers. It needed to know 'why' and 'who' – answers that wouldn't come easy, if they came at all. With the lack of immediate answers, a traumatized and stressed mind would inevitably start creating its own ... and it would create an army of them. It didn't matter if those answers sounded absurd or not. It didn't matter if they sounded like a crazy fantasy or not. To a mind at the brink of breaking, they would all sound plausible because the desperate need for answers would overwhelm rational thinking, and as those answers started sounding like the real deal, the mind would initiate a new, very damaging, line of questioning – the 'what ifs' and 'should haves'. Those types of questions *always* brought two of the most destructive feelings with their answers – guilt and regret. It wasn't a question of if that happened to Troy. It was a question of when. Hunter knew that from experience. And once the mind started creating its own army of answers, the thin line between reality and fantasy would get lost.

Hunter needed to try to ask Troy a few questions before that happened.

Thirty-six

The house was humble – single-story and sat back from the street, with a small lawn up front where an individual pink trumpet tree took center stage. Troy's Ford pickup truck was parked on the driveway, just behind a white VW Golf.

Hunter parked on the street, right in front of the house, but took a moment to collect his thoughts before walking up to the front door. He needed to go back to the subject of the note that the killer had left behind, and since there was no denying that the underlying theme of both notes was love, or some strange permutation of it, Hunter's questions to Troy would have to be delicate, especially considering the state that Troy was in. They involved asking him about previous relationships and partners from both sides, any problems they might've been having in their actual relationship, and the toughest subject of all because no matter what, people always lied about it – affairs ... lovers ... flings ... crushes ... one-night stands ... work flirts ... anything of that nature. At this stage, nothing and no one could be discarded.

Hunter's intention wasn't to try to identify if there were any cracks in Troy and Kirsten's relationship. What he was looking to do was to try to establish some sort of connection between the two victims, and at the moment, the only thing Hunter had that linked them together was the theme of the two 'love' quotes, or so it seemed.

Ninety-nine percent of murderers who pre-selected their victims did so for a very specific reason – there was always some sort of criteria that the victims needed to fulfill. Sometimes it was something simple, like an aesthetic match – hair color ... eye color ... height ... body type ... breast size ... etc. Sometimes it was a personality trait, or a mannerism – the sound of their voice ... how they played with their hair when they were nervous ... the way in which they threw their head back when they laughed ... it could be just about anything, from simple to complex, but whatever it was, that was the trigger. It was what initiated the entire process inside the killer's head, and that was really where the problem with identifying such criteria lay, because whatever that trigger was, it didn't have to have any meaning or make any sense to anyone else but the killer.

Before stepping out of his car, Hunter checked his phone for any messages from Garcia, who had gone to the taxi company to have a chat with the cab driver who had dropped Melissa Hawthorne off at her house after she left her friend's birthday party.

No messages.

At the house's front porch, where most of the yellow paintwork had cracked and chipped to reveal a very old and discolored green coat of paint underneath, Hunter rang the doorbell and waited. He had called ahead and spoken to Mrs. Foster. At first, she had been very reluctant to agree to Hunter's visit, which was understandable. She told him that Troy was in a very bad headspace and questions at this time would not only make everything much worse for him, but also probably get Hunter no good answers. Hunter hadn't disagreed, but had calmly explained the issue with timing and post-traumatic stress. If he was to stand any chances of obtaining more reliable answers, this couldn't be delayed.

Hunter was about to ring the doorbell again, when he heard tired footsteps approaching from the inside. A moment later, Mrs. Foster pulled open the door.

Hunter had met her in the early hours of the morning, when she and Troy's brother, Brett, came to collect him from his house in Alhambra. She looked quite different from what Hunter remembered. From how puffy her eyes looked, he knew that she had spent most of the day crying.

After making Hunter promise her that he would be as brief as possible and that the questions would stop if Troy felt that they were too much, Mrs. Foster finally showed him into her living room, which seemed too small for the amount of furniture and objects in it.

'Please, have a seat,' she said, indicating the area with a sofa and two armchairs. 'I'll go get Troy.'

As she left the room, Hunter turned his attention to some of the many framed photographs that decorated the walls. They were all family photos, and it took him only a second to realize that they followed a chronological order, moving from left to right. Mrs. Foster was, undoubtedly, a very proud wife and mother.

Hunter recognized Troy straight away, even in the photos where he looked to be only about two or three years old. From the pictures, it was clear that Troy and his brother had both developed a very strong physique quite early on. Both of them had played for their high school football teams and by the looks of it, Troy had also tried his hand at surfing. Judging by the photos alone, Troy seemed to have been a happy kid, displaying a bright smile in at least ninety percent of the photos he was in.

Hunter had just started looking at a set of photographs of Troy holding a surfboard, when he heard dragging footsteps come from behind him.

'My dad used to love taking us to the beach.'

Hunter turned to find Troy standing by the door that connected the living room to the hallway that lead to the rest of the house. Mrs. Foster was standing right behind him.

In the space of less than a day, Troy seemed to have shrunk to half of his original size. It was like his body had curled in on itself, shoulders drooped with his chin dipped, almost bowing forward beneath the invisible weight of grief and loss. His blonde hair was a mess and his eyes were puffy and sore. As Hunter looked back at him, Troy snorted a breath through a congested nose and pulled the sleeves of his green sweatshirt up to his elbows. The look was completed by black gym trousers and blue sliders over black socks.

'You surf?' Hunter asked in reply, indicating one of the photos.

Troy's head dipped left as his eyebrows lifted. 'I tried. I wasn't very good at it.'

'Santa Monica beach?' Hunter asked, knowing that Santa Monica was a great beach for surf beginners.

'Yes.' Troy nodded. 'We used to go there a lot when my dad was alive.'

Hunter felt a knot start forming at the base of his throat. The last thing he wanted was to remind Troy of another painful loss.

'I'm sorry.' That was all he could say, though his words were sincere. He stepped away from the wall and the photos and approached the sofa.

Troy followed.

'Let me get you both something to drink,' Mrs. Foster said. 'How about some peach ice tea?'

'I'm OK, Mom,' Troy replied, pausing by one of the armchairs. For a moment he looked like he couldn't remember why he was in the living room.

'Detective?' Mrs. Foster's gaze moved to Hunter.

'That would be very nice. Thank you so much.'

'I'll bring you some anyway, Troy,' she said, addressing her son. 'And I'll make you a sandwich too – pastrami, cheese and mustard on rye – your favorite.'

'I'm not hungry, Mom.' Troy's voice was just a whisper.

'You *need* to eat, Troy.'

That was a mother's command, not a suggestion.

Troy looked like he just didn't have the strength to argue about anything. Instead, his sad eyes found a spot on the rug he was standing on and just stayed fixed on it.

'Sandwich, Detective?'

'No, thank you, ma'am. I'll be fine with just the ice tea.'

As soon as Mrs. Foster left the living room, Troy blinked and looked at Hunter.

'Anything yet?' he asked, his voice quivering, his eyes beginning to glass over again.

'It's been less than twenty-four hours, Mr. Foster,' Hunter replied.

'My father was Mr. Foster.' Troy's thumb stabbed toward the photos on the wall. 'I'm just Troy. And that means "no", right? You guys don't have anything.'

'How about we have a seat?' Hunter said, indicating the sofa and the armchairs. 'I'd like to show you something.'

That made Troy pause, his interest renewed. 'What? What have you got?'

'Please,' Hunter insisted.

Troy took one of the armchairs. Understandably, he wanted answers and he wanted them immediately, but Hunter had been in this same exact situation way too many times, and he knew that people in Troy's position tended to be a lot more willing to answer difficult questions, like the ones Hunter needed to ask him, if they saw that some sort of progress was being made with the investigation. The best way to do that was to drip-feed information – give a little, get a little. It was a psychological trick that, more often than not, worked pretty well.

Hunter sat at the far left edge of the sofa, closer to the armchair that Troy had taken. As he did, he retrieved the printout and the facial composite of 'Sleazy Mark' from his pocket.

'I know that these aren't the best of images,' Hunter began.

'But unfortunately they're all that we've managed to come up with so far.' He handed them both to Troy. 'I'd like you to have a look at them and tell me if you have ever seen this person before.'

Troy took the printout and the composite, but barely looked at them.

'Is this him?' he asked, his voice quivering again, but this time with a different emotion. 'Is this the motherfucker who did that to Kirsten?'

That was always the biggest peril in showing a person in Troy's position an image like the one on the printout. Because his brain demanded answers, it would automatically try to simplify whatever it could into a binary 'yes/no' answer.

Hunter was expecting it.

'You *know* that it's not that simple, Troy.'

Psychological trick number two – Hunter emphasized the word 'know' to indicate to Troy that he wasn't patronizing him. On the contrary, he was giving him credit for his knowledge.

'Every investigation is like a live jigsaw puzzle.' Hunter's voice was even. 'We need to link individual pieces together until we have the full picture, or just a better picture. A single piece on its own never really completes the puzzle.' Hunter pointed to the printout in Troy's hand. 'At the moment, the person on that image is a single, loose piece that we'd like to identify and talk to.'

'Why?' Troy's forehead creased. 'How's he a piece of the puzzle?'

Troy's mind was skipping hurdles again.

'That's the thing,' Hunter replied, motioning for him to slow down a little. 'He might have nothing to do with *our puzzle*. We won't really know until we find him and talk to him.'

'Alright,' Troy accepted it. 'But what's his connection to what happened to Kirsten? Where did you get this image?'

Because Troy's mind was desperate, if Hunter revealed

everything at once, there was a chance that it would maybe start creating memories and images that weren't really there.

Hunter didn't want to run that risk.

Give a little – get a little.

'Please.' Hunter once again nodded at the printout. 'Have a look at the images first and I'll clarify everything for you in a moment.'

Troy finally gave in and studied them both.

'Maybe you've seen him somewhere on your street, or maybe even at your gun shop.'

'My shop?' Confusion coated Troy's words. 'Why would he be in my shop?'

Another long shot.

Hunter and Garcia had already come to the conclusion that whoever this killer was, he had shadowed not only Kirsten, but Troy as well. The fact that he had struck when Troy was out of town, and that he so happened to drive the same pickup truck as Troy's, was no coincidence, but that was also the sort of information that Troy didn't really need to know.

'I'm just keeping an open mind here,' Hunter explained. 'What I mean is – don't try to remember if you've seen him only around your street. It could've been anywhere ... your local supermarket ... the park ... the gym ... your gun shop ... it doesn't matter.'

'Are these the only images you have?' Troy asked, after spending almost a minute staring at the printout.

'Unfortunately, yes.'

Troy's gaze reverted back to the two pieces of paper for another instant before he breathed out despair. 'My head is a mess, Detective. Nothing makes sense in here anymore.' He tapped his index finger against his skull. 'Neither of them is bringing anything back.'

'I understand. It was worth a try.'

'How come this is such a bad image?' Troy asked indicating the printout, a pleading quality to his tone. 'Where did you get it? And why do you think that this dude, whoever he is, could be a piece of our puzzle?'

Troy was on board. He had just used the pronoun 'our' of his own accord.

Drip-feed again.

'The image comes from the CCTV camera in a hotel lobby downtown.' Hunter immediately lifted a hand to pause Troy. He didn't want him imagining that Kirsten might've been using a hotel in central LA for some sort of affair. 'This is in relation to a different crime scene . . . a different investigation, one where there might be a link.'

'What?' Troy's eyes became two giant marbles. 'How? What kind of link? What other crime scene?' The questions came like stabs.

Before Hunter could clarify, Mrs. Foster returned to the living room, bringing with her a floral-print tray with a jug of ice tea, two glasses, and a plate with a sandwich neatly cut into four triangles.

'Here we go,' she said, placing the tray down on the coffee table between the sofa and the armchairs. She then handed Hunter a glass and poured him some ice tea. She did the same for Troy.

'Thank you so much,' Hunter said. 'That's very kind of you.'

'Don't mention it,' she replied, handing Troy the sandwich.

'Mom, I told you, I'm not hungry.'

'It's cut into quarters, Troy,' she said back. 'Have at least one of them.'

'Maybe later.' Troy returned the plate to the tray.

Mrs. Foster gave him a look that only a mother could.

Troy waited, but instead of leaving, Mrs. Foster planted herself on the second armchair.

'Mom,' Troy said, locking eyes with her. 'We're sort of in the middle of something here, if you don't mind.'

'Not at all,' she replied, sitting back and crossing one leg over the other. 'You boys do your thing. Don't mind little old me here.'

Troy's gaze darted to Hunter then back to his mother. 'No, Mom. What I mean is – can you give us a moment, please.'

'Oh, you want me to leave?' She did her best 'surprised' face.

'Yes. If you don't mind.'

From the look on Mrs. Foster's face and the way in which she squared her shoulders, Hunter could guess what was coming.

'This is my house, Troy. I can sit in whichever room I damn well please.' She pointed at Hunter. 'Detective Hunter here promised me that he wouldn't upset you with his questions. It's not that I don't trust him.' All of a sudden, Hunter was at the receiving end of another 'motherly look'. 'But if it's all the same to you, I'd like to sit – *in my living room* – and judge for myself.'

Troy puffed out a breath. 'I don't need babysitting, Mom. I'm a grown man.'

'I know you are,' came her reply, which was immediately followed by her finger pointing upwards. 'But you know what that is, right above your head?'

Hunter bit his lip. This was an argument that Troy would never win.

'My roof,' she said. 'The key word here, Troy, is "my".' In a split second, her tone went from imposing to ultra-tender. 'I'm just being a mother, Troy.' Tears seemed to have caught in her throat. 'It breaks my heart to see you hurt like this, son, and I don't know what to do to make it better.' The tenderness in her eyes was disarming as well as contagious.

Troy reached out for her hand, as he fought off tears. 'I know, Mom. I know.'

Mrs. Foster sucked in a breath through her nose and recomposed herself. 'I'll be quiet. I promise. I'll just sit here.'

Troy let go of her hand and his attention returned to Hunter.

'You were about to tell me about some other crime scene and a possible link. What crime scene? What link?'

Mrs. Foster's face practically turned into a question mark.

Hunter reached into his pocket for a brand new image. This time, a photo of Melissa Hawthorne, which he handed to Troy. 'Do you know who this woman is? Have you ever seen her before?'

Curiosity got the better of Mrs. Foster and she leaned right, stretching her neck to have a look.

Troy stared at it for a long moment.

Hunter had a sip of his ice tea and nodded at Mrs. Foster. 'This is delicious. Thank you.'

The reply came with a proud smile. 'Homemade. And you're welcome.'

'No, I can't say I know who she is,' Troy finally admitted, with a subtle shake of the head. 'I don't think I've ever seen her before. Who is she?'

'Her name is Melissa,' Hunter told him. 'Melissa Hawthorne. Do you know the name? I mean, have you ever heard it before?'

Troy took another moment, his eyes narrowing as he searched his memory.

'No. I can't say I have.'

'So you couldn't really tell me if she was a friend of Kirsten's or not?' Hunter insisted.

Troy refocused his attention on the photo. 'If she was, I never met her.' He looked back at Hunter. 'Why? Was she?'

'We don't know,' Hunter explained. 'We were hoping you could either confirm or deny it.'

Another look at the photo.

'If they were friends, they weren't close,' Troy assured Hunter. 'I've never seen her before. Does she work at the hospital?'

'No. She was a hairstylist. Do you happen to know where Kirsten used to get her hair done? Her nails? Pedicure? Anything like that?'

Troy nodded, but before answering, he had to swallow the lump that seemed to have lodged itself in his throat.

'Kirsten used to go to a place just down the road from our house. It's called . . .' The tips of his fingers grazed against his forehead for a moment. 'Something "cut". MixedCut, or MixCut . . . something like that. I can't remember, but it's easy to find. It's in the Japanese mall at the corner of South Garfield and Valley Boulevard. Is that where she works?' He nodded at the photo before handing it back to Hunter.

Before Hunter could reply, Troy's phone, which was on the coffee table in front of them, beeped twice, announcing a new text message. Troy turned his head to have a look at its screen and immediately did a double take. The message had come from an unknown number. It was its preview that had caught his eyes.

'Kirsten'.

The message preview also indicated that there was a video attached to it.

Hunter was sitting too far away to see the screen.

'Excuse me for a second,' he said, reaching for the phone. While Troy unlocked his phone and tapped on the message, Hunter had another sip of his ice tea.

As the video started playing on Troy's cellphone screen, his eyes seemed to lose whatever life they still had in them.

'Oh my God!'

His hands were trembling even before the words had escaped his lips.

That was when it hit Hunter – the video that the killer had sent Melissa's sister the day after her murder.

So much had happened in the past few days . . . so many puzzle pieces to try to link together and make sense of, that one of them had managed to completely escape Hunter's memory – the fact that this killer had a seventh stage to his MO.

Thirty-seven

In the space of a single breath, the walls in the furniture-packed living room seemed to have closed in on Troy. His legs threatened to buckle under him, as life … existence … the universe … all of it were lost in a blur.

Hunter didn't know that what Troy was looking at were moving images, until he heard sounds coming from the tiny speaker on Troy's phone. The volume on it was low and Hunter was sitting too far away to be able to hear it properly, but the first sound he heard sounded like a car engine revving up.

Saliva gathered at the back of Troy's throat. Bile pressed up against his esophagus and he dry-retched, dropping his cellphone onto the coffee table even before the video had finished playing. He had watched only about five to six seconds of it.

A split second after dropping his phone, Troy let out a scream so guttural, so full of pain and agony, that it made even the hairs on the back of Hunter's neck stand on end.

The scream made Mrs. Foster jump back on her chair, frightened.

'Troy,' she cried out, the rasping sound of air catching and scraping the back of her throat. 'What's wrong? What happened?' Her eyes looked lost as they moved from her son, to the phone on the table, to Hunter, and then back to Troy.

Troy brought both hands to his face, covering his eyes, as a new scream escaped his throat. This one carrying as much anger as it did pain.

Hunter quickly reached for the phone on the coffee table before its screen timed out. Though the video had ended by then, the last frame remained frozen on the screen. It showed a message containing only six words. As he read them, his heart sank.

Yes, Hunter had completely forgotten that this was this killer's seventh stage when it came to his MO: the aftermath – the psychological torturing of the victim's loved ones. The levels of complexity at which this killer operated were truly something unheard of, and the video he'd just sent Troy was proof of that.

Mrs. Foster, despite being terrified, still jumped to her feet and tried hugging her son, her tiny arms not quite long enough to go around his strong frame.

'Troy, what's going on?' she asked, her voice weak, her eyes filled with tears.

No answer.

She looked at Hunter. 'What is it? What did he get sent?'

Hunter shook his head at her. Just a gentle movement to let her know that it would be better if she didn't know the details.

Mrs. Foster carried on trying to cradle her son in her arms.

With Troy's phone in hand, Hunter stepped away, putting some distance between him and Troy before pressing the 'play' button. Still, he kept the volume down to a minimum.

The video had been edited to show five different segments, and the collage was nothing less than grotesquely evil.

The first segment, which was about six seconds in length, showed Kirsten, naked, lying on the ground, with the whole rope-chain-hook set-up already in place. The rope was attached to the back of a vehicle, ready to start dragging her by her wrists against what looked to be a deserted stretch of road. Hunter could see asphalt underneath her body, but no road marks. Lighting didn't come from lampposts, but from what seemed to be either a flashlight or some cheap video lighting unit.

The vehicle couldn't really be seen, but it was obvious that the camera and the lighting unit had been set up at the back of it, angled in such a way that Kirsten's whole body was visible. And that was where Hunter felt as if his heart had been stabbed.

Kirsten was alive, lying on her back, with her arms stretched out above her head. Her terrified eyes, overflowing with tears were wide open and looking up at the camera. She was shivering in such a way that it looked like she was convulsing. Hunter had never seen so much fear stamped across a person's face before.

Kirsten's lips moved – one single word – but her vocal cords were too petrified to emit any sounds.

Hunter read her lips – *please* – that was all she said.

All of a sudden, the car engine was turned on and revved up. That was where the first segment ended.

The cut from the first segment to the second was rough. No fading out . . . no fading in, just an amateurish jump from Kirsten being on the ground, terrified, begging for her life, to the vehicle that was pulling her along already at high speed.

From then on, the footage was simply sickening.

The second segment was a little longer than the first one – around eight seconds in total – and it showed Kirsten's body being dragged with so much momentum that it rolled and bounced chaotically against the asphalt like an enormous slab of meat. As her body kept on hitting the ground with force, small chunks of skin and flesh could be seen flying up in the air, together with mists of blood.

Hunter took a deep breath.

Throughout his career, he had seen a lot more than his share of brutality. He had witnessed the kind of evil that humans are capable of, and attended more sadistically violent crime scenes than anyone in the entire Los Angeles Police Force, but the cruelty depicted on those images was so inhumane . . . so raw . . . so repulsive . . . that he felt a chill sink into the marrow of his bones, sending a shiver rippling beneath his skin. Right then, he too felt the acidity of bile burn at the back of his throat.

Exactly how long into the dragging that particular segment had been shot was anyone's guess, but it must've been right at the beginning of it all – *less than a minute after the vehicle had started moving*, Hunter thought, because in the footage, Kirsten's body still had most of her skin on and she was still alive.

All of her agonizing screams were muffled by the sound of the vehicles engine.

Another amateurish cut.

The third segment was about four seconds long, but it had been edited to show a slow-motion effect.

As the segment started, it zoomed in on Kirsten's face, but the zooming in didn't seem to have been done at the camera end, which means that it was done afterwards, using a video-editing suite.

The killer had clearly searched the footage for these few particular frames, chosen for their shocking effect and for the fact that it somehow captured Kirsten in one of her very few conscious moments throughout the whole ordeal. They showed her once again on her back, as she rolled with the momentum of the drag. By then, her face had been dragged against the asphalt several times. Some of the skin had already been scraped off, showing the flesh beneath it, which was raw, cut and bloody. Her nose, also heavily scraped and bleeding, looked broken and her lips were severely lacerated, but the zooming-in motion had her eyes as its main focus. Despite the amount of blood that covered her face, her eyes could still be seen, full of despair and pain. Those few frames caught them just as the back of her head hit the asphalt . . . hard. That seemed to have been the decisive moment, because whatever little hope was still left in those eyes was suddenly lost, and as they began to close, Hunter knew that Kirsten had given up the fight ... she had run out of hope. No one was coming to save her ... and she knew it.

That wasn't the moment that Kirsten's life was extinguished. At least Hunter didn't think so. That was the moment that she was knocked unconscious, but from then on, it would be just a matter of minutes ... maybe seconds. With Kirsten unconscious, her head would've collided against the hard surface of the road under her countless times. At the speed that she was being dragged, those collisions would've undoubtedly shattered her skull, creating an endless number of splint fractures. From there, there was no coming back. Death was a certainty.

As her eyes finally closed and the slow-motion footage ended, so did the third segment.

The fourth segment was around the same length as the first and it worked as an outro to the entire sequence. After another abrupt edit, it started with the vehicle, once again, at a standstill. It was over. What was left of Kirsten's severely mutilated, disfigured and broken body lay on the road, lifeless and completely covered in blood.

Staring at those images, Hunter could feel his heart beating franticly against the inside of his chest because it confirmed what he and Dr. Slater had alluded to at the crime scene – that the killer had carried on dragging Kirsten's body against the harsh asphalt long after her life had left her.

Hunter was sure that Kirsten had died shortly after the end of the third segment. Probably just moments after she had lost consciousness. From the amount of skin still left on her body during that third segment, Hunter could tell that it had been right at the beginning of her ordeal, but in the fourth segment, as the sequence ended, she was unrecognizable. She had lost maybe eighty to eighty-five percent of the skin on her body, together with a vast amount of muscle tissue and flesh. All of her limbs seemed broken, with both legs showing exposed fractures. Her body was so bloody … so deformed … that it resembled an animal carcass after being picked over by a flock of vultures.

To achieve that level of mutilation, Hunter guessed, the killer must've carried on driving for at least another ten minutes after Kirsten was dead.

But the video hadn't ended yet.

And the fifth and most destructive segment was still to come.

Thirty-eight

Still at the sitting area of her living room, a desperate Mrs. Foster had her arms around her son, frantically trying to console him. She looked lost, confused and scared all at the same time, trying her absolute best not to become hysterical. Her tearful eyes were fixed on Hunter, in an attempt to understand what could have caused Troy so much pain.

What the hell was in that message?

The question didn't need to be asked. It travelled silently through the air from the look in her eyes.

But Hunter didn't give her an answer ... he didn't even hold her stare.

In her uncertainty of what to say or do, Mrs. Foster kept on repeating the same two words over and over again, in a voice strangled by tears: 'Please, Troy ... please ...'

Troy still had both hands cupped over his face. Every time he took a breath, his whole body shivered almost uncontrollably.

How could anyone be that monstrous ... that evil? Hunter thought, as he watched the dying seconds of the clip.

It ended with another abrupt edit, cutting from the image of Kirsten's mangled body on the ground to a still shot of her face. The shot had clearly been filmed before the dragging had started because she wasn't hurt. No scrapes ... no wounds ... no cuts ... no swelling ... nothing ... other than the desperate look of fear in her eyes.

Then, at the bottom of the image, six words appeared that Hunter knew would annihilate whatever was still left of Troy's sanity:

'*LIKE AN OLD SLAB OF MEAT.*'

A fraction of a second later, the video ended.

For a moment, Hunter felt paralyzed. There was no real sense in what this killer was doing. People who enjoyed inflicting psychological pain and torture onto others usually got their pleasure out of watching their victims as they suffered. Their victims' pain was their pleasure. Narcissists were a great example of that, but this was levels above even cognitive psychological gratification. This killer had practically created a whole new category of sadism.

'Why?' Troy yelled the word, bringing Hunter out of his mini-trance.

Troy's hands had finally left his face. His voice was angry and pain-stricken. Though his attention was on Hunter, his eyes seemed lost.

On Troy's cellphone, Hunter quickly tapped the icon to share the video before entering his own cellphone number and pressing 'share'.

'Why?' Troy yelled again, breaking free from his mother's embrace and moving toward the detective.

Hunter wasn't about to try to explain to Troy the psychology behind extreme sadism and the unrelenting compulsion that came with it.

Instead of answering Troy, Hunter reached for his own phone and speed-dialed Shannon Hatcher, the leader of his research team back at the LAPD headquarters.

'Shannon,' he said, as the call was answered at the other end. 'It's Robert. I need you to try to trace the location of the last message that was sent to the number that I am about to send you. Call me back as soon as you get anything.'

Hunter quickly found Troy's number on his phone before forwarding it to Shannon.

This was, once again, another very long shot. Hunter didn't really believe that this killer would be likely to make that sort of amateurish mistake, but he had to try.

'Can I have my phone back?' Troy said, as soon as Hunter had disconnected from the call.

Hunter hesitated. He knew that Troy hadn't watched the video in full. He hadn't seen the killer's final message to him, and Hunter so wished that it would stay that way, but he also knew that there was very little that he could do to stop Troy from replaying that clip over and over again, if he so wished. It was his phone after all.

'Detective,' Troy said again, his trembling hand out in front of him. 'My phone?'

'Please, Troy, don't watch this video again,' Hunter pleaded, his voice calm. 'Don't let this creep get into your head. That's what he wants. That's why he sent you this video. Don't give him that pleasure. Don't let him win. You're stronger than this. These are not the sort of images you want rolling around inside your head . . . ever.'

The problem with what Hunter had just asked of Troy was the undesirable reverse psychology effect that unfortunately came with his words. Tell or ask somebody *not* do to something and more often than not, that somebody would get an almost uncontrollable itch to do the exact opposite. Hunter understood that well, but he had no other alternative.

'What else is in the video?' Troy asked, his voice faltering, as tears streamed down his face.

Hunter shook his head. 'Nothing good. Trust me.'

Troy looked down at nothing, his focus lost, his mind clearly divided.

'What video?' Mrs. Foster asked, clearly confused, her eyes wet, her voice thin.

Hunter, once again, just shook his head.

'Let me delete the message, Troy,' he said, trying to seize the opportunity. 'Please. I've already forwarded it to my phone so that we can analyze the video frame by frame back at headquarters. I'll get all of our tech guys on this. You don't need this message sitting on your phone.'

'I don't know what's in that video, son,' Mrs. Foster said, once again approaching Troy and trying her best to hug him. 'But I'm sure that the detective's right. If the message and the video were sent by the person who took Kirsten from us, then there can be nothing good in it. This person is pure evil and the detective is right – he wants to get into your head. Don't let him do that, son. You *are* stronger than this. Don't let this creep win.'

Troy looked troubled, as he visibly fought the curiosity devil inside his head. On one hand, the inquisitive side of his brain wanted . . . needed to know how Kirsten had died. On the other, his brain's defense mechanism, knowing how destructive those images would be, was fighting for self-preservation.

'My phone, Detective,' Troy said again, his hand still shaking.

'Please, Troy,' Mrs. Foster begged him.

'I'll delete it myself,' Troy said, giving Hunter a nod.

There was nothing else Hunter could do. He handed the phone back to Troy, who for a long, fraught moment stared at the list of messages on his screen. The killer's message to him was the first one at the top. His deliberation was almost painful to watch.

Finally, Troy placed his index finger on the message until it highlighted, indicating that it had been selected. He then tapped the 'delete' icon.

'It's gone,' he said, showing Hunter his phone. 'See?'

'Are you sure?' Hunter asked, sounding half apologetic. 'Some phones will automatically save any received photo or clip attachments into its gallery, as soon as you open them for the first time.'

'Yes, I know that, detective.' Anger now joined the cocktail of emotions in Troy's voice. 'That feature is disabled on my phone.'

Hunter wasn't about to antagonize Troy. He had to trust him.

'I'm sorry, Detective, but I think that we should end this right here, don't you?' said Mrs. Foster, her voice as authoritarian as only a mother's voice could be.

Troy's eyes had returned to his cellphone screen. He was looking at it as if he'd regretted what he'd just done. He nodded, without meeting Hunter's stare. 'Yes, I don't think I can do this anymore today, Detective. I'm sorry.'

Even though there was still so much that Hunter wanted to ask Troy, he had to agree that enquiring about possible hidden affairs and ex-partners right at that moment was not a good idea.

'Of course,' he said before walking back to the coffee table to retrieve Melissa Hawthorne's photo. As he did, he turned and handed Troy one of his cards.

Hunter had already given him a card outside his house in the early hours of the morning, but there was no harm in reassuring him.

'Troy, if you get any new messages . . . or anything at all relating to Kirsten, please contact me straight away, OK?'

Troy didn't look up. Grief seemed to be eating away at everything. 'I already have your card, Detective.'

'I know,' Hunter replied, placing the card on the coffee table. 'I'll leave it here, anyway. Also . . .' He paused and waited until Troy had looked back at him. 'If you need anything . . . and I mean, absolutely anything, please don't hesitate to call me at any time . . . day or night. My cellphone is on the back.' He nodded at the card.

Troy looked down at it with dead eyes.

'Thank you once again for the ice tea,' Hunter addressed Mrs. Foster, who simply nodded back at him.

Right at that moment, his cellphone vibrated inside his jacket pocket. It was Shannon Hatcher.

'Shannon,' he took the call. 'Anything?'

As he listened to her reply, his mouth dropped half open and his eyes dashed in the direction of the window.

'Jesus Christ!' Hunter whispered to himself before shooting toward the front door like a bullet train.

Thirty-nine

After entering the phone number that Hunter had given her into the Unified Police Force GPS Tracking System, requesting it to try to pinpoint the origin of the last SMS message sent to it, Shannon Hatcher sat back on her chair and waited, not holding much hope. Eight out of every ten GPS searches that she ran for the UVC Unit came back with nothing at all. Either the sender's phone had no GPS system, or it had been disabled.

Nowadays, even the most amateurish of petty criminals knew about GPS tracking. Hardly anyone made that mistake anymore.

It was for those reasons that Shannon's eyes almost popped out of their sockets when, in less than two minutes, her computer screen updated to show a location.

'No freaking way,' she said to herself, jumping up on her chair and immediately typing another command into the system. Once the screen re-updated, she reached for the phone on her desk.

Hunter answered the call within the second ring.

'*Shannon*,' he said. '*Anything?*'

'Robert, you're not going to believe this, but I got a hit. The phone is unregistered and it isn't active anymore, I just checked it, but the last SMS message received by the phone number you gave me originated from the corner of Dronfield Avenue and Herron Street in Sylmar.'

'*Jesus Christ!*'

Forty

With his phone still firmly pressed against his ear, and to Mrs. Foster and Troy's total surprise, Hunter dashed through their living room and out of their front door as if a fire had broken out. Mrs. Foster's house sat right at the corner of Dronfield Avenue and Herron Street in Sylmar. The killer had sent the message from just outside her home.

'Shannon,' Hunter said into his phone once he was outside, his eyes searching left then right. 'How precise is that pinpoint?'

'*Pretty accurate, Robert. No more than five yards, if that.*'

It was just past two in the afternoon, but being residential roads, traffic on both Dronfield Avenue and Herron Street was minimal. Hunter's eyes searched everywhere. Though there were several cars parked up and down both roads, he could see no black pickup truck and no one was standing on the sidewalk, observing the house. In fact, as far as Hunter could see, there were very few pedestrians out and about – a woman across the street, carrying a couple of bags of groceries, two kids riding their bikes and another two on skateboards. That was it. No one else.

Directly across from where Hunter was standing, on Dronfield Avenue, there was a gated parking lot to a private condo.

He quickly crossed the road in its direction.

'*Robert, are you OK?*' Shannon asked, clearly picking up the anxiety coming from Hunter.

'I'm here, Shannon.'

'*Here where?*'

'At the location you just gave me. I'm right at the corner of Dronfield Avenue and Herron Street in Sylmar.'

'*What? How did you get there so fast?*'

'I didn't. I was already here when I called you.'

Shannon had questions, but she clearly chose not to ask them. '*I've set up a twenty-four-hour scan on the phone. We'll get an alert if it ever goes live again, but I wouldn't hold my breath.*'

The gate to the private parking lot was shut. Access would come only through remote control, or by entering a number code onto the metal keypad on the wall, but it was a simple metal-bar gate, which allowed Hunter to see inside. At that time in the afternoon, there were only eight cars parked in the lot – none of them was a black pickup truck and there was no one sitting inside any of the other cars.

Hunter crossed the road back to Mrs. Foster's house.

'Shannon, are you still there?'

'*I'm here, Robert. How can I help?*'

'Can you track my cellphone and compare my location to the result you got? Tell me how close to the sender's actual position I am right now.'

'*No problem. Give me just a minute.*'

Hunter heard the clack of keyboard strokes as he waited. His eyes never stopped searching both roads.

'*OK, I've got you on my screen, Robert,*' Shannon finally said. '*The message was sent from across the road from where you are and a little to the right ... maybe three yards. Pretty close to the northwest corner of the road.*'

Hunter ran a hand over his mouth and breathed out frustration. The killer was looking directly at Mrs. Foster's house when he sent that message. He was right there, just a few yards away. He could've even have crossed the road and tried looking into the house through one of the windows because . . . why not? He was definitely bold – much more than what Hunter had initially thought.

Forty-one

Forty-five minutes after leaving Sylmar, Hunter arrived back at the UVC Unit office. Garcia was already at his desk, his gaze locked onto his computer screen, his expression somber.

'If this isn't total madness,' he said, his concerned eyes moving to Hunter, 'then I don't know what is.'

'I'm assuming you're talking about the video,' Hunter replied.

On his way to the PAB, Hunter had forwarded the video clip that the killer had sent Troy to Garcia and to the Cyber Forensics Lab.

'This is so fucked up,' Garcia commented, cringing, as his attention switched back to his computer screen. 'This goes way beyond grotesque, and sadistic, and vile, and sickening, and monstrous, and whatever other words you can think of.'

'I know.' Hunter replied, his tone hopeless.

'And you were right there?'

Hunter nodded. 'A few yards and a couple of walls away from him.'

Garcia sat back on his chair. 'Do you think he knew? Do you think the killer knew that you were in the house?'

Hunter shrugged and took a seat at his desk. 'Possibly. That depends on how long he'd been waiting outside before sending Troy the video. I'd been in the house for about ten, maybe fifteen minutes tops when the message came through. From then on, my timekeeping got a little blurred,' Hunter admitted. 'I'm not quite sure how long it was between Troy getting the message and Shannon calling me back with the location, but I don't think that it was any longer than three or four minutes. By then he was gone.'

'Do you think that he's fucking with us?'

Hunter looked back at him, cautiously.

'The reason I ask,' Garcia said, 'is because . . .'

Hunter read the question in his partner's eyes. 'Because he left the GPS on this time.'

'Exactly. The killer sent Janet a similar message yesterday. No GPS. Then today he sends Troy one and, what? He forgot the GPS was on? I don't buy it. Not for a second. He wanted us to know that he was right there, which means I think he knew you were in the house, Robert.'

'Shannon told me that the phone was turned off straight after the message was sent.'

'I don't know, Robert, but I think this killer's compulsion might go beyond his sadism. Maybe he wants the challenge. Another freak for the "catch me if you can" game. God knows we've met plenty of those. I wouldn't be surprised if all of a sudden this killer started contacting us directly just for the fun of it.'

'Me neither,' Hunter admitted. 'I've already contacted the Traffic Division in Sylmar, inquiring about traffic cameras near Mrs. Foster's house.' A shake of the head. 'We'll give it a try. I'll ask Research to have a look at the footage, but I don't think that we'll get anything. The closest cameras aren't close enough – Hubbard Street and Foothill Freeway, both of them about three blocks due east and north from Mrs. Foster's house. Too many different routes out of there that would've escaped them both. That's problem one. Problem two is that we don't even know which vehicle to search for.'

Garcia raised his eyebrows at Hunter.

'Yes,' Hunter accepted, 'we do know that the killer used an

identical or very similar pickup truck to Troy's when he took Kirsten on Monday night, but this guy is clever. Probably a lot more than we think. The chances of him having stolen, rented, or even acquired a similar truck just so he could use it exclusively on that night are very real. Today, in Sylmar, he could've been on a motorbike, for all we know.'

'Yeah, that's another piece of bad luck for us,' Garcia said, returning to his computer and opening another file on his screen. 'With that same thought in mind, I've also started checking stolen auto reports, vehicle rental companies, and used car dealers.'

'OK?'

'Well, Troy drives a Ford F-150 pickup truck, 2014 Model.'

'Yes, that's correct.'

'So come have a look at this.' Garcia gestured his partner closer.

Hunter rounded his desk to get to Garcia's.

'That's the Ford F-150 pickup truck, 2014 model,' Garcia explained, indicating the photo on his screen.

'Alright.'

'Front view,' Garcia said before clicking onto the next photo. 'And rear view.'

Hunter could already guess what was coming.

'Now check this out.' Garcia clicked again. New photo. 'That's a 2014 Chevy Silverado 1500. Front view and . . .' Another click. 'Rear view.'

Hunter sighed. The Ford F-150 and the Chevy Silverado 1500 looked extremely similar from both angles.

Another click from Garcia.

'This is 2014 GMC Sierra 1500. Front view . . . rear view.'

Also eerily similar.

Another click.

'This is a 2014 Ram 1500 – front-view . . . rear-view.'

Click.

'2014 Toyota Tundra – front-view . . . rear-view.'

One last click.

'And finally a 2014 Nissan Titan – front-view . . . rear-view.'

Hunter's face was one of defeat. All five pickup trucks were similar enough from both angles to confuse most people, unless you were a pickup truck aficionado.

'The killer could've used any of these on the night he took Kirsten,' Garcia continued. 'And any neighbor, either walking by or looking out their window, like Mr. Hennessey, would've fully believed that they were looking at Troy's Ford F-150, especially at night. And I'm sure that the killer knew that.'

Hunter nodded slowly. 'Like I said, this guy is clever.'

'Very,' Garcia agreed, as he walked over to the coffee machine on the corner. 'The video is another example of that – five extremely short segments, filmed at very tight angles and under shitty light conditions. You can barely see the road under her. We have two chances of identifying that location – zero and none, unless Cyber Forensics performs a miracle.'

Hunter wasn't sure that that would happen either.

'Coffee?' Garcia offered.

'Please.'

Garcia poured two large mugs and handed one to Hunter. He then turned to face the picture board. 'If we thought that the clip that this killer had sent Janet yesterday was a mind-fuck . . .' He chuckled humorlessly. 'This video hits that ball clear out of the park. I can't even imagine how Troy . . .'

'He didn't watch the full clip,' Hunter interrupted him, before explaining what had happened.

'So he never saw the written message at the end of it?' Garcia asked.

'Not while I was there.'

Garcia frowned at his partner. 'But you just told me that you saw him delete the video.'

'I did.'

'So it's gone, or do you think that the killer is going to send him another one?'

Hunter told him about the feature that automatically saved message attachments to a phone's memory.

Even though Garcia had that exact feature on his phone, he had forgotten it existed.

'Troy told me that that feature was disabled on his phone.'

Garcia sipped his coffee and studied Hunter for a second. 'You think he was lying?'

He knew that Hunter was levels above everyone else when it came to picking apart body language, words, micro-expressions, gestures, eye-movements, skin-flushing, voice fluctuation ... anything and everything that could give away if someone was lying or not.

'Perhaps not,' Hunter replied.

'So that's a good thing, right? It means that he won't get to see that message – because that is the final boss of mind-fucks.'

Hunter nodded, but he knew that there was a false dichotomy there, one that led most people to make a dangerous assumption – just because someone wasn't lying, it didn't mean that they were telling the truth.

But despite how good he was at it, Hunter hadn't been able to properly read Troy for a very obvious reason: everything about him – his body language, his voice fluctuation, his eye movements ... everything had been completely unreliable as a telltale sign because all of it had been altered by grief, pain and the shock of the images he'd just seen.

'You have the video on the big screen?' Hunter asked.

'Yeah,' Garcia replied, as he pointed at the computer monitor on his desk. 'Be my guest. I don't think I can watch that again. Hands down, one of the sickest and saddest things I've ever seen in my life.'

Hunter couldn't disagree.

'How did you get along with the cab driver?' he asked, as he moved over to Garcia's desk. 'Anything?' He pressed the space bar on Garcia's keyboard and the video played from the beginning. Watching it on a twenty-seven-inch screen seemed to give new depths to the sadism depicted on those images, especially during the third segment, when the footage zoomed in on Kirsten's eyes. On the big screen, Hunter could clearly see the light of hope disappearing from them. She knew that that was the end.

Garcia waited until the video had played through before answering his partner.

'Nothing from the driver,' he said, having another sip of his coffee.

'Really? He couldn't give us anything?'

'She,' Garcia replied, putting down his coffee and picking up a notepad from his desk. 'Linda Evans. Very sweet woman. Forty-five years of age. She did remember picking Melissa up from the Freehand Hotel in the early hours of Sunday morning. Her records showed that the pick-up occurred at 1:29 a.m.'

'Yeah, that's also what we have,' Hunter agreed, returning to his desk.

'The drive from the hotel to Melissa's house in Leimert Park,' Garcia continued, 'lasted just short of half an hour. Drop-off was at 1:58 a.m.' He flipped a page on his notepad. 'Mrs. Evans said that Melissa was quite drunk. She exited the cab and couldn't even close the door properly – even after a couple of tries. Because she seemed so drunk, Mrs. Evans waited until Melissa had gotten into her house before driving off.'

'That was nice of her,' Hunter commented.

'She has a teenage daughter. She told me that she'd heard too many stories of single women being attacked as they arrive home, especially after they've been drinking. Every time she drops off a woman by herself . . . drunk or not . . . night time or not . . . she waits until they get in before leaving, just in case.'

'We need more people like her in this city.'

'Since she waited until Melissa go in before driving off,' Garcia carried on, 'I asked her if she had noticed if Melissa had forgotten to close the front door.'

'Did she?'

'No, she said that as soon as she saw Melissa disappear into the house, she drove off. But we've been to the house. It's set back from the street, remember? From inside a car parked on the road, at night, if Melissa left the door just ajar instead of wide open, you would've needed the eyes of a hawk to see it.'

'True,' Hunter agreed. 'But the killer never said that Melissa forgot to close her front door. He said that she forgot to lock it. She might've closed it and simply forgot to turn the key, which brings me to the next question.'

Garcia guessed it. 'Did Mrs. Evans notice anyone close, or around Melissa's house at that time?' It was his turn to give Hunter a defeated headshake. 'She said that as far as she could remember, the street was quiet. I also asked her if she had noticed any cars following them from the Freehand Hotel. She said that there was no one. The whole time that she was parked in front of Melissa's house – between Melissa managing to get out of her cab, struggling with closing the door, stumbling to her house and finally getting inside – we're talking nearly five minutes. That whole time, Mrs. Evans told me that she couldn't remember a single car driving up or down the road. She would've seen the headlights.' Garcia returned the notepad to his desk. 'Which means that we've got nothing so far.' He finished his coffee and slumped himself onto his chair again.

'I know,' Hunter said, before trying to reassure him. 'But there's still a lot of people to talk to. The possibility that this killer has had some sort of romantic contact with both victims is still very real. We're going to have to plough through both of their lives and see if we can find a link between them because there's no way that they've been victims of chance.'

Garcia agreed, pulling himself closer to his desk again. 'I was just about to start sieving through their social media looking for—' he threw his hands in the air '—I don't know, anything that could connect them, really, when I got your message forwarding the video.' He massaged the back of his neck. 'I'm not going to lie, Robert. It has unbalanced me. This level of brutality is just disturbing ... even for people with our experience. I know that we believe that there's some sort of meaning to everything that this killer does, but seriously?' He nodded at his monitor. 'What kind of meaning could be behind this other than "I'm fucked in the head and I want to hurt people like no one has before"?'

Hunter had to agree. As the LAPD UVC Unit, he and Garcia had chased murderers whose cruelty didn't seem to belong to this world.

This killer was surpassing them all.

Forty-two

Grace Bauer hugged herself on the couch to stop her from shaking. She was sitting up in a tense position, her knees pressed tightly against each other ... her shoulders rigid ... her neck muscles straining.

'I swear I thought I would be stronger than this,' she said, her voice tired and raw. 'And just look at me. I'm falling apart on our first ever session, but I no longer know what to do or how to act. The drugs simply aren't working anymore.'

Josie Griffith sat by the window in the oxblood-colored chesterfield armchair that faced Grace. Her left leg was crossed over her right one, her posture relaxed, her hands resting on her thighs, together with her notepad. According to Grace's consultation factsheet and to what she had told Josie so far during their session, Grace had been on prescribed antidepressant medications like Paxil and Brintellix for a little over ten months now, and though they'd helped, they still were no match for the overwhelming darkness that seemed to rule her thoughts on a daily basis. Despite being diagnosed with severe depression and anxiety eighteen months ago, this was Grace's first ever psychotherapy session, and as far as she could remember, the first ever time in her adult life that someone had truly listened to her for anything over five minutes.

'Every day is the same,' Grace continued, as tears gathered

along the lower rims of her eyes, threatening to spill over at any second. 'I don't feel like getting up in the mornings. I don't want to go to work. I don't want to eat. I don't want to get into bed with my husband at night. I don't want to talk to my friends. I don't want to go out. I don't want . . .' She paused and looked down at her arms folded around her body, the tears finally overpowering her will not to cry again. 'I don't want this life anymore.'

Josie glanced out the window of her second floor office in Downtown LA, at the tall office tower directly across the road from her. For a second, she wondered how many people in those offices really wanted to be there. How many of them were doing a job that they really wanted to do. Her gaze moved to the street and to the line of cars waiting for the traffic light to go green on the intersection down below. She wondered how many of those sitting inside their cars were going somewhere where they really wanted to go. How many of them would be returning to a home, or even to a relationship, that they really wanted to be in. The ugly truth, Josie knew, was that few people on this planet had the luxury of doing a job that they really wanted to do. Few lived a life they really wanted to live, even those who were fabulously rich.

Sitting there, listening to Grace, made Josie think back to how lucky she was to have someone like Oliver in her life . . . how lucky she was to be so in love with him and he so in love with her.

'*I don't want this life anymore.*' To a psychotherapist, a statement like that was the mother of all red flags.

'Have you thought about hurting yourself, Grace?' Josie asked calmly, looking over at her.

Grace looked away and nervously ran her tongue across the edge of her teeth. She used the tips of her fingers to gently wipe away her tears. She chose not to reply.

'Have you thought about hurting someone else?' Josie tried a different approach, still keeping her voice calm and her posture steady and in control.

Grace coughed to clear her throat, but her mouth felt like sandpaper, and her words caught in the roughness of it. 'I just want this horrible feeling inside to go away. I don't want to feel like this anymore. That's all I want.'

To Josie, that sounded like an evasive answer. People tended to show telltale signs – they'd look away, coughed, scratched some part of their body that didn't need scratching, blushed, licked their lips, something – when a truth that they didn't want anyone else to know about was mentioned. Josie didn't want to call Grace out for being evasive, not on their first session, but she needed to pursue this subject because it was truly worrying her.

'Tell me about this feeling inside, Grace. What is it like? Why is it horrible?'

Grace once again looked back at her psychotherapist, but the look in her eyes seemed hollow . . . soulless even, as if behind those beautiful dark eyes there was nothing left but pain.

'The feeling of nothing inside,' she replied in a lifeless tone. 'This terrible emptiness everywhere. The worthlessness that I feel every day.'

Josie watched tears well up in Grace's eyes yet again.

Grace was in her mid to late forties and still very attractive, with a perfect slope to her nose and cheekbones, wavy mahogany hair, and round, dark-as-night eyes. Physically, she also looked to be in great shape.

Throughout their session, Grace had told Josie a lot about herself and her life. She had told her that at the age of twenty-two, she had married her husband, Dayton Bauer, twelve years her senior and already tremendously wealthy, having made all of his fortune on the stock market. At first, Grace had convinced herself that she was as happy as she could possibly be, but now, over twenty years later, with her beauty and physical presence just beginning to fade, or so she believed, she had finally decided to face the fact that she had never been in love with the man she'd married, nor was she in love with her fake lifestyle. She had allowed beauty and wealth and materialistic things to drag her away from her true self, and now she had no idea of how to get back to the person she once was, or whether there would be anything left for her to get back to.

'Doesn't your job give you some sort of fulfillment?' Josie asked. 'A small but very important bridge over some of this void you feel inside? Don't you enjoy what you do?'

Grace had already told Josie that she ran her own interior decorating business. She explained that quite a few years back, she had managed to secure a few contracts to redesign the houses of several Hollywood stars. That had been the push she needed because once she got a few prestigious names onto her roster of clients, more business followed almost automatically, and it had never stopped.

Grace chuckled dismissively, as she finally unhugged herself and rested her hands on her lap. 'I'll let you in on a little secret, darling. Are you ready?' She readjusted herself on the couch. 'I don't know the first thing about interior design. My husband pushed me into it, probably because he was sick of me being at home all day with nothing to do. He said I had a good eye to make a room look "neat".' Grace paused and nodded at Josie, sarcastically. 'Yes, "neat" really was the word he used. I'm a fraud. I'm no interior decorator. What I can do is match colors and put furniture items together in a way that it won't look like someone has puked all over the room.'

Josie let a smile part her lips.

'I'm serious,' Grace reinforced her argument. 'You'd really be surprised if you could see inside some of these houses. Matching colors and furniture together seems like something that very few people in this city can do, especially the rich and famous. They just go out and buy, buy, buy. Then they throw everything together in a room and think that just because they spent a fortune on the crap they bought, everything will look good, regardless.' She shook her head disapprovingly. 'The first few celebrities I managed to get into my portfolio came to me because of my husband and his contacts, not because I was good at what I did.' She shrugged. 'And in a city as fake and as shallow as LA, that's all you need to get started. The rest will follow like sheep. You know how it goes, right?' Grace put on an overly nasal voice. '*Oh, she's decorated so-and-so's house. She must be awesome. Let's hire her, honey.*'

Another smile from Josie.

For a heartbeat, Grace seemed to curl in on herself, her chin dipped, almost bowing forward beneath some invisible weight. Guilt? Shame? Something between the two?

'Truth is,' she said, her tone apologetic, 'I'm not awesome at all. Far from it. I'm just not stupid or blind when it comes to arranging colors, furniture and items in a room, that's all.'

Josie couldn't help but wonder what Grace thought of how she had decorated her office. For a split second, she glanced left then right. Was the office too dark? Too bright? Too colorful?

As her gaze settled upon her office window again, she absent-mindedly glanced down at the street two stories below.

That was when Josie saw him.

On the sidewalk, leaning back against the building across the road, a tall and well-built man was just standing there. His black jacket was zipped up all the way to his neck, with a hoodie pulled tightly over his head and his hands casually tucked into his pockets. In truth, there was nothing really different about the man, except for the fact that he seemed to be looking straight up at Josie's office window. For a moment, their eyes met, but the man quickly blinked and looked away.

Josie blinked as well, and just like that, the man was gone. She searched left then right, but he had blended into the crowd like a shadow. She blinked again and brought her attention back to Grace, who had just placed her right hand over her left wrist. Her fingers brushed the face of the expensive-looking watch she was wearing.

'These things,' Grace said, touching the small butterfly pendant hanging from the chain around her neck. 'Do you know what they are?'

Josie thought about replying 'terribly expensive by the looks of them', but she held her tongue, instead answered in her favorite manner – with a question.

'What are they to you?'

Grace looked away again, when she looked back at Josie, her eyes had a hint of anger in them. She chuckled.

'They are reminders of the mistake I made ... of the prison that I voluntarily walked into all those years ago. I was young and very, very poor. The kind of poor that led me to foolishly believe that materialistic things like these would, somehow, make me happy.' She indicated her jewelry again. 'Well they don't. They never have. I hate them, and I truly hate myself for being so naïve and stupid ... so gullible.'

Grace's words made Josie wonder just how dark and harmful her thoughts really were. In the space of just a few minutes she had avoided answering if she had ever fantasized about hurting herself or others, she had compared her life to a prison sentence, and she had used the word 'hate' twice – one of those, in relation to herself. Josie wondered how much those thoughts could be pushing her toward something truly destructive. The impression that Josie was getting, not only from Grace's words, but from her demeanor, her facial expressions, her tone of voice, and her gestures, was that Grace seemed to really be struggling against an ever-growing impulse to hurt herself – the proverbial 'ticking time-bomb'. Josie wonder if that was why Grace had finally decided to seek the help of a psychotherapist – because she was at the brink of something very, very bad. In the face of all that, Josie had to try again.

'Do you sometimes feel overwhelmed by everything around you?' she asked. 'By the life you lead?'

'Ha!' Grace laughed. 'Sometimes? Try "all the time". I told you – I hate this life. I don't want it anymore.'

And there it was again.

Josie wrote something down on her notepad.

'And what do you think about during those times?' she asked. 'Do you feel like you need to punish yourself in some way? Punish others?'

Grace looked down at her hands, which she had clasped together, before regarding Josie with a deep probing gaze.

Josie waited but all Grace did was check her watch.

'Can we continue this next week, if you have a free slot?' she asked, reaching for her handbag. 'I really have to go now.'

Grace was evading having to answer the question again.

Josie kept her attention on her patient. She was fully aware of the time.

'We still have fifteen minutes to go in this session, Grace.'

'Do we?' Grace stood up.

Josie didn't. She wanted to state the fact that it was Grace who was walking away. It was Grace who had declined to go deeper into what was really going on inside her head.

'We do,' Josie reconfirmed, but it didn't deter her patient.

'Unfortunately I really have to go,' Grace said again, this time with a little more determination. She took three steps toward the door before pausing and facing Josie one last time.

'I can guarantee you,' she said, holding Josie's gaze, her voice measured . . . her tone tender. 'I'm in no way a danger or a threat to myself, or anyone else. I have never had any sort of harmful or destructive thoughts involving me or others, and that includes animals.'

Boom.

It was as if a nuclear bomb had just gone off inside Josie's office.

Josie felt the sound of those words crawling along her nerve endings. She blinked twice, wondering if she had heard right, because what Grace Bauer had just done right there was what was known in psychiatry as a 'contract for safety' – the words a potentially dangerous patient had to *voluntarily* speak in order to avoid being compulsorily taken into hospital and committed to a secure psychiatric ward.

Suddenly, Josie had the impression that Grace Bauer knew a lot more about psychiatry and psychoanalysis than she had let on. She knew that the session was being recorded and that her 'contract for safety' was now on tape. Unless Grace voluntarily nulled that contract by *explicitly* verbally contradicting what she had just said, no matter how dangerous to herself or others she might appear to be in subsequent sessions, Josie could not have her committed. Not after a 'contract for safety'.

'Thank you so much for your time,' Grace said with a lingering smile. 'Hopefully I'll see you next week. I'll call to book another appointment.'

Several seconds after Grace Bauer had left her office, and still trying to process what had just happened, Josie, in one of those instinctive movements, turned and once again looked out her window. She wasn't really sure what she was expecting to see, or what that would accomplish. She just wanted to have one last look at Grace before she disappeared, maybe into a chauffeur-driven car, or just walking off into the crowd down below – but Josie never spotted Grace. She did, however, spot the man she had seen earlier. He was back in the same spot he had been before. Just standing there . . . hands tucked into his pockets. Josie stood up to try to get a better line of sight, but as she did, just like that, the man once again blended himself back into the crowd, disappearing like thin smoke in the air.

Forty-three

Back at the UVC Unit's office, Hunter and Garcia had just come back from another meeting with Captain Blake when a new email came through to both of them. The sender was Martin Carr. The subject had been left blank.

'This will be the transcripts from Kirsten Hansen's cellphone,' Garcia announced, as he quickly opened the email.

Hunter did the same.

The body of the email contained two words – '*As requested*'. That was it – no greeting, no explanation, no beating around the bush. It was followed by Martin Carr's digital signature under the words 'Kind Regards' and the AT&T Corporate logo. Just like the email they'd received concerning Melissa Hawthorne's cellphone, this one also only had two zip attachments – Phone conversation transcripts and SMS text messages.

'Is he kidding me?' Garcia asked, as soon as the email opened on his screen.

'No video file,' Hunter said, guessing the root of his partner's frustration.

'Exactly.'

'Maybe the killer didn't send Kirsten one. Let's have a look.' Hunter clicked the attachment titled SMS text messages.

'I really hope not,' Garcia said back, his tone annoyed. 'Because if I have to go back to him with a new warrant to ask for any sort of image file that he's failed to include here, I'll be one fucking angry customer.'

'Yeah, I can see that,' Hunter said, as his eyes moved to the top of the SMS messages transcript file. The last text conversation Kirsten Hansen had had was initiated at 00:29 on Tuesday morning from an unknown number.

Garcia was right on it as well.

UNKNOWN NUMBER: *Rough day at the hospital today, Kirsten? How was the pizza?*

KIRSTEN HANSEN: *Who is this?*

UNKNOWN NUMBER: *I'm am an educator, Kirsten ... a mentor, if you will.*

'Yep,' Garcia commented, as soon as he read that line. 'It's our killer alright, sticking to his MO.'

They both read the remainder of the file in silence.

'No video file,' Hunter said, sitting back on his chair.

'Nope,' Garcia agreed. 'No emojis either.

'None needed,' Hunter said, 'because the first lesson – fear – is quickly achieved.'

'Indeed.' Garcia agreed, as he pointed to his screen. 'Right from the start he mentions the pizza. That would've already worried her. How did he know she had pizza? From there, he loses no time in telling her that she would die that night. And all of that in what?' He checked the timestamp on the messages. 'Within two minutes of Kirsten receiving his first text.'

'Exactly,' Hunter agreed.

'Then,' Garcia continued, 'right in his next message, he mentions the fact that the kitchen window was left unlocked. If she had noticed that, then she's back to the same question as the pizza – how does he know? If she hadn't noticed, then fear comes from doubt, because what should she do? Get out of bed and go check? Stay in bed and pray that this is all just a joke? Fear would set in, regardless.'

'Like I said,' Hunter commented. 'Objective achieved.'

Garcia scratched his chin. 'So do you think that the kitchen window really was his point of entry, or was he lying? Forensics reported nothing about the kitchen window. No forced entry. Could Kirsten have forgotten to lock the window earlier in the day, or is this just something he uses to scare his victims even more? He used the same tactics with Melissa – unlocked front door. Maybe he wants them to believe that it's their fault for being careless about their homes.'

'I don't know,' Hunter said, his expression pensive. 'It's possible, but that's not exactly what he tells Kirsten. He never tells her that she forgot to unlock her window, like he did with Melissa. He tells her that *he* is the reason why the window was left unlocked. But he did give us something that we didn't know before,' he added, reaching for the phone on his desk.

Garcia's eyes narrowed at him.

'I don't think he was lying when he told Kirsten that he was hiding either under her bed or inside the wardrobe. Like he said, those were the only two possible hiding places inside her bedroom.' Hunter dialed the number for Dr. Slater at the forensics lab.

The phone rang five times before she picked it up.

'Susan, it's Robert – UVC Unit.'

'*Robert.*' It sounded like Dr. Slater was chewing on something. '*How can I help?*'

'Kirsten Hansen's crime scene . . .' Hunter said, but before he could say anything else, Dr. Slater began reporting.

'*Yeah, just a second.*' She paused and Hunter heard the sound of wrapping paper being ruffled. '*Sorry about this, Robert. It's been a crazy day so far.*'

'Did I catch you on your lunch break?' He checked his watch. It was past three in the afternoon.

'*I wouldn't quite call it a break ... or lunch, for that matter. Just a few minutes for a quick sandwich, but I'm all done now.*' More paper ruffling. This time, it sounded more like a napkin against her lips. 'OK, *we're still working on the little we got from the scene, but I can tell you that you were right. The killer did wrap her body in something before bringing her back into the house and placing her on the bed. The fibers we've retrieved are cotton. Though they were soaked in blood, we were still able to identify its original color – light beige. Unfortunately, they match the grade and structure of the cotton fibers used to manufacture regular dustsheets. The kind you can buy in just about any home improvement store.*'

'Thanks, Doc,' Hunter said in return. He hadn't been expecting much to come from those fibers. 'I really appreciate it, but I'm calling to ask you to send a couple of agents back to Kirsten Hansen's house.'

'*Really? Why?*'

'I know you and your team are always very thorough with every crime scene you're assigned to but I'm guessing that you didn't really fine comb under her bed or inside the wardrobe, did you?'

There was a quick, thoughtful pause. '*I know we checked it, but I don't think that we fine-combed it. Why?*'

'The killer was hiding either under the bed or inside the wardrobe,' Hunter clarified.

'*Hold on ... how did you figure that out?*'

'He told us.'

'*Umm ... what? What do you mean, he "told" you?*'

'It's part of his MO,' Hunter quickly explained about the text messages.

'*Are you serious?*' A mixture of shock and disbelief slid into Dr. Slater's voice. '*He actually frightens his victims first before taking them?*'

'Yes.'

Hunter heard Dr. Slater take a deep breath. *'The evils that humans are capable of never fail to impress me.'*

'Yeah, me neither, Doc.'

'Give me a sec, Robert.'

Hunter heard the faint clacking of computer keys.

'I can't really interrupt what I'm doing at the moment,' Dr. Slater explained. *'But I can get one, maybe two agents to the house in . . . two and a half to three hours. Not before.'*

'That works,' Hunter said. 'Also, in the text that he sent the victim, he told her that he entered the house via the kitchen window. I know that your team reported no forced entry anywhere, but could we have a second look at that window?'

'Yes, of course.'

'Thanks, Susan. I might drop by the house to have one more look myself, but I'll wait until your team is there.'

'Sure. I'll let you know when they're on their way.'

As soon as Hunter ended the call, his cellphone rang on his desk. He reached for it and checked the display screen. There was a number showing, but no name.

'Detective Hunter, LAPD UVC Unit.'

Whoever it was at the other end of the line sounded desperate. Even Garcia could hear the frantic yelling from his desk.

'Hold on,' Hunter said into his phone. 'Please take a breath and say that again.'

Garcia's curiosity heightened.

'When?' Hunter asked, the word coming out heavy, full of pain.

Hunter listened for a couple more seconds before closing his eyes and allowing his head to drop, defeated. His lips moved but no sound came out.

Garcia couldn't lip read, but anyone could understand Hunter's silent word.

Fuck!

Forty-four

With sirens blasting, Hunter and Garcia made the trip back to Sylmar and Mrs. Foster's house in under twenty-five minutes. A police cruiser was parked in front of her driveway, while several of her neighbors were standing on the street outside, their expressions solemn, their conversations not much louder than a whisper. A uniformed officer was standing by the house's front door.

Garcia pulled up by the black-and-white unit and he and Hunter dashed into the house, quickly flashing their credentials at the officer outside as they stormed past him.

Mrs. Foster was sitting on the sofa in the living room. Her clothes, her arms, her hands and part of her face and neck were stained with blood. Tears streamed down her pain-stricken face as her body trembled. Troy's brother, Brett, was sitting next to her, his strong arms wrapped around his mother's tiny body, trying his best to comfort her, though he was shaking almost as much as she was, with just as many tears running down his cheeks.

Sat in one of the armchairs opposite them was a woman dressed in blue jeans, a white blouse and a dark business blazer jacket. Her dark hair was combed straight behind her ears and held in place by two alligator hairclips. She had a notepad in her hands.

As Hunter stepped into the room, Mrs. Foster's eyes met his in a silent exchange. Her head tilted to her left, her mouth opened slightly, as if she was about to say something, but no words came out. Instead, she emitted a high-pitched shriek so full of pain and agony that both Hunter and Garcia's bodies tensed at its sound.

A second uniformed police officer was standing by the entrance to the corridor that led to the rest of the house. Hunter's gaze moved to him and the officer's eyes drifted toward the corridor.

'In there,' he said.

Hunter rushed into the hallway, quickly followed by Garcia. They came to the first door on the right and stopped. Sadness and desperation lingered in the air like a giant, invisible cloud, infecting whoever came close.

Garcia grimaced, as his and Hunter's eyes took in the scene.

The room was square in shape, with a double bed pushed up against the far wall, a wardrobe to its left and a chest of drawers by the door. On the bedside table to the right of the bed they could see an open bottle of bourbon. Three quarters of it had been consumed. The bed covers, its headboard, the bedside table, two of the walls and part of the ceiling were splattered with blood. On the floor, to the right of the bed, Troy Foster's body lay in a pool of his own blood. His face was completely deformed, with at least one third of his head and cranium gone. They could see no weapon anywhere, but there was still a faint smell of gunpowder in the air.

'Jesus Christ!' Garcia whispered, allowing his arms to sink to his sides, as he inflated his lungs with air.

Hunter stood numb, his eyes lost, his throat dry.

They both heard footsteps coming toward them from the living room, but neither detective looked away from the scene.

'I'm Detective Louisa Carson with the LAPD Valley Bureau,' said the dark-haired woman who had been sitting in the living room with Mrs. Foster, as she joined Hunter and Garcia by the bedroom door.

For a moment, neither detective said anything back.

She waited.

Garcia was the first to make eye contact. 'Sorry. I'm Detective Carlos Garcia and this is Detective Robert Hunter – LAPD UVC Unit.'

'Yes' Carson said. 'I was told you guys were coming.'

'Different investigation,' Garcia half explained. 'He was the fiancé of the victim.'

'Oh my God!'

Garcia nodded. 'Yeah, it's complicated.'

'It always is,' Carson said, as her head tilted in the direction of the living room. 'I was trying to find out what happened from his mother and brother . . .' There was sorrow in her voice. 'I mean, trying to find out about the circumstances that led to what happened. Protocol, you know. But they are in shock and you can see why. I really didn't manage to get anything out of them.'

'We can file the report, if you like,' Garcia told her. 'Has the medical examiner been informed?'

'Yes. About twenty minutes ago.'

'Has anything been disturbed?' Garcia indicated the room.

'Well, yes. I've been inside the room to take a closer look. Again, protocol. You know this. If a firearm has been used in a suicide, it needs to be bagged for forensics.'

'Of course. Can we have a look at it, though?' Garcia asked.

'Sure, give me just a minute,' Carson replied before walking back into the living room.

'The phone,' Hunter said, nodding in the direction of the bed.

Garcia followed his stare. On the covers, half hidden by the pillow on the left side, he could see the edge of a smartphone.

They fully entered the room and rounded the bed.

Hunter reached into his pockets for a pair of latex gloves.

Garcia did the same.

'It's Troy's phone,' Hunter said, remembering it from earlier. He retrieved it from the bed and pressed the screen to activate it.

Locked. A message at the bottom of the screen read: 'Use fingerprint to unlock'.

The two detectives exchanged an *I guess so* look before Hunter walked over to Troy's side of the bed, being careful to avoid the pool of blood. His breathing became shallow, as his gaze drifted toward Troy's fatal head wound. He had clearly used a very powerful handgun. The entry wound was located just under his chin. The bullet had ripped through his skull and brain, devastating everything in its path, before exiting at the top of his cranium, creating an exit wound roughly the size of a grapefruit. Gray matter and bone splinters were splattered everywhere – the bed sheets, the walls, the floor ... even the ceiling. The damage to Troy's skull, brain and cranium had been so severe for such a close range impact, he had to have used a high caliber, hollow-point, expanding bullet.

Hunter squatted down, still avoiding all the blood by the body, brought the cellphone to Troy's right hand and carefully placed his index finger on the reading pad. A split second later, the screen came alive and Hunter felt a knot grab hold of his throat. The last application Troy had used was still loaded onto the screen – the video player. The first frame of the last video he'd watched was displayed. At the bottom of the screen, there was a button that read: 'Play Video'.

Neither Hunter nor Garcia needed to tap the button to know which video that was. They both recognized that first frame. Instead, Hunter tapped the 'back' button at the top left corner of the screen, which took them back to the video folder inside the phone's image gallery.

Hunter felt the knot on his throat begin to tighten.

'Fuck!' Garcia breathed out, as he shook his head. 'So the feature that automatically saves a video attachment to the phone's memory wasn't turned off on his phone, like he told you it was.'

'I should've checked,' Hunter said back, his voice quiet and full of sorrow.

'No,' Garcia replied, his tone firm, as he stared his partner down. 'Don't do that, Robert.'

'I should've checked, Carlos.'

'You told him not to watch the video.' Garcia sounded like a teacher lecturing a student. 'You asked him to delete it. You saw him do it. You reminded him that the 'auto-save' feature existed and he told you it was disabled on this phone. This is not your burden to carry.'

Hunter's gaze moved down to Troy's body on the floor.

'This shouldn't have happened.'

'You're right,' Garcia agreed. 'It shouldn't have happened, but it did, and guess what, Robert, it was completely out of your control.' He took a breathing pause. 'Look, it was out of pure luck that you so happened to be here at the same time that he received the video from this psycho. What if he had received the message with the video after you left? Or before you got here? There's nothing you could've done then to stop him from watching it, Robert.' He lifted his index finger at Hunter. 'And here's something that you understand and know much better than I do – human curiosity … the human urge to "know" is a hell of a powerful one. Very few people have the kind of willpower needed to curb it. Troy Foster didn't. He chose to watch the video, Robert. Not you.'

'What video?' Carson asked, as she walked back into the room, carrying three transparent evidence bags in her right hand.

Garcia shrugged at her. 'Like I said, Detective, it's complicated.'

Carson understood the hint and didn't push any further.

'Well,' she said, offering the first of the three evidence bags she had with her to the two detectives, 'he certainly didn't pack light.'

Inside the bag was a Desert Eagle .50 AE Magnum semi-automatic pistol – one of the most powerful handguns in the world.

Hunter took the bag and lifted up against the light before

Carson handed him the second evidence bag. It contained the Desert Eagle's magazine.

'Six rounds remaining in the seven-round capacity clip,' Carson informed them. 'They're all hollow-point, expanding rounds. He didn't stand a chance.' She nodded at the bedside table. 'And this was found inside the drawer.' She handed Hunter the final evidence bag. Inside it was a small seal-grip plastic bag containing residues of some white powder. 'It's cocaine,' Carson told them.

Sorrow completely intoxicated the room and for a long moment, no one said a word.

'Are you sure that you want to file this report?' Carson finally asked.

'Yes,' Hunter replied. 'We'll take it. It's not a problem. Thank you for your help, Detective Carson.'

After Carson left, Garcia waited outside for the coroner's van to arrive, while Hunter sat in the living room with Mrs. Foster and Brett for a few minutes.

Mrs. Foster had stopped crying. In fact, she had fallen into the loudest of solemn silences, her eyes lost and without focus, her expression morbid, her grief immeasurable and devastating. Her mind was probably fragmenting right there, right in front of Hunter, and there was nothing that he could do to stop it from happening.

Hunter had seen that same lost look in other people's eyes before. He'd certainly seen it in his own more than once. It happened when all that his mind could do was replay a scene over and over in an endless loop. In Mrs. Foster's case, Hunter could only imagine the images that would torment her for the rest of her days – she, sitting in the living room and all of a sudden hearing what would have sounded like a cannon going off under her roof. Desperate, scared, and completely confused, she would've rushed into Troy's room and into the most devastating day of her life. The images she saw, as she looked down at her son's lifeless body on the floor, would never, ever leave her.

As Hunter observed them, all he could do was silently hope that Mrs. Foster and Brett would both somehow find the strength to survive this.

Forty-five

The next couple of days went by in a heap of frustration, with no meaningful developments.

The two-men team that Dr. Slater had sent back to Kirsten and Troy's house to re-examine under the bed and inside the wardrobe had found a few hair strands and a number of different fibers, most of them from inside the wardrobe. The hair strands had already been processed. They all belonged to either Kirsten or Troy. The fibers were undergoing infrared spectrophotometry to try to determine their generic and sub-generic classes, but the problem with those was that they could've come from any of the many garments that Kirsten had hanging from the rails inside her wardrobe . . . and she had quite a selection. A positive match could take days. All in all, full analysis from the forensics lab was expected to be a laborious and slow process, and so far they had come up with nothing of any real significance.

The kitchen window and its lock had also been re-examined – definitely no signs of forced entry, but the agent had told Hunter that the lock was several years old and not of great quality. Breaching it without causing any damage to the lock or the window itself wouldn't be too much of a problem. All that the perpetrator would've needed was a firm and thin piece of wire and the knowledge of what to do.

Dr. Hove had also been in contact with Hunter and Garcia with two reports.

First – with rigor mortis finally subsiding, she was able to perform the post-mortem examination on Kirsten Hansen's body. The results confirmed what Hunter had deduced – death had come as a consequence of brain trauma and cerebral hemorrhaging, which was, in turn, brought on by countless powerful strikes against her head, fragmenting her cranium and her skull and with it, creating an endless number of splinter fractures. Those perforated her brain at different points, causing a river of hemorrhages. Blood toxicology had revealed traces of a fast-acting sedative called Triazolan – the same sedative that showed in Melissa Hawthorne's blood exam. That was clearly how this killer subdued his victims before taking them.

Dr. Hove explained that unfortunately, Triazolan was an easy drug to obtain. The Internet was full of outlets that would sell the drug without requiring a prescription.

Second – the law in California stipulated that any deaths from suicide required a post-mortem examination to be performed, regardless of how apparent the cause of death was. In Troy's case, the examination revealed what everyone was expecting. Death came from a single gunshot wound to the head that caused fatal mutilation to the skull, brain and cranium. The partial toxicology report also came back as expected. Troy's blood alcohol levels were off the charts. Toxicology for drugs would still take a few days, but other than the cocaine bag found by Detective Louisa Carson, Hunter had also found an empty bottle of oxycodone hydrochloride on his bedside drawer. Oxycodone hydrochloride was an opioid-based medication used in the treatment of chronic pain. Despite it being a prescribed drug, like so many opioid-based compounds, oxycodone was highly addictive and it was used by many as a drug to get high on.

Unsurprisingly, Troy had done his best to numb his body and brain before ending his own life.

Forty-six

Garcia pushed his chair away from his desk, rubbed his tired eyes and checked his watch. It was coming up to 7 p.m.

'OK, I'm done here,' he said before having a last sip of his coffee and allowing his gaze to move to Hunter, who was sitting at his desk, engrossed in something on his computer screen. 'If I read any more Facebook or Twitter posts today, I'll probably turn into one.'

Hunter angled his body to look past his computer monitor and back at his partner.

'Anything?' he asked, knowing that Garcia had been trying to find something . . . a friend, a location, an activity . . . anything that would maybe constitute some sort of link between Melissa Hawthorne and Kirsten Hansen.

Garcia stretched his arms above his head before twisting his torso from side to side to try to loosen some of the tension in his muscles.

'Absolutely nothing,' he replied, his tone giving away how unsure he was of what else to do. 'And I've checked everything that I could check. I looked at their "check-ins" to see if they maybe visited the same places around the same time. I've cross referenced their likes in movies, music, TV shows, books . . . everything. I've looked at events they attended. I've checked groups that they belonged to. I've looked at every photo I could . . .' His shrug was a defeated one. 'All that I managed to find was that they liked some of the same music artists ... a couple of the same films ... but that was about it. If their social media is a true reflection of their lives ...' His eyebrows arched. 'Melissa and Kirsten were strangers as strangers can be.'

Hunter shared his partner's frustration. Everywhere they looked turned out to be a dead end. In the past couple of days, he and Garcia had also talked to several of Melissa Hawthorne and Kirsten Hansen's friends, asking about old boyfriends, flings, people who they might've rejected after a romantic advance ... anyone who could've held a grudge against them, probably because their feelings toward either of the two victims weren't reciprocated. The end result was nothing.

'Most of Melissa Hawthorne's posts were just funny memes,' Garcia explained. 'Or photos of her clients' freshly cut and styled hair. Kirsten Hansen's posts were a little more serious, talking about her days at the hospital ... the operating procedures ... how difficult they had been ... how well they'd gone ... etc. She posted a ton of pictures of her and Troy together, always mentioning the upcoming wedding. She also posted several photos of her hometown back in Denmark ... some of her and her parents ... a few of her with friends ... all the usual stuff. I've gone back a year so far on of all of their accounts, read every post and every comment – no arguments with anyone, no disputes, no bullying, nothing that seemed worth looking into.'

Hunter nodded, as he too pushed his chair away from his desk. 'Go home, Carlos. It's Friday. You've pulled extra hours every day this week. There's nothing else to do here at the office. Go home, pick Anna up and maybe take her out to dinner somewhere. It's still early.'

'Yeah, I know,' Garcia said, as he checked his watch once again. 'I actually do have to go.' He got to his feet and nodded at Hunter. 'And I *am* having dinner out with Anna ... together with the in-laws.'

'Oh, OK!' Hunter paused for a second. 'Tell them I said "hi". Your mother-in-law is a riot.'

Garcia chuckled. 'She is, yes.' A little head tilt. 'Her husband, not so much.' All of a sudden, Garcia snapped his thumb and forefinger and pointed at Hunter. 'Geez, I almost forgot again.' He reached for his cellphone.

'Forgot about what?'

Garcia copied something from his cellphone onto a piece of paper and placed it on Hunter's desk.

'That's Denise's phone number. She asked me to give it to you after the barbecue on Sunday, but with everything that's happened since then, I keep on forgetting.'

'Who?' Hunter asked.

'Don't you start that shit again,' Garcia said, pulling a face at Hunter, whose only reply was a coy smile. 'I'm serious, Robert. You should give her a call. She would love that, and I'm sure that she'd also love to meet you for dinner. Like you said – it's still early. And I know that you have no other plans for tonight.'

'Really?' Hunter challenged. 'And you know that how?'

'Because you never do, Robert.'

The glaring contest didn't last long.

'I'm not kidding,' Garcia pushed, pointing at the piece of paper he had just placed on Hunter's desk. 'She really did ask me to give you her number, Robert. And you pulled extra hours every day this week, too. You've said it yourself – there's nothing else to be done here at the office. Our brains are fried.' He indicated the board. 'Going over these photos, or rereading the lines that the killer left at the scene for the zillionth time won't make a difference because right now, we can barely think straight. We both need time off to recharge – move the thought process somewhere else, then bring it back.' He reached for his jacket. 'You need to eat, right? And you sure as hell could do with a night off and some good company. It's Friday night and we're not supposed to be in again until Sunday, though I'm sure that you'll be work-ing, somehow.'

Hunter stayed silent.

'Seriously, Robert, give her a call. She's fun, she's intelligent, she's beautiful . . . *and* she's single.' He paused, pretending he was trying to remember something else. 'Oh yes . . . and Denise loves whisky. When was the last time that you had a drink with a date who truly appreciates a nice Scotch?'

Hunter's mind tripped, caught in the past for half a heart-beat. *Tracy*. The name automatically popped into his head, but he didn't say it out loud. He didn't have to. Garcia read it in his eyes.

At the door, Garcia paused and faced Hunter once again.

'You couldn't have prevented it, Robert.'

Hunter looked back at his partner.

'I know what you're thinking about,' Garcia told him. 'You couldn't have stopped Troy.'

Hunter said nothing in return, but the look in his eyes was pure sadness.

'Do yourself a favor, friend – get your head off the case for a day. Call Denise. You'll be thanking me come Sunday. If nothing else, she'll make you laugh. I guarantee.'

'I wouldn't be good company to anyone tonight, Carlos,' Hunter replied, meeting his eyes again. 'My head wouldn't be in it, and that wouldn't be fair to whoever was out with me, especially for the first time.'

Garcia nodded. 'Yeah, but that just means that you would have to go out again on a second date. You know the saying right? If at first you don't succeed . . .' He paused for effect. 'Then skydiving is not for you.'

Hunter's stare stayed on his partner.

Garcia waited.

Hunter kept the same blank stare.

'Wow, nothing?' Garcia asked. 'Not even a tiny stretch of the lips? Did you even get the joke?'

Hunter nodded back. 'I got it. And yes, it was a good joke.'

'I could tell by the way that you were cracking up.' He used both hands to retighten his ponytail. 'Seriously, take the night off, man. You need it. Go for a drink with Denise. You need to get out of this office. You need to get out of your own head.'

As the door closed behind Garcia, Hunter's gaze shifted over to the piece of paper on his desk. It had been a while since he'd been out for dinner, or even a drink with someone.

Though the thought began gaining strength inside his head, there was also the knowledge that Garcia had read him like a book. Hunter had been thinking about Troy. He had been thinking about Janet Lang a lot too. He'd been in contact with Tom everyday, checking on Janet's mental state, but Garcia was right. At the moment, what Hunter needed more than anything was to try to disconnect from the case, even if only for a few hours. His brain did feel fried and going over everything they had so far for the zillionth time would only feed his frustration.

He checked his watch – 7:11 p.m.

If he were to meet Denise for drinks or dinner, he would need to drive home, have a shower, and change clothes. Maybe he could meet her for nine o'clock.

He sat back on his chair and crossed his arms over his chest. He looked again at Denise's number.

'Well, why not?' he said to himself at last, but just as he reached for his cellphone, it vibrated on his desktop. He checked the screen. There was a number showing, but no name.

He took the call. 'Detective Hunter, LAPD UVC Unit.'

'*Detective, it's Roger Wynn – bartender at the Broken Shaker bar – Freehand Hotel. We spoke on Monday?*'

'Roger,' Hunter said, as he shook his head momentarily. 'The Broken Shaker. Yes, of course.'

'*Well.*' There was a shrug in Roger's tone. '*You gave me your card and asked me to holler at you if I ever spotted that dude you were asking about. You know, the one that was here at the bar, talking to the lady you said was murdered?*'

'Yes, that's right.' Hunter sat up on his chair. 'Have you seen him?'

'*Yep. I'm actually looking at him right now.*'

'What?' Hunter was already up on his feet. 'Where are you?'

'*I'm at the Shaker,*' Roger said. Hunter could hear music playing in the background. '*He's here with some other woman ... quite young ... quite pretty. They're having dinner at the Exchange later.*'

'The Exchange?' Hunter asked.

'*Yeah, that's the restaurant here at the hotel,*' Roger explained. '*The dude and his date came up to the Shaker for a pre-drink before dinner.*'

'And how do you know he's having dinner at the hotel?'

'*Because when he came to order his drinks, he asked me if they could be put on a tab and then transferred to the Exchange. He said that they had a table booked for seven-thirty this evening.*'

Hunter instinctively checked his watch again. It was 7:15 p.m.

'*Though the Shaker and the Exchange are both here at the Freehand,*' Roger continued, '*neither is actually part of the hotel chain. The space is rented out, so we're talking two completely different owners and companies. The bills can't be shared.*'

'I see.' Hunter reached for his jacket. 'And you're absolutely sure that it's him? The same man that you saw sitting with Melissa Hawthorne at the bar on Saturday evening?'

'*It's him alright,*' Roger confirmed, his tone confident.

'OK. I'm at the Police Administration Building, which is just about a mile from you and I'm on my way. I'll be there in five ... ten minutes tops, but do me a favor, Roger – keep an eye on him for me. This is very important.'

'Sure. I'll do what I can, but there are two parties happening here tonight. One started at seven and the other is booked for seven-thirty. Guests are coming in by the buckets already. I'll try not to lose him.'

'Thank you.'

They disconnected.

A split second later, Hunter was rushing out of his office.

Forty-seven

Hunter had been so surprised by Roger Wynn's call that in his calculation of time, he forgot to take into account that it was a Friday night in the City of Angels. A city where going out, having a drink and partying until you dropped was practically embedded in everyone's DNA.

Traffic wasn't so bad, since the Freehand Hotel really was just over a mile from the PAB. It was finding a parking space in the vicinity of the hotel that became a problem. There weren't any. Hunter rounded the block twice before having to settle on a multi-story car park on South Olive Street. Still, he had to drive all the way up to the third floor before he found a spot.

Adding the time that it took him to run downstairs, out of the car park, around the corner, into the Freehand Hotel, and then take the elevator all the way up to the roof terrace – door-to-door – it took Hunter a little over twenty minutes to get to the Broken Shaker.

There were three bartenders working that night. Roger was completing a drinks order for one of the tables when he spotted Hunter zigzagging his way through the tables to get to the bar. Roger quickly gestured for Hunter to go over to the area reserved for waitressing service only.

Hunter did.

'Detective,' Roger said, his tone semi-apologetic. 'You just missed him by about five minutes or so.'

'He left?'

'He left the bar, yes,' Roger explained. 'But like I said on the phone, he had reservations for dinner, so he's in the Exchange restaurant down on the ground floor.'

'Are you sure?'

Roger nodded confidently, giving Hunter a proud smile. 'Yeah, I went downstairs to check. Blue shirt, dark trousers with a matching blazer jacket and a Panama hat. He's sitting with a short-haired brunette on table sixteen. That's toward the back of the restaurant floor.'

Hunter breathed out a sigh of relief and thanked the bartender before rushing back to the elevators.

Forty-eight

Downstairs, at the entrance to the Exchange restaurant, Hunter encountered no line of people waiting to be seated.

'Good evening,' said the restaurant host, greeting him with a bright and welcoming smile. He was a stocky man whose red hair came with the stereotypical pale skin and freckles of the Irish.

Hunter quickly explained that he was meeting a friend, who was sitting at table sixteen.

'Table sixteen is at the end of the floor,' he host indicated. 'On the right, by the window, just around that corner.'

'Thank you,' Hunter said. 'I'll find it, but just to be sure, could you please confirm the name on the booking?'

'Of course,' the host replied, checking his screen. 'Umm ...' He frowned at Hunter. 'The booking was made under the lady's name – Sarah Hartley.'

Hunter nodded. 'Of course it was.'

As he entered the restaurant, he was greeted by the delicate and inviting aromas of oriental spices being cooked with garlic and chilies. The mouthwatering smell was intoxicating, which prompted his stomach to loudly remind him that he'd had no dinner yet.

The man sitting at table sixteen was facing the other way. His hair was short and parted sideways. His blazer jacket was resting on the back of his chair.

The woman he was sitting with looked to be no older than

thirty, and she was indeed very attractive. As Hunter made his way to their table, the man reached for the half-drunk bottle of Cabernet Franc that was sitting in front of him and refilled both of their glasses before reaching for the woman's hand.

'Mark?' Hunter asked, coming up from behind him.

The man and his date looked back at Hunter curiously.

Every detective in America knew that a composite sketch was, at best, flaky. Generally, the human brain was terrible at describing faces from memory, and that was really all a sketch was – a memory locked inside the brain of a victim or a witness. The reason why the human brain was so bad at describing faces from memory was because the brain processed human faces holistically, rather than on the level of individual features, which was how a sketch artist worked – drawing part by part – eyes, nose, lips, eyebrows, etc. When trying to describe individual parts from a memory that had been stored as a whole, the brain would usually falter, but right then, Hunter was very impressed. Roger, the barman, had done an amazing job in remembering the man's facial attributes. The strong jawline, the round nose, the upturned eyes, the hairstyle, the noticeable widow's peak, the slope of the forehead – most of it was all there.

'I'm Detective Robert Hunter of the LAPD.' He flashed Mark his credentials. 'I was wondering if I could have a quick, private word with you?'

The woman's gaze crawled from Hunter to her date.

The man put down his wineglass. His expression stayed relaxed and unconcerned. The smile on his lips went nowhere.

'Umm . . . are you sure you've got the right person here, pal?' he asked, indifferently. His eyes flicked to the brunette for a heart-beat before returning to Hunter.

Slowly, she pulled her hand back from under his.

'I am, yes,' Hunter replied. No hesitation. 'I'm just not sure if your name really is Mark.'

'We're about to have a romantic dinner here.' The man, once again, smiled at his date. 'And you're completely killing the vibe, if you haven't noticed. What is it that you want, Detective ...?'

'Hunter. Robert Hunter.' This time, it was Hunter's gaze that flicked over to the brunette. It stayed on her for a couple of seconds before returning to the man. 'It's a delicate matter. I think that it would be better if we could talk privately.'

The woman grabbed Hunter's hint, reaching for her handbag and instinctively checking her watch.

'Umm ...' She looked uncertain. 'I'll go outside for a cigarette ... maybe two.' She got to her feet, but her eyes stayed on her date.

'Don't go too far, sweetheart,' he said, winking back at her. 'The food will be here shortly and I'm sure that Detective Hunter here won't stay too long.' The stare he gave Hunter right then could've curdled milk.

As the brunette turned the corner in the direction of the restaurant entrance, the man breathed out, annoyed. 'Way to kill it, pal.'

Hunter stayed silent, taking the now vacant seat across the table from the man.

'Oh, by all means, have a seat, why don't you, Detective?'

'Thank you,' Hunter replied calmly.

For a moment, they both assessed each other with eyes that moved like a scanner. If Hunter made the man nervous, it didn't show, not even a little bit.

'How about we start with a name?' Hunter hit first. 'Is it really Mark, or is that just the one you use out on dates?'

The man chuckled, unperturbed. 'You come in here, interrupt my dinner, ask my date to go for walk so you can find out what my name is? I don't do guys, if that's what you're after.'

Once again, Hunter said nothing in return. All he did was stare at the man across the table from him, whose body language and expressions seemed to be expertly controlled.

Hunter switched most of his attention to the man's hands.

In his experience, a person's hands and fingers could reveal a lot just by the way they moved. They drummed against surfaces, they fidgeted, they stilled nervously, they covered mouths, they rubbed, they picked, they plucked, they trembled ... there were just so many tells.

Once Hunter had taken his seat, the man had sat back, crossed one leg over the other and placed his hands on his lap. His chair was far enough from the table for Hunter to be able to see them – right hand resting on his left one, but in a somewhat unnatural position. His fingers were bent at the knuckles with his thumb folded in. Not exactly tense, but not really relaxed either.

'Mark *is* my real name, yes,' the man finally gave in. 'Satisfied?'

Hunter waited for Mark to offer his last name, but the offer never came. Instead, he pushed Hunter for an explanation.

'So if you're not here just to find out my name or ask me out ...' Mark reached for the brunette's wineglass and poured its contents into his. ' ... What's this all about then?'

'For the record,' Hunter began, his voice loud enough for Mark to hear it, but quiet enough so it wouldn't reach any of the neighboring tables. 'Could I have your full name?'

Mark had a sip of his wine then scratched his left cheek.

Hunter got the impression that Mark had been in this position before.

'Well,' Mark said, his expression calm. '*For the record*, I don't need to give you my full name, unless you are actually here to arrest me for something, which you're not, or else you would've done it already.'

'You're right.' Hunter's expression matched Mark's. 'I'm not here to arrest you. This is more like an informal chat. I prefer it that way, but if you like, I can certainly kick this up a notch or two and take you down to the station for something a little less informal.' Hunter angled his head slightly to the left, as he shrugged.

'But let me tell you, if I do that it might get a little embarrassing for you and for the restaurant because I'll be sure to make a scene, you know? Handcuffs ... raised voices ... might even pull out my weapon and pretend that you are resisting ... get you to lay on the floor ... hands behind your head and all that jazz ... we can even make it Hollywood style. Great spectacle. Maybe your date will be impressed.' He nodded toward the window. 'Your call.'

Mark's tongue rolled around inside his semi-open mouth. 'Why is it that every cop in this city is also a dick? Pun intended.'

Hunter gave him an eyebrow shrug. 'It's part of our training.'

Mark smiled in a way that told Hunter that he knew that Hunter wouldn't really do any of what he'd just threatened, but he still lifted his hands in surrender. 'My name is Mark Waller.'

Somehow, that didn't ring true.

'Any ID?' Hunter asked. 'Just to confirm it.'

Mark chuckle. 'Nope.'

'A credit card with your name on it will do.'

'I didn't bring my wallet with me.' Mark's head angled toward the window before his stare moved to the wine bottle on the table. 'She's buying.'

Hunter nodded.

'So, Detective,' he said, 'are you going to tell me what this is all about now, or are we going to keep on playing this ridiculous game? The food will be here any minute now and if you were gone by then, that would be great.'

As if on cue, a petite waitress with a bright smile approached their table.

'Could I get you something, sir?' she addressed Hunter. 'Shall I bring you a wineglass?' Her gaze flicked back from the bottle on the table.

'No thank you,' the reply came from Mark. 'He won't be staying.'

The waitress' surprised eyes moved from Mark to Hunter.

'I'm OK for now,' Hunter said, sending a warm smile her way. 'Thank you.'

'I'm still waiting, Detective,' Mark said, once the waitress had moved out of earshot. 'So far you've interrupted my date, threatened me, wasted about three to four minutes of my time and I still have no idea why you're here.'

'I'm here because of Melissa ... Melissa Hawthorne.'

Mark's eyes narrowed at nothing, as he clearly searched his memory. A few seconds later, he gave up.

'I'm sorry, who?'

Hunter's gaze didn't swerve from Mark's face. 'Melissa Hawthorne,' he said again, this time retrieving a photo of Melissa from his pocket and placing it on the table in front of Mark. 'You met her last weekend at the Broken Shaker, upstairs. You sat at the bar with her ... the two of you chatted for a little while ... you got her phone number?'

Mark's full attention dropped down to the photograph, where it stayed for just a couple of seconds.

'Oh! Her?' He blinked at Hunter then reached for his wineglass. 'Yes, I remember her ... last weekend, upstairs, that's right.' He had another sip. 'What about her?'

'What happened after the two of you left the bar upstairs?'

Mark frowned then gave Hunter a slight shake of the head followed by a mouth twist. 'Nothing. We didn't leave together.' He shrugged. 'Don't get me wrong. I wanted to, but she said no, so ...' His eyes narrowed again. 'As far as I can remember, she left and I think I left just a little after her. It was late, the crowd up at the Shaker was dying down, so I went home.'

'You didn't follow Melissa home?' Hunter asked.

Mark looked confused. 'What do you mean, "follow her home"? Like how?'

'Like jumped in a car, or a cab,' Hunter said back. 'And followed her cab back to her place without her knowing?'

Mark almost choked on his wine. 'What? Why the hell would I do that for?'

Hunter was still studying Mark – his movements . . . his expressions . . . his voice . . . even his silences. There was no panic in him. No fear either.

'Maybe because she said "no" to you?' Hunter replied with a question. 'Maybe you don't deal well with rejection and hers kind of hurt your pride? Maybe you wanted to –' the pause that came was deliberate because Hunter wanted to emphasize his next few words '– teach her a lesson?'

Mark put down his wineglass and exaggerated a jaw drop at Hunter. 'Are you serious, right now? And what the hell do you mean by "teach her a lesson"?'

Hunter's facial expression was a blank sheet, unreadable, cool, assessing.

Mark looked down at the photo on the table again. 'Look, she's a pretty woman. There's no doubt in that, but c'mon, Detective. Have one look at me . . . have one look at the woman who was sitting right there, where you are.' He chuckled. 'I have women who look like that lining up at my door. All of them dying to get a piece of this action.' He pointed at himself. 'You got this back to front, Detective. I don't chase women. They chase me. And there was no "rejection", like you put it. She was more than willing. She gave me her phone number and all. She was just playing hard to get . . . probably hoping that I *would* chase her. Well, I didn't.'

As Mark spoke, Hunter nodded along, his hand folded on his lap. 'So you went home after you left the bar upstairs on Saturday night?'

'That's what I said, isn't it?'

'And home is where?'

Mark chuckled. 'Home is where the heart is, Detective, didn't you know that?'

'Do you have anyone who can corroborate that?'

'What? That I went home?'

Hunter nodded.

'No,' Mark calmly said back. 'I live alone.'

'Did you get a cab home? Maybe the driver remembers you.'

'No, I walked. It was a nice night.'

'Did you call her?' Hunter nodded at the photo. 'Message her?'

Mark didn't reply. Instead he twisted his body to look out the window to his right.

'You said that Melissa gave you her number,' Hunter pushed. 'Did you call or message her at all?'

Another frown from Mark, as he thought about it for just a couple of seconds. 'No, I don't think I ever did. My week was pretty booked up as it was, you see? I was out on Wednesday ... I'm out tonight ... I have something arranged for tomorrow evening, which will probably carry on until Sunday ...' The edges of his mouth upturned in a humorless smile. 'I'm a guy in demand, Detective, what can I say?' He shrugged. 'Maybe I *will* give her a call sometime, she's pretty enough.'

'So you date a lot of women?' Hunter continued.

Mark chuckled, confidently. 'Yeah, I guess you can say that.'

It looked and sounded like Mark's narcissistic personality was about to swallow him whole, but despite his poker-face being very good, Hunter still had one more weapon in his arsenal. He reached into his pocket for another photograph. This time, of Kirsten Hansen. Without saying a word, Hunter placed the photo on the table right next to the one of Melissa, his attention on Mark's face and eyes.

Mark's stare shifted to the new photo and he studied her face for several long seconds.

'Very pretty,' he said, nodding in an approving way. 'Who is she?' The shrug was followed by another sip of his wine.

'You don't know her?'

A careless shake of the head. 'No. Why? Should I?'

'She's not one of the many women you've dated?' Hunter asked. 'Maybe a while back?'

Mark's attention went back to the photo before he once again shook his head at Hunter. 'No, I don't think so. A face this pretty I would remember.' He paused and checked his watch. 'Seriously, Detective, what the hell is this all about? Like I've said, you came over here, you completely killed the romantic atmosphere that I had going on with Sarah.' His head jerked toward the window. 'You show me a picture of a woman I talked to for about half an hour on Saturday night. Asked me a bunch of stupid ques—' Mark paused, glared at Hunter then lifted his hand. 'Hold on. Just hold on a minute here. Can I see that badge of yours again?'

Hunter placed it on the table in front of him.

'Homicide? You're LAPD Homicide?' Mark said the words a little too loudly, prompting the couple sitting at the table to his left to turn and look at him.

In silence, Hunter picked up his badge and returned it to his pocket.

'You're kidding right?' Mark tried to sound shocked, but there was no sincerity in his tone. 'This woman.' He tapped Melissa's photo with his index finger. 'The one that I talked to at the bar on Saturday night, are you telling me that she's dead? When?'

'That same night,' Hunter told him. 'After she left the bar upstairs.'

Mark's chuckle was hard to decipher. 'And you think I had something to do with that? That's why you're here? That's why you asked me if someone could corroborate that I went home that night? You've gotta be joking, right?'

Hunter allowed his facial expression to do the replying.

'Look,' Mark said, sitting up on his chair and placing both elbows on the table, his voice still. 'I'm sincerely sorry to hear about her death. I truly am, but you suggesting that I had some-thing to do with it simply because I had a conversation with her at a bar, is just ludicrous. Are you making those same sort of accusations to everyone who was there on Saturday night? Everyone who talked to her?' Mark didn't wait for a reply. 'Yeah, I didn't think so. So if you'd excuse me, Detective, I've got a date to go back to.'

Hunter didn't move. 'You said that you were out on a date this past Wednesday? Three nights ago?'

'Yes, that's right, so?'

'How about on Tuesday night?'

'What?'

'Were you out on Tuesday night at all? Maybe another date?'

Hunter was bombarding Mark with questions for a reason, but Mark's steadiness was unflinching and Hunter once again got the impression that he had been in similar situations before. He flashed Hunter a smile that was more a baring of teeth than anything else.

'I think we're done here, Detective.'

'It's a simple question.'

'To which you got a simple answer,' Mark replied. 'We are *done* here.'

Hunter knew that there was nothing else he could do. It was clear that Mark wouldn't be answering any more questions. At least not tonight.

Hunter nodded his understanding, collected the photos from the table and stood up, but as he turned to leave, his right hand brushed against Mark's wineglass, tipping it and spilling most of its contents onto Mark's lap.

'Oh, really?' Mark laughed, getting to his feet. 'Wow, that's just cold, man.' His tone was a lot calmer than Hunter expected.

'I'm so terribly sorry,' Hunter said, quickly grabbing a napkin and placing it over the small puddle on the table.

'Sorry? Really?' Mark shook his head as he reached for another napkin. 'I saw you move, Detective, and that was done on purpose.'

Mark's trousers were soaked in red wine, especially the groin region.

Hunter reached for the tipped wine glass before it rolled off the table, being careful to grab it by its base, using the palm of his hand, not his fingers. 'I'm really, terribly sorry about this. I'll get the waitress to bring you a brand new bottle of wine.'

Mark smiled back at Hunter, carelessly. 'It's OK, Detective. I can afford another bottle, if I so wish. I'm sure this bottle is a few steps above your pay grade.'

'I thought your date was buying it tonight.'

'She is,' Mark shot back. 'And she can afford it too.'

From the corner of his eyes, Hunter saw the waitress and the restaurant host quickly making their way to their table.

'I'm terribly sorry about this,' Hunter apologized to them. 'It was a clumsy accident.'

'Yeah, right,' Mark said. 'Will you just leave, now?'

While everyone busied themselves with cleaning up after Hunter's mess, he stepped away from the table, quickly reached for his cellphone and snapped a couple of shots of Mark without him noticing it.

The waitress and the restaurant host also failed to notice that Hunter never handed them the wine glass he'd taken from the table.

Forty-nine

Oliver Griffith wasn't used to being home alone, at least not overnight. Since he and Josie had met each other, seventeen months ago, and even more so after they'd gotten married, they'd practically spent every evening together. They really did love each other's company. They were into the same type of music. They liked the same movies and the same kind of food. Their sense of humor seemed to have been tailor-made because they were constantly making each other laugh. They were into the same sexual kinks . . . in short, they were as perfect for each other as perfect could be. Sleeping alone in their bed was a brand new experience for Oliver, one that he didn't like at all.

Josie and her friends had left for Stacey's *hen-night extravaganza weekend* in Vegas early yesterday morning. Last night – game night – Oliver tried making the most of it. He invited a few friends around to watch what turned out to be the closest of games between the LA Lakers and the San Antonio Spurs. Unfortunately for them, the Spurs won by four – 110 to 106.

Once all his buddies had left, and with the house all to himself, Oliver had felt a little lost, not really knowing what to do. He'd thought about giving Josie a quick call, but he'd known she'd be out with all the girls, having a blast, and he sure as hell hadn't wanted to come across as the needy husband who missed his wife too much. Instead, he'd poured himself a few more shots of whisky and allowed the alcohol to act as a sleeping aid for the night, a decision that he had thoroughly regretted this morning. His head had hurt with such intensity, he'd thought that he could actually hear his brain sloshing around inside his cranium and knocking against its walls every time he moved his head. It was only by about 11:30 a.m., after a Spanish omelet and a detox smoothie, that Oliver's hangover began to subside.

The rest of the day went by lazily. Josie called him at around one in the afternoon, and by the sounds of it, her hangover trumped his by a few thousand points, but she and the girls were in great spirits. At that time, they were all at the Mandalay Bay Beach Hotel for lunch, but they had the entire day planned out, culminating in dinner at the Edge Steakhouse followed by the big surprise night for Stacey, Josie's best friend and the bride-to-be.

'Umm . . . would that involve strippers, by any chance?' Oliver had asked, his tone playful, but with a concerned edge.

'*We're in Vegas, honey,*' Josie had replied. '*What do you think? They don't call this place "Sin City" for nothing.*'

'Oh, OK . . . I'm sure you'll all have a great time.' Oliver had tried to sound breezy, but Josie knew him way too well.

'*Aww, honey, you're jealous?*'

'Nope. Not at all. I'm good.' Oliver's reply had been too curt, something that was very unlike him.

'*Oh, that's so sweet.*' Oliver could hear the smile in Josie's tone. '*But you know that you have zero reasons to be jealous, right?*'

Oliver had stayed quiet.

'*For starters . . .*' Josie's voice had gone soft and sexy, in a way that she knew would make Oliver's legs go weak at the knees. '*You know that I love you more than anything or anyone, right?*'

. . .

'*Right?*'

'Yes.' Oliver finally gave in.

'*And you're the only one who can get me going the way you*

do. You know what I'm talking about.' Josie had delivered those sentences like a pro, sending a shiver slithering across Oliver's skin. '*No one comes even close to how much you pleasure me, baby, so why would I even bother?*'

Oliver breathed out frustration. 'Yep, now you're making me horny.'

Josie chuckled. '*Put some ice on it, honey, and hold that thought until tomorrow evening when I get back. I promise that I'll make it worth your while.*'

Oliver had had to readjust himself inside his trousers. 'That's a deal.'

Josie's reply had been a pleased and teasing laugh.

'Enjoy yourself tonight, baby,' he said, 'and get some pictures of the surprise night.'

'*Oh, I will, honey. Trust me. This will be duly documented for posterity. I love you.*'

'I love you more.'

They disconnected.

Thanks to an unexpected hot air current blowing in from the west, the day turned out to be relatively warm for mid-February, something not at all that surprising for Californian "winters", so in the afternoon, Oliver simply lazed around outside by the pool with a large glass of ice tea. It wasn't quite hot enough for a swim, but it sure felt good to be lying out in the sun for a couple of hours, most of which were spent dozing off on the chaise longue.

At around five in the afternoon, Stuart, one of Oliver's only unmarried friends called, asking him if he wanted to meet up for a drink later on, but the simple mention of more alcohol made Oliver's stomach rock like a ship in high waters. He decided that the best thing to do would be to give his liver a break and simply stay in.

There was another game on TV tonight, starting at seven. This time, the LA Clippers would play the Phoenix Suns in Arizona.

Oliver could watch that and afterwards, depending on how tired he felt, he would either call it a night or try for a film.

About half an hour before the game started, Oliver drove up to his favorite burger joint – the Habit Burger Grill – just around the corner from his house, to pick up a Santa Barbara Char Combo, to which he always added an extra slice of pineapple with a spoonful of guacamole. That had been something that Josie had taught him and it had become their secret ingredient to what they called 'the best burger on the planet'.

Back in his living room, Oliver got comfortable on his couch, ready for another thrilling game, but what he got was a 'walk-through'. At the beginning of the second quarter, the Suns were already leading the Clippers by twenty-two points, and there was no hint of the Clippers getting back into the game.

With a full stomach and a boring game, it was no surprise that by half time, Oliver was already drifting in an out of that weird 'limbo' stage between wakefulness and sleep ... dream and reality. It was then, as his mind floated into half unconsciousness that he heard a familiar sound coming from somewhere in front of him.

With his brain still heavy and slow, Oliver scanned the room, searching for the source.

Was that a buzzer in the game? he thought, quickly checking the TV screen.

It didn't look like it, but the Clippers were down by an extra six points.

As his eyes crawled back from the screen, Oliver caught a glimpse of a flashing light at the top left edge of his cellphone, which was resting on the coffee table between the couch and the TV set.

He reached for it.

A text message.

'Unknown Number.'

Oliver used his index fingerprint to unlock his phone and tapped on the message preview.

Warmer than expected today, huh, Oliver?

Oliver found the message just a little strange. First, because it was an unknown number. Second, because all of his friends always called him Ollie, not Oliver.

He shrugged and reached for his glass of ice tea, which wasn't icy anymore, but his mouth felt a little dry, so he finished the glass in two gulps before typing a quick reply back.

It sure was. Great to be outside again without the need for a jacket. BTW, who is this?

It didn't take long for a reply to arrive, but it wasn't what Oliver was expecting.

Yes, warm enough to even leave the windows open while doing a quick burger-run, huh?

'What?' Oliver breathed out the word, as he shook his head, trying to wake himself up a little more. He read the message again. 'What the fuck?' He sat up and squared his shoulders before typing the same question again.

Who is this?

Several seconds went by before Oliver heard anything back.

You do know that you left the windows unlocked and open while you went to pick up your burger, right?

The text prompted Oliver to look up, his gaze sweeping the room from wall to wall. Both living room windows were, in fact, ajar and he did remember opening them as he went outside to lie by the pool. He'd wanted to get some fresh air into the house.

'Yeah, so?' Oliver asked out loud before a thought entered his mind. *Was this Mrs. Miles from across the road being nosey, like always?* But the idea was dismissed just as quickly, because *how would Mrs. Miles have his cellphone number?*

This time Oliver used all capitals: *WHO IS THIS?*

The sender finally complied with a more suitable answer.

To you . . . I'll be a mentor, Oliver.

Oliver chuckled at the text. 'Yeah, right. A mentor. Of course.'

This was definitely one of his buddies. Probably Stuart, because he didn't go out for a drink.

Stu, is that u, u idiot? Are you drunk already? Where are u? He paused as a new and relatively worrying thought came to mind. He typed an extra line: *And how the hell do u know I went to grab a burger and that my windows were left open?*

The reply came back in no time at all. *No, this isn't Stu. Like I said, to you I'll be mentor, Oliver, because really, what this is, is a lesson.*

Oliver wasn't impressed.

'Yeah, fuck off.' He laughed. 'A lesson. OK then.'

Stu, u r a dick, not a teacher, he typed back. *Lesson my ass. U need to put down the booze and go get laid, or something. Leave me be, dude. I'm watching the game.*

The reply from the Mentor arrived quickly: *You weren't watching the game, Oliver. You were falling asleep by half time. You didn't even finish all your fries.*

That made Oliver's shoulders tense on the spot. This had just crossed the thin line between 'funny' and 'creepy'. Instinctively, his eyes circled the room before settling on one of the open windows.

'What is this bullshit?' he asked himself. 'How the fuck does he know about my fries, or about me falling asleep?' He placed his cellphone back down on the coffee table and got to his feet. As he did, he felt a little too woozy, as if he'd been boozing for a couple of hours. 'What the fuck is going on here?'

Oliver steadied himself and blinked the brain fog away before approaching the window. Mrs. Miles's house lights were all off. So were her neighbors' on both sides.

After spending a few seconds checking the street outside, Oliver pulled the window to and locked it. He quickly did the same to the other one. As he got back to the couch, his phone beeped and vibrated again. At the same time, the dizziness in his head moved up a level.

He picked up the phone and checked the message.

It's not bullshit, Oliver.

Oliver squinted at those words. He hadn't typed his question in a text. He had said it out loud. This couldn't be a coincidence.

Ding, ding. New message.

Unfortunately it's a little too late to close and lock the windows now, don't you think?

Oliver's stomach knotted, as his eyes, not really knowing what he was looking for, swept the room from left to right.

Nothing.

Ding, ding.

And I'll tell you how I know about your fries and you falling asleep, Oliver.

As Oliver finished reading that last text message, his vision blurred for just a couple of seconds. Something definitely wasn't right. Why was he so dizzy?

Ding, ding.

Because I'm already inside your house. Look behind you.

By then it was too late.

Fifty

Oliver coughed and finally spluttered awake. As his senses began to slowly come back to him, so did the pain, ferociously rushing through his bloodstream like a contaminated river. Every muscle, every bone, every joint in his body ached, as if they had been individually pounded to an inch away from breaking and rupturing . . . and then there was confusion – thick and dark like a heavy storm cloud. His brain, numb. His thoughts, lost.

Despite trying, Oliver had no idea of how long he'd been unconscious. He couldn't remember where he was either. In fact, it had taken him several seconds just to remember *who* he was.

Through the pain, he tried to force his eyes open. Identifying his surroundings would certainly help with the debilitating confusion, but his eyelids felt too tired . . . too heavy to move. All he got from them was a drowsy flutter before they collapsed back to their starting position.

Oliver's mouth also felt desert-dry, with his glands struggling to produce any saliva. The little they did produce would die on his tongue way before hitting his throat, which felt as if he had gurgled with crushed glass.

Oliver coughed again – a natural reflex to clear the airways – but that rush of pressure felt as if a bomb had gone off inside his skull, compressing his brain and making him dizzy again, the pain so intense that even breathing became a struggle.

It was then that he heard a noise.

Thud, thud,.

It came at him faintly, but in perfect timed intervals, as if a maestro was conducting a beat.

He tried to think, but nothing made any real sense.

Was this a dream? A nightmare?

It had to be. That was the only plausible explanation. How else would he be here? Wherever the hell 'here' was.

Thud, thud.

The metronome-precise sound came again and it seemed to be getting louder . . . closer even.

Fear began taking over.

Thud, thud.

Despite the pain, Oliver breathed in a lungful of air that felt warm and stale, heavy with an odd smell that he couldn't quite identify.

Thud, thud.

As the sound kept on repeating itself, Oliver finally realized that it wasn't coming from around him . . . it was coming from inside him. That pounding noise was the sound of blood powerfully thundering through his eardrums, and with each thud he felt his entire head pulse along with his heart, connected by the rush of blood.

What ridiculously crazy nightmare is this?

Splash.

All of a sudden, ice-cold water splattered against his face like an angry backslap, prompting Oliver to finally let go of the fearful cry that had been readying itself in his throat since he had regained consciousness.

The scream echoed loudly around him, a clear indication that he was surrounded by solid walls.

Desperate, he gasped, swallowing air as if he was trying to drink it.

This isn't a nightmare, he thought, his body shivering, his heart about to explode out of his chest. *This is real. All of it. What the hell is happening?*

The unexpected slap of freezing water to his face brought on a multitude of immediate physical reflexes – shivering, tightening of the muscles, constriction of the diaphragm, skin turning into gooseflesh and, worst of all, a brand new avalanche of fear – because now Oliver knew that wherever he was, he wasn't alone.

As the water dripped down his face, onto his bare chest and down to the floor beneath his feet, a hacking cough wrenched through his body, sending the pain at the base of his skull crashing through his ribs and down into his pelvis and thighbones.

But the icy water also served to shock him into an even higher state of alertness. His eyelids fluttered again, but this time he managed to find the strength to finally flick them open. As he did, he was immediately greeted by blurred shapes, his brain still heavy and foggy, but fear had its own special way of accelerating physiological responses. A fraction of a second later, his eyes began to regain their focus.

Concrete flooring.

That was what Oliver seemed to be looking at – polished concrete flooring.

He took in another mouthful of air. His ribcage lifted then fell slowly, as his lungs took in the much-needed oxygen. His eyes were still adjusting to the poor light, but he was sure that he was staring at polished concrete flooring.

It took his brain an extra two seconds to connect the dots. Oliver was in an upright position, with his head slumped forward, his chin almost touching his chest. What he was staring at was the floor underneath his feet, because his feet weren't touching the ground.

Suddenly, pain exploded from both of his hands and arms, travelling all the way from his fingertips to his shoulders, where it spread like wildfire onto his neck and back. That was when Oliver finally realized the exact position he was in. He was upright, but he had been tied onto a large, X-shaped wooden cross. Also known as a Saint Andrew's cross.

His wrists and ankles were being held in place by thick, leather straps that had been buckled as tight as they would possibly go without actually cutting the blood circulation to his hands and feet. The straps at his wrists were dotted with blood. The reason why his arms, shoulders and neck hurt so desperately was because his arms were supporting most of his weight, as his feet couldn't quite touch the ground.

It was at the same moment that Oliver realized that he was completely naked.

Splash.

Another splatter of ice cold water against his face.

Another shocking round of immediate physical reflexes.

The straps around his wrists bit deeper still into his flesh.

'Wakey, wakey, sleepyhead.' Oliver heard a voice say. The tone was smooth, underlined by such serenity it was disturbing. There was no rush in the words . . . no anger . . . no emotion. Just a stillness that was as soothing as it was unnerving.

It took Oliver an effort of will to lift his head up, trying to see who was talking to him. As he did, bright light burnt into his eyes and he immediately squinted, his head recoiling back like a fired weapon.

Where is that voice coming from?

He blinked, once again, giving his eyes time to adapt. It didn't take long for the burning to dissipate and a shape to finally begin to take form before him – a figure, tall, athletic – but the harsh light was still there, coming from behind it, which meant that all he could really make out was a silhouette . . . a shadow looking back at him.

Oliver tried to focus on the silhouette's face, but there was nothing there other than a dark oval of shadow. Oliver couldn't make out the eyes . . . the nose . . . the lips . . . nothing.

'Who . . . are you?' Oliver tried to say, but his vocal cords didn't quite respond like they were supposed to. All that came out of his lips was a barely audible rasp.

The shape before him shifted from one leg to the other, but remained in darkness.

'The headache . . .' the shadow said. Once again, the voice was calm and controlled. 'The muscle pain . . . the dizziness . . . the burning throat . . . all of those are mainly side effects from the drug I slipped into your ice tea when you fell asleep. Your arms hurt because they are holding the bulk of your weight. The side effects of the drug should wear off in a few minutes.' There was a pause. 'But trust me when I tell you that you'll wish they hadn't.'

There was something evil in the way that the shadow delivered that last sentence.

Oliver ran his tongue against his cracked lips, trying to collect a few drops of water to sooth his agonizing throat. With that, he somehow managed to fight the fear . . . the pain . . . the exhaustion and find the strength needed to finally activate his vocal cords.

'Who . . . are you?' he asked again in a labored breath.

This time, Oliver's voice finally reached the shadow's ears. 'I've already told you who I am,' it said. 'Don't you remember?'

Oliver heard a smile somewhere between those words.

'To you . . . I'll be a mentor, Oliver . . . . a teacher of sorts.'

Oliver's memory blinked inside his head, tripped, blinked again. Where had he heard that before?

To you . . . I'll be a mentor, Oliver.

Oliver concentrated with everything he had, until some of his memory finally came back to him. He hadn't heard those words before. He had read them . . . in a text message.

Another flash of memory – he had been sitting in his living room, watching a basketball game, when his phone beeped.

It hadn't been a dream.

'Would you like a drink of water?' the Mentor asked.

Oliver desperately needed water, but fear kept him from replying.

The Mentor read him like a book.

'Don't worry, Oliver. This isn't drugged. There's no need for that anymore.' The Mentor poured some water into a plastic cup and had a sip before approaching Oliver. 'See?'

As the Mentor finally stepped out of the shadows, Oliver's eyes eagerly tried to take in everything he could.

What he saw looked like a nightmare.

The Mentor was dressed all in black, wearing what seemed to be a neoprene diving suit. The hair was also covered, completely tucked away under the diving suit's hoodie, but the face was exposed. Oliver concentrated on it – the eyes, the lips, the nose, the cheekbones, the shape of the chin ... whatever he could see. He tried hard, urging his brain to respond. It took several long seconds before his memory told him that it had no idea who the person standing in front of him was. He had never seen the Mentor before and that only served to fill Oliver with even more confusion and fear.

The Mentor held the plastic cup to Oliver's lips, who drank its contents in small, but hungry gulps. At first, the water scratched his throat as if he was drinking liquid sandpaper, but it soon felt like the nectar of the gods.

'Nice place you've got here,' the Mentor said, looking around the room they were in. 'This has saved me a lot of time and effort.'

Oliver swallowed the last drop of water from the cup and tentatively allowed his gaze to scan his surroundings. He'd been so frightened, so confused since he'd regained consciousness that he had concentrated all of his attention on his assailant. The room he was in had come a very distant second on his list of priorities, but now that his eyes began taking in the walls, the ceiling, the corners, the furniture, the props ... despite the dim lighting and the shadows, it took him only a moment to realize where he was. His sense of smell also seemed to finally wake up, registering the faint smell of leather mixed with latex.

The Mentor, once again, read Oliver's expression.

'Yes, Oliver, this is your basement, and I must admit that I'm impressed.' The Mentor looked left then right. 'This is one hell of a well-equipped dungeon. You and your wife must be into some very kinky shit, huh?'

Both Oliver and Josie enjoyed all different kinds of sex play, including BDSM, role-playing and mild to moderate pain. It was all a big part of their sex life. Just before their wedding, they managed to find a house with a reasonably large basement, something that was considered a rarity in Los Angeles. It took them two months to transform the basement into a very well-equipped dungeon, with wall and ceiling metal rings, used for tying each other up, a vast selection of mild punishing implements and all different kinds of whips, canes, ropes, straps, and chains. There were also two different restriction chairs and the St. Andrew's cross that Oliver was now tied to. This was their playroom.

What the hell is happening here?

Fear slapped Oliver across the face with an angry hand and he could feel his whole core shaking. Pain tugged at his arms again, but he pushed through.

'We ... we don't have that much money.' His weak voice filled the space between him and the Mentor. 'Some savings ...'

The Mentor placed a gloved finger on Oliver's lips.

'Shhhhhhh! You think this is about money?'

Their gaze found each other's, and Oliver saw something burn inside the Mentor's eyes that he had never seen before in anyone's eyes. Something dark and dense like a black hole full of anger. If there was any truth in the phrase 'the eyes are a window to the soul', then the Mentor didn't have one. All Oliver could see was darkness.

The Mentor smiled before walking back into the shadows.

Oliver could feel panic starting to craw along his skin.

'This won't be pleasant,' the Mentor said. 'At least not for you. Here we go. Lesson number one.'

That was when Oliver noticed what the Mentor had picked up.

Fear and panic rolled into a single ball of terror that made him gasp for air.

'No . . . wait . . . please . . .'

The Mentor smiled again.

'Well, if this scares you, Oliver, then I can't wait until you see the real surprise.'

Fifty-one

Garcia had been right – Hunter did end up working on what was supposed to have been their day off. Despite his best efforts, his brain simply couldn't disconnect, always finding a way to bring his thought processes back to the investigation. This, he knew, was like fighting insomnia. It was a pointless effort because he knew he wouldn't win.

As his 'day off' began, Hunter took a trip to the LAPD Criminalistics Lab at California State University, in the University Hills district. There, he dropped off the wine glass that he had taken from 'Sleazy Mark' at the Exchange restaurant the night before, putting in a request for DNA and fingerprint analysis. Sure, as of yet, they didn't have a DNA sample or any fingerprints from the Mentor. Hunter was simply playing the odds game.

In his head, Hunter had replayed his conversation with Mark more times than he cared to admit, and he could recall everything – Mark's voice intonation, his movements, his expressions, the look in his eyes, what he'd said . . . all of it.

Mark was a womanizer. There was no doubt about that, but during those few minutes that they sat face-to-face, Hunter got the impression that Mark had somehow managed to assert almost total control over his physiological and psychological motor responses – something that was terribly hard to do.

Hunter had caught glimpses of Mark's ability throughout

their conversation, but it was really when he had showed Mark Kirsten Hansen's photograph that it became more apparent. As Mark's eyes had settled on the photo for the first time, they had widened ever so slightly, which didn't indicate recognition. With recognition, a person's eyes tended to narrow – sometimes almost imperceptibly, sometimes visibly. The interrogator would have to be specifically looking for it to pick it up and even then, it could be easily missed.

Narrowing of the eyes indicated concentration. It happened when a person searched his or her memory for an identical or similar image – 'recognition' – but the real giveaway would usually come with the movement of the eyes. Up and to the right denoted that the person was trying to engage their memory for visually remembered images – something they'd seen before. Up and to the left suggested that the person was trying to access their visual constructive cortex – creating an image or memory that was never there in the first place.

At the Exchange restaurant, Mark's eyes had narrowed before barely moving up and to the right when Hunter had first showed him Melissa Hawthorne's picture. He clearly remembered seeing her somewhere and was trying hard to place her. With Kirsten Hansen's photograph, Mark eyes had moved neither left nor right – they had stood perfectly still, but also widened almost imperceptibly. Hunter had only caught it because he was looking straight at Mark. Widening of the eyes indicated surprise or shock, but it was also an indication of admiration or approval – the kind a person shows when they see someone who their brain perceives as attractive. Mark had followed the widening of his eyes with a comment that had sounded totally natural and unforced, also indicative of his womanizer personality – that Kirsten was 'very pretty'.

Those types of automatic reactions and micro-reactions were examples of physiological and psychological motor responses to stimuli. Most of us don't even know we do it, that's why they are so difficult to control. How do you control something you don't even know is there?

But Hunter also knew that though difficult, it *was* possible to control them. It took a lot of concentration ... tens, maybe hundreds of hours of practice ... and a lot of discipline, but it could be done. And if those reactions could be controlled, then they could also be altered to give out the wrong signal.

There was a lot that Hunter still didn't know about this killer, but what he did know was that the Mentor was tremendously disciplined, systematic, creative and patient. That, in itself, was an indication that the Mentor had above average intelligence, something that Hunter knew was an absolute must if anyone wanted to develop the ability to control their physiological and psychological motor responses.

Fifty-two

On Sunday, Flight WN167 from Las Vegas to Los Angeles was scheduled to land at 5:15 p.m., but due to a minor delay at boarding time, it touched down at LAX twenty-six minutes late. Deplaning was quick, but Josie still had to wait almost fifty minutes before everyone in their group had collected their suitcases.

A Barbie-pink stretch-limo had been arranged to take everyone back home. It was all part of the 'door-to-door hen-night extravaganza', which Josie had helped organize, but there was no doubt that the limo trip back home was very different than the outbound one.

On their way out, on Friday morning, spirits were high. Everyone was rested and totally ready to party. This was going to be a weekend that no one would forget. Two days later and the almost-no-sleep, all-partied-out, six-strong group of women barely had anything left in them. All they wanted to do was sleep.

As soon as they got into the limo, all six of them collapsed onto the seats.

As all the girls began dozing off, Josie tried calling Oliver again. She'd tried three times already, once before leaving the hotel and twice from McCarran International, but the calls went straight to voicemail, every single time.

She had already left two messages, but Josie still hadn't heard a word from her husband, which was strange and totally unlike Oliver.

They'd spoken on the phone yesterday and he'd sounded fine. Yes, he was clearly a little jealous about the 'stripper surprise' that she had arranged for Stacey, but Oliver wasn't really the jealous type, and neither was Josie. They trusted each other, they trusted themselves, and they trusted their love.

'Baby, it's me again,' Josie whispered into her cellphone so as not to wake up Stacey, who was asleep right next to her. 'I'm not sure if you got my previous messages. If you did, why haven't you at least texted me back? Is everything alright? I hope you're not still upset about the strippers, honey.' She drew a breath. 'Anyway, I wanted to let you know that we've landed safely and that I'm on my way home. We're all in the limo and I am drop-off number five, so it will still be at least an hour and a half before I'm home. Can't wait to see you. Miss you and love you.' She disconnected.

'Still haven't heard from Ollie?' Stacey asked, with only her right eye open.

'Sorry, honey, didn't mean to wake you up,' Josie said, still keeping her voice quiet.

'Not really sleeping,' Stacey came back. 'Just resting my eyes.'

Josie shook her head. 'No, not even a text message. That's not like him. I'm not sure what's going on.'

Stacey stretched her arm, placing her right hand on Josie's knee. 'Don't worry, babe. He probably . . . lost his phone or something. He did it before, didn't he?'

Josie nodded. She had thought about that possibility. 'Yes, twice,' she confirmed. 'He can be an airhead sometimes. Especially when he's out drinking with the gang. But if he lost he phone, he could've messaged me through Facebook from the computer at home.'

Stacey opened her left eye as well. 'Would you like me to call Scott and ask him if he knows anything? They were together on Friday night, watching the game.'

Josie pondered the idea for just a second. 'Nah, it's OK. We'll all be home soon, but thank you anyway, honey.'

'Or maybe he's got some sort of surprise waiting for you when you get back,' Stacey added. 'That would be totally Ollie-like.'

Josie's perfect eyebrows arched.

Oliver did love surprising Josie with gifts, notes, messages, poems, flowers ... anything and everything. He was truly the romantic type. Even on this trip. At their hotel, Josie had opened her toiletries bag to find a note that Oliver had slipped into it without her seeing. The note depicted a make-believe dialogue between the two of them. It read:

JOSIE: 'Ollie, I want you to yell, as loud as you can, that you love me, so that the whole world can hear.'

OLLIE: *scoots over and whispers in Josie's ear* – 'I love you.'

JOSIE: *looking confused* – 'Why did you whisper it into my ear?'

OLLIE: 'Because you are my whole world.'

The note had brought a tear to Josie's eyes.

'Yeah, that *would* be totally like him,' Josie admitted it.

Josie had been pretty close to right on the money when she'd estimated it would be an hour and a half before she was home. With traffic on the freeways surprisingly better than expected, it took the driver one hour and twenty-seven minutes to get to her place in Santa Clarita. Josie kissed Stacey and grabbed her suitcase.

Oliver's black Mercedes was parked on their driveway, right next to her Mini Cooper.

Just to be sure, Josie checked her cellphone again. No messages. No missed calls. It was 8:38 p.m.

'Really, Ollie?' she asked herself in a half annoyed, half disbelieving voice.

Josie hated arguing with her husband. In fact, since they'd met each other, they'd only gotten into two arguments, and both of them had been for silly reasons, but if Oliver didn't have a great explanation for his total silence since yesterday, he would definitely get a piece of her mind.

Josie carried her suitcase up to the front door and searched her handbag for her house keys, but as she tried pushing the correct key into the keyhole, the door swung open. It had been left unlocked and ajar.

'What the hell?' Josie frowned. Now she was getting worried. 'Ollie?' she called from outside.

No reply.

Their front door opened into a small anteroom, where they usually left their shoes, so as not to dirty the carpets.

Josie quickly kicked off hers and closed the door behind her.

Next was the living room, where all the lights were off. Josie reached for the switch to the right of the door and flicked it on.

'Oliver, are you in here?' she called again, louder, this time.

Silence.

'Oliver?'

The house sounded dead.

Josie looked around the room. Nothing seemed to be out of place. The cushions on their sofa were all piled up against one end, but that was about it. It was only when she put down her suitcase that she finally noticed it. On the floor, about two feet from the door that led from the living room into the kitchen, she could see . . . red rose petals?

She straightened up her body and tilted her head slightly to the right before frowning. She wasn't seeing things. There really were red rose petals scattered on the floor, but not in a messy way. They had been arranged to form a single line, leading from the living room into the kitchen.

Stacey's words came back to Josie:

Or maybe he's got some sort of surprise waiting for you for when you get back. And that would be totally Ollie-like.

Josie couldn't fight the smile that sprung up on her lips. Nevertheless, Oliver could've messaged her back and still have kept this a surprise. The radio silence had worried her and he should've been a little more considerate.

'The surprise is in the kitchen?' she asked herself, as she started toward the line of rose petals.

Maybe Oliver had cooked her dinner.

Oliver wasn't really the chef type, but he had managed to master a few dishes, including Josie's favorite – beef goulash with potato pancakes. To her, this would be an amazing surprise because the hangover had finally subsided and she was feeling positively hungry. The problem was, she wasn't picking up any smells coming from the kitchen, and every time Oliver cooked beef goulash, the mouth-watering smell would fill the entire house for hours.

'Ollie, babe,' she called again, her voice a little less stressed than moments ago. 'Are you in the kitchen?'

No reply.

Josie got to the door and reached for the light switch on the inside. As the lights came on, her forehead creased with concern.

Oliver wasn't in the kitchen and there were no signs that any cooking had taken place in there – no pots on the stove, no dishes in the sink or on the dish rack, no mess on the worktop, and no smell of food. The rose petals, though, carried on in a jagged line, as if they were breadcrumbs left behind by Hansel and Gretel. They moved left then right, past the small cooking island and in the direction of the basement door – their dungeon.

'Oh, I see,' Josie said, as her arms slumped by her sides. She loved playing their sexy games. She had been the one who had truly advocated for their home dungeon. She had chosen all the furniture and most of the playing props that they had down there. She was a highly sexed woman, but mood played a huge part in the type of games and role-plays that she and Oliver enjoyed. One needed to be prepared and in the correct frame of mind to be kinky, and right at that moment, Josie's frame of mind and mood were after one thing only – sleep. Maybe a pizza before sleep, but not much else.

Josie followed the petals to the dungeon door and pushed it open. The mood-setting fairy lights that contoured the red-carpeted stairs had been left on, dimly illuminating the steps. She paused at the top and drew a deep breath.

She really didn't want to put a damper on Oliver's surprise. Whatever he had planned for them downstairs, she was sure it would be something hot and very sexy, but her mood really was all wrong for tonight. She felt so tired that she ran the risk of dozing off whilst role-playing or having sex, and that would be a very big 'no-no'.

'Ollie, babe, are you downstairs?' Josie used her best soft-velvety voice. 'You know I love you right? And that I'm never one to shy away from playing.' She took the first two steps going down. 'But I'm truly exhausted, babe. It was a crazy weekend. Could we just have cuddles in bed tonight, instead? I promise you I'll make it up to you . . . with interest. You know I'm good for it.'

She finally reached their basement dungeon, where all the lights were off. The fairy lights on the stairs behind her weren't powerful enough to illuminate anything past two to three feet from where Josie was standing, which made the whole set-up feel odd, but what truly made her frown was the smell. Something alien to their playroom. It wasn't the smell of latex or leather. Josie knew those too well to get them confused with anything. No, this smelled like something metallic – iron, maybe. First impressions were that it wasn't really to her liking.

'Ollie,' she called as she reached for the light switch. 'What have you got down here that smells . . .'

The light flicked on at the same time that her toes touched something wet on the floor.

The horror of what was down in their dungeon hit Josie all at once with the power of a buffalo stampede, paralyzing her every muscle.

Her eyes were immediately filled with tears. Her pupils seemed to dilate, eating up most of the green in her irises. Her core shook with fear and disgust before her whole existence was swallowed by a black hole of confusion. At that moment, Josie let out an anguished howl so disturbing that not even she would recognize it as coming from herself. It pulsated against the walls, returning to her in vibrating waves that slammed into her chest like a hammer.

She wanted to run, but her legs didn't respond.

She wanted to think, but her brain wouldn't engage.

Shock was shutting her body down.

She let go of a second scream and all of a sudden, the entire room began spinning around her. Too fast for her to control it. Too powerful for her to stop it.

Her legs weakened. Her knees buckled under her body and in an awkward half-spin, Josie collapsed to the floor, but just before her eyelids came together . . . just before darkness took over . . . she realized that she wasn't alone. That was when she saw a figure appear behind her, right at the base of the stairs.

Fifty-three

The address that Hunter was given took him to a small cul-de-sac street on the north quadrant of Santa Clarita. Even at that time at night on a Sunday, traffic through the canyon was slow and it took him almost an hour and fifteen minutes to make the forty-five mile journey.

The house in question was the third on the left, but Hunter could see the flashing blue and red lights lighting up the sky from almost a block away.

The outermost perimeter had been set right at the top of the street. This was not the forensics (inner) perimeter. That one had been set just around the house, including the front lawn, the driveway, the garage and the natural stone pathway that led from the sidewalk to the house's front door.

As Hunter arrived, he couldn't see any press vehicles or professional-looking cameras anywhere, at least not yet, but there were plenty of onlookers crowding the entrance to the road. It looked like most of the residents from the neighboring streets had also come out to see what was going on.

Hunter geared down and slowly maneuvered his way through two groups of people to get to the police barriers blocking the street entrance, where two deputies from the LA County Sheriff's Department stood guard.

Hunter rolled down his window just as the shorter of the two approached his car.

'Could you do me a favor, Deputy?' Hunter asked, as he showed the deputy his credentials. 'Could you please turn the blue-and-reds off?' He nodded at the Sheriff's Department SUV that was parked to his right. 'All that those lights are doing is attracting more of a crowd.' He indicated the mob of people behind his car. 'I could see them flashing from a mile away, and so can the whole neighborhood. As a crime scene, the less public attention we get here, the better.'

The deputy acknowledged Hunter's credentials with a matter-of-fact nod. 'Sure.' He signaled the other deputy to move one of the barriers out of the way. 'Do you guys live in the same street, or something? Could've shared the ride.'

'Excuse me?' Hunter frowned at the deputy.

'Some other detective from the UVC Unit has just arrived,' the deputy explained, pointing past the barriers. 'Less than a minute ago.'

'Is forensics also here?' Hunter asked.

'Yep. They've been in the house for at least forty-five minutes now.'

As Hunter drove past the barriers and into the street, he checked his rear-view mirror. The deputy he had just talked to had repositioned himself by his partner. The lights on his SUV were still flashing.

Ahead of him, Garcia had parked on the street, just past one of the other three Sheriff's Department vehicles that were at the scene. He quickly spotted Hunter and signaled him to pull up just in front of his Honda Civic.

'The deputy told me that you just got here,' Hunter said, as he jumped out of his car.

'Yep,' Garcia confirmed, instinctively checking his watch. 'About a minute ago.' As he looked back toward the barriers he chuckled sarcastically. 'They're still on.'

'What are still on?'

'I asked the deputy to switch off the blue-and-reds,' Garcia explained. 'They're bouncing off the houses and lighting up the sky like a crowd beacon.'

Hunter nodded his agreement, but said nothing in return. He clipped his badge to his belt and he and Garcia both turned to face the two-story, beige-fronted house that had been isolated from the neighboring ones by black and yellow crime-scene tape. To its right, there was a two-car garage. A red Mini Cooper and a black Mercedes Benz were parked side-by-side on the wide driveway. Outside the front door, another deputy stood guard, while on the street, four other ones seemed to be just hanging around by their units.

'LAPD UVC, right?' The question came from a woman who seemed to have appeared out of nowhere. Her sharp but not unattractive features were framed by straight auburn hair, hanging to shoulder length. Her hazel eyes sat behind frameless glasses that were perched high on a petite nose. She looked to be in her mid to late thirties.

'That's right,' Hunter replied, as both detectives turned to look at her.

She wore a standard issue LA County Sheriff's Department uniform. The three chevrons on her sleeve told Hunter and Garcia that she was a sergeant.

The woman was a head shorter than Hunter's six foot, but she had a way about her that made it seem that it was others who had to look up to her.

'I'm Sergeant Jacqueline Logan with the LA County Sheriff's Department,' she said, offering her hand.

Hunter and Garcia shook it in turn, as they introduced themselves.

'Were you first at the scene?' Hunter asked.

'That's correct,' Sergeant Logan confirmed. 'I got the call

from Dispatch at around ten past nine this evening – possible homicide – Dispatch wasn't one hundred percent sure because the caller was borderline hysterical.' Her gaze pinged to the house. 'And truthfully, that's no surprise, considering what's in there.'

Hunter and Garcia stayed quiet, allowing the sergeant to continue.

'I was on night patrol when we got the call,' she explained. 'We were just about eight blocks away from here. That's Deputy Suarez and myself.' She indicated the house again, as reached for her pocket notepad. 'He's upstairs with the victim's wife, her friend and the friend's fiancé. The victim's name is Oliver Griffith – thirty years old. He worked as a creative director for an advertisement agency located somewhere in Playa Vista.'

'Oliver Griffith?' Garcia asked. 'The victim is male?'

The question made Sergeant Logan's gaze bounce from one detective to the other. She had clearly picked up the surprise in Garcia's tone.

'That's correct.' She readjusted her glasses on her nose. 'I really don't have much here. I didn't want to start asking questions in a case that clearly would be bumped up to you guys, but the story I have is that Mr. Griffith was alone in the house. His wife, Josie Griffith, was away for the weekend. Vegas. A two-night hen party for a friend.' Sergeant Logan's index finger indicated the house once again. 'That's the friend who's upstairs with Mrs. Griffith right now. Her name is Stacey Green. Her fiancé, Scott Summers, is also there with them. The hen-night party group – six of them in total – left on Friday morning and got back this evening. Upon arriving at LAX, they all jumped in a limo that had been pre-booked. The journey here took about an hour and a half. Mrs. Griffith arrived at her home at around 8:40 p.m. She entered the house, went downstairs to the basement and ...' The Sergeant drew a deep breath. 'Found her husband.'

'So Mrs. Griffith was the one who called 911?' Hunter asked.

'Actually, no.' Sergeant Logan explained. 'Her friend, Stacey Green did. When Mrs. Griffith was dropped off by the limo, she left her work phone behind, on the seat. Miss Green noticed it just as they got to the top of the road. She asked the driver to stop and wait, while she ran back here with the phone.' She flipped a page on her notepad. 'According to Miss Green, she was about to ring the doorbell when she heard a scream coming from inside. The door had been left unlocked, so she entered the house. That was when she heard a second scream, which came from the kitchen. She rushed in there, then down into the basement where she found Mrs. Griffith on the floor, together with everything else that's down there.' She paused to recompose herself. 'And what's down there is seriously the creepiest shit I've ever seen.'

'Thank you,' Hunter said, as all three of them began making their way to the house.

'Like I said,' the sergeant continued, returning her notepad to her pocket. 'We got the call at around ten past nine and we were here in less than ten minutes, but you just have to have one look at that scene to know that this isn't staying with the Sheriff's Department. At least not with a small branch like ours.' They all stooped under the crime-scene tape to enter the inner perimeter. 'I called my captain and we both agreed that this had to go either to the LAPD UVC or the FBI. We went with the UVC, which according to the forensics lead was the right call.'

They paused just a few feet from the front door.

'What do you mean?' Garcia asked.

Sergeant Logan shrugged. 'The first thing that the forensics lead said after she took one look at the scene and saw those words was, "We need to call the LAPD UVC. This is their case".'

'Words?' Hunter asked. 'What words?'

There was a look of disbelief in the sergeant's eyes. 'Ummm . . . the killer left some sort of note down there . . . written on the wall.' Her stare moved past Hunter and settled on the house for a couple of seconds before returning to the detective. 'And if those words don't creep you out – wait until you see what was done to the victim.'

Fifty-four

At the house's front door, Hunter and Garcia were given dispos-able forensics jumpsuits. They suited up in silence, signed the crime-scene manifest and entered the house.

In the living room, a forensics agent was dusting the windows for latent prints. Just like with their previous two crime scenes, there were no signs of a struggle anywhere in that first room. Hunter and Garcia greeted the agent with a head nod before moving left, in the direction of the door that led into the kitchen, but they both stopped almost immediately.

'What the hell?' Garcia said, his gaze on the forensics evidence identification marker on the floor, displaying '1' in black ink. 'Are those rose petals?'

Hunter nodded. 'They look to be.'

They both understood the reason for the identification marker as soon as they stepped into the kitchen.

'It's a trail,' Garcia said, his tone more surprised than confused. 'The killer left a rose petals trail leading down to the basement? This is new.'

Hunter got down on one knee and picked up one of the rose petals.

'Not fake,' he said, bringing it to his nose. He picked up a slight fragrance.

Other than the rose petals on the floor, nothing seemed to be out of place in the kitchen.

The trail led to an open door on the left, just past the cooking island. Hunter and Garcia could hear voices coming from downstairs. The one that they immediately recognized belonged to Dr. Slater.

The narrow steps, twelve in total, were now fully lit, courtesy of the powerful forensics crime-scene light that had been set up at the top of the stairs. Hunter and Garcia took them slowly, being extra careful to avoid the several other identification markers on eight of the steps, each next to a full or partial bloody footprint. Once they reached the basement, they both stopped dead, their breaths catching on their throats as their brains tried to take in the enormity of the scene before them.

It was clear that the basement had been transformed into a sex-play dungeon, with different props everywhere and a vast selection of implements hanging from the wall to their left. On the wall to their right, just like Sergeant Logan had told them, someone seemed to have left a message, written in large, red letters, but the true horror down in that basement . . . what really made Hunter and Garcia's hearts beat to a different tempo, was the victim's body and the manner in which it had been posed.

Positioned directly in front of them, just a few feet from the back wall, Oliver Griffith's naked body was spread-eagled against a large X-shaped wooden cross. His wrists and ankles were held in place by thick leather straps that sprung out of the cross's wood beams. Another thick leather strap looped around his waist, pinning his core down. His head was slumped forward. Inside his wide-opened mouth, Hunter and Garcia could see a red ball-gag, also secured in place by a leather strap that had been buckled up behind the base of his skull. His torso looked to be untouched – no cuts, no marks. It was from his waist down where things seemed to go completely insane.

There was blood everywhere.

Starting from his groin region, it caked both of his legs before spilling down onto the floor beneath his feet, forming a huge pool of coagulated blood that extended to just about a foot from where Hunter and Garcia stood. The blood on his groin, legs and feet had already dried, but despite the sheer amount, there was no mistaking the wound that had caused such intense hemorrhage.

Oliver Griffith had been viciously castrated.

His penis and testicles had been severed at their base, leaving behind a large, raw, exposed flesh wound, made to look even worse by the position of his legs – widely spread apart on the X-shaped cross.

Though the savagery of the scene before them had made Garcia grimace, his eyes never left the victim, and despite the strong forensics light illuminating the whole of the basement, he was still unsure about what he was looking at.

'What . . . the hell . . . are those?'

The question, which stumbled out of his lips, was intended for Hunter, but it was heard by Dr. Slater and both of the forensics agents already working the scene.

'I imagine that you're referring to the lobsters.' The answer came from Dr. Slater, who had been standing just a little to their right.

'That's what it looks like from here,' Garcia said back, his gaze moving to her for just a second before returning to the body. 'On his legs?'

'As crazy as that may sound and look,' the Doctor confirmed, 'that's exactly what they are – lobsters.'

With their bodies pressed against each of Oliver Griffith's upper thighs, the killer had pinned two raw lobsters in place – one to each thigh. Their antennas and antennules had been made to stick up and out, away from their bodies, creating a disturbing thorn-like effect. Their pereiopods, or walking legs – eight on each lobster – had been spread out to mimic their walking motion, as if both crustaceans were crawling up Oliver's thighs. But the really ominous detail came from their claws. With both of their heads pointing toward the wounds on Oliver's groin, their crusher claws had been positioned to give the impression that the lobsters had severed the victim's organs. The one on his left thigh had its crusher claw against the lacerations to his testicles, while the one on his right leg had its claw at the base of the penile wound.

The overall visual effect was as sickening as it was shocking.

'Please tell me that that's not really what the killer used to . . .' Garcia left the sentence unfinished, ending it with a shake of the head.

'No.' This time, the answer came from Hunter. His voice sounded somewhat calm, but there was disbelief in his tone. His gaze remained on the victim. 'Lobster pincers aren't powerful or sharp enough to cut through muscle in that way. In fact, they don't actually cut at all. They crush and pinch. That's why they're called "pincher" and "crusher" claws. The crusher claw is the stronger of the two, but even if it were sharp enough, it wouldn't be powerful enough to sever the organs from his body.'

'Robert is right,' Dr. Slater confirmed, stepping around a restriction chair to join both detectives. 'I left everything as we found it so that the two of you could see the crime scene in situ.' She indicated the body on the cross. 'This would be hard to explain even with photographs, but I was able to quickly examine the wounds. The cuts seem razor-sharp clean.'

'Knife?' Hunter asked.

'A very sharp one, sure,' Dr. Slater replied. 'The perp might've also used something like a scalpel, or even a pair of shears . . . maybe large scissors. If the killer has left whatever instrument he's used behind, we haven't found it yet.'

The answer made Garcia press his legs against each other, like a kid who was dying to go to the bathroom. The grimace on his face intensified.

'Maybe the killer was looking for the shock effect with the

lobsters,' one of the forensics agents ventured. 'Because this is one hell of a shocking image.'

'I don't think so,' Garcia countered. 'Just look at this setting.' He indicated the victim on the cross. 'It's shocking enough without the lobsters, and you've seen this killer's previous crime scenes, right?' He addressed Dr. Slater. 'This guy doesn't need gadgets or gimmicks to make his murders shocking. They simply are.' A sliver of exasperation slid into his voice. 'Like Robert has mentioned before – we might not understand it now . . . we might even never understand it, but there's got to be a meaning behind all this . . . including the lobsters.'

Hunter stepped around the pool of blood on the floor to get a closer look.

Garcia did the same.

Hunter first studied the victim's neck, where he saw no hematomas, no bruises, no ligature marks . . . no signs of any choking or strangulation. The ball-gag in his mouth, together with his lips, were plastered with dried bile and food residue that had dripped down to his chin and bare chest, indicating that Oliver Griffith had vomited during his ordeal . . . probably more than once. Hunter didn't need to move the ball-gag to see that there was still vomit inside his mouth. The sickening smell was strong enough to make his eyes water.

Garcia instinctively took a step back and brought a hand to his face to cover his nose and mouth.

Hunter squatted down to have a look at the fatal wound and at the two lobsters pinned to Oliver Griffith's thighs. The killer had used two large T-shaped taxidermy pins through their bodies to fix them in place. The incisions to both wounds did look very clean and precise.

From his squatting position, Hunter looked up at Oliver. His eyes were closed, but his face was contorted in an expression that gave away the tremendous physical pain that he had gone through – unbearable ... devastating ... final – not to mention the panic ... the horror ... the fear that had undoubtedly taken over Oliver once he'd realized what the Mentor was about to do to him. In his mind, Hunter could practically hear the desperate screams, muffled by the ball-gag in his mouth, as Oliver tried to beg and plead with his attacker.

'Did he bleed out?' Hunter asked, his eyes leaving the body and moving to the pool of blood on the floor.

'That's the assumption,' Dr. Slater explained. 'Just like I mentioned before, the cuts are clean and right at the base of both the penis and the scrotum. The whole of his penile arterial and venous supplies were severed and left undressed. Despite the arteries and veins that form both supplies being small in comparison to the body's major ones, if left unattended ...' Her gaze shifted to the pool of blood on the floor before going back to Hunter. 'In time, the hemorrhage would be fatal.'

'In time?' Garcia asked. 'How long would he have lasted?'

'Very hard to tell,' Dr. Slater replied. 'It would've depended on several factors – his general health, the condition of his heart, and so on. Those would've also dictated how many times he would've lost consciousness. Even without any help, or the use of his hands to try to lessen the bleeding, he could've bled for over an hour before he'd lost over forty percent of his blood. At that point, most of his major organs would've shut down.'

'Any guesses to the time of death?' Hunter asked.

'Just like with the previous victim, the body is already in full rigor mortis, so easily over twelve hours, but given its temperature, I'd say less than twenty. He died sometime in the very early hours of this morning.'

'This is just insane,' Garcia whispered.

'No doubt,' Dr. Slater agreed. 'And then you still have this to add to the insanity.' She called their attention to the words that had been written on the wall.

Hunter got back on his feet and joined Garcia. Their attention finally refocused on the wall to the right of the stairs.

Across a portion of it, about six feet from the floor, fifteen words had been written in large red capital letters that seemed to measure around six to seven inches each.

If there were still any doubts that the atrocities down in that basement belonged to the Mentor, those doubts vanished once both detectives read what was clearly a new line from his 'poem':

'THROUGH THIS SOUL, NO PAIN WILL EVER BE GREATER THAN THE PAIN OF LOSING YOU.'

Hunter unzipped his jumpsuit and reached for his cellphone before snapping a couple of shots of the new line. That done, he approached the wall to have a closer look.

'This is blood,' he stated, instead of asking, an uneasy shiver caressing the back of his neck.

'It is, yes,' Dr. Slater confirmed.

Hunter stepped back from the wall and allowed his stare to crawl back to the pool of blood on the floor.

'The victim's blood.' Once again, not a question.

'Presumably, unless this killer brought a couple of bags of somebody else's blood with him.' Dr. Slater's head tilted slightly right. 'Which given what we have here and what we've seen in his previous crime scenes, wouldn't really surprise anyone, would it? Anyway, for confirmation you'll need to wait for the lab results.'

'This is another change to his MO,' Hunter said, addressing Garcia, who nodded.

'You mean, using blood as ink?' the doctor asked. 'Writing the quote on the wall, instead of on a piece of paper?'

'Yes, that too,' Hunter agreed. 'But there's something else, which is a lot more significant. With the previous two crime scenes,' he explained, 'the killer *forced* his victims to write down the verses from his "poem" before killing them, but this line is written in blood . . . *presumably* the victim's own.' Hunter shook his head. 'No way that the victim wrote that.'

'Not a chance,' Garcia agreed.

'So that must be the killer's handwriting,' Dr. Slater said.

Hunter nodded. 'And that's also probably the reason why the whole line is in block letters, instead of cursive writing. It makes graphology analysis a lot harder.'

The room went quiet for a moment before Garcia spoke again.

'The severed body parts,' he asked, instinctively looking around. 'Have they been found?'

Dr. Slater paused to wipe some of the perspiration from her forehead. The heat from the forensics light was gradually transforming the basement, which had been soundproofed, into a sauna.

'Not yet.' She shook her head. 'But we're looking.'

'How about the victim's cellphone?' Hunter, this time. 'Has it been found?'

Another head shake from Dr. Slater. 'Not down here, in the living room or in the kitchen. We haven't looked through the rest of the house yet.'

Hunter rounded the pool of blood to get back to the stairs. 'We'll get out of your hair and let you guys finish down here, Susan, but I'll stick around for a while, so please let me know if you come across anything new.'

'Of course,' Dr. Slater replied. 'Will you be outside?'

'Eventually, but I need to go talk to the victim's wife first. From what I understand, she found the body.'

'That's also my understanding,' the doctor agreed. 'But she's in shock, Robert. You won't get any info out of her . . . not today.'

'I'm not going to question her,' Hunter said, taking the first step back upstairs. 'I'm going to warn her.'

Fifty-five

As Hunter and Garcia came up from the basement into the kitchen, Garcia's attention moved back to the rose petals on the floor and he let go of a heavy breath.

'You know?' he said, his voice sounding tired. 'A moment ago, when I told the CSI agent downstairs that there would be a reason why this killer had pinned two, full-sized lobsters, to his victim's thighs . . .' He shook his head. 'I'm not sure if I really believe that, or if that was just me going into "automatic cop-talk".'

Hunter paused and looked back at him, his stare analytical.

Garcia shrugged. 'I don't know, Robert. We have two crime scenes prior to this one and there was no animal, or sea creature, or insect, or any other extinguished life forms other than the victims themselves, and that was already mind-boggling on its own.' He leaned against the kitchen sink. 'I'm starting to think that there might not be any meaning behind any of this. What if this killer is just plain nuts, trying to outdo himself with every murder? What if all this . . . the brutality . . . the super-complex MO . . . the quotes he leaves behind . . . the lobsters downstairs . . . the crazy, over-the-top kill methods . . . what if all of this is just to mess with us? Because nowadays, anyone who watches any TV knows that detectives can't disregard anything that's found at a crime scene.' He broadly indicated the rose petals on the floor. 'And now the killer has chosen a male victim. Another complete jump from what we had.' Garcia used both hands to scratch his chin. 'There's some crazy part of my mind that can actually picture this freak sitting in a room, licking the cream out of Oreos and talking to himself like . . .' He put on a silly voice. ' "*I know, I'm going to drop by the supermarket, grab me a couple of lobsters and leave them at the next crime scene. Let's see what kind of crazy shit the LAPD makes of it.*"'

Hunter could easily understand his partner's frustration, but he also knew that frustration was something that they had to deal with every day. It came with the job. And Garcia knew that too.

'Hey,' he asked. 'Are you OK? Everything alright?'

Garcia pulled down his jumpsuit hood and ran a hand through his hair.

'Yeah,' he replied, after a few silent seconds. 'I'm fine. Just . . . feeling a little helpless, you know?' He gestured toward the basement.

'Yes, I know . . . and some of those same thoughts have bothered me as well, but all of this seems way too personal for it to be some madman just trying to outdo himself . . . even the seemingly crazy, over-the-top kill methods.' Hunter used the fingers in his right hand to indicate the victims. 'Victims one and three were murdered in two completely different ways, but in their own houses . . . victim two was also murdered in a very different way, but she was taken away, killed somewhere else, then brought back to her house . . . why? Why go through all that trouble and risk?'

Garcia took a moment. 'Because the killer wanted them to die in that specific way. No other way would do.'

'Exactly,' Hunter agreed. 'These crazy, over-the-top kill methods have been specifically tailored to each victim. There's got to be a reason behind it other than simple madness.'

Garcia nodded. 'I really hope so, because right now, I feel like I'm the one losing my mind.' He took a deep breath and recomposed himself. 'Do you need me upstairs with you?'

Hunter checked the time – 12:33 a.m.

'No, I don't think it's necessary,' he replied. 'I won't be long.'

'I'll be outside then,' Garcia said back, gesturing toward the window. 'Some of the neighbors are clearly awake, so we might as well have a shot at a few quick questions now. I'll co-ordinate the efforts with the Sheriff's Department and the LAPD. Whoever we don't talk to tonight, we'll come back to in the morning.'

'Good idea. I'll meet you out there in a few.'

Garcia stopped by the kitchen door. 'You know that it won't really matter if you warn her or not, right?' His eyes moved to the ceiling to indicate upstairs. 'Human curiosity will trump any explanation you give her. No matter how clear.'

Hunter nodded, knowing that his partner was probably right. 'All I can do is try, Carlos.'

This time, Hunter knew that Garcia had noticed the worry in his voice.

Fifty-six

In the living room, before taking the stairs up to the second floor, Hunter got rid of his forensics jumpsuit. The last thing that Josie Griffith needed right then was for a stranger dressed like 'Doctor Death' to walk into her room.

As he reached the landing upstairs, he could hear hushed voices coming from the room at the far end of the corridor, where a door had been left ajar. To his right, there was a dresser where a vase displayed a beautiful flower arrangement of red roses and purple azaleas. Hunter picked up one of the roses and brought it to his nose. A very faint fragrance – the same fragrance he'd picked up from the petals on the kitchen floor. Forensics would have to come dust upstairs as well.

Surrounding the vase was a selection of photographs in expensive looking frames – wedding pictures, Josie as a cheerleader in high school, Josie graduating from university, Oliver posing with a tennis racket and with a group of friends – a typical 'couple in love . . . happy home' display.

Hunter returned the rose to the vase and made his way down the corridor.

'Mrs. Griffith?' he called at the door, his voice not too loud. His knock, despite being gentle, managed to push the door open a little more, just enough for him to be able to see inside.

Lying on a large four-poster bed, facing away from the door, was a tall, blonde woman. She was hugging a pillow, which she also had her face buried into, but she wasn't asleep. Hunter knew that because he could see her shoulders move as she sobbed. Even with her face hidden, Hunter recognized Josie Griffith from the photographs he'd just seen.

A shorthaired brunette woman sat next to her, her right hand gently caressing Josie's hair.

In hearing Hunter's voice, the brunette woman turned to look at him. She too was crying. Her tears had made her mascara and eyeliner run down her cheeks, creating a criss-cross of thin black lines that disappeared under her chin.

According to Sergeant Logan, this would be Josie Griffith's best friend, Stacey Green.

Across the room from where the door was, a tall and skinny man stood by the window. Stacey's fiancé, Scott Summers. He also turned to look at Hunter. The look in his bloodshot eyes was anxious . . . disbelieving . . . full of fear.

There was no one else in the room, which meant that Sergeant Logan and her partner had probably already left.

Neither Stacey nor Scott said anything. Their desperately sad stares simply settled on Hunter, as if they were waiting for even more terrible news.

Hunter greeted them with a courteous nod before taking a step into the room.

'Has she been sedated?' he whispered.

'Yes, but nothing too heavy,' Stacey whispered back before wiping new tears from her smudged face. 'She's not asleep.'

'Mrs. Griffith,' Hunter said again, his tone soft but steady.

Josie didn't move.

'I'm Detective Robert Hunter with the LAPD.' He paused and waited.

Josie still didn't move.

'I'm terribly sorry for your loss,' Hunter said, filling in the pause. 'I'm also terribly sorry for having to disturb you at this hour, but I really need a moment of your time.'

That seemed to wake up Scott.

'Sorry, Detective,' he said, taking a step toward Hunter. His voice was shaky. 'But couldn't this wait? I know that you are just doing your job and you need a whole bunch of questions answered, but—'

'I'm not here to ask Mrs. Griffith any questions.' Hunter interrupted him before addressing Josie again. 'I just really need you to listen to me . . . please. It's terribly important.'

Josie finally let go of the pillow and twisted her body on the bed to look at Hunter. Her eyes were so red and puffy, it looked like she'd been in a fist-fight . . . and lost. She was still sobbing.

Hunter took a moment to gather himself. He needed to choose the right words.

'Will you be staying with your friends?' he first asked. His nod made it clear that he was referring to the couple in the room.

'Yes.' The reply, once again, came from Stacey, who nodded first at Hunter, then at her fiancé before looking at Josie. 'You'll be staying with us, honey.' She bent down to give Josie a hug, but Josie didn't respond, her body, rigid . . . her stare, borderline catatonic.

The reason for Hunter's question was because the information he was about to share was sensitive to the investigation. The fewer people who knew about it, the better, but he still had to make it sound as if what he was about to tell them wasn't a certainty.

'I know that this will sound strange,' he began, 'but the reason why I'm here . . . the reason why the LAPD is taking over from the Sheriff's Department is because there are a few similarities between the crime scene downstairs and a previous one that we are already investigating.'

The surprise around the room was uniform.

Scott seemed ready to ask the first question, but Hunter paused him with a hand gesture.

'Let me please explain everything first. If you have any questions, I can answer them all at the end.'

Scott took a step back.

'Do you have your phone with you, Mrs. Griffith?' he asked.

It took Josie's brain a couple of seconds to register the question.

'Yes,' she replied, her voice faltering. 'It's in my handbag.' She aimlessly looked around the room. Her stare was so distant and lost that it went over her handbag, which was on a chair by the door to the en suite bathroom, and she didn't register it. 'I don't know where it is. Why?'

Hunter breathed out. This next part would be tricky.

As simply and as calmly as he could, Hunter explained to Josie that if this was the same perpetrator that they were after, she would get a message sometime in the next day or two. He told her that the message would come from an unknown number and that the first word in the message, so it showed on her screen preview, would most probably be *Oliver*, all in capital letters, to truly grab her attention. He then explained that the message would probably contain footage of something that she really did not want to see or hear . . . or maybe just a photo, or a recorded sound. Something that would add considerable weight to the psychological battle that she was already fighting.

As Hunter told her all this, he saw everyone's expression go from lost and desperately sad to total confusion and disbelief.

'Why?' Scott asked, his gaze bouncing from Josie to Hunter. 'Why would anybody send such a message?'

'We don't know the reason why he does it,' Hunter replied, his voice balanced, his tone sincere. 'But we do know that he does it.' He addressed Josie again. 'And that's why I'm here, Mrs. Griffith – to ask you to not look at the message. Don't read the words. Don't look at any images. Don't play any video

footage. Don't listen to any audio files . . . no matter how entic-
ing the message title is.' From his pocket, he retrieved a couple of
calling cards. 'If you receive such a message, please, contact me
straight away, whatever time of day or night.' He placed one of
the cards on the bed, in front of Josie, and handed the other one
to Stacey.

Josie's eyes moved to the card, where it stayed for several long
seconds, but once again, her stare seemed distant and lost. She
was clearly struggling with logic, trying to comprehend what
seemed incomprehensible. When her gaze went back to Hunter,
he could tell that she had a million questions that she wanted to
ask, but right then, it looked like she would fail to put even the
simplest of sentences together. Instead, Josie collapsed back onto
the bed, burying her face back in the pillow.

There was nothing else Hunter could do, other than hope that
he'd done enough. As he stepped out of the room, Scott rushed
out after him.

'Detective?'

Hunter turned to face him.

'Is Josie at risk?' he asked, as he pulled the bedroom door
closed behind him. 'You know, this whole thing about this message . . . about whoever did that to Ollie, sending Josie a photo,
or a video, or an audio file . . . does that mean she's in danger?'

Hunter met his pleading stare.

'Please, Detective, don't bullshit me. I'm an attorney.'

Hunter failed to see why Scott's profession would have any
relevance in him telling Scott the truth or not.

'As far as we know,' Hunter replied, 'no. So far, this perp
hasn't targeted his victims' loved ones, but the contents of the
message that he sends them are truly devastating.' He nodded
at the bedroom door behind Scott. 'Right now, and understandably so, Mrs. Griffith's state of mind is skating on very
thin ice. The killer knows this. The message that he sends is

like a heavy hammer on that ice. It will create cracks every-where, with a very real possibility of sending her through.' Hunter paused, giving Scott a few seconds to grasp the urgency of it all. 'That's why it's terribly important that she doesn't look at this message, and that she contacts me straight away, if she ever gets it.'

Scott shifted his weight, trying to find balance. 'I know that Stacey will stay with Josie twenty-four seven. I'll reinforce the importance of it all to her.'

'Thank you.'

As Scott turned to return to Josie's bedroom, Hunter stopped him.

'How well did you know Mr. Griffith?'

Scott blinked, angled his head and shrugged. 'Ollie was one of my best friends.'

'I assume that you have been downstairs?'

Scott looked down at his shoes before bringing both hands to his face and cupping them over his nose and mouth. He nodded, unable to meet Hunter's eyes.

'Was Mr. Griffith allergic to shellfish?' Hunter asked. 'Lobsters in particular. Was he scared of them? Or maybe they were his favorite dish? Do you know?'

Scott breathed in and out to steady himself. 'Josie would be able to give you a more definite answer here, but as far as I'm aware, none of that's true. I know that he wasn't allergic to them because we've had them at a couple of restaurants before. He also wasn't scared of them. As for his favorite dish, I'm pretty certain it was pasta.'

Hunter's instinct had been that the answer to the lobster conundrum wouldn't be anything as simple as that, but he'd had to try.

'If I could ask you one last question,' he ventured. 'I take it that you also saw what was written on the wall in the basement.'

A new nod from Scott, but this time it carried no conviction. 'I did, but I can't really remember what it said.'

That was all the answer Hunter needed. If Scott couldn't remember the words, then the quote meant nothing to him.

Fifty-seven

By eight o'clock the next morning, Hunter and Garcia were both back at the Police Administration Building. By nine-thirty, they'd already printed all the crime-scene photographs that were taken by Dr. Slater's forensics team. Half an hour after that, Captain Blake was standing, dumbfounded, in front of the picture board inside the UVC Unit's office.

'What the . . .' She shook her head, as she turned to look at both detectives. 'Are those real lobsters?'

'Yep,' Garcia replied.

'And a male victim, this time,' the captain continued, her gaze skipping from Garcia to Hunter. 'Why? Why the change all of a sudden?'

'To us it might look sudden, Captain,' Hunter replied. 'But it wasn't to the killer.'

'How would you know that?'

'Because this killer pre-selects his victims. We've figured that much out. He studies them, he observes them, and he plans ahead. There's something very personal about everything he does, especially his victim selection.'

'Are you telling me that you think that these victims aren't strangers to the killer?' Captain Blake asked. 'He knows them?'

'Yes,' Hunter said. 'I believe he does.' His head tilted sideways in a somewhat frustrated gesture. 'We're still working on how and to what degree.'

The captain nodded before facing the board again. 'And those are the victim's only wounds? No head trauma? No strangulation marks? No other cuts? Nothing?'

'That's correct.' Garcia again. 'We need to wait for the autopsy report to be sure, but the theory is that he bled out.'

Captain Blake's gaze moved to a close-up photo of both of Oliver Griffith's wounds, but it only managed to stay there for a couple of seconds before her stomach knotted. She cringed and looked away. 'And what's the theory on the lobsters? Because this just looks crazy.'

Garcia glanced at Hunter, who in turn, looked back at him, but neither offered the captain an answer.

'I mean,' she pushed, 'it's obvious that the killer didn't really use the lobsters to inflict those wounds, so what's the deal here? Was this part of the killer's "fear lesson"? Did the victim have a phobia of lobsters? Were they used as some sort of psychological torture to heighten his terror?'

'We don't know the reason for the lobsters yet, Captain.' Hunter replied. 'You're right, this killer does feed on his victims' fear, but the victim didn't have a phobia of lobsters. I checked. He wasn't allergic to them either.'

Captain Blake took a step back from the board. 'And we're sure that nothing similar to this was found in any of the previous two crime scenes? Maybe hidden away somewhere, instead of on the victim's body?'

'We're sure,' Garcia confirmed.

The captain's hands came up in a 'what the hell' gesture. 'So the only thing that links all three crime scenes together . . . all three murders, is this?' She pointed at a photo of the words that had been written on the wall inside Oliver and Josie Griffith's basement. 'Lines quoted from something, and we have no real idea what the source is.' Her hands dropped by her sides, as if she was giving up. 'How sure are we that this is really the same perp?'

'One hundred percent sure, Captain,' Hunter countered. On the board, he indicated the list that showed the seven stages of the killer's modus operandi. 'His MO is too complex to be copied . . . too complex for freaky coincidences. This is the same killer. No doubt.'

Captain Blake quickly read through the simplified list on the board.

One – fear.
Two – capture.
Three – note/poem.
Four – torture.
Five – murder.
Six – staging.
Seven – aftermath.

'Well, I've got questions,' the captain said, her eyebrows lifting at Hunter. 'The first stage, fear. Has that been confirmed with this new victim?'

'We're waiting on the files from Mr. Griffith's cellphone provider, Verizon,' Garcia said, joining Hunter and Captain Blake by the picture board. 'I put in a request first thing this morning, and I made it very clear that if there are any photos, videos, or audio files attached to any messages that he might've received in the forty-eight hours prior to his death, that they *must* be included.'

'Timeframe?' the captain asked.

'Tomorrow, if we're lucky.'

Her gaze shifted back to the list. 'OK, new question – why would this killer, all of a sudden, change some of his MO? Like on the third stage. This time he didn't force the victim to write down the line from his poem, or whatever it is, onto a piece of paper. He splattered it all over the wall.'

'And the assumption is that the killer used the victim's blood as ink,' Garcia added. 'Also waiting for confirmation from the lab.'

The captain's head dipped left as she looked back at Garcia. 'So that means that the victim didn't write this. The killer did?'

'That's the assumption.'

'Which would constitute a sizable change from his original MO, wouldn't it?' Captain Blake's question was aimed at both detectives. 'At least when it comes to stage three. Why would he do that?'

'We were discussing exactly that when you arrived, Captain,' Garcia replied.

'OK, and?'

'And we haven't reached any conclusions yet,' Hunter took over. 'But if you think about it, it's not exactly a change to his MO, Captain. It's almost as if he's . . . adapting.'

'Adapting?'

Hunter nodded. 'He's done it before – from the first murder to the second, and now from the second to the third.'

The captain's stare skittered back to the board, first to Melissa Hawthorne's note, then to Kirsten Hansen's, and finally to the one in Oliver Griffith's basement.

'I don't follow,' she said. 'Both of the previous notes were written onto a piece of paper, and we've also confirmed that both notes were written by the victims themselves. Where has the killer "adapted" from the first to the second note?'

'The location,' Hunter explained, indicating on the board. 'With his first victim, the killer hid the note inside the victim's body. The note was only found at the autopsy examination. With the second victim, the killer left the note securely in the victim's hand. The note was found at the crime scene by the forensics team.' He looked at Garcia. 'We were there when they found it.'

Garcia nodded.

'And this time, no paper and no victim's handwriting. The note was written on the wall.'

'OK, I see that, but why? What is he adapting to? And what difference does it make where he leaves the note?'

'I'm not exactly sure,' Hunter said. 'That's where we were getting to when you got here.'

Captain Blake lifted her hands, as she took a step back. 'By all means, do carry on. Don't let me stop you.'

Hunter unpinned all three photographs from the board and placed them on his desk in the correct sequence, showing how the 'poem' read so far:

*Through these eyes, no one will ever look as perfect
    as you did.*
*Through this heart, no love will ever surpass my
    love for you.*
*Through this soul, no pain will ever be greater than
    the pain of losing you.*

Hunter indicated each picture as he spoke: 'Melissa Hawthorne – placed inside her body. Kirsten Hansen – placed in the grip of her right hand. Oliver Griffith – written onto the wall.'

Captain Blake's gaze bounced from one detective to the other. 'And that tells us what?'

'My first thought,' Hunter ventured, 'was that maybe the words in each line would give us a clue to why the killer changed locations from one note to the other, but I've read them a million times and can't see it. Can anyone?'

Garcia and Captain Blake reread all three lines.

'Not really,' the captain replied.

Garcia agreed.

'So maybe the answer isn't in the lines themselves,' Hunter suggested. 'Maybe it's something a lot simpler.'

'Like maybe the killer is just messing with us?' Captain Blake asked, a hint of disdain creeping into her tone. 'Because just look at these lines. It's clear that they read like a love poem, but now, after three victims and three verses . . . this can't be about love. This killer is fucking with us, guys. He's been doing it from the start.'

'There's always a chance of that,' Hunter admitted. 'But with such complex MO . . . such violence . . . such preparation before every attack . . . this killer seems to have a hell of a lot more pur-pose than "just messing with us", Captain.' He paused. 'And I'm sure you know this, but most serial killers who employ things like love or religious symbols, for example, are not actually killing in the name of love, or in the name of God. They grab onto those symbols as an excuse . . . a justification for their compulsion, but it's the compulsion itself that makes them kill, not the love or the religious impulse.'

'So what do you suggest, Robert?' she asked.

Hunter faced the board again and as he did, an odd feeling came over him. It was as if he knew that the dots were all there. Dots that lined up to a shape he couldn't yet see . . . that his brain couldn't yet connect because he had missed something. He knew that he needed to go back and look at everything from a different perspective.

'Well,' he began. 'We've worked plenty of cases before where perpetrators have left notes behind . . . hidden at the crime scene . . . in plain sight . . . inside victims' bodies . . . etched on their skin . . .'

'Yes, I know,' Captain Blake agreed. 'But never something like this.'

'That's what I mean, Captain,' Hunter came back. 'Ignore the words in the killer's notes for a moment. The primordial reason why perps leave any sort of note behind is communication. Yes, it's an odd way of doing so, but that's what they're doing – communicating. The key question here would be – with whom?' He lifted a finger to halt all the questions for a second. 'Nine out of ten times, the killer is communicating with the investigating team – local PD, Sheriff's office, FBI, whoever. But what if that isn't the case here? What if this "poem" isn't meant for us?'

The thoughtful silence that followed lasted a few seconds longer than Hunter had expected.

'Who then?' the captain asked. 'The victims?'

'That's a possibility,' Hunter agreed. 'But if these verses are meant for the victims themselves, then I'm afraid that their true meaning dies with them.'

'What other options do we have?'

'We've got two,' Hunter replied, lifting two fingers. 'The victims' loved ones, or the media.'

'The media?'

'It makes a weird sort of sense,' Garcia, this time, finally riding Hunter's train of thought.

Captain Blake turned to look at him.

'In all fairness, Captain,' Garcia explained, 'this killer has no real way of knowing if his "notes" have been found or not. Think about it. The first note was left inside the victim's body. Like Robert explained, it was only found at the post mortem examination, but it could've been missed. We've all worked cases where important clues weren't picked up at the post mortem, for one reason or another.' He shrugged at the captain.

'The only way the killer would've known for certain if that first note had been found or not,' Hunter took over again, 'was if he had a contact within our unit, which he doesn't, or if something had appeared in the media.'

'Which it didn't,' Garcia again. 'Because we never mentioned anything. The only ones who knew about it were Dr. Hove and us. Not even the forensics team that attended that first scene were aware of it.'

'Now let's suppose that the killer thought that his first note hadn't been found,' Hunter continued. 'So with the second murder, he decides to make things a little simpler and places the note somewhere that would be easier to find – in the victim's hand – but again, nothing shows up in media.'

'Hold on . . . hold on.' Captain Blake halted him. 'If the killer wanted his notes to appear in the media, wouldn't it be a lot easier to just send it to them, anonymously? That's happened plenty of times before.'

'True,' Garcia agreed. 'But the media wouldn't be able to print or report anything without coming to us first for confirmation, because whatever they'd received, anonymously, could be a hoax . . . someone looking for attention. That's happened plenty of times before, too.'

Captain Blake couldn't argue with that.

'And if we wanted to keep the notes from being publicized,' Garcia continued, 'so as not to cause an unnecessary hoo-ha around the city, all we had to do was deny it.'

'But the second note was found at the crime scene,' Hunter moved on. 'By Dr. Slater and her team, which means that the circle of people who knew about the killer's notes increased by a few numbers. And as we all know – the more people who knows about something restricted, especially in a homicide case, the bigger the chances of a leak to the press.'

Captain Blake, at last, began to catch on. 'But even though the circle of people who knew about the notes grew, nothing showed up in the media.'

'Exactly,' Hunter agreed. 'Because people who knew about them were still very reliable. No one from Dr. Slater's team would've leaked that sort of info to the press, or anyone else, for that matter. Which means that after the second note, the killer still had no real way of knowing if his notes, or quotes, or whatever, were having the desired effect, because let's face it, Captain,' he indicated the three photos on his desk, 'any perp who leaves something like this at a crime scene is looking for some sort of effect.'

'So with the third victim,' Captain Blake said, now fully on board, 'the killer puts the note on the wall, which would expand the circle of people who have seen or heard about the note exponentially.'

'That's right,' Hunter agreed again. 'The first officer at the scene, plus everyone else who went down to that basement – deputies and detectives from the Sheriff's Department, family friends, the clean-up team, not to mention everyone who those people would've told. Something like that won't stay a secret for too long.'

The captain's fingertips brushed against her temples before she looked back at Hunter. 'Alright, so let's say that you're correct about this, Robert. Why would this killer want the media attention on this? What would he gain?'

'That's the million dollar question, Captain. Maybe he wants to grab the attention of someone else . . . someone unrelated to the crimes. Someone to whom these quotes would mean something.'

Captain Blake thought about that for an instant. As she did, her mouth twisted to the right. 'That's a pretty crazy theory, don't you think, Robert?'

'Maybe,' Garcia jumped back in, broadly indicating the whole of the picture board. 'But what part of this doesn't seem crazy to you, Captain?'

Hunter's attention returned to the three verses on his desk. 'Or maybe not someone unrelated.'

'What?' The captain faced him again.

'I said that maybe the killer wanted the attention of someone else ... someone unrelated to the crimes. Maybe that someone isn't unrelated.'

'Robert.' Captain Blake looked at him sideways. 'If you could start making sense right about now, that would be great. I've got a busy day ahead.'

'With the two first lines,' Hunter explained, 'the only people who have seen them outside the investigating team has been the person who has found the victim's body – Melissa Hawthorne's sister Janet, and Kirsten Hansen's fiancé Troy. They were the ones who identified the handwriting as belonging to the victims themselves, but ...' He looked back at the board, then at the three verses again. 'But they'd only seen the line that was left at the crime scene that they were relevant to. Never the other ones. Janet Lang only saw the first verse. Troy Foster only saw the second. I never showed them both.'

Captain Blake and Garcia both paused, as they mulled over Hunter's words.

'Maybe they are supposed to see everything. The whole poem.'

Garcia and Captain Blake glanced at each other thoughtfully.

'Last night,' the captain asked. 'The person who found the body – the victim's wife – did the line on her wall mean anything to her?'

'We don't know,' Hunter replied. 'I didn't really get to talk to her. She was in total shock.'

'Well,' Garcia said, his voice leaden, 'unfortunately we can't ask Troy Foster anymore, but we can pay Janet Lang a visit.' He nodded at Hunter. 'It's worth a try.'

Hunter read the look in his partner's eyes, and the unspoken ending to Garcia's sentence: *It's worth a try ... because we've got nothing else.*

Fifty-eight

Having to revisit and re-question any person who had discovered a body at the site of a brutal homicide was always a very delicate matter.

In Janet Lang's case, it had only been eight days since she had walked into her sister's house and into the worst nightmare of her life. The magnitude of the trauma that her loss, together with what she saw that morning would bring her, was yet unknown, but it would be life-changing.

Despite the countless times that Hunter and Garcia had found themselves in this exact situation, neither of them had ever grown accustomed to it ... neither of them believed that they ever would ... but neither of them could escape it. It came with the job.

Hunter called ahead to check if Janet would be home and if she could spare just a few minutes of her time. The call was once again answered by Tom, her boyfriend, who was reluctant at first, arguing that Janet had already been through too much – she was now struggling with post-traumatic stress and night terrors, and more questions could only make matters worse for her. However, after Hunter promised him that they really only needed to ask Janet one single question, and no more, Tom finally agreed.

It was past midday when Tom showed Hunter and Garcia into the apartment. Janet was sitting at their table in the living room, staring blankly out the window.

'That's all she's done for the past week,' Tom informed both detectives. 'If she's not locked in our room, crying her eyes out, she sits by the window and stares at nothing at all. She barely eats. She barely sleeps, and when she does, chances are that she'll wake up screaming and shaking. It's breaking my heart because I don't know how to help her.'

There was no sound advice that either Hunter or Garcia could offer. Grief was a very individual feeling, one that came with no expiry date and everyone dealt with it differently. What worked for one person wouldn't necessarily work for someone else. The only common factor was always time, and that was something that only Janet could give herself.

Hunter reached into his pocket for a card.

'I know that Janet probably won't want to leave the house for some time,' he said, as he handed the card to Tom. 'But this is one of the best psychologists in LA, who specializes in post-traumatic stress. She can and she will help Janet, whenever she's ready to see someone. Please give her a call.'

'Thank you, Detective,' Tom said, taking the card. 'But I don't think we can afford one of the best psychologists in LA . . .'

Hunter shook his head. 'She's a very good friend of mine. I've already talked to her. She'll see Janet without charge. Just give her a ring whenever Janet is ready, OK?'

In silence, Tom stared at the name on the card for several long seconds before placing it in his back pocket.

'Baby,' he called. 'Detective Hunter is here to see you.'

Janet broke eye contact with the window to look back at her boyfriend and his two guests. She wore pajama pants and a high school football shirt, under a pink and white bathrobe. She looked to have lost at least fifteen pounds in the past week.

'Hello Miss Lang,' Hunter said, greeting her with a head nod. 'This is my partner, Detective Carlos Garcia.'

'It's a pleasure to meet you, Miss Lang,' Garcia said, stepping forward and offering Janet his hand, but she simply stared at it for a couple of seconds before turning to face the window again.

'Have you caught the monster who murdered my sister, Detective?' The question was thrown at Hunter with the force of an angry whip. 'Or are you here to tell me that "you're doing the best you can" . . . again?'

'I'm here to ask you for your help, Miss Lang,' Hunter replied. His voice carried a tone that spoke of importance.

'My help?'

Hunter stepped forward while Garcia took a step back.

'I want to ask you if you could please have a look at something for me. See if you maybe recognize it . . . if any of it means anything to you at all.'

Janet's gaze skipped to Hunter . . . darted away . . . darted back to him. Her hair was a mess. Her skin seemed dried and blotchy, and Hunter could almost see each sleepless night in the thin criss-cross of veins beneath her sad eyes.

She studied him for several silent seconds.

'What is it that you want me to look at?' she finally asked.

Hunter reached into his jacket pocket for the piece of paper where he had written all three lines from the Mentor's 'poem'. He thought that it would be better not to show her the photographs of the original writing found at each crime scene for two very strong reasons. One – because the first example carried her sister's handwriting, and that could trigger an avalanche of undesirable images in her mind. And two – because the third example had been written in blood.

He placed the piece of paper on the table in front of her.

'This reads like a poem, Miss Lang,' he explained. 'But it could be just about anything . . . the lyrics to a song, some sort of riddle, a love letter . . .' With a shrug, Hunter allowed the sentence to evaporate in the air. 'We're not really sure. We can't find any reference to any of it anywhere.'

As Janet's attention moved to the piece of paper, Tom circled around Hunter and Garcia to get to the table.

Hunter's stare stayed on Janet, looking for an eye twitch, a lip bite, a movement of the mouth, an arching of an eyebrow . . . anything that could signal some sort of recognition. He saw a frown, followed by a slight angling of the head.

Tom, on the other hand, kept a puzzled expression throughout.

'Didn't you show me this before?' Janet asked. 'Isn't this what you told me was found in my sister's house, in her handwriting?'

Hunter nodded. 'Yes, I did show you this before, but not all of it. The first of the three lines was found at your sister's house. I know that you said you didn't recognize it at first, but I thought that maybe, now in a more complete form, it might trigger a memory, or something.'

'I'm a little confused,' Tom said, lifting a hand at Hunter. 'You just said that you couldn't find any reference to any of this anywhere. So where did the other two lines come from then?'

'That's a good question,' Janet joined forces with her boyfriend. 'What aren't you telling us, Detective?'

Hunter and Garcia exchanged a look that seemed like a conversation.

'That first line was found in your sister's kitchen,' Hunter began, remembering the story he had spun when he first showed it to Janet and Tom. 'Left by the stove.'

The look Garcia gave his partner was subtle enough not to be noticed by either Janet or Tom.

'At first,' Hunter continued, 'we didn't know if there was any real connection between those words and what happened that day. Especially because, as you told me, the line was in your sister's handwriting. It could've been something that she copied out of a book, or something, and left by the stove the night before . . .'

'At first?' Tom questioned.

Hunter's gaze dropped to the piece of paper on the table, as he nodded. 'The other two lines were found at two other, separate crime scenes.'

'*What?*' The question came from Janet and Tom at the exact same time.

'Both new lines followed the same pattern.' Hunter had to go with another white lie. 'What I mean is – they were found close enough to the victim, they carried the victim's handwriting, and as you can see by the first three words in each of them, they seem to belong to the same composition.'

Janet and Tom, both allowed their eyes to return to the piece of paper on the table.

Hunter and Garcia waited.

'Hold on a sec,' Janet said, looking completely unsure. 'Are you trying to tell me that my sister was the victim of a serial killer?'

'That's what it seems like,' Garcia confirmed.

Anxiety filled the room.

'Why?' Janet asked, her desperate stare bouncing from person to person without a final destination. 'Why my sister?'

'That's what we're trying to find out, Miss Lang,' Hunter replied. 'But the truth is, only her attacker really knows why he chose your sister over someone else. He could've seen her walking down the road and become obsessed with her. They could've met in a coffee shop, or in a lounge and she rejected his advances. There really is no telling, and more often than not the reasons behind such choices are only logical to the attacker.'

'In most cases,' Garcia added, 'it's like their brains are wired differently. Some feel a lot more rage and anger than most of us, making them much more violent. Some feel absolutely nothing at all – no sympathy, no remorse, no pity ... nothing.'

Hunter could tell that Janet was struggling to hold herself together.

'I really don't want to take much more of your time, Miss

Lang,' he said, before indicating the piece of paper yet again. 'Do any of those verses mean anything to you … separately or together? Maybe something that your sister might've shown you at some point, or maybe commented on?'

Janet questioned Hunter with a half confused look.

'I thought that this could possibly have been a poem,' he explained. 'Something that an ex-boyfriend, or an admirer gave her. Someone who might've been desperately in love with her?'

Janet's head shook before her lips moved. 'No. None of it means anything to me. And I don't remember my sister ever showing me or even mentioning anything about anyone sending her or writing her something like this, either. This is just crazy.' Her tears finally became too much for her.

Hunter offered her a paper tissue.

'Thank you.'

Janet dabbed her eyes and took a few seconds to recompose herself. 'Who were the other ones?' The pleading tone in her voice matched the look in her eyes. 'You said that the other two verses were found in two separate crime scenes. Who were the other victims?'

Hunter and Garcia both knew that that question would come. Hunter reached for his cellphone and loaded up a photo of the Mentor's second victim.

'This is Kirsten Hansen,' he said, as he offered his phone to Janet. 'She was a nurse at the Los Angeles Surge Hospital in Westlake. She used to live in Alhambra. She was the same age as your sister.'

Janet took the phone from Hunter's hands and stared at the photo for just a few seconds.

'I've seen this photo before,' she said. 'Tom showed it to me a couple of days ago.'

'I know,' Hunter agreed. 'I sent it to him and asked him to ask you if the woman in the photo looked familiar at all.'

'Yes, and I told him she didn't.'

'Are you certain that she wasn't a friend of your sister's?' Garcia jumped in. 'She doesn't look familiar in any way?'

Janet shook her head once again. 'No, I've never seen her before.'

'Are you sure?' Garcia prodded. 'Please take your time.'

'She's a very pretty woman,' Janet replied. 'Very easy face to remember. If she was a friend of Melissa's, I never saw them together.'

Hunter reached for his phone, loaded up a photo of Oliver Griffith and returned the phone to the table.

'This is Oliver Griffith,' he told them. 'He worked for an advertisement agency in Playa Vista and lived in Valencia, in Santa Clarita. He too was the same age as Melissa.'

This time, Janet and Tom looked back at Hunter with surprise in their eyes.

'A guy?' Tom asked. 'One of the victims was male?'

'That's right,' Garcia confirmed.

'Hold on,' Tom said, his eyes moving back to the photo, then to the verses on the table. 'Is this normal? I mean, don't serial killers usually stick to the same type of victim – all blondes, or all blacks, or all men, or something?'

'Not exactly,' Garcia replied. 'That's a misconception that gained a lot of strength through movies and TV series. In reality, the only rules serial killers follow, if they do follow any, would be the ones that they create themselves, and those can change at any time. In a lot of cases, what triggers them – what guides them to pick one victim over another – could be something that not even they understand themselves. It's an urge . . . a drive that they can't really control.'

'Does his face look familiar at all?' Hunter pushed, driving Tom and Janet's focus back to the photo.

'No,' Janet replied first. 'I can't say I've ever seen him before.

His name doesn't sound familiar either.' She looked at her boyfriend, who shook his head.

'No,' Tom said. 'I don't recall ever seeing him either.'

For a brief moment, Hunter's gaze dropped to his shoes before he nodded and collected his phone from the table.

'Thank you both for your time,' he said. 'We appreciate you having a look at these.'

'What do you suggest we do now, Robert?' Garcia's frustrated question came as soon as he and Hunter got back to his car. 'We can't go ask Troy Foster to have a look at those lines, or the photos. Do you want to try the same with Josie Griffith?'

Hunter sighed. 'I'd love to, but it's too soon to approach her. It's been less than twenty-four hours since she found her husband. Chances are, she either didn't sleep a wink last night, or she's been sedated to a zombie state. Either way, her brain will be mush. Words and images won't make much sense to her right now. We'll need to give it a few days.'

'My thoughts exactly,' Garcia said, as he got behind the wheel. 'So where to?'

Hunter buckled up on the passenger's seat. 'How about we go back to the Griffiths's house for a second look? It's a big house and we didn't get to really look around last night.'

Garcia nodded as he turned on his engine. 'Sounds good to me.'

Fifty-nine

In the hour and a quarter that it took Garcia to drive from Leimert Park to Santa Clarita, the sky above Los Angeles went from beach blue to doomsday gray. Heavy clouds had gathered from all corners, promising the rain that could already be seen falling in the distance, over Los Padres National Forest.

'Wow,' Garcia said, zipping up his jacket, as he once again parked on the road in front of Oliver and Josie Griffith's house. 'That's one hell of an angry-looking sky.'

'It is,' Hunter agreed, his eyes scanning the clouds. 'But the wind is blowing north and we're south-east from that.' He pointed west, toward the rain. 'If we're lucky, we might not get the full force of the downpour.'

'I really hope you're right. With heavy rain, the canyon becomes an aqueduct. We really don't want to get stuck there.'

The house was still surrounded by black and yellow crime-scene tape. At the door, a very bored-looking Sheriff's deputy with a peppery horseshoe moustache got both detectives to sign the crime-scene manifest.

'Clean-up team hasn't been in yet?' Hunter asked.

'They're scheduled to be here in about two hours,' the deputy replied, giving Hunter a single shoulder shrug.

Back inside the house, Hunter and Garcia started with the basement. Despite the body not being there anymore, the air was still heavy with the unique smell of death – an ever changing, odd, and very hard to describe scent that tended to scratch the nostrils and knot the steadiest of stomachs – but that wasn't all. The whole atmosphere at the bottom of those stairs seemed saturated with something else . . . something that made the air dense and a little harder to breathe, as if Oliver Griffith's fear and desperation had stayed behind, clinging to the walls like old paint. The pool of blood still covered most of the floor. The words that the Mentor had scribed onto the wall were still there – ominous . . . challenging.

'Of all the crime scenes I've revisited in my life . . .' Garcia said, turning to face the X-shaped cross where they'd found Oliver's body. 'This one, somehow . . .' He shook his head, unable to find the right words to finish his sentence.

Hunter tucked his hands into his pockets. 'Neither of us really know what we're looking for in here, Carlos. If we spread out . . .' His eyes moved up to indicate the rest of the house. 'We can cover more ground in less time and maybe we can get out of here before the rain catches us. What do you think?'

Garcia didn't need any further persuasion.

'Fine by me. I'll look around upstairs.'

Hunter didn't take long in the basement. It was true that he didn't really know what he was looking for, but he did know that Dr. Slater's team would've been as thorough as humanly possible. If there were something else to be found down there, they would've already found it.

This time, Hunter also didn't try to visualize what had happened. There was no real mystery to it. The Mentor had simply strapped Oliver Griffith to the St. Andrew's cross, mutilated his body and left him to bleed to death.

Back upstairs, Hunter met Garcia on the second floor landing, by the dresser with the photo frames and the vase displaying roses and azaleas. The roses looked to be dying, but the azaleas were in full bloom.

'You OK?' Hunter asked, noticing the look in his partner's eyes.

'I didn't know that they were practically newlyweds,' he said, indicating a photo of Oliver and Josie on their wedding night. 'It's dated six months ago.' He consulted his watch for the date. 'Actually, it would've been exactly six months in four days.'

Hunter's attention moved to the photo.

'Six months, Robert,' Garcia continued. 'They were still in that amazing honeymoon period, where everything is still just awesome. You're still discovering stuff together ... stuff about each other ... making crazy plans for the future ... maybe they were even planning on having kids.'

Hunter knew that Garcia was thinking of his wife, Anna. It was another natural, neurological reflex. When faced with any sort of tragedy to which they could somehow relate, the human brain would, most often than not, think of the people we loved the most.

'They looked to be a very happy couple,' Garcia added, indicating another photo.

But Hunter's attention had moved three frames to the right of the picture that Garcia was talking about, making him pause, as he frantically searched his memory for something that he knew was there, he just needed to find it.

One ... two ... three seconds.

There it was.

One single piece.

One single connecting piece that reshaped the entire puzzle.

Garcia was quick to see the change in his partner's demeanor.

'Are *you* OK?' he asked. 'You look like you're waiting to go see a dentist.'

Hunter didn't look back at him. All he did was mutter a single sentence in a tone that sounded full of regret.

'We've got this so wrong, Carlos.'

'What?' Garcia blinked, trying to follow Hunter's gaze. 'What do you mean, Robert? What are you looking at?'

Hunter indicated a specific item, on a specific photo. 'Look familiar?'

Garcia didn't see it at first. It took his brain an extra couple of seconds to make a partial connection, but even a partial connection was enough to shake his core. He looked back at Hunter wide-eyed.

'Sonofabitch!'

'Yep.'

Sixty

'Detectives?' a very surprised Tom Foster said, as he, once again, opened the door to his and Janet's apartment to face Hunter and Garcia. 'What brings you back so soon?'

This time, Hunter hadn't called ahead.

'We're sorry to turn up at your door unannounced,' Hunter replied. Though his voice was gentle, it left no room for argument. 'But we really need to ask Miss Lang a couple more questions.'

'What about?' Tom asked, as he held the door semi-open, his body blocking the way in. 'Those crazy quotes again?' There was annoyance in his tone.

'No,' Garcia said. 'Not this time.'

Tom breathed out in a huff. 'Look, it took Janet almost two hours to stop crying after you left.' He checked his watch. 'It's almost six o'clock and she's finally managed to eat something and put her head down for a few minutes. Like I said before, she's barely sleeping at night, so this is a treat for her. I'd really rather you not upset her again, especially with questions that she just can't help you with.'

'That's just it, Mr. Foster,' Garcia again. 'This time, Miss Lang's pretty much one of the very few who can help us.' He kept his tone cordial, but firm. 'Once again, we promise that we won't take much of her time, but this really can't wait.'

'What is it that you need to ask her?' Tom insisted.

'You can sit in, if you like,' Garcia said.

'Oh, I will. There's no doubt about that.'

'Who is it, Tom?' Janet's voice came from somewhere deep within the apartment.

Tom's head dropped, as he pressed his lips together. 'Great,' he whispered. 'You've woken her up.' He turned away from Hunter and Garcia. 'It's the detectives again, baby. They want to ask you something else.'

Janet appeared behind Tom. Her eyes were dry, but still puffy and red. She was still wearing pajama pants and a high school football shirt, under her pink and white bathrobe. Her eyebrows lifted at the detectives, as if she had recognized the seriousness in their expressions. 'Is it about that poetry again?'

'No,' Hunter assured her. 'Something else entirely.'

Janet stood still for a couple of seconds before pulling her bathrobe tightly around her and crossing her arms over her chest. 'I guess you better come in then.'

Tom finally stepped out of the way, allowing both detectives back into the apartment. 'Please don't upset her,' he whispered as Hunter and Garcia walked past him. There was legitimate concern in his tone.

They all returned to the living room table.

Janet, once again, took the chair by the window.

Hunter lost no time.

'Could I ask you, where did you go to school, Miss Lang? Junior high . . . high school . . . was it somewhere around here?'

'No. I didn't live around here when I was in school.' She looked down at the football shirt she was wearing under her robe. Its logo was a large 'G' letter in green, with the face of a black panther coming from its center. Janet pointed to it. 'I went to Gardena High. That's where we lived at the time.' Her head tilted right. 'Well, from eighth grade onwards, I mean. Before that we lived in Inglewood, so from lower school all the way to seventh grade, I went to Morningside.'

'Your sister as well?' Hunter nodded at Janet's shirt.

'No. Mel never went to Gardena High,' Janet explained. 'She stayed in Morningside, even though we moved neighborhoods. She was three years ahead of me, which means that when we moved from Inglewood to Gardena, she was just about to start her senior year. It would've been crazy for her to change schools then.' She shrugged. 'Graduating with a whole bunch of students she just met, while all of her school friends graduated just a few neighborhoods away? For Mel? Not a chance.' She chuckled softly. 'I can remember the arguments she had with Mom about not transferring to Gardena High. Drove Mom nuts, but Mel was Mel, so of course in the end, Mel won. She would wake up like at 5 a.m., sometimes earlier, just to hop on the bus to go back to Morningside. Actually, two buses. And she did it every day . . . for the whole of her senior year.' Her eyes went sad again. 'Mel was a very determined person. If she decided that she wanted to do something . . . she'd just do it.'

'In school, were you part of a tight group of friends?' Garcia asked.

Janet looked at him inquisitively.

'Well,' he tried to clarify, 'in school, especially high school, most kids tend to always hang out with the same bunch of friends . . . the same gang. Do things together, go places together. You know what I mean, right?'

Janet looked confused for a moment. 'Like I said, Mel didn't go to Gardena High. Plus, she was three years ahead of me. We didn't really hang out together in school . . .'

'No, no,' Garcia explained. 'Not you and your sister. Just you. Did you always hang out with the same group of kids when you were in Gardena High?'

Janet frowned and looked at Tom.

'Detectives,' he said, no effort to hide his irritation. 'Could we please just drop the small talk and get to the real questions? That's why you're here, isn't it? So let's just get it over with . . . please.'

'We're not making any small talk,' Garcia said, looking at Hunter.

Hunter reached into his jacket pocket for his cellphone. Already loaded onto its screen was the photo that he had snapped of one of the picture frames on the dresser display on Oliver and Josie's second floor landing.

'Do you, by any chance, recognize this person?' he asked, placing the phone on the table before indicating.

Janet and Tom's intrigued eyes moved to the picture, while Hunter and Garcia studied their expressions. Tom frowned, then twisted his lips, then slightly shook his head. No recognition there.

Janet, on the other hand, paused. Her gaze stayed on the photo for at least five seconds before she blinked.

'Yes, I knew her,' she said, giving both detectives a single nod.

The image on Hunter's screen showed a young Josie Griffith in a white cheerleader uniform, holding a couple of green pompoms. The logo across the front of her uniform was a large 'G' letter in green, with the face of a black panther coming from its center. She had been a member of the Gardena High cheerleading team.

'That's Jo.' Janet revealed. 'Josie . . .' She took a few seconds to remember her last name. 'Moss . . . I think her name is Josie Moss. We were in Gardena High together – same class.' Another pause, this time with an added eyebrow lift. 'I mean . . . until the end of our freshman year. Jo moved to a different school after we finished ninth grade.'

'I take it that you're not in contact with her anymore,' Garcia asked.

Janet chuckled. 'No, not at all. To be honest, I never saw her again after she left Gardena High.' She paused and lifted both hands to signal her slight confusion. 'Hold on . . . why? Why are you asking me about Jo?'

Hunter flicked to another image on his phone. This time, it was the same photo of Oliver Griffith that he had showed her earlier.

'Well,' he explained, 'Josie Moss was her maiden name. That changed about six months ago, when she married Oliver Griffith.' He pointed to the photograph.

Janet's mouth dropped open.

'Wait up,' Tom said in confusion. 'Isn't this the male victim you showed us earlier?'

'That's correct,' Garcia confirmed.

'I'm not sure I understand,' Janet said, her uncertain gaze gravitating from Garcia to Hunter. 'What is going on?'

Instead of answering, Hunter, once again, reached for his cellphone and loaded up a new photo. 'How about this person? Do you recognize him at all?'

This was almost a second-by-second repeat of moments ago: Tom frowned, twisted his lips, then shook his head, but Janet simply stared at the image unblinkingly for several long seconds, and even before she said anything, Hunter saw clear recognition light up in her eyes.

'Yes, of course I recognize him. He was one of the stars of Gardena High's football team when I was there.' Janet shifted on her seat. 'His name is Troy ... umm ... Troy Foster, if I'm not mistaken. He was also in my class.'

In the car, on their way back to Janet and Tom's apartment, Hunter had placed a call to Mrs. Foster, with an odd request. Back in Oliver and Josie's house, when Hunter made the connection between Josie's cheerleading uniform and the shirt that he had seen Janet wearing under her robe, something else had flashed up in his memory. Something that took him three whole seconds to fully remember – another photo. He had seen it when he had visited Troy Foster in his mother's house in Sylmar a few days ago, before Troy had ended his own life. The photo was of Troy running with a football, just about to score a touchdown ... and his football shirt had been identical to the one that Janet was wearing now. That was what had made Hunter's heart triple in speed. That had been the connecting piece.

Hunter had asked Mrs. Foster if she could take a snapshot of that photo and send it to him.

She had.

'Was he in your class during the same years as Josie Moss?' Garcia asked.

Janet blinked at him.

'You said that she left at the end of your freshman year, right? Was Troy Foster in that same ninth grade class with the two of you?'

Janet thought about it for a single heartbeat before nodding. 'Yes, he was in my class throughout the whole of high school. In fact, they were both there when I joined Gardena, in eighth grade.' The perplexity in her voice was mimicked by the look in her eyes. 'Why? Why are you now asking me about Troy? What do Josie and Troy have to do with any of this?'

On his phone, Hunter loaded up another photo, one that Janet and Tom had already seen – Kirsten Hansen.

'Troy Foster,' Hunter finally explained, 'was Kirsten Hansen's fiancé. They were supposed to get married in seven months' time.'

Hunter's words hung in the air, ominously, while Janet and Tom's faces melted into bottomless dishes of doubt and confusion.

'This is the other victim.' Tom didn't phrase it as a question.

'Yes,' Garcia confirmed.

'I . . .' Janet's hands came up in a defensive gesture while tears streamed down her face. 'I don't understand. What does all this mean?' Her tongue scrapped against her lips. 'What is it that you're trying to tell me here?'

'Miss Lang . . .' Garcia began, but Janet cut him short with an angry stare.

'Janet.' She was just a couple of decibels short of a yell. 'My name is Janet. I hate being called Miss Lang.'

'I apologize,' Garcia said. 'And in answer to your question – to be perfectly honest, we don't exactly know what all this means. Not yet. We only just unearthed all this information about an hour and a half after we left here earlier today, but the one thing that we do know … the one thing that years and years of experience has taught us, is that in our line of work, coincidences don't really happen, especially ones like this.'

Hunter offered Janet a new tissue and he and Garcia waited as she dabbed her tears.

This next part would be complicated.

Sixty-one

Hunter and Garcia had been lucky back in Santa Clarita. The wind had carried the heavy rain that they had seen over Los Padres National Forest in the opposite direction from where they were, but the weather had changed since then. New, dark clouds had formed over the North Pacific. Though nowhere near as menacing as the ones that they had seen a few hours ago, those new clouds, helped by a fresh wind front coming in from the ocean, had turned the sky outside Janet's window into a dirty-ash color, and as she dried her tears, the first drops of rain drummed against her windowsill.

Janet crumpled up the tissue in her hand and dabbed it against her nose. Her uncomfortable stare shifted from person to person around the table, until it settled on Hunter.

'Would you like a glass of water?' Hunter asked.

Janet swallowed the lump in her throat before nodding. 'Yes, please.'

'I'll get it,' Tom said, getting to his feet. 'Would anybody else like some?'

Both detectives declined.

Tom brought the water to Janet, who took a tiny sip before placing the glass on the table in front of her.

'This is where we need to go back to the first question I asked you,' Garcia began, commanding Janet's attention. 'During your time in school, did you always hang out with the same group of students? And if so, were Josie Moss and Troy Foster part of that group?'

The veins in Janet's hand danced as she reached for her water again. This time, she took a gulp instead of a sip.

'Well ... yes ... kind of.' Her eyes darted away from both detectives.

'What does "kind of" mean, exactly?' Garcia prodded.

'Umm ... yeah, I guess that you could say that at first, we did hang out together a little.'

Though Hunter and Garcia were expecting Janet to carry on, she didn't.

'At first?' Hunter, this time.

'Yeah. What I mean is – mainly in eighth grade, you know, junior high. Back then, we did hang out together in school ... sometimes out of school as well, but in high school ...' She stared into her glass as she said those words. 'We sort of drifted into different groups.'

'Any particular reason why you drifted apart and into different groups?' Hunter asked.

Janet paused before shrugging. 'No.' Her eyes moved up then left. 'I guess the main reason was because we went from junior high to high school. Things kind of change for students with that transition, don't they?'

Neither Hunter nor Garcia could argue with that logic. Both of them knew from experience that things did change, sometimes quite a lot, when students graduated to high school. Many teenage students in the USA saw that particular hurdle as the beginning of their adulthood. They would, undoubtedly, go through a festival of physical and psychological changes, and dropping old friends for new ones wasn't really that uncommon.

'Troy joined the high school football team,' Janet continued. 'And just like that ...' She snapped her fingers. 'He had a new crowd to hang out with. I remember that he truly became the pro-verbial "sports jock". All the girls wanted to be his girlfriend . . . all the guys wanted to be his friend.' She had another sip of her water. 'Jo was an extremely attractive girl. At the beginning of our freshman year, she tried out for the varsity cheerleading team. She got in easy, and that was it – new hot cheerleading friends means goodbye old, not-so-hot junior high friends.' Janet lifted her hands in a gesture of surrender, indicating that she wasn't without blame either. 'But I started hanging out with other kids as well. I started dating this guy in ninth grade . . . my first high school boyfriend . . .' She looked at Tom, who didn't really look bothered. 'And started hanging out with his crowd . . . and that was that, basically. We all found new friends to hang out with.'

'OK,' Garcia accepted it. 'So let's, for a moment, go back to your time in eighth grade. You said that that was when you hung out with Troy Foster and Josie Moss quite a bit, right?'

'Yeah.'

'And how long ago was that?'

'Umm . . .' She blinked a couple of times as she thought about it. 'I was . . . thirteen, so thirteen years ago. We graduated from junior high in 2009.'

Garcia took note before continuing. 'And was there any one else in that particular group other than you, Josie and Troy?' He lifted a hand before Janet could reply. 'Please, think about this carefully because this is very, very important.'

'We weren't exactly a super tight group,' Janet clarified. 'We did hang out together quite a few times, but we had other school friends as well.'

'Still,' Garcia pushed. 'When you guys did hang out together, was there anyone else you can think of other than you, Troy, and Josie?'

Janet used the tissue against her tears once again. Her gaze moved to a random spot on the table, where it stayed for only a few seconds. 'Sophie,' she said with a nod. 'Sophie hung out with us a lot too.'

'Sophie?'

'Yes. Well – we called her Sophie, but her real name was Sofia . . .' Janet scratched her left cheek. 'Umm . . . we were always making fun of her because her last name sounded like "Ravioli".'

'She was Italian?'

'She was born here, but I think that her parents were Italian.' It took Janet another few seconds to remember the name. 'Risoli,' she said, snapping her fingers again and pointing at Garcia. 'Her name was Sofia Risoli.'

'Great,' Garcia said, writing the name down.

'Did Sofia also drift away from everyone else once you started high school?' Hunter asked.

'She did,' Janet confirmed. 'She went a bit strange, actually.'

'What do you mean by "strange"?' Hunter asked.

'Oh, she got in with the hairy crowd,' Janet explained. 'You know . . . long hair dudes, dressed mainly in black, listening to metal, or goth, or emo, or some heavy, screaming stuff that shouldn't really be called music.'

Garcia peeked at Hunter. There was a smile in his eyes.

'I take it that you also lost contact with her after you left Gardena High,' Hunter said.

'Yeah. Never saw her again after we graduated.' Janet paused. 'Never saw any of them again.' She looked back at both detectives with eyes still full of doubt.

'Anyone else you can remember that was part of that group?' Garcia insisted.

The next five silent seconds ended with a shake of the head from Janet. 'No, I don't think so.'

'Another boy, perhaps?' Hunter suggested.

Janet looked back at him, one eyebrow lifted just a little higher than the other.

'We're talking about school kids here,' Hunter explained. 'The group you've just mentioned was comprised of three girls and a boy. We don't know Sofia Risoli, but you and Josie Moss were attractive young women, which would lead me to believe that Sofia was too?'

Janet nodded. 'She was attractive, yes.'

'In junior high,' Hunter continued, 'a boy who's always hanging out with three attractive girls doesn't go unnoticed by his friends. And to be honest, if that boy was one of my friends when I was in school, I'd go an extra mile to get closer to him and into that group. Do you know what I mean? I'd want to hang out with the pretty girls too.'

From the corner of his eye, Hunter saw Tom half nodding in agreement.

Janet angled her head to one side, as she went back into thinking mode. A few seconds later, she blinked at Hunter.

'Maybe Pedro,' she said, giving both detectives a careless shrug. 'He and Troy were good buddies and he did have a thing for Sophie. Thinking about it, he did hang out with us whenever he could, which wasn't all the time. His family was pretty strict. I remember that. He always had a curfew ... church every Sunday ... you know, typical religious family, so he couldn't really come out as much.'

'Can you remember his last name?'

Janet tried but gave up after a short moment. 'It was some odd Mexican name. No chance I'll remember it, but Troy will.'

Garcia kept a steady face, but Hunter's eyes dropped to the floor for just an instant. No one but Garcia noticed it.

'It's OK, we'll find it,' Garcia assured her. 'Anyone else at all?'

Janet shook her head. 'No. Like I said, we weren't exactly a tight group, but when we did hang out together, it was usually the four of us ... Pedro came along whenever he could.' Before another question came her way, Janet threw her hands up.

'Stop . . . please. I don't get it. What does all this have to do with my sister? She didn't even go to Gardena High.'

Hunter reached for his cellphone, which was still on the table, and returned it to his pocket. 'Well, this is where we really need your help, Janet.' Hunter waited until she had locked eyes with him again. 'Whoever is doing this . . . whoever this killer is . . . he's clearly somehow linked to your eighth-grade group of friends.'

'Linked? Linked how?'

'We don't know yet,' Hunter replied. 'And that's why we need your help. We need you to think back to that time . . . to the group . . . to the things you did together. Did something happen?'

'Something?' Janet shook her head as her jittery eyes moved from Hunter to Garcia then back to Hunter. 'Something like what?'

This was the delicate part.

'Something that would've involved all of you,' Hunter tried to explain, deciding to use himself as an example. 'Look, just like most kids in school, I used to mainly hang out with the same group of friends when I was in junior high too. In my case, there were four of us, all boys. We hung out at the mall, we went to the cinema, we went to parties . . . same as most kids.'

Garcia nodded in support.

'But we also did a few things that at the time might've seemed cool,' Hunter continued, knowing that he had to tread carefully. 'You know, "kids will be kids" kind of stuff. Sometimes we did things that we thought would make us look badass . . . trying to be rebels and all that, but now, thinking back, I'm not really proud of some of the stuff we did.'

Janet looked doubtful. 'Like what?' she challenged. 'Having a drink in the park? Smoking a joint? Lifting some cash from another student's locker? What?'

'No,' Hunter replied. 'Silly things . . . but things that could've offended, or even hurt others, like, for example . . . sometimes we used to pick on other students ... sometimes we used to pick on ...' The pause that came was deliberate. 'Teachers. We used to make fun of them for one reason or another – their haircut, their weight, their looks, the way they dressed, how bad a teacher they were ... kids do stuff like that. And that's what I'm talking about, Janet. Was there a teacher, a student, or even multiple students, who your group usually picked on ... made fun of ... maybe even played pranks on a lot of the time?'

Janet looked surprised. 'Are you talking about bullying?'

'Maybe,' Hunter sounded serious.

'So you're asking me if we used to bully other kids.'

'Did you?'

'No,' she said, decisively.

'How about just a few jokes?' Garcia pushed. 'Maybe making fun of someone for some silly reason. Kids do that.' He paused for effect. 'This really is important, Janet.'

Janet tried to refocus her thoughts, but she didn't do it for long. 'Look,' she said, the sadness in her voice beginning to give way to irritation. 'Yes, of course there were times when we made jokes about someone's clothes, or their haircut, or how fat they were, or something. We made jokes about teachers too. We even did it amongst ourselves ... quite a lot, actually. We played a few pranks on other students as well, just like every student in the country does, but I'm guessing that what you're talking about here would be someone who we "always" made fun of, right? Someone who was "always" the target? And something really, really bad, like the kind of bullying you see in films, right?'

'Possibly, but not necessarily,' Hunter explained. 'It would all depend on that person's mental strength. Sometimes a single act is enough, and that's why I need you to think about this carefully, Janet.' Hunter knew that right then, he needed to reassure her. 'Please understand that we're not here to judge you on anything that might've happened all those years ago. Like I've said, kids will be kids. I did it.' He placed his palm against his chest. 'I picked on other kids and I picked on teachers when I was in school, and I did it just for fun. I even made other students cry at times. I'm not proud of it, but I did it. Things like that happen. They happen in every school and they happen every day. It's a fact.'

Hunter searched Janet's eyes for understanding, but all he saw was confusion, so he carried on.

'If there is someone who you guys, as a group, picked on . . . even in a way that for you might've not seemed so bad, that someone might be the link that we're looking for.'

Garcia kept a steady poker face, but he knew that Hunter wasn't being exactly truthful. In school, Hunter had been the outsider, the geeky, skinny kid who sat alone at lunchtime. He had been the one who others made fun of, not the other way around. But Garcia also knew why Hunter had told Janet that he used to pick on other students. Most people had trouble admitting guilt, no matter to what degree. If Janet believed that Hunter had done something similar to what she and her group might've done, especially with him being an LAPD detective, it could counteract enough of her guilt, if any, for her to tell them something.

'Like I've said,' Janet tried explaining it again. 'Of course we made jokes and played pranks on other students from time to time. Probably all of our eighth grade class at one time or another, but we weren't bullies, you know? We didn't constantly pick on specific students just for the fun of it.'

'How about a teacher?' Garcia pushed. He wanted to solidify the idea that they weren't talking exclusively about another student. 'Any teacher you guys joked a lot about?'

'Probably all of them,' Janet admitted. 'But nothing truly horrible, and we never did it to their faces, we just joked around in the group, you know – "I hate that class" . . . "Mr. So-and-so smells" . . . that kind of silly thing.'

'How about the other way around?' Hunter asked. 'Was there a teacher who sort of picked on you guys? Or on a specific member of your group?' He shrugged. 'Teachers can do that too.'

This time Janet paused, biting her lip and clearly searching her memory. 'Not that I can remember,' she finally said. 'None of us was a straight-A student, but we were alright. Our relationship with our teachers, as far as I can remember, was normal.'

'Any of you ever flunked any of your junior-high classes?' Hunter insisted, trying a different approach.

'I know I didn't,' Janet answered. 'I can't be certain about the others, but I don't think so.'

'Hold on just a minute here,' Tom interrupted, waving his hands at both detectives. 'Are you trying to tell us that the LAPD's goddamn theory on this is that there's someone torturing and killing people out there – three so far – because he was bullied in school some thirteen years ago?'

'It could also have been a teacher.' Garcia threw that in the mix again, just for good measure.

'What we're trying to do, Tom,' Hunter replied, 'is cover every possible angle. Like we've explained. The fact that all the victims were closely related to members of this eighth-grade group that Janet has mentioned *isn't* a coincidence. There's a link there and we need to find it.'

'Maybe,' Tom agreed. 'But it sounds nuts.'

Hunter remembered the video that the killer had sent Janet the day after Melissa Hawthorne's murder. He remembered the words that the killer had used to end the footage. He didn't really want to remind Janet of it, but he had no choice.

'In that awful video clip that you were sent,' he asked. 'The sender wrote – *just like a fish* – at the end of it. Does that mean anything to you at all? Did you ever play a prank on anyone that involved a fish?'

Janet looked back at Hunter as if he were from outer space. 'A prank with a fish . . . what?'

'I don't know,' Hunter tried to clarify. 'Maybe you, or someone from that group could've left a fish hanging inside another
student's locker as a silly joke.'

Tom's eyebrows arched at Hunter.

'Or stuffed a fish inside someone's bag,' Hunter continued.
'Or lunchbox, or something? You know ... just a kid's prank ...
anything involving a fish?'

Janet shook her head decisively. 'No. Never. Never played any
kind of jokes, or pranks involving a fish, or any sea creatures for
that matter. Not even a seashell. Are you guys for real?'

'Yeah, alright.' Tom threw his hands up to stop everyone. 'This
is now starting to sound a little more than just nuts. It's starting to
sound plain stupid. Are you guys high? Have you been smoking?'

An awkward moment fell upon the room before Garcia tried
a different avenue.

'How about someone who wanted to be part of your group?'
he asked. 'Someone who wanted to join your crowd, but you guys
sort of rejected him? Did that happened at all? Like Detective
Hunter said – other kids must've been falling over themselves to
hang out with you guys.'

This time, Janet thought about that question for a little while.
'I don't think so.' Her chin dropped to her chest. 'You're making
it sound like we were some sort of fraternity taking submissions
for membership, or some sort of special group, like that vampire
crowd in *Twilight*. We were just a bunch of eighth graders – thirteen and fourteen years old that *sometimes* hung out together,
that was all. We did what kids do. Nothing more, nothing less.
There was nothing special about us.'

Hunter's stare pinged around the room before pausing on the
bookshelf that was pushed against one of the walls.

'You wouldn't happen to have kept your junior high yearbook,
would you?' Hunter asked. Another long shot.

The look on Janet's face was half surprised, half sarcastic. 'My junior high yearbook? Definitely not. I don't think I even bought one.' Her eyes narrowed a touch, as she tried to remember. 'Yeah, I don't think I did because ... who does? Nobody really cares much about junior high. All you're doing is going from middle school to high school ... *in the same school*. Nothing really changes. You start the next school year pretty much with the same crowd you finished the one before. It's not like you're going off to college and you might never see your friends from school again.'

It was true, both Hunter and Garcia knew that. Most students in America didn't much care for the jump from middle school to high school. If the junior high yearbooks weren't handed out for free, and very few schools could afford to do so, a lot of students would choose not to purchase their junior-high yearbook. The high-school yearbook was a different ball game altogether.

Hunter knew that at that moment, there was nothing else that they could ask. Pushing for more, right then, would only enrage Janet.

'Thank you for your time, Janet,' he said, as they got to their feet, but he paused just before turning away. 'You know, the human memory works in funny ways. Sometimes when you push it, it gives you nothing but blanks. Then, when you're thinking about something else entirely, it brings back something that was hidden somewhere in your subconscious. If anything or anyone does come to mind – for any reason at all – please contact us straight away.'

There was no reply, but as they got to the front door, Hunter could hear Janet starting to sob again.

Sixty-two

'Do you think she was hiding something,' Garcia asked, as they got back to his car. 'About the bullying, I mean?'

'I didn't get that impression,' Hunter replied. 'Janet did accept that they played pranks and made a few jokes at the expense of other students. Maybe one of those pranks or jokes affected someone a lot more than she knew. The old case of – to one person it's just a joke, to another it develops into psychological trauma.'

Garcia nodded and checked the time.

'It's almost seven-thirty,' he told Hunter. 'What do you want to do? Call it a day for today and start again tomorrow morning, or what?'

Hunter ran a hand through his hair and looked up at the sky. The rain had stopped, but the clouds were still there.

'I guess that at this time,' Garcia added, 'the only thing we could still do would be to try to pay Josie Griffith a visit and hit her with the same questions we've just asked Miss Lang upstairs.' He paused and rolled his tongue inside his mouth. 'Problem is, like you've said earlier, it hasn't even been twenty-four hours since she lost her husband. Getting reliable answers out of her right about now, would be kind of a miracle.'

'Yeah, I know. I don't think that there's much more that we can do tonight. Tomorrow, first thing, I'll ask Research to track down Sofia Risoli and Pedro "whatever his last name is". Once we find them, I'm sure they'll probably be able to remember more about their eighth-grade group than Miss Lang and Mrs. Griffith.'

Garcia nodded. 'Their brains won't be struggling with grief.'

'Exactly,' Hunter agreed.

'We should also talk to Troy's brother,' Garcia suggested. 'Chances are that he went to the same school in Gardena. He might be able to tell us something.'

'I'll have a poke around online tonight.' Hunter unzipped his jacket. 'But let's add him to tomorrow's list, after we've taken a trip down to Gardena High. I'd like to have a look at their junior high yearbook from 2009 first, maybe talk to a few teachers, janitors, staff, admin ... whoever is still there from that time.'

'And if there's no one?'

'Then we'll track them down.'

Garcia nodded and unlocked the car, but before they could get inside, Hunter received a new phone call.

'*Detective*,' a female voice said, as Hunter answered his phone. She sounded distressed and tearful. '*This is Stacey Green ... Josie's friend. She's staying at my house at the moment.*'

'Hello, Miss Green,' Hunter said back. 'Is Mrs. Griffith OK?'

'*Josie is asleep. She's spent most of the day sedated, but last night, back in her house, you asked Scott and I to keep an eye on her phone. You asked us to get in touch with you if she received any odd messages coming from any unknown numbers.*'

Hunter signaled Garcia to get into his car.

Inside, Hunter quickly switched the call to speakerphone.

'That's right. Did she get a message?'

Both detectives heard Stacey sniffle, as she tried to steady her voice, but it didn't quite work. Instead of uttering words, all she could do was sob.

'Miss Green.' Hunter kept his voice steady. 'Just take a deep breath. Are you at home?'

More sniffles. '*Yes.*'

'Can you get yourself a glass of water? Or maybe ask your fiancé to get it for you?'

'*Scott isn't home right now.*' There was a pause followed by more sniffles. '*I'll be OK.*'

'Are you sure?'

'*I'll be OK.*'

'Alright. Just take your time.'

It took Stacey a few more seconds to compose herself.

'*Yeah ... well ... I guess bad news travels fast, you know?*' she said, her voice still feeble. '*Josie's been getting quite a few messages from unfamiliar numbers today. All of them saying how sorry they were to hear about what had happened.*'

'Has she shown you all the messages?' Hunter asked.

'*Like I've said – Josie's been sedated and asleep for most of the day, but I know her passcode, so while she's resting, I've kept her phone by my side.*'

'Smart,' Garcia mouthed the word at Hunter.

'*But about half an hour ago ...*' Stacey continued, '*she got another message from an unknown number.*' She paused, as her voice became strangled by tears.

'What did the message say?'

'*Well ... just like you mentioned yesterday, the sender used two words – "From Oliver" – all in capital letters, so it would appear on the screen popup.*'

'Did you have a look at the message?' Hunter asked, but from the way that Stacey was crying, he already knew what the answer would be.

'*Yes. I did.*' Stacey exploded into sobs. '*There was ... there was an attached vid—*' Her voice faltered and she was unable to finish the sentence.

Hunter closed his eyes, as if in pain.

'*Why ...?*' Stacey asked. '*Why would someone send that ...*'

'Miss Green,' Hunter said. 'Please, go into your kitchen and pour yourself a glass of sugary water. Just one spoon of sugar in the glass will do. It will help calm you down.'

Hunter and Garcia heard Stacey take in the deepest of breaths through a clogged-up nose. They then heard what sounded like a zippo lighter flicking open then closed, followed by the sound of someone taking a long drag.

'*I'm OK,*' she finally said. '*What do you want me to do now?*'

From her tone of voice, it was clear that Stacey wasn't really OK, but there was very little that Hunter or Garcia could do.

'Do you still have Mrs. Griffith's phone with you?' Hunter asked.

'*Yeah. I've got it right here.*'

'Good. What I need you to do right now is forward that whole message to me. Including the attached video. Do you know how to do that?'

'*Yes, of course.*'

'Please do it now,' Hunter told her. 'Don't play the video again, just select the message from the list, click on the forward button, enter the same phone number you just dialed and send it to me.'

'*OK . . . hold on.*'

Hunter and Garcia heard faint keypad tones come through the speakerphone.

'*It's done. Did you get it?*'

Three seconds later, Hunter's phone vibrated once.

'Yes, I got it. Thank you. Now, there are a couple more things that I need you to do for me. And this is very, very important.' Hunter wouldn't make the same mistake as he had with Troy.

Stacey followed Hunter's instructions as he guided her on how to completely delete the message and the video from Josie Griffith's phone.

'*OK . . . it's gone,*' she told him, in between sobs.

To be one hundred percent sure, Hunter asked Stacey to check everything once again.

'*It's gone,*' she reassured him. '*It's not here anymore.*'

'Miss Green, can I ask you one more question before you go?' Hunter asked. 'How do you know Mrs. Griffith? Did you by any chance attend Gardena Junior High with her?'

Another deep breath from Stacey. '*No. I met Josie at UCLA. We were both psychology majors. We graduated together.*'

'How about the other women from your group of friends?' Hunter asked. 'The group that was in Vegas for your bachelorette party? Do you know if any of them knew Mrs. Griffith from her time at Gardena Junior High?'

'*Umm ...*' Stacey didn't really have to think about it for too long. '*No. None of them. I think that Lucy and Aimee knew Josie from high school, but they didn't go to Gardena. They went to South High, in Torrance.*'

'OK, thank you,' Hunter said, rubbing his tired eyes. 'I'll call you tomorrow to check on how Mrs. Griffith is doing, alright?'

'*Yeah,*' Stacey whispered back.

'You did great today, Miss Green. Thank you.'

Immediately after they disconnected, Hunter opened the text message that Stacey had sent him. The message itself contained only four words, grouped in pairs and separated by six line breaks. The first two words, just like Stacey had told them, read: 'FROM OLIVER'. That's what had showed on the message popup. The last two words read: 'TO JOSIE'.

'Clever,' Garcia said. 'With a message like that, how would you not want to watch the attached video, a day after losing your husband?'

Hunter nodded.

'OK,' Garcia said, taking a deep breath to steady himself. 'Let's see what we've got this time.'

Hunter pressed 'play'.

Sixty-three

The next day started like most days, with a progress meeting at the UVC Unit's office, but before Captain Blake arrived, Hunter and Garcia made a few changes to the picture board. Now, a portion at the far right corner of the board showed three new photographs – Janet Lang, Troy Foster, and Josie Griffith – all connected by a single red line.

Captain Blake listened in total silence for twenty minutes, as both detectives updated her on everything that they'd come across in the last twenty-four hours. Once they were done, the captain took a step back from the board, her eyes moving from photo to photo, as if she was trying to navigate a complex labyrinth . . . one where she couldn't yet see the exit.

'And there's a new message from the killer,' she said, her whole body already assuming a defensive posture. 'A new video?'

'That's right,' Hunter replied, indicating his computer monitor. He had already transferred the video from his cellphone to his hard drive.

'I'm going to go grab a soda,' Garcia said, as Captain Blake approached Hunter's desk. 'I'm not watching that again.' He paused by the door. 'Anybody want anything?'

Both Hunter and Captain Blake shook their heads.

As Garcia closed the door behind him, Hunter took a deep breath. 'This is . . . deeply disturbing,' he warned the captain.

'Judging by what we've had so far,' Captain Blake replied, looking at the board, 'I wouldn't expect anything less.'

Hunter selected the clip and pressed 'play'.

This time, the video clip was a little – twenty five seconds. It started with a fade-in – a close-up shot of Oliver Griffith's face. His eyes were so lost ... so full of sadness ... so lacking in hope ... that it was easy to overlook how red, and puffy they were. Tears ran down his cheeks until they dripped off his chin. Every breath he took seemed shallow, as if the air around him was too thin to breathe.

The shot lasted about eight seconds and it ended with his trembling lips moving, but no sound was heard.

None was needed.

Even a child could've read his lips: *Please ... don't*.

The next shot had clearly been filmed several minutes after the first one. It too started with a fade-in on a close-up of Oliver's face. His eyes were still red, and puffy, and wet, and lost, but there was a new overwhelming quality in them – total and utter terror.

A leather-strap ball-gag now kept Oliver from screaming ... from begging ... from saying a word.

The shot then zoomed out to show Oliver's entire body firmly strapped to the Saint Andrew's cross in his basement. He was naked, but still untouched. The two lobsters were nowhere to be seen.

All of a sudden, Oliver went completely rigid, every muscle in his body tensing almost to the point of cramping. His head recoiled back in a jerk, at the same time that his eyes widened with so much fear it nearly paralyzed him. The ball-gag did a great job at muffling the raw scream that had erupted from his throat.

Oliver tried to fight. He tried to kick. He tried to wiggle his body free, but the straps were too tight ... too strong for him. All he was able to do was shiver in place.

'Jesus Christ!' Captain Blake said, cringing with anticipation.

Hunter's eyes moved away from his monitor. He already knew what was coming and, like Garcia, he didn't want to watch it again.

On the screen, the clip faded-out then in again. The new shot, just like the previous two, was another close-up, but not of Oliver's face. This was a close-up of his groin region.

Suddenly, coming in from the right side of the screen, a pair of long-blade garden shears appeared.

'Oh fuck!' Captain Blake's hands palmed her entire face, but her fingers spread out just enough for her to be able to still see the screen.

Hunter simply closed his eyes and waited for the sound that he knew was coming.

It happened fast. The blades opened then closed with a sickening *shluck* sound that made Captain Blake stop breathing for a second. The precision of the cut had been impeccable, severing Oliver's penis clean off at its base.

'Fuck!'

This time, the captain did squeeze her eyes firmly shut, burying her face in her hands.

On the screen, blood could be seen gushing out of the freshly open wound, like water flowing out of an open faucet.

Oliver's body was shaking as if he had been electrocuted, and despite the tight ball gag in his mouth, the most feral of screams managed to find its way through it.

If the sound of the blades had made Captain Blake stop breathing, Oliver's scream made her sick to her stomach.

The Mentor barely waited a second before the blades were back on the job.

Shluck.

Cut number two was as precise as the first one, severing Oliver's scrotum with tremendous ease.

His body convulsed once . . . twice . . . three times before a final awkward jerk. His muscles finally relaxed. Then nothing. No more movement. Oliver had passed out from pure pain.

Captain Blake's hands came up to cup her mouth. Her gaze moved to Hunter for a split second before going back to the screen.

The sequence faded-out again, only to fade back in for the last segment – a full shot of Oliver on the 'X' cross. Blood had cascaded down his legs, forming a viscous and sticky crimson pool on the floor. His groin region was a mess of raw flesh and blood. His body was limp, held in place only by the leather straps around his wrists and waist. His head was down, as if its weight had become too much for his neck muscles.

The shot zoomed in onto his face one last time. His eyelids were semi-open and the camera was angled in such a way that allowed the viewer to see his eyes. They were moving erratically – left, right, left right – not exactly as fast as REM, but almost.

Oliver was clearly in a state of delirium, induced by pain, shock, and the loss of blood.

Suddenly he coughed, his whole head lurching up then down with the effort.

As a consequence of the ball-gag blocking his mouth, his cheeks puffed out like a blowfish, but at the same time, something spurted through the edges of his mouth . . . something more than just saliva. Oliver had vomited, and the vomit had nowhere to go.

'Oh screw this,' Captain Blake said, vigorously shaking her head and turning away from the screen. 'I'm done here,' she told Hunter. 'Turn it off.'

Hunter paused the clip. 'There isn't any more,' he said. 'That's where it ends, except that the killer has added the words "CLACK, CLACK, CLACK" across the bottom of the screen.'

The captain's attention returned to the monitor on Hunter's desk. '"Clack, clack, clack"? What's that supposed to mean?'

'Probably a sound reference to a lobster's pincer opening and closing,' Hunter replied.

The effort of watching that twenty-five-second video seemed to have completely exhausted Captain Blake. She straightened and breathed deeply, her ribcage rising then falling as she tried to collect herself. She crossed her arms across her chest in a new protective posture, one she didn't even notice that she was doing.

'Is it over?' Garcia asked, as he pulled the door open and paused by it, a can of Dr. Pepper in his right hand.

Hunter nodded, but Captain Blake just shook her head.

'I need a minute,' she said, her voice trembling, something that Hunter and Garcia had only heard once or twice before. 'Just give me a minute,' she said again, as she walked past Garcia, heading toward the bathroom.

Sixty-four

It took Captain Blake a lot longer than a minute to recompose herself. When she finally got back to Hunter and Garcia's office, Hunter noticed that her eye makeup looked a little different – a little smudged under her lower eyelids, but that wasn't all. Now, together with the sadness and the disgust, there was a new emotion in her eyes – anger.

'Are you OK?' Garcia asked. He and Hunter were back standing in front of the picture board.

'As much as I can be after watching probably the most sickening clip I've ever seen in my life.'

'Tell me about it,' Garcia replied, as the captain joined them.

She regarded the board once again, this time doing her best to follow the red lines that had been drawn onto it, connecting the series of photographs.

'So,' she said in a voice that lacked conviction. 'If I got this right from your briefing earlier, what you were telling me was that the new UVC theory is that this killer, whoever this psycho is, has some sort of . . . "beef".' She nodded sideways in a dubious look. 'And not with any of the actual victims that he's tortured and murdered, but with someone who was closely related to them.'

Garcia was about to say something, but Captain Blake halted him with a single hand gesture.

'A "beef",' she continued, 'that according to you, has its roots some thirteen years ago, while these people –' she pointed to the corner of the board with the three new photographs '– were in junior high, in Gardena.' She indicated the rest of the board. 'So all this – including that absolutely vile video clip that I just watched – is nothing more than payback ... punishment for something they did when they were ... how old?'

'Janet Lang was thirteen at the time,' Garcia clarified, indicating as he spoke. 'Troy Foster and Josie Griffith were both fourteen, and like we've said, there are apparently two other members to that group – Sofia Risoli and Pedro "something". We've haven't had time to find them yet, but Research is working on it as we speak.'

'Thirteen ...' The captain's wide eyes settled on Garcia. ' ... And fourteen.' Her attention shifted to Hunter.

'Maybe the person we're looking for wasn't another student,' Hunter said, which made Captain Blake pause, her attention returning to the board, specifically to the snapshots of the text messages between the killer and the victims.

'He calls himself the "Mentor",' she said.

Garcia nodded. 'Probably for a reason.'

'So you think that this might be one of their teachers ... from thirteen years ago?'

'We know how this all sounds, Captain,' Hunter said.

Captain Blake chuckled as she played with her left earing. 'I think that the word you're looking for is "desperate", Robert.'

'Every investigation into serial murders is desperate, Captain,' Hunter hit back. 'A desperate race against time. In essence, we're after someone who is freely walking the streets, murdering people to an agenda and a timeframe that only he knows. The longer it takes us to get to him, the closer he gets to another victim. Time is *never* on our side.'

'You think I don't know that, Robert?' Captain Blake replied, allowing a sliver of annoyance to grace her tone.

'I know you know that, Captain,' Hunter countered, his tone, on the other hand, serene. 'And I also know that you know that a triple coincidence like this . . .' He indicated the three new photos on the board. 'It doesn't actually happen. Not in the world of Violent Crimes.'

Looking at the board, Captain Blake felt something tighten inside her chest. 'It's just . . .' She shook her head, as she bit her bottom lip. 'Crazy, really, having to wrap my head around the thought that there's someone out there, torturing and killing innocent people, in the vilest ways, as retribution for something that apparently happened thirteen years ago, while they were all in junior high. They were all kids, for Chrissakes. What could a bunch of thirteen and fourteen-year-olds have done to warrant this kind of payback?'

Garcia chuckled. 'You're underestimating what kids are capable of nowadays, Captain.'

'It's not nowadays, Carlos,' she volleyed back. 'It's thirteen years ago.'

'Still.'

'It's pointless speculating,' Hunter said. 'Knowing or not knowing whatever happened thirteen years ago won't change the fact that we need to catch this killer, and this group of students from Gardena Junior High is the link that we were looking for. We figure out the connection and we'll catch this guy.'

At that exact moment, the phone on Garcia's desk rang. He rushed to it.

'Detective Garcia, UVC Unit.'

He listened for a few seconds before reaching for his notepad. After taking down a few notes, he suddenly stopped.

'What?' His troubled gaze moved to Hunter. 'When?'

There was a pause, and then Garcia exhaled, dropping his pen on his desk. 'OK. Just email me everything you've got. I'll also need that police report.'

'What was that?' Captain Blake asked, once Garcia ended the call.

'Research,' Garcia informed them.

Hunter's ears perked up.

'We've got an address for Sofia Risoli,' Garcia continued. 'It took them a while longer to find her because her last name isn't Risoli anymore.'

'She's married,' Hunter said.

'She is,' Garcia confirmed. 'Her name is now Sofia Elliot.' He read from his notepad. 'Twenty-seven years old. Her husband – Lucas Elliot – is a project manager for T-Mobile.'

'Any kids?'

'No.'

'Brothers?' Captain Blake insisted. 'Sisters?'

'One sister,' Garcia informed her. 'Older. She lives in Frisco. Her parents, though, live in LA.'

'Where?'

'They still live in Gardena, where she went to school.'

'How about Sofia Elliot?' Hunter, this time. 'Where do she and her husband live?'

'El Monte in San Gabriel Valley.'

Hunter checked his watch at the same time that Garcia checked his computer. The email from Research had just arrived.

'And what does Mrs. Elliot do?' Hunter prodded.

Garcia scrolled down on his screen. 'She's an accountant. Runs her own practice from home.'

'How about the other kid that used to be in their group?' the captain asked. 'A boy, right?'

Garcia nodded and Hunter recognized the defeat in the movement. 'His name was Pedro Bustamente.' He spelled it out loud before pausing and locking eyes with his partner. 'Unfortunately, he committed suicide about a year ago. He was twenty-five years old.'

'Suicide?' Captain Blake asked. The surprise in her expression was mirrored in Hunter's face.

Garcia opened the police report file that Research had attached to the email.

'That's correct,' he confirmed, his eyes scanning through the file, knowing exactly where to look. 'His body was found in his apartment in Pomona by his landlord.'

'How did he end his life?' Captain Blake asked, as she and Hunter rounded Garcia's desk to have a look at the file. The name of the Pomona PD Detective who attended the scene was James Lee.

'He sliced his wrists in the bathroom,' Garcia informed them.

'According to Detective Lee,' Hunter said, reading from the file, 'there were no signs of foul play. No investigation was initiated. Did we get an autopsy report?'

Garcia went back to the email. 'Yep.' He clicked on the attachment.

Hunter scrolled down to toxicology and read their findings. 'Alcohol and Tramadol in his blood.'

'Most people numb their brains before taking their own lives, Robert,' Captain Blake commented, unsurprised. 'You know that.'

'True,' Hunter agreed. 'But he had enough of both in his system to knock him down for at least half a day.' He indicated the numbers.

'Are you thinking that he didn't really kill himself?' the captain asked.

'I don't know,' Hunter replied.

'I'll get in touch with Detective Lee,' Garcia said. 'We need a little more information about this.'

'Good,' Hunter agreed. 'El Monte and Pomona are both in the San Gabriel Valley, so why don't you take both of those. Talk to Detective Lee in Pomona and to Sofia Elliot in El Monte.'

'On it.' Garcia reached for his jacket.

'What are you going to do?' Captain Blake asked Hunter.

'I'm going to take a drive to Gardena Junior High, have a look at their 2009 yearbook and talk to whoever I can, including Sofia Elliot's parents. The yearbook should also give us a few more names for Research to track down. Somebody's got to remember something. After that, I'll try to pay Josie Griffith a visit. Hopefully she'll be able to answer a few questions about their old school group.'

'Alright,' the captain said, checking the time as she moved toward the door. 'I need to brief the Chief of Police this afternoon, so keep me in the loop, whatever happens.'

'Will do.'

Hunter grabbed his jacket and he and Garcia were out the door.

Sixty-five

Gardena High was located just across the road from the famous Roosevelt Memorial Park, on West 182nd Street. With almost fifteen hundred students, a full-sized football field, and over twenty buildings in its complex, the school grounds were enormous, covering almost two entire city blocks.

At the gates, Hunter got directions to the middle-school principal's office from one of the security guards. A quick two-minute walk from the entrance, the office itself was spacious, with the walls decorated by a variety of framed achievements and awards, a few student pictures, and a large photo of the current US President. Two secretaries sat at different desks, both typing fiercely on their keyboards. On a bench, pushed up against the east wall, a male student sat with a gloomy look on his face.

As Hunter entered the office, the secretary at the desk closest to the door, a middle-aged African American woman with cornrows in her hair, looked up at him.

'Good afternoon, sir,' she said, giving Hunter a warm smile. 'How can I help you today?' Her voice was high-pitched.

Hunter approached her desk, showed her his credentials, and in hushed voice explained that he needed to see the principal.

'She's on a phone call at the moment,' the secretary explained. The smile on her lips vanished, replaced by an overall look of concern. 'But she shouldn't be long. If you'd like to take a seat, I'll let her know that you're here.'

As Hunter sat at the bench, next to the gloomy-faced student, the secretary wrote something down on a Post-it note before entering the principal's main office. Two seconds after that, Hunter's cellphone rang in his pocket. The call was from Garcia.

'Carlos,' Hunter took the call. 'Where are you?'

'*El Monte,*' Garcia replied. '*Just outside Sofia Elliot's place and about to make my way to Pomona to go see Detective Lee.*'

'That was quick,' Hunter said. 'What happened with Sofia Elliot? Did you talk to her?'

'*Nope. That's why I'm calling. Big update.*'

Hunter readjusted himself on the bench.

'*Sofia Elliot and her husband, Lucas, flew to Italy two days ago. It's her grandfather's eighty-fifth birthday.*'

Hunter paused for a moment. 'How did you find that out so quickly?'

'*Her neighbor. I got here, rang the bell then knocked – no answer. As I was trying to look in through the window, the next-door neighbor came out. After I explained who I was – and that took some talking – she told me that they had left for Italy a couple of days ago. The neighbor is cat-sitting for them.*'

'*As far as she's aware, Sofia's whole family flew out with her. That means her father and mother too. So don't bother trying to drop by their place after you leave Gardena High.*'

Hunter thought about that for a moment. 'That could be a good thing.'

'*That's exactly what I thought,*' Garcia agreed. '*No loved one left behind for the Mentor to go after.*'

'When are Mrs. Elliot and her husband back? If the neighbor is cat-sitting for them, she must have an idea.'

'*She does. The husband is due back in three days' time, on*

Saturday morning. Sofia should be staying a few more days, but she's not one hundred percent certain.'

'We'll need to put an undercover tail on him the second he lands at LAX,' Hunter said.

'Yep, I was thinking the same. If the Mentor is going for a loved one, the husband is the best bet. It perfectly fits his MO, down to the victim being alone at home while the other party is away.'

'Did you ask the neighbor if anybody else came looking for either Sofia or her husband in the past couple of days?'

'Oh, damn!' Garcia said, trying his best to keep his tone serious. *'No, I forgot. Shall I go back?'* He paused for effect. *'This isn't my first rodeo, Robert. Of course I asked her and no, she hasn't seen anyone else at their door, or around their house. I've also checked door locks and windows. Nothing seems to have been tampered with.'*

'Not yet,' Hunter said back.

'You're thinking the same as I am, aren't you? We should put the whole house under surveillance.'

'Absolutely,' Hunter agreed, as he saw the external-line light on the intercom on the secretary's desk go off. 'I'm about to go into the Gardena Junior High principal's office. You said you're on your way to Pomona, right?'

'Just getting into my car now.'

'OK, so could you give Captain Blake a call?' Hunter asked. 'Give her Sofia Elliot's address and ask her to organize a surveillance team ASAP. This needs to be in place before the end of the day today.'

'On it. I'll talk to you later.'

Less than ten seconds after they disconnected, the door to the principal's office was pulled open by an average height woman with a plain, round face. Her hair color fell into that indistinct category between blonde and brunette, the strands of which were pulled back into a neat chignon.

'Mr. Hunter,' she said, clearly deciding not to address Hunter as 'Detective' in front of any students.

Hunter stood up to shake her hand.

'I'm Principal Martinez,' she said, as she gestured. 'Please, come into my office.'

Before following Hunter inside, Principal Martinez looked down at the boy sitting at the bench. 'Mr. Goodwood. Why am I not surprised?'

'I ain't done nothing, Mrs. Martinez,' the boy replied, shaking his head at the principal.

'So you keep telling me. Your teachers, though, seem to always disagree with you.'

The boy didn't meet her stare.

'Just sit tight, Mr. Goodwood. I'll be with you in a moment.'

The boy sulked, as Principal Martinez returned to her office and closed the door behind her.

Inside, the conversation between Hunter and the principal didn't last long. Mrs. Martinez had taken over the middle school principal's position eight years ago, after the retirement of Joseph Greer, who had been Gardena's middle school principal for nearly twenty years. That meant that Mrs. Martinez had never met Melissa, Troy, Josie, or anyone else from the class of 2009. Hunter did enquire about Principal Greer, but Mrs. Martinez informed him that unfortunately, he had passed away from cancer three years ago.

'Any of your teachers or staff members who are still here from 2009?' Hunter pushed. 'Or even earlier?'

'I think I might have a couple,' Principal Martinez replied, as she scrolled down on her computer screen. 'I'm just checking that now.'

In anticipation, Hunter reached into his jacket pocket for his notepad.

'Being a schoolteacher has become harder and harder over the years, Detective,' Principal Martinez explained, as she continued searching. 'I'm sure you can imagine. The yearly curriculum demands a lot from everyone . . . the students demand a lot from everyone . . . the parents demand a lot from everyone . . . and the educational board demands a lot from everyone. Tough hours, with a lot of work to take home and not enough pay.' She gave Hunter a shrug. 'In my experience, most middle-school teachers either burn out within eight to ten years, or they find something else that's less demanding and better paid. Career teachers aren't as easy to find anymore.' She paused and nodded at her screen. 'But yes, I was right. Mr. Hartley, the eight-grade homeroom and history teacher, and Mrs. Anderson – eighth-grade English – were both here in 2009. Though at the moment, Mrs. Anderson is on leave for medical reasons. She had surgery less than a week ago.'

Hunter noted both names down. 'But Mr. Hartley is on campus today, right?'

'Yes, he is.'

It took Principal Martinez another five minutes to find out about staff members, but it turned out that only a handful of them had been with the school for over thirteen years – the head janitor, two of the security guards, three people who worked at the school canteen, and one of the school gardeners.

'I'd like to speak with all of them today, if that's alright,' Hunter said. 'Particularly with Mr. Hartley.'

'Yes, of course,' Principal Martinez replied, as she consulted her watch. 'The problem is, I have no one to take over Mr. Hartley's class at the moment. If you don't mind waiting, I'm sure he'll be glad to speak with you as soon as he gets a break, but that might not be until the final bell.'

'I can wait,' Hunter replied. 'It's not a problem.'

Principal Martinez reached for a pen. 'OK, let me get you the names of all the staff members I just mentioned.' She quickly wrote the seven names down. 'I don't have their work schedule for the day, but I can ask Brenda to radio them and ask each one to come meet you here, in the office.' She gestured toward the door, indicating the anteroom with the two secretaries.

'Thank you,' Hunter said, getting to his feet. 'But I'd like to have a look at the 2009 junior-high yearbook first, if I could. Photographs work much better than names when it comes to remembering people.'

'Sure, that won't be a problem,' the principal said, handing Hunter the piece of paper with all the names. 'You'll find a copy of the yearbook in our library.' She paused, as she thought better of her suggestion. 'Actually, maybe it would be best if I send them to meet you in the library. You should have more privacy there than here in the office.'

'That works for me,' Hunter agreed. 'Before I go, could I ask you for one more favor?'

'Of course.'

'Is there a way that you can find out if any of these five students –' he handed Principal Martinez a piece of paper with the five names '– from the junior-high class of 2009 flunked any of their classes during that school year?'

The principal took the paper from Hunter's hand and silently read through the five names.

'Sure.' She sat back down behind her desk. 'Give me a minute and I'll pull their records.'

It didn't take long for Principal Martinez to find out about their grades.

'Umm . . . no. It doesn't look like any of them flunked any of their classes. Some below par grades, for sure – a couple of "D"s here and there, but they all passed.'

'Those records wouldn't happen to show any teacher annotations against any of their names, would they?' Hunter tried. 'Any sort of complaints . . . fights . . . incidents . . . anything?'

Principal Martinez shook her head. 'No. Nothing like that.

We're talking kids here, Detective – thirteen- and fourteen-year-olds. For something to be noted onto their junior-high record, it would have to have been something substantial, like being expelled or something. We don't keep a record of reprimands. If we did, in a school with fifteen hundred students, we could fill a library every year.'

Back in the anteroom, Principal Martinez instructed the same secretary who had greeted Hunter to give him directions to the library building and, when he was ready, to radio the seven staff members whose names were on the list she'd given him.

As the secretary retrieved a school-grounds map from one of her drawers, Principal Martinez kept the door to her office open, placed her hands on her hips and looked back at the student who was still sitting at the bench.

'Mr. Goodwood.' Her head angled in the direction of her office. 'Shall we?'

Sixty-six

Garcia chuckled to himself as he switched off his engine. Every dull, stripped-down detail about the squat police station that he had parked in front of in Pomona screamed government-owned, suburban property.

Garcia had called ahead to make sure that the trip wouldn't be wasted. Detective Lee, who looked to be about ten years older and a whole foot shorter than Garcia, was sitting at his desk, going over a mountain of paperwork when he arrived.

'Please, have a seat,' Lee said, indicating one of the two metal and polyester-cushioned chairs in front of his desk.

Lee was dressed in a tight, pinstripe suit. His black hair was gelled back and his stubble created a dark, charcoal shadow on his squared jaw. His eyes seemed kind, housing a look that could easily be associated with substance and intelligence.

'On the phone you mentioned that this was about a suicide case,' he said, as Garcia took a seat. His voice was low and soothing, what Garcia imagined a smooth jazz radio DJ would sound like. 'Something that happened about a year ago?'

'That's right,' Garcia confirmed. 'The victim's name was Pedro Bustamente.'

Faint recognition flashed across Detective Lee's face. The name had clearly sounded familiar, but he couldn't exactly place it yet.

'I have the case file number, if it helps,' Garcia said.

'If you don't mind,' Lee replied, pulling himself closer to his desk.

From his notepad, Garcia read a combination of letters and numbers, while Lee typed them into his keyboard. Once he hit 'enter', it took less than two seconds for the file to load onto his screen. As it did, he nodded, sitting back on his chair.

'Oh yes . . .' He shrugged. 'I remember it now. The kid cut his wrist open in the bathroom using a kitchen knife. Horrible job. He only sliced through one wrist.'

'Really?' Garcia found that strange.

Detective Lee nodded. 'Very deep cut. He almost amputated his hand, and that's probably the reason for the single wrist job. After that cut, there was no way he could've gripped onto anything with his left hand. His tendons had all been severed.' He used his mouse to drag something across his screen. 'The scene was a mess. There was no bathtub in his apartment, so he just sat on the floor and hacked at his hand. There was blood absolutely everywhere. His landlord found him when he went over to collect the weekly rent.' His eyes scanned a little more of the file. 'That was about it, really. There wasn't anything unusual with the scene to make it stand out – just another terribly sad suicide case. The kid was just twenty-five years old.'

Garcia nodded, solemnly.

'Unfortunately,' Lee continued, 'suicide amongst young people is on the rise, Detective. I'm sure you are aware of that. Especially young men.'

'You just said that there was nothing unusual about the scene,' Garcia prodded. 'But didn't the single-wrist, super-deep cut look unusual to you?'

'Not when you've attended as many suicide scenes as I have,' Lee replied. 'There's no real "how-to" rulebook when it comes to suicide, Detective. Sure, people can research it on the Internet, but that's up to them. In this case, kid wants to cut his wrists open but he's got no real idea of how much pressure to put on the knife, or even where to cut exactly. So he puts knife to wrist—' Lee used his right hand over his left wrist to demonstrate '—and *whack*. Instead of a simple cut, he puts too much force onto the slicing movement ... maybe because he's way too nervous ... maybe because he really has no idea at all ... I don't know, but too much force with a razor-sharp, long-blade instrument against soft tissue and that's the result.' He indicated his computer monitor. 'Single-wrist, deep-cut suicides happen a lot more often than you'd imagine.'

'There was no medical history attached to the file we got,' Garcia explained. 'Is there one attached to your records? I mean, was the victim known for having depressive episodes? Did he suffer from borderline personality disorder? Did you check with his family ... his doctor?' Garcia was careful to keep his tone inquisitive, but not demanding or accusatory.

'Umm ...' Lee returned to his computer to recheck what he had. There was no medical file attached, or a mention of any history of depression reported by Pedro Bustamente's family or his doctor. 'I can't exactly remember, but no, we probably didn't check. No investigation was initiated because there was nothing to investigate. No signs of foul play. It was an open-and-shut suicide case, and to speak candidly ...' He met Garcia's stare. 'Unearthing the reasons that could've led anyone to terminate their own lives isn't really our job, Detective.' He indicated the pile of paperwork on his desk. 'We have enough on our hands as it is.'

Garcia agreed with a nod.

'But speaking from experience,' Lee continued, 'nowadays, a growing number of suicides amongst young kids – and I include Mr. Bustamente in my definition of "kids" – occur from lack of social approval, generated by the craziness of social media and the madness that "cancel culture" has become, not a history of depression or a chemical/hormonal imbalance in the brain. Most of the sadness that goes around the world today, especially amongst teenagers and young adults, is electronically generated – delivered straight into their psyche via social media.' Lee rattled his fingers on his desk. 'Nowadays, more and more people are searching for validation from complete strangers, comparing themselves and their lives to individuals, who they've never met and probably never will. When they don't match up, and they *never* do because they are essentially comparing themselves to a lie, they get low ... sometimes this low.' Lee indicated Pedro Bustamente's suicide file on his screen once again.

Garcia studied the detective sitting before him.

'I guess that what I'm trying to explain to you here,' Lee said, placing his elbows on the arms of his chair and interlacing his fingers together, 'is that their own families, their own friends, even their own doctors usually have no clue that these kids are falling apart. They have no clue that they're feeling low or depressed. They have no clue of what these kids are about to do to themselves. The truth is that most people out there, especially younger people, don't know how to ask for help. What they do know how to do, and they do it really well, is put filters on everything, masking their sadness and selling the illusion that all is perfect – and the first person that they sell that illusion to is themselves. They pretend that all is fine, just for a false feeling of belonging.'

Garcia couldn't disagree with him. 'How about the autopsy report?' he asked. 'Didn't it make you wonder?'

Detective Lee frowned at him. 'I never saw the autopsy report. There was no need. Like I said, Detective, it was an open-and-shut suicide case. No signs of foul play. No investigation was initiated. In the case of suicide, the law demands that a post mortem examination is carried out. You know that. The autopsy report is then added to the death certificate for the benefit of the family.'

But Garcia's question did tickle Detective Lee's curiosity. 'Why?' he asked. 'Did the autopsy report make *you* wonder?'

Garcia nodded. 'It did. Very high levels of alcohol and Tramadol.'

The surprise on Detective Lee's face had an added sarcastic edge to it.

'You can't be this naïve, Detective Garcia,' Lee said, and paused for a moment. 'Ninety-nine percent of all people who commit suicide show great quantities of either alcohol or drugs in their system. Usually a combination of both. What they're about to do to themselves is final. And I mean *final* final. There are no do-overs.'

'Yes, I understand that but—'

'Let me pause you there for a moment, Detective.' Lee didn't give Garcia a chance to counter. 'Why is the LAPD UVC interested in a Pomona suicide victim of a year ago?'

'His name popped up in one of our investigations,' Garcia explained. 'We're trying to gather as much info as we can.'

'Well, I don't think there's anything I can tell you that isn't in the report you got,' Lee said, sitting back in his chair again.

'You're sure that his landlord was the one who found the body?' Garcia insisted. 'Not someone else . . . a loved one like a partner . . . girlfriend . . . boyfriend . . . member of the family?'

'Yes, I'm sure.' Lee scrolled down on his screen. 'It says so in the occurrence sheet. The landlord, a Mr. Juan De Bastila, went over to collect the weekly rent, as he did every Thursday. The time was 8:10 p.m. There was no reply at the door. Mr. De Bastila then used his key to gain access to the property, with the intention of leaving a note reminding Mr. Bustamente that his rent was due. Upon entering the apartment, he discovered Mr. Bustamente's body on the floor inside the bathroom, practically floating in a pool of blood. He then proceeded to call 911.' Lee paused, as he read something new on his screen. 'Though . . .'

Garcia noticed the uncertain look in Lee's eyes and moved his chair around just enough to be able to peek at his screen. 'Though what?'

'Though I made an annotation against the file,' Lee explained, indicating on his monitor, 'that the assumption was that this had probably been the consequence of a broken heart.'

Garcia read the annotation that Lee had indicated.

'Because of a handwritten note?' Garcia looked back at Lee in surprise. 'He left a suicide note? That wasn't mentioned in the file we received.'

All Detective Lee could do was shrug.

'Where's this note?' Garcia asked. 'What did it say? You at least have a record of it, right?'

'Umm . . .' On his screen, Detective Lee clicked back to get to the case root folder. 'We probably have a photo of it somewhere.'

One of the subfolders was named 'Photos'. Lee opened it to find that it contained only twelve images. He started at the top. The photo that they were looking for was number eight on the list. It showed a white, ruled piece of paper that had been left on the sink, inside the bathroom. On it, there was a single, handwritten line of text – twelve words that made the hairs on the back of Garcia's neck stand on end.

Detective Lee noticed the change in Garcia.

'Something wrong, Detective?'

Garcia's unflinching eyes stayed on the note.

'You've got to be kidding me.'

Sixty-seven

The library at Gardena High was much bigger than what Hunter had expected. The 'Yearbooks' section was located on the second floor and the first yearbook on the shelf dated back to the class of 1948. Hunter fought the urge to leaf through it, just for curiosity's sake, and reached for the 2009 junior-high edition, which had a light blue cover, with a black panther at its center.

Yearbook in hand, Hunter found an empty table in the library's sitting area and quickly flipped through the pages until he got to the graduating class of 2009.

It wasn't unusual for a school with such a high number of students, like Gardena, to have more than one class per grade. During the 2008/2009 school year, Gardena Junior High had four separate eight-grade classes – 8A, 8B, 8C and 8D. 8A had fifty-one students, 8B fifty-two, 8C fifty and 8D also fifty-two.

Since they were the graduating class, eighth-graders had more yearbook pages allocated to them than any of the other grades. There was also an entire section – almost forty pages – dedicated to either showing student life in general, or highlighting specific students and their achievements in academics, sports, school clubs, student board, etc.; but what Hunter was really interested in was the class pages. Those looked just like any other yearbook in America – plastered with small headshots of every student in the class, with their names showing under each photo – an authentic Class of 2009 'who's who'.

Hunter slowly scanned through all four pages of the 8A class, where he found none of the five students that he was looking for. Still, he grabbed his cellphone and snapped a photo of each page before moving on to the 8B class.

This time there were five pages of ID-sized photos. The first four pages showed four rows with four photos each. The last six student photos were spread, unevenly, over the fifth and last page.

Hunter found Janet Lang and Troy Foster right on the first page of the 8B class. He didn't even need to check the names to correctly identify them.

On the next page, Hunter found Pedro Bustamente's photo. He had been an average-looking kid, with midnight-black curly hair, dark eyes, chubby cheeks and a smile that didn't look forced, as if he had actually enjoyed having that photo taken, something that most junior-high students certainly did not.

The very first photo on the third page was of Josie Moss. Her hair was a little shorter and a shade darker than when Hunter first met her, two days ago, but he still had no problems recognizing her. Her beauty hadn't exactly changed in thirteen years, but it had clearly matured. From that one photo alone, it was easy to see that every boy, in all four eighth-grade classes, would probably have done anything just to grab her attention.

The fifth photo on the page was of the last student in their group – Sofia Risoli. She too was an attractive girl. The fringe of her long, straight dark hair fell over enigmatic deep brown eyes, framing a delicate, heart-shaped face. The braces on her teeth took nothing away from a smile that seemed warm and friendly. Hunter wondered if her beauty had matured in the same way as Josie Moss's.

Out of pure curiosity, Hunter browsed through all the student photos of the two remaining eighth-grade classes – C and D.

When he was done, he checked his watch and quickly returned to Principal Martinez's office to tell Brenda, the secretary, that he was ready to see the seven members of staff on the list that she'd been given by the principal. Ten minutes later, back in the library, Hunter met Mr. Barros, the head janitor.

Mr. Barros was a sixty-four-year old, tall and slender man, who'd been working at Gardena High for twenty-five years, fifteen of them as the head janitor.

Hunter showed him the five yearbook photographs – Janet, Troy, Josie, Sofia and Pedro.

The first one that Mr. Barros recognized after just a couple of blinks was Troy Foster.

'Oh yeah,' he said in a voice that sounded as kind as the look in his eyes. 'I remember him. Football player, right? Wide receiver. Fast as hell and very strong. This kid was going places.'

Out of the other four, the only one that Mr. Barros was able to vaguely remember was Josie Moss, but only because she had been part of the cheerleading team.

Hunter tried asking him about Troy and Josie together, if he remembered anything else about them other than football and cheerleading, but Mr. Barros could offer nothing else. Sounding apologetic, he explained that he was an old man now and that his memory wasn't the same, but he was also just a simple school janitor. Students walked by him while he was cleaning the hallways, the classrooms, the bathrooms, etc., but very few ever spoke to him. He told Hunter that he did his job and tried as best as he could to keep himself to himself – students' lives were none of his business. He said that he remembered Troy and Josie because he loved sports and whenever possible, he would watch the school games – junior-high and varsity.

After Mr. Barros, Hunter met the three members of the school canteen, the school gardener and one of the security guards. The second security guard was off that day.

All five of them were able to remember Troy, the football player, but none of the others, not even Josie. Hunter tried asking them all about school bullying, fights, pranks, anything that might've stood out. Something that maybe Troy had been involved in, since he was the only one they all remembered, but none of them could recall anything and they all gave Hunter a very similar answer. First, they were talking about thirteen years ago, which was quite an ask for anyone's memory. Second, in a school with about fifteen hundred students, fights, pranks, and bullying happened every day, and that was not an exaggeration. It was a fact – physically stronger students bullied the weaker ones. Sports students bullied the ones that didn't play any sports. Girls bullied other girls because of their hair, or their clothes, or their shoes, or any of a million silly excuses to be bitchy. That was also one of the biggest reasons why students hung out in groups. If anyone came across as a loner, or an outsider, that person would be picked on.

Just as Hunter finished his short interview with the security guard, the last of the available members of staff on the list he had, his cellphone vibrated inside his jacket pocket.

'*Robert*,' Garcia said, as Hunter took the call. '*You're not going to believe this.*'

'You found something?'

'*Yeah, I'd say so.*'

'I'm listening.'

'*Pedro Bustamente's death wasn't suicide.*'

There was a split second pause from Hunter. 'Is that what Detective Lee told you?'

'*No. Detective Lee is certain that it was suicide,*' Garcia replied. '*Classic open-and-shut case, but I found something that wasn't mentioned in the file we got this morning.*'

'Really? What?'

'*There was a handwritten suicide note ... left on the sink inside the bathroom. Written in Mr. Bustamente's handwriting. His mother confirmed it at the time.'*

Hunter felt his jaw muscles tighten. 'OK, and what did it say?'

'Are you sitting down?'

'Yes. What did it say?'

'"*Through this darkness, no light will ever burn as bright as yours.*"'

Sixty-eight

Hunter sat still, his cellphone firmly against his right ear, his unfocused eyes staring at nothing at all … his brain, though, was working overtime, trying to piece together a sequence of events that at last, at least for him, was starting to make some sort of sense.

'*Robert*?' Garcia called after seconds of dead silence. '*Are you still there*?'

'Yes, I'm here.' There was another short, thoughtful pause. 'This means that Mr. Bustamente was the very first victim of the Mentor.'

'*I'm sure he was,*' Garcia agreed. '*It's the only way to explain why he was killed instead of a loved one. It's not because he was a loner and had no one. I thought of that too, but according to Detective Lee, Pedro was very close to his parents, especially his mother. His parents live in Covina, not that far from here. I'm going to try to pay them a visit as soon as I leave Pomona.*'

'Great idea,' Hunter agreed.

'*Pedro being the very first victim,*' Garcia continued, '*also explains why the Mentor made it look like suicide instead of using the kind of brutality we witnessed in every single one of his crime scenes. When the Mentor went after Pedro Bustamente, there was no MO … there was no plan … there wasn't even a "Mentor" – just a very angry person lashing out. This first* murder ... this wasn't calculated, or thought through. *This was emotional. This was pure rage.'*

'I agree,' Hunter said. 'That would also be why it took the Mentor over a year to strike again. He didn't like how he handled his first attack – the make-believe suicide. There was no suffering, no pain, no torture ... nothing. That wasn't good enough for him, but he only realized that after he took Pedro's life. After that, he needed to get organized ... he needed a plan of action ... and he needed to track down the other members of the group.' Right then, Hunter heard the school bell ring. It was time to go talk to Mr. Hartley.

'*If we're right about this, Robert, and this first attack was really an emotional lashing-out ...'*

'It means that the Mentor probably wasn't as careful as he's been with his last three attacks.' Hunter said, anticipating what his partner was about to say. 'It means that there were probably clues left at the crime scene ... forensic clues. Was the scene documented?'

'No.' Frustration dripped from Garcia's answer. '*It wasn't viewed as a crime scene – open-and-shut suicide case, remember? In total, Pomona PD has twelve images and an occurrence sheet. That's all.'*

'Get them to email us whatever they have. Every file. Every photo. You never know.'

'*Done already.'*

'Good job.'

'*How's it going at Gardena Junior High? Any luck?'*

'Not yet, but I'm just about to go talk to a teacher who actually taught the class of 2009.'

'*That's promising. I'll finish up here in Pomona and head to Pedro Bustamente's parents' place. I'll call you after I talk to them.'*

Hunter disconnected from the call, but still didn't move. His

mind was too busy shuffling things around and creating theo-
ries out of thin air. He'd worked cases before where the serial
perpetrator had shown similar behavior – the first murder had
either been pure rage or a spur-of-the-moment attack, followed
by a long dormant period, in which the aggressor took the time
to organize himself and to devise a plan. In those similar cases,
there had always been one constant – rage would never again
supersede rationale.

Out of curiosity, Hunter flipped the yearbook to the back
cover, looking for its library checkout card. It was completely
empty. No one had ever taken that yearbook out.

He glanced at his watch again. It really was time to go see Mr.
Hartley, but as he reached out to close the yearbook, he noticed
that its final four pages were part of a students' special section,
one that he hadn't noticed until then.

Hunter quickly read through the section and studied the twelve
student photos on those pages – nothing of any real significance,
but something on the very last page of that final section sparked
a brand new thought in Hunter's mind. Another very long shot.

He quickly got up and returned to the yearbook section. This
time he picked up the Junior High, Class of 2010 edition.

Standing by the bookshelf, Hunter flipped the yearbook open
to the last few pages, seeking the same special section he'd just
found in the Class of 2009 yearbook. There it was – seven pages
this time, instead of four. He read through the pages and studied the photographs – nothing. Another long shot that didn't
pay off, but as he was returning the yearbook to the bookshelf,
he paused.

'Hold on a sec,' he whispered to himself. 'I might be looking
at the wrong yearbook here.'

His eyes scanned the shelves until they found the other 2010
edition – the one for Gardena High School, not the Junior High.

'This would make a lot more sense.'

Hunter reached for the book and once again flipped it to the last few pages, until he found the section that he was looking for.

The high-school yearbook was considerably thicker than the junior high one. The final, special section had twenty-one pages in total, but Hunter didn't get to look at them all. As he flipped the pages to the beginning of the section, he froze in place, barely believing what he was looking at.

'No goddamn way.'

Hunter's disbelieving words fell into the empty space between him and the bookshelf. A crazy theory started taking shape inside his head, but he quickly discarded it, due to the absurdity of it all.

'It can't be this.'

His words, once again, reached no one else's ears but his own.

He quickly returned to his table and studied the three photos on the page before reopening the Junior High, Class of 2009 edition. With both yearbooks open on the table in front of him, his gaze bounced from one book to the other, as he cross-referenced what he had found. It took him less than a minute to match it.

Another few flips on the Gardena High, Class of 2009 edition and he paused at a photo, the young boy on it looking back at him with terribly sad eyes.

Hunter felt his heart beating at the bottom of his throat as he reached for his cellphone.

'*Robert*,' Garcia said, as he answered his partner's call. '*What's up?*'

Silently, Hunter read the name underneath the photo. 'Carlos', he said, 'I think I know who we're looking for.'

'*What?*'

'The Mentor . . . I think I'm looking at him right now.'

Sixty-nine

After leaving Gardena Junior High, Hunter had to fight the urge to go confront Janet Lang and Josie Griffith with what he had found out back in the school library. He knew that he would have to do that eventually, but he first needed Research to confirm some of his theory. He was experienced enough to know that when faced with a truth that they didn't want revealed, most people's natural instinct was to lie, regardless of the consequences.

Hunter had been the first to get back to the Police Administration Building. Garcia arrived about half an hour after him, just a couple of minutes ahead of Captain Blake, whose meeting with the Chief of Police and the Mayor of Los Angeles had run a little beyond schedule.

'You found him?' she asked, surprised, as she busted through Hunter and Garcia's office door. 'You found the killer? How? Who is he?'

Once the captain had stepped out of her meeting, she'd received two urgent messages. The first was from Garcia, quickly explaining about Sofia Elliot's trip to Italy and requesting a surveillance team to stake out her house, effective immediately. The second had been from Hunter.

'We've got a name,' Hunter replied, turning from the picture board to face her. 'No location yet.'

Captain Blake approached the board. 'OK, I'm listening. Who is he?'

'His name is Michael Williams,' Hunter said, taking a step to his left and indicating one of the new images now on the board. It was a reprint from a photo from one of Gardena High yearbooks. It showed a physically strong kid, with fair skin, light-brown eyes and a pointy nose. The long fringe of his straight black hair was swept left, partially covering his eye. On the photo, the edges of his lips were slightly curved up, as if he was trying hard to force a smile that was never really there to begin with.

'Mr. Williams was seventeen years old when that photo was taken,' Hunter continued. 'That was thirteen years ago. He graduated class of 2009 from Gardena – the high school, not the junior high. We still haven't managed to find a more recent image anywhere, but Research is working on it.'

'No social media?' Garcia asked. He too was standing before the board, right between Hunter and Captain Blake. 'There's got to be something.'

'So far, Research has come across tens of Michael Williams on three different social media platforms. Unfortunately, the name Michael is the fourth most common male name in the US.'

The captain chuckled. 'Typical . . . and let me guess, with our luck, so is the family name Williams, right?'

'Top three,' Hunter confirmed. 'With over two million Americans sharing it, but truthfully, the problem with social media is that people can create a profile with whatever name they wish, so Michael can become Mike, Mick, Mc, or whatever. He can call himself "Papi" if he wants to.' Hunter's head tilted right. 'We're hoping he didn't, but that's why Research is running a facial image recognition key-points test against not only every "Michael Williams" social media account they find, but also against all California State driving licenses.' Hunter's pause was leaden. 'No matches so far, but they've only just started. They're also running his name against a few address databases – homeowners, car owners, utility bills, credit cards . . . the works.'

'How about tracking his parents down?' Garcia asked. 'They'll probably know where to find him.'

'Research is on that too.'

'Hold on a second,' the captain said, her eyebrows lifting slightly at Hunter at the mention of driving licenses. 'You said that he graduated class of 2009, right? Driver's ed was still taught in high schools back then, wasn't it? If I remember correctly, they only started phasing it out of school curriculums around 2012, 2013?'

'That's right,' Hunter confirmed. 'And I checked when I was there – Michael Williams never took driver's ed when he was in school. I also checked his home address from the time that he was at Gardena High. He didn't live that far from the school.'

'No luck, I presume,' Garcia said.

Hunter shook his head. 'The Williams family moved out in 2010. They lived in a small block of flats on West 156th Street. I talked to everyone in the building who answered their doors. Nobody remembered them.'

'*Nobody?*' Captain Blake looked at Hunter a little sideways.

'Twelve apartments in the building,' Hunter explained. 'All of them owned by the same landlord who, according to the tenants I've spoken with, rents them out at not very friendly rates. In places like that, Captain, few people or families will rent for over three to four years, if that. No one in that building has been there for twelve. None of them even met the Williamses.'

'Have you spoken to the landlord?' the captain asked.

'Only on the phone. He said that they were a nice family and that they paid their rent on time. His records showed that they moved out in February 2010. He had no forwarding address for them.'

It was only then that Garcia's brain picked up on something that Hunter had mentioned a few moments ago.

'Hold on,' he said, lifting a hand and pinning Hunter with an inquisitive stare. 'You said that he graduated class of 2009 ... from the high school, not the junior high?' He indicated the photo on the board. 'And that he was seventeen years old when this picture was taken ... in 2009?'

'That's what I said, yes,' Hunter confirmed, already knowing that Garcia had caught on. By the look on Captain Blake's face, she was just about to.

'So when Janet, Troy, Josie, Sofia and Pedro were thirteen or fourteen and finishing eighth-grade,' Garcia continued, now indicating the photos of the Gardena Junior High group of students, 'Michael Williams was seventeen years old and a *high school senior.*'

'That's correct,' Hunter confirmed again.

The captain finally saw what was wrong with that whole scenario.

'Hold up,' she said, taking a step forward. 'There's no way that a group of eighth-graders were bullying a seventeen-year-old high-school senior, especially when he looks like this.' She indicated the photo on the board. 'He's built like a boxer.'

'Right again,' Hunter confirmed. 'They didn't bully him.'

The hint came in the way that Hunter had delivered his last sentence.

Seventy

A few hours earlier – Gardena School Library.

Hunter flipped the yearbook to the back cover, looking for its library checkout card. It was completely empty. No one had ever checked out the 2009 Junior High yearbook.

He checked his watch. It really was time to go see Mr. Hartley, but as he reached out to close the yearbook, he noticed that its final four pages were part of a special section – dedicated to students who had unfortunately lost their lives during the school year. The section was titled – 'In Loving Memory Of'.

Those four words caused a rollercoaster of thoughts inside Hunter's head.

He knew from his own experience and from so many years as a homicide detective that nothing could make the human psyche more vindictive than loss. So what if he and Garcia were wrong? What if the Mentor wasn't going after the group of Gardena Junior High students because he had been bullied and humiliated when he was in school? What if he was going after them because of a terrible loss, a loss that he somehow blamed on that group of students?

Hunter flipped through the four pages in the section.

There were twelve photos in total, displaying four

students – three boys and a girl. Each page focused on a single student, with three large color photographs per page. On every page, there was also a dedication, loving words written either by a member of the family, a teacher, or both. Two of the boys were brothers – nine and eleven years old – who had passed away on the same day. The girl had been a ten-year-old fifth-grade student, and according to the date at the top of the page, she had lost her life just a couple of weeks before the end of the school year. The last of the four students had died at the age of nine. He was a fourth-grader.

None of those four kids had been an eighth-grade student. None of them belonged to the Class of 2009, but something on the very last page of the 'In Loving Memory Of' section, cause Hunter's thought-rollercoaster to take off on a new spin.

The fourth-grader, the boy who had died at the age of nine, had passed away in August 2008, but Hunter was looking at the junior-high yearbook of 2009 – almost a whole year after his death. So why was he featured in the 2009 edition? The answer was simple – the boy had died just after the end of the previous school year, 2007–08. The junior-high yearbook for 2008 had already been printed – they were usually ready by the end of June. That meant that if any students lost their lives during their school break, while transitioning from one grade to the next, their 'In Loving Memory Of' page would feature in the next yearbook edition.

Hunter got up and returned to the bookshelf. This time, he picked up the Junior High, Class of 2010 edition and flipped it open to the last few pages, until he came across the 'In Loving Memory Of' section. In the 2010 edition, there were seven pages, instead of four. Once again, every page featured a different student, showing three large color photographs per page, together with a dedication.

Hunter read through the pages and studied the students'

photos. None of them had been an eighth-grader. None of them belonged to the graduating class of 2009. Just another long shot that hadn't paid off, but as he was returning the yearbook to the bookshelf, he paused.

'Hold on a sec,' he whispered to himself, realizing where he might've gone wrong. 'I might be looking at the wrong year-book here.'

If a student from the Class of 2009 had lost his or her life after the end of that school year and before the beginning of the next one – around July, August or September of 2009 – their 'In Loving Memory Of' page would appear in the 2010 edition, but not the junior high one. In 2010, the graduating students from the 2009 class would be in their first year of high school. They'd all be ninth-graders – sophomores. Logic dictated that their 'In Loving Memory Of' page would appear in the high-school yearbook, not the junior-high one.

Hunter's eyes scanned the shelves until they found the Gardena High School 2010 yearbook edition.

'This would make a lot more sense.'

He reached for the book and once again, flipped it to the last few pages.

The high-school yearbook was considerably thicker than the junior-high one. The 'In Loving Memory Of' section had twenty-one pages in total, but Hunter didn't get to look at them all. As he flipped the pages to the beginning of the section, he froze in place. The page that he was looking at belonged to a fourteen-year-old girl, with shiny black hair, almond-shaped brown eyes and a disarmingly kind-looking smile. She had sadly passed away in July 2009, just a few weeks after she had graduated from the junior high's Class of 2009.

But what had made Hunter's stomach drop to the floor and his mouth go desert-dry was the dedication text on the page.

Through this darkness, no light will ever burn as
   bright as yours.
Through these eyes, no one will ever look as perfect
   as you did.
Through this heart, no love will ever surpass my
   love for you.
Through this soul, no pain will ever be greater than
   the pain of losing you.
Through this life, nothing else matters
   without you here.

The signature at the bottom of the dedication belonged to a boy who had graduated from Gardena High in 2009. He was the one who had written those verses. His name was Michael Williams. The girl who had died in July 2009 was his sister. Her name was Genesis Williams.

Seventy-one

Captain Blake and Garcia listened in stunned silence as Hunter ran them through how he'd found out about Michael and Genesis Williams. With every new name and new description he mentioned, he indicated a new photo on the board. The one that mesmerized everyone was the yearbook page printout with Michael's dedication to his sister.

'So these lines that he leaves behind at each crime scene,' Captain Blake said. 'They weren't meant for the victims at all. They're all about his sister?'

'In truth,' Hunter replied, 'they *are* about his loss ... his pain ... his anguish. It's a poem about his own suffering.'

'How did she die?' Captain Blake asked.

Hunter looked at his partner and Garcia felt his heart speed up inside his chest. He knew the answer even before Hunter said a word.

'She committed suicide.'

Seconds of silence ruled the room.

'How?' The captain again.

'She sliced her wrist open.' The answer came from Garcia, who was beginning to connect the dots.

Hunter nodded his agreement. 'I talked to their old homeroom and history teacher. He still teaches at Gardena and he remembers when he heard the news during the school break – July 2009.' The look in Hunter's eyes turned sad. 'She slit her wrist inside a bath-tub . . . in her family's bathroom, but here's the peculiar thing.' Hunter's gaze returned to Garcia.

'She only cut one wrist open,' Garcia said, his stare never leaving Hunter. 'Her left one . . . so deep it almost severed her whole hand off.'

Hunter nodded again.

Captain Blake pinched the bridge of her nose. 'So the logical conclusion would be that these five over here,' she indicated the photos of Janet, Troy, Josie, Pedro and Sofia, 'bullied this little girl back in 2009 to the point that she couldn't take anymore.'

'Presumably,' Hunter confirmed. 'And that's probably the reason why he isn't targeting them directly. He's going after their sisters . . . girlfriends . . . husbands . . . whatever, but not them.'

The captain paused. 'Wait a second. Why is that?'

'Because in a way,' Hunter replied, 'dying is easy. He doesn't want easy. He doesn't want them dead.'

'Easy?' Captain Blake's forehead creased.

'When you die, you cease to exist, Captain,' Hunter clarified. 'You cease to be, and so do all your emotions . . . all your feelings. You don't feel any pain anymore . . . or love, or anger, or remorse, or guilt, or shame . . .' He shrugged. 'There's no more suffering once you're dead. Suffering is done by those who are left behind.'

'And he wants them to suffer,' Garcia said, picking up from Hunter. 'He blames these five people not only for what happened to his sister, but also for what happened to him . . . for everything that he's had to go through for the past thirteen years.'

'Carlos is right,' Hunter confirmed. 'He does blame them. Maybe he blames others too. We don't really know how far his blame game reaches, but what is clear is that he doesn't want them dead. What he wants is for them to experience loss . . . pain . . . emotional turmoil . . . anguish . . . suffering . . . everything that comes with having someone you love taken away from you.'

Hunter paused, his tongue scraping along the roof of his mouth, finding the ridge there and pressing against it to center himself. 'How do you kill someone without actually killing them?'

Garcia looked back at Hunter with trepidation.

'You empty their soul,' Hunter answered his own question, 'only to refill it with pain. You take away what they love the most.'

Those words made Captain Blake's thought process stutter.

'Why does that sound familiar to me?' she asked, her left hand reaching for her nape. 'And why did it make me so uncomfortable to hear it?'

'Lucien Folter.' The reply came from Garcia.

Captain Blake's heart skipped a beat. 'What?'

'That's what he told Robert after killing Tracey's parents, remember?' Garcia replied.

Hunter's reaction was to look down at the floor.

'You're not actually suggesting that . . .'

'No,' Hunter said before the captain was able to finish her question. 'Lucien doesn't have anything to do with this, but the thought behind these crimes is the same. If you truly want to make somebody suffer, don't kill them – take away what they love the most and let them live the rest of their lives with the psychological torture that the loss will bring them.'

'And that has to be why the Mentor torments them with the aftermath messages,' Garcia added. 'The videos he sends them the day after the murder. He does it to completely mess them up psychologically. To let them know how much their loved ones suffered. If they can't handle the pain . . . if they prefer death to suffering . . . they have to do it themselves, like Troy Foster.'

'Like Genesis Williams,' Hunter said.

Captain Blake placed her hands on her hips and allowed her eyes to circle the board once . . . twice . . . three times.

'OK,' she said in a deflated breath. 'So now I have a few new questions . . . like – if this little girl, Genesis Williams, took her own life in July 2009 and her brother blames this group of students for it, why is he only going after them now, thirteen years later? Why did he wait this long?'

'The most logical conclusion,' Hunter began, indicating the photos as he explained, 'is that whatever it is that Michael Williams found out that made him blame this group of students for his sister's suicide didn't happen until about a year ago. Before that, he probably blamed no one. That's why he was inactive.'

Captain Blake bit her bottom lip, as she pondered her detective's words.

'We don't really know what happened to him right after his sister passed and he left Gardena High,' Hunter continued. 'Yes, thirteen years later he's going around torturing and killing people in the most sadistic of ways, but that doesn't necessarily mean that he lost it straight after his sister's suicide. Once he left Gardena High, he could've gotten a job and worked himself to the bone so he didn't have to think about what happened ... he could've gone off to college somewhere ... he could've taken a break and left California, or even the country, trying to put some physical distance between him and his sister's death. We don't know, Captain, but no matter what ... no matter how well or badly a person is handling his or her loss, the number one question that absolutely everyone asks when faced with suicide – loved ones or not – is "why?"'

This time, it was Captain Blake's eyes that found the floor. Neither Hunter nor Garcia knew about it, but before she became the LAPD Robbery Homicide Division's captain, one of her closest friends had taken her own life one Sunday afternoon. To this day, Captain Blake still asks herself, 'Why?'

'The problem is,' Hunter carried on, 'in most cases, there's very rarely an answer that will suffice, even when a note is left behind, because truthfully, the only person who really knows why they did it is the person who is gone. Everything else is speculation ...

but unfortunately, the human brain can't help but do exactly that. We humans need answers to things we don't understand. It's our natural behavior.'

'And when we can't find the real answers to ease the pain,' Garcia offered, 'we tend to fabricate them ourselves.'

'We do,' Hunter agreed. 'And I'm sure that in his head, Michael Williams has answered that question a million times, with a million different answers, but deep down most of us know that the answers that we fabricate in our heads aren't real and that means one thing – we never stop asking "why".' He tapped his right index finger against Michael Williams photo on the board. 'He never did.'

Captain Blake thought about the thousands of scenarios that she had created in her head over the years about what happened to her friend that Sunday afternoon. Why did she do it? What was really going through her mind in the moments preceding her death? Why didn't she reach out for help?

'And twelve years later,' Garcia said, bringing the captain's attention back to the room, 'Michael Williams obviously came across something he never knew before. Maybe he bumped into an old friend of his sister's . . . maybe he bumped into one of them.' He indicated the photos of the five members of the Gardena Junior High group.

'Possible,' Hunter agreed. 'And if he did, my guess is that he bumped into Pedro Bustamente and that would be why he was the first victim . . . why he died instead of a loved one.'

'That was about to be my next question,' Captain Blake said. 'Everything you just said about suffering and the killer making them go through the ordeal of losing a loved one doesn't apply with the first murder, does it? If it really was a murder instead of a suicide.'

'It was,' Garcia confirmed, before quickly running her through his meeting with Detective Lee. He explained about the first verse of Michael Williams's dedication to his sister, which was found on the sink, in Pedro Bustamente's bathroom, and how it was easily mistaken for a suicide note. He then explained about the single wrist cut.

'Pedro Bustamente was the beginning of it all,' Garcia said. 'Before Mr. Bustamente there was no "Mentor", there was no strategy, there was no revenge, and there was no MO. This first attack –' he pointed to the photo '– wasn't exactly planned or thought out. At least not like the rest of them. This first attack was emotional. It was Michael Williams lashing out in total anger after discovering the truth about his sister's suicide.'

By the look in Captain Blake's eyes, Hunter could see that in her head, things were finally starting to make some sense.

'So after that first murder,' she concluded, 'he decided to hunt them all down.'

'Exactly,' Hunter agreed. 'But once he was finished with his first victim, he realized that he wasn't happy with what he'd done. Faking a suicide didn't quite satisfy his anger ... his thirst for revenge.' Hunter ran a hand over his mouth. 'And it's easy to see why. Pedro Bustamente was dead – no more suffering ... no more pain ... nothing, but Michael Williams was still alive ... a tortured soul for twelve years ... still hurting ... still suffering ... still angry. How was that fair?'

'So he takes his time to devise a plan.' The captain again. 'How he could make them suffer in the same way that he's been suffering.'

'Do to them what they did to him,' Garcia said with a nod. 'An eye for an eye.'

'Humans have always wrongly believed that through vengeance, they can be made whole again,' Hunter said. 'Just look at history.'

Captain Blake sighed. 'So now all we have to do is actually catch him.'

'We've got his name, Captain,' Garcia came back. 'We know who he is and it looks like we know who's next on his list.'

'Sofia Elliot's husband,' Captain Blake nodded. 'And before you ask, yes, surveillance on their house is starting from tonight.' She checked her watch. 'SIS are probably already there now.'

The LAPD Special Investigation Section – or SIS – was the country's elite, tactical surveillance squad. Even the FBI sometimes used them for short-term, high-tech surveillance.

'Then it should be only a matter of time before we catch him,' Garcia replied.

'Have you taken this to Janet Lang or Josie Griffith yet?' Captain Blake asked.

'No, not yet. I want to get as much information as I can on Genesis and Michael Williams before confronting them with all this. They are both battling the worst kind of emotional pain there is, Captain. They have not only lost someone who they loved, but they were also the ones to have found the bodies. Their minds are at the brink of breaking, if they haven't yet. Confronting them with this – the idea that all this madness,' Hunter indicated the picture board, 'is possibly in retaliation for something that they did thirteen years ago while in junior high – it could easily push them to that breaking point. This is what the killer wants. He wants them to know that this is *their* fault.'

Once again, Captain Blake studied the new pictures on the board. This time, her attention settled on the three color photographs of Genesis Williams. There was only one full-body picture of her, where she was standing with her back against a brick wall. Her right leg was bent at the knee, with her foot flat against that same wall. Her thumbs were hooked through the belt loops of her blue jeans, which were ripped at both knees – rock and roll style. Her black hair was loose, framing her delicate face. It didn't look like a forced pose. The undeniable kindness that resided in her eyes made her seem peaceful, as if very little could ever faze her.

'In these photos,' the captain said, her expression curious, 'she looks like a very sweet girl. The kind that makes friends easily.'

'Took the words right out of my mouth, Captain,' Garcia agreed. 'Why did they pick on her? She was definitely pretty enough to join their group.'

Hunter's eyebrows lifted at both of them. 'You haven't noticed anything different about her?'

Garcia and Captain Blake's eyes returned to the photos, trying to take in every detail.

To help them, Hunter hooked his thumbs through the belt loops of his black jeans.

That was when they finally noticed Genesis Williams's hands.

Seventy-two

The studio apartment was small, just a tiny kitchen, a bathroom and a living/sleeping room not much bigger than a parking space. The bed was one of those, which folded into the wall, so that a foldable table could be pulled out. That was how the room currently looked – bed in, but table out, where a half empty bottle of Heaven's Door bourbon whiskey sat next to a half empty glass, a couple of photographs and a half-eaten sandwich. The sky outside the only window in the room had darkened a couple of hours ago, but the night was starry, with a bright, honey-colored moon.

Sitting by the table, facing the window, the Mentor carefully placed the items that had been laid out on the floor into a travel bag before zipping it up.

There had been a change of plans. That LAPD Detective was making progress a lot faster than initially anticipated. Sure, that first encounter had been expected ... planned even, but not the one that happened today. That meant that the LAPD was getting close ... maybe too close.

What had happened in the afternoon hadn't exactly been an encounter. In fact, it had been a huge stroke of luck.

The Mentor had already managed to make a copy of the key to Sofia Elliot's house. That had been relatively easy. Sofia's neighbor Mrs. Perks had kindly agreed to cat-sit while Sofia and her husband were away in Italy, and she had hidden Sofia's house keys – probably to make certain she didn't forget where she'd put them – under a plant pot, around the side of Sofia's house. While staking out the house, the Mentor had spotted the hiding place the morning after Sofia and her husband had left for Italy.

Taking the keys, making copies, and returning the originals to the plant pot before Mrs. Perks had to feed the cat again had been a walk in the park.

This afternoon, the plan had been to use the keys to enter Sofia's house for a thorough inside recon of the space. Knowing beforehand the best places to hide inside the victims' houses had been one of the Mentor's greatest assets so far, but today's plan hadn't quite worked out.

The Mentor had been parked on the road for less than five minutes, three houses away from Sofia Elliot's place, when the LAPD detective pulled up in front of her house, exited his car and rang the doorbell.

No answer.

The detective had just moved to go check the windows, when Mrs. Perks came out to talk to him.

This wasn't in the original script, at least not for a few more days. If the LAPD knew about Sofia Elliot, it meant that they were slotting the pieces into the puzzle faster than expected, and that was why a change of plans was needed.

It had taken fourteen months of preparation, together with tremendous patience and discipline, to be able to spend day upon day . . . night upon night, observing and studying every victim . . . learning their habits and their time schedules . . . finding out exactly when they'd be home alone and for how long, so that they could get what was coming to them . . . what they truly deserved.

The new plan wasn't perfect . . . it wasn't polished and meticulously detailed like the original. It was also a lot riskier, but it would work because it had to.

The Mentor refilled the glass on the table and paused by the window before gulping the drink down. The alcohol burn was welcome ... appreciated ... needed.

The wait was finally almost over; but first, there was one more thing that needed to be done.

Seventy-three

Due to the camera angle and the fact that Genesis Williams had hooked her thumbs through the belt loops on her jeans, her hands weren't exactly noticeable. It was only after Hunter's hint that Garcia and Captain Blake saw it, but still, even after craning their necks forward to get a closer look, neither of them could be one hundred percent sure of what they were actually looking at.

'What's wrong with her hands?' the captain asked, squinting at the photo. 'Is she missing a finger?'

'It's called ectrodactyly,' Hunter explained. 'It's a congenital disorder, characterized by the absence or malformation of one or more of the fingers and toes. Mr. Hartley told me that only Genesis Williams's hands were affected, not her feet. In her case, the index and the middle fingers on both of her hands never developed.' Hunter indicated on the board. 'You can't really tell from this photo because of the position of her thumbs, but according to Mr. Hartley, her thumbs were curved inwards, at the knuckles, and her ring and little fingers were webbed together, giving the illusion that on both hands, she only had her thumb and one finger.' He walked over to his desk and picked up a new printout. 'I looked it up. Ectrodactyly is divided into six levels of severity. A curved thumb together with webbing of the only two fingers left on the hand is considered level five.'

'In other words,' Garcia said, 'quite severe.'

Hunter nodded. 'Yes, but she'd still have relatively good use of her hands. She would've been able to write, draw, type, drive a car, grip objects, etc.' He pinned the printout to the board. 'This is how her hands would've looked.' The image had come from a specialized medical website and it showed a hand affected by ectrodactyly, where the ring and little fingers were webbed together and the thumb was curved inwards at the knuckle.

Hunter gave Garcia and Captain Blake a few seconds to study the printout before dropping the bomb.

'Due to how the condition causes the muscles of the hand to atrophy and the bones to reshape,' he explained, as he indicated, 'ectrodactyly is also referred to as "lobster claw syndrome".'

Two pairs of wide, surprised eyes moved to him.

'Are you joking?' Garcia asked, knowing full well that Hunter wouldn't joke about something like this.

Hunter gave him a subtle shake of the head.

Garcia's attention moved to the photos of Oliver Griffith's crime scene. 'Now this is finally starting to make some sort of sense.' He pointed to the pictures with the lobsters pinned to Oliver's thighs.

'They were clues,' Hunter told them. 'But not directed at us. Directed at the person who the killer knew would find the body.'

'Oliver's wife,' Garcia said. 'Josie.'

'Precisely,' Hunter agreed. 'He wanted her to know why her husband had died. That's why he used the lobsters. That's why he left the line on the wall. They were clues. He wanted her to remember.'

'So he's playing a goddamn game,' Captain Blake said, her tone moving toward angry. 'A "catch me if you can" game.'

'More like a charade,' Hunter said. 'Like a "who am I" kind of game.'

'But why leave clues only in the last of his four crime scenes?' the captain asked.

'That's just it,' Hunter clarified. 'He didn't. He left a line at each of the four crime scenes, but none of the people who were supposedly able to identify it, did. Maybe there were other clues as well – the posing of the bodies, the way in which they were murdered, props that were used.' Hunter shrugged. 'We don't know because like I've said, the clues weren't directed at us. They were directed at the people who knew Genesis Williams.'

'Did her teacher tell you that there was a bullying problem?' Captain Blake asked. 'Were other students mean to her?'

'He said that he never saw it happening in his classroom,' Hunter explained. 'And that he doesn't remember it being a problem, but he also agreed that just because he never saw it happening, it doesn't mean that it didn't happen at all.'

'We've said it before, Captain,' Garcia commented. 'Kids will be kids – and what I mean by that is kids can be assholes sometimes. Even if bullying wasn't a recurring problem, I'm sure that mean comments ... name-calling ... stupid jokes ... notes in the locker ... all that kind of shit would've popped up every now and then.'

'Enough to push her over the edge and make her want to end her own life?' the captain asked.

'It would all have depended on her state of mind,' Hunter took over. 'But understandably, kids with physical disorders or abnormalities – congenital or not, severe or not – tend to struggle a lot more with depression and anxiety, especially during their teenage years. That's when they first start worrying about their looks and about their bodies – girls start to notice boys, boys start to notice girls. You know how it goes. Genesis Williams knew she looked different and at that age, when she might've been getting the hots for someone for the first time, that knowledge would've played havoc with her confidence and her self-esteem, making her state of mind even more fragile. Even if she wasn't really being constantly bullied, like Carlos said – mean comments ... name-calling ...

stupid jokes . . . all that kind of stuff would have popped up here and there, and unfortunately, things like that don't just go away. They stay with you. They accumulate in your mind.'

'That's so terribly sad,' Captain Blake said, as she took a step back from the board. 'But still, it doesn't justify her brother going on a manic killing spree.' She checked her watch – it was getting late. 'Do you think we'll manage to locate him tonight?'

'Hard to say,' Hunter replied. 'Research is doing their best. The facial image recognition software will be running all night, or until it hits a match. If we still have nothing by the morning, we'll use aging software on the yearbook photos we have of Michael Williams to hypothesize what he looks like now, thirteen years on. We'll then APB those images to every police station in LA and Greater LA.'

'But the advantage has tipped our way now, Captain,' Garcia jumped in. 'Because if we're right about his next victim being Sofia Elliot's husband, Lucas – and I do think we are – he's not back from Italy until Saturday morning. It's Tuesday, which gives us three full days to track Michael Williams down. But even if we somehow fail to locate him, we'll have eyes on Mr. Elliot from the second he touches down at LAX. His house is already under surveillance. The only way that the Mentor, Michael, or whatever crap name he wants to call himself is getting to Lucas Elliot before we get to him is if he becomes invisible.' Garcia shook his head. 'And he's not doing that. His game is over.'

Seventy-four

As Hunter parked in front of his apartment building in Huntington Park, he checked the clock on the dashboard of his old Buick – it was coming up to 11 p.m. He rested his head on the steering wheel and breathed out – a mixture of exhaustion, tension, anticipation and apprehension, all in one.

Despite all their efforts, Research still hadn't managed to locate Michael Williams, but Hunter knew that in a city with a population of almost nineteen million, even with a name and a recent photo, it could take days, sometimes weeks to track someone down, especially if that someone didn't want to be found.

Before going up to his third floor apartment, Hunter checked with the undercover SIS surveillance team parked on Sofia and Lucas Elliot's road. He was sure that if Michael Williams were to break into Sofia's house and hide inside, like had happened with his previous three crime scenes, he wouldn't do it until around twenty-four hours before Lucas was expected back from Italy – either the day or the night before – and that wasn't until Saturday. However, Hunter also knew that the Mentor was disciplined and systematic, probably almost to the point of being obsessive. If he hadn't yet, he would've felt the need to check on every detail before acting. He would've wanted to know every inch of the inside of Lucas's house to minimize the possibility of a mistake, and what better time to do that than while the house was completely empty and no one was expected back for days?

No luck yet. Other than the neighbor going in to feed the cat, no one else had approached the house.

After having a shower and a quick microwave dinner, Hunter poured himself a large dose of GlenAllanchie, 15-year-old single malt Scotch whisky, and took a seat on the sofa in his living room. He chose to keep the lights off. It was more relaxing that way.

He brought the glass to rest against his lips and savored the burn of the alcohol in his nostrils for a moment, picking up hints of butterscotch and sweet spices, before finally sipping the auburn-colored liquid. The smooth Scotch warmed in the heat of his mouth and he allowed it to sit there for a prolonged instant, until the aromas had developed into flavors.

The whisky helped with some of the tension in his muscles, and slowed down the avalanche of thoughts in his head, permitting him to unwind just enough to be able to doze off. And so he did, right there, on his living room sofa.

That night, for some reason, his insomnia finally decided to leave him alone, because Hunter slept there on the sofa for just a little over four hours. What woke him up wasn't any of the many nightmares or dark thoughts that had tormented him since he was a kid. It wasn't his brain screaming for him to come back to reality, or even his phone ringing. This time, what woke him up was a regular dream . . . nothing special . . . nothing scary . . . just a dream about him placing flowers on his parents' graves, something that he did, on average, every two weeks.

Hunter jolted awake, blinking rapidly before checking the time – 4:53 a.m.

He hadn't forgotten the flowers this month. He'd been at the cemetery just a few days ago – the previous Saturday. That wasn't why the dream woke him up. It was the idea that the dream had given him.

Despite the visits, Hunter paid a yearly fee at the cemetery so that one of the keepers would look after his parents' graves – small repairs, clean-up after heavy rains, looking out for growing weeds ... general maintenance stuff. What that really meant was that the administration office at the cemetery where his parents were buried had his contact details on file – name, current address, phone number and email. He was the one that they would contact in case of a problem, or if something was needed.

With that in mind, it wasn't too unrealistic to assume that someone whose sister meant so much to him – someone who had been going around murdering people to avenge her death – would visit and even place flowers on her grave from time to time. If that was true, then there was also a chance that Michael Williams, just like Hunter, paid an annual fee so that his sister's grave was looked after 365 days a year. All Hunter needed to do was find out in which cemetery Genesis Williams was buried and hope for the best.

In the USA, the government kept a specific burial records database which wasn't open to public access. The database was run by a branch of the Department of Health and Human Services called the Health Care Agency. Hunter logged in as a law enforcement officer and ran a search, hopping that Genesis Williams hadn't been cremated instead of buried.

It didn't take long for a result pop up on his screen – 2.6 seconds to be precise. Genesis Williams hadn't been cremated. She'd been buried and in the exact same cemetery as Hunter's parents, which wasn't that much of a surprise. Rose Hills Memorial Park in Whittier was the largest cemetery in North America, with over 450,000 graves.

However, as the page loaded onto Hunter's computer screen, he paused, his unblinking eyes staring at the words in front of him. He read them three times before the tips of his fingers moved to his temples.

'This can't be right,' he whispered to himself before quickly running another search.

Same result, which could only mean one thing.

They were wrong again.

Seventy-five

Rose Hills Memorial Park opened its gates to the public every day at 8 a.m. sharp, but Hunter had been such a regular visitor over so many years that he knew that despite its opening time, there was always someone either at the administration office or at the mortuary from 7 a.m. onwards. He also knew that several of the cemetery's gravediggers and maintenance workers started their daily duties at least a couple of hours before that. That was why at 6:30 a.m., Hunter was already standing directly in front of the main gates to the 1,400 acre cemetery on Workman Hill Road. Aware he was too early, he rang the intercom anyway, just in case he got lucky.

No reply.

Hunter was about to return to his car and wait when Rafael Ramos, a slight sixty-three year-old man who'd been one of the cemetery's ground workers for over thirty years, drove past the gates in his little green maintenance cart. He saw Hunter's headlights and came to meet him.

'I'm sorry, sir,' he said, his voice made hoarse through years of smoking, his Mexican accent still heavy. He gave Hunter a courteous smile. 'The cemetery only opens at eight.'

'I know,' Hunter replied, reciprocating the smile. 'But I'm here on official business.' He showed the old man his credentials. 'I was just hoping that maybe someone from admin would be here early.'

Ramos readjusted his thick glasses on his nose and squinted at Hunter. Recognition danced at the back of his eyes.

'I've seen you here before, haven't I?' he asked, taking a step to his right to escape the glare of Hunter's headlights.

'Possibly. I come here a lot. My parents are buried here.'

Ramos thought about it for a couple of seconds. 'Garden of Peace, right?' he said, proud of his own memory.

At Rose Hills Memorial Park, the allocated ground spaces for burials were divided into plots, and each one carried a name, not a number. There were three different types – Gardens, Terraces, and Lawns. Hunter's parents were buried in a plot named 'Garden of Peace'.

'That's correct,' Hunter confirmed. 'I was here on Saturday.'

'Yeah, I'm sure I saw you.' The old man shook his index finger at Hunter. 'Early in the morning, right?'

'I prefer early mornings.' Hunter nodded. 'I sometimes like to walk around the gardens after visiting my parents. It's quieter at that time . . . peaceful.'

'It's always peaceful here, but I know what you mean.' Ramos shifted his weight from one leg to the other and his tone changed from casual to concerned. 'Is that why you're here? Is there a problem with your parents graves?'

'No, not at all,' Hunter replied and quickly explained that he was after the details of the person registered as the contact for one of the cemetery's other graves.

'Oh, OK!' Ramos's expression relaxed a little. 'Which one would that be?'

'The name on the tombstone is Genesis Williams,' Hunter replied. 'Which plot and grave number I'm not sure.'

'Oh, I can help you with that,' the old man said, lifting his hand at Hunter while walking back to his cart to retrieve his work tablet. 'Genesis Williams, you said?'

'That's right,' Hunter confirmed.

Ramos typed the name onto the search box on his tablet and tapped 'enter'. Two seconds later, he had a results page.

'We actually have two Genesis Williams,' he informed the detective on the other side of the gates. 'Genesis A. Williams, who is at the Terrace of Faith and Genesis Williams, no middle initial, who is at Parkview Lawn. Genesis A. Williams has been a guest here since 1956; Genesis Williams, no middle initial, since 2009.'

'That's the one I'm looking for,' Hunter said. '2009.'

Ramos gave Hunter an apologetic look. 'Unfortunately, the information available through this is very limited.' He lifted his tablet at Hunter. 'I won't be able to pull any details on the person who's registered as the contact for her grave. You'll need to go to the main office for that.' He threw his right thumb over his shoulder. 'But I can show you the grave if you like? It's not that far from here.'

'Yes,' Hunter replied, giving Ramos a firm nod. 'If that's not too much trouble, I'd really like to see it.'

'No trouble at all, sir.'

The old man checked his watch before keying a six-digit code onto the keypad at the gates.

'Parkview Lawn is the one directly behind the Hillside Chapel. Do you know how to get there?'

'I do,' Hunter confirmed, as he got to his car.

'I'll meet you there, sir,' Ramos said, jumping back onto his green cart.

Less than three minutes later, Ramos was guiding Hunter through the grave paths on Parkview Lawn.

'It's right over there,' he said, pointing ahead. 'Just past those trees.'

They walked for another thirty seconds before Ramos paused and indicated the grave directly in front of him, one with two fresh bouquets of yellow and white flowers. 'Oh, this is the one. OK.'

There was a clear tone of recognition in Ramos's voice, but Hunter missed it, as he stood completely still, his full attention locked onto the tombstones before him.

GENESIS WILLIAMS.

19 MARCH 1995 –
14 JULY 2009
AGED 14

BELOVED DAUGHTER AND SISTER.

THROUGH THIS DARKNESS, NO LIGHT
WILL EVER BURN AS BRIGHT AS YOURS.

THROUGH THESE EYES, NO ONE WILL
EVER LOOK AS PERFECT AS YOU DID.

THROUGH THIS HEART, NO LOVE WILL
EVER SURPASS MY LOVE FOR YOU.

THROUGH THIS SOUL, NO PAIN WILL EVER BE
GREATER THAN THE PAIN OF LOSING YOU.

THROUGH THIS LIFE, NOTHING ELSE
MATTERS WITHOUT YOU HERE.

YOU WILL ALWAYS BE REMEMBERED.

From his search back in his apartment, Hunter already knew what he would find, but seeing the real grave and reading the words on the *second* headstone, sent shivers up and down his spine.

Michael Williams

25 May 1992 –
02 October 2010
Aged 18

Beloved son and brother.

Now taking care of his
sister up in heaven.

Rest in peace, my angels.

Somehow, the words on those tombstones seemed to chill the already cold air around Hunter even more.

'All the graves on this lawn are attended to by Mario,' Ramos explained. 'I can go get him if you like. He started at five today. Same time as me, but I take care of many of the graves on Vista Lawn.' He pointed right, indicating the plot directly across the driving path from where they were. 'I've seen her around here many times. The flowers on this grave are always fresh, and I mean *always*.' He paused and scratched his forehead for a second. 'Actually, I'm pretty sure that she was here yesterday, late afternoon. I saw her while I was doing some maintenance on Vista. That's why the flowers are so fresh.'

Hunter's jaw dropped open as he looked back at Ramos, full of disbelief.

'She?'

Ramos nodded. 'Yes, the lady who visits this grave. She's a total regular.'

Seventy-six

By the time Garcia got to the UVC Unit's office at 8:45 a.m., Hunter had already spent over an hour up on the fifth floor of the Police Administration Building, working with his research team.

Back at the admin office at Rose Hills Memorial Park, Hunter had found out that the person registered as a contact for Genesis and Michael Williams's grave was John Williams – their father – but it had been Mario Castro, the cemetery maintenance worker who took care of Parkview Lawn, who had supplied Hunter with the most important information.

'What's all this?' Garcia asked, as he stepped into the office, indicating the new photos and documents that Hunter was about to pin to the board.

'No wonder we couldn't find him,' Hunter said, without deviating his attention from all the printouts on his desk. 'We were searching for the wrong person.'

'What?' Garcia placed his jacket on the back of his chair. 'What do you mean – the wrong person?'

'Michael Williams . . .' This time, Hunter paused to look at his partner. 'He's dead.'

'*What?*' Garcia's entire expression morphed into confusion. 'When?'

'2010,' Hunter replied. 'Just over a year after he graduated from Gardena High. He was eighteen years old.'

Garcia's pause was hesitant. 'Are you sure?'

Hunter reached for one of the new photos on his desk and handed it to Garcia. It was one of the images that he had taken at the cemetery. It showed Genesis and Michael Williams's headstones.

Garcia stared at the photo in silence for a long moment. When he looked back at Hunter, he looked like he was made of questions.

'Yeah, I know.' Hunter nodded.

'What happened? How did he die?'

Hunter reached for another printout on his desk.

'Knowing the exact day of his death,' he explained, 'makes it much easier and faster to trace the autopsy report.'

He handed the printout to his partner.

'OD?' Garcia said, incredulous.

'Heroin,' Hunter confirmed.

Garcia's gaze flicked back to the printout for an instant. 'Hold on a sec. How did you figure all this out overnight? How did you know where to look?'

'I didn't,' Hunter replied, before quickly running his partner through the idea that his dream had given him. He also told him what he'd found out at the admin office at Rose Hills Memorial Park.

'So we're now looking for a John Williams, instead of a Michael Williams,' Garcia said, interrupting Hunter's account. 'You do realize that John is an even more popular name than Michael, right? If we were struggling to find a Michael Williams—'

'We're not after him,' Hunter said, cutting Garcia short. 'He's not the one doing this.'

'And you know that how?'

'Because he isn't the one visiting Genesis and Michael's grave,' Hunter replied. 'He's not the one placing flowers on it every couple of weeks or so . . . their mother is.'

Garcia blinked at Hunter.

'Her name is Linda Williams.'

Garcia's brain took a couple of seconds to process all this. He shook his head at Hunter, as if waking up. 'Hold up. Are you telling me that you think a woman is doing all this?' He broadly gestured at the picture board. 'A *woman* is being this cruel ... this vicious?'

It had been well documented over the years that women murderers were a lot less sadistic than their male counterparts. They tended to use less violent methods, like poisoning and strangling, as oppose to mutilation, or any approach that could cause heavy bleeding and disfiguration. History had also shown that they almost *never* tortured their victims prior to murdering them.

'Evil doesn't always wear an ugly mask, Carlos,' Hunter said. 'You know that. It often hides in plain sight ... it parades beneath the guise of friendliness ... of righteousness and helpfulness ...' He shrugged. 'But what we're talking about here is a severely broken woman and a very, very angry mother, so yes, I think a woman is doing all this.'

Garcia's attention returned to the board ... to the carnage of all the crime scenes. 'And how did you find out about her?'

'Mario Castro,' Hunter replied. 'He works at Rose Hills Memorial Park – ground work, maintenance, looks after graves ... that kind of stuff. He takes care of most of the graves on Parkview Lawn. That's the plot where Genesis and Michael's grave is located. He's been there for eighteen years.'

Garcia leaned back against his desk. 'So what did he say?'

'He told me that he wasn't the ground worker for either of the two funerals, but he's seen their mother, Linda, at the cemetery hundreds of times over the years. He told me that on average, she's there at least twice a month – she brings flowers, she cleans the grave, sometimes she even brings a flask and sits there for hours.'

Garcia's eyes widened at Hunter. 'So all we need to do is stake out the grave and wait.'

'Maybe,' Hunter accepted it. 'But she was there last night. The flowers on the grave were fresh this morning and she was seen by another ground worker. That means that she won't be back for a couple of weeks, at least. Lucas Elliot will be back from Italy in three days' time. I'm sure she won't wait long to go after him.'

'True,' Garcia agreed. 'But we also have his house under watch and we'll have eyes on him the second he touches down at LAX.'

Hunter breathed out doubt. 'And what if there are others on her kill list that we don't know about?' he asked. 'What if she blames more people than we believe she does? What if the next name on her list isn't Lucas?'

Garcia nodded as he bit his bottom lip. 'Then we have a problem.'

'We need to find her fast. We can't wait.'

'So what else do we know about her?'

'Well,' Hunter began, 'Mr. Castro told me that he's spoken with her a few times over the years. Like I've said – he's seen her there hundreds of times, so it was only natural for him to say hello or good morning – just being friendly, you know. He told me that at first, all those years ago, she was rarely alone. She'd always visited the grave with who he assumed were her husband and son. Then, and he couldn't be sure of the time lapse, but now we know that it would've been a year, the son dropped out of the picture and Linda started visiting the grave accompanied only by her husband. That was when Mr. Castro noticed that the grave that she visited had become a shared one – sister and brother. A little while after that, and again, he couldn't be exact of how long, she started turning up alone.'

Garcia tilted his head to one side. 'Divorced?'

'Could've been, we don't know yet, but the information I have is that, unfortunately, her husband, John Williams, has also passed.'

He didn't give Garcia a chance to ask a question. 'We don't know when and we don't know how yet. Research is working hard to try to confirm it, but that's what she told Mr. Castro in one of their brief conversations. He told me that one day, maybe eight or nine years ago, she approached him and told him that she wouldn't be able to come to the cemetery for a few weeks. She asked him if he could take care of Genesis and Michael's grave while she was away. He confessed that she paid him directly, instead of going through the cemetery's administration. In passing, she told him that she was a widow then.'

'None of the neighboring graves to Genesis and Michael belong to a John Williams?' Garcia asked.

'Nope. And that's the only grave she visits at Rose Hills Memorial Park. If he really is dead, I don't think that he's buried there.'

'Cremated?'

'I checked with the cemetery records,' Hunter replied. 'If John Williams was cremated, it wasn't at Rose Hills either, but here comes the good part.'

Garcia's eyebrows lifted at Hunter.

'The reason why Linda Williams was going away for a few weeks all those years ago, kept on repeating itself, over and over, in all the subsequent years . . . until just over a year ago, when she stopped travelling altogether.'

'Pedro Bustamente,' Garcia said. 'The beginning of her killing spree.'

'It appears so,' Hunter agreed. 'And when she told Mr. Castro she was a widow, she also told him why she had to go away so often. Linda Williams used to be an A&E trauma nurse at Gardena Memorial Hospital, but a few years after Genesis took her own life, she quit her job and started travelling the country.'

'Travelling the country? Why?'

'She was visiting schools, including special schools for disabled and handicapped kids, doing single-day lectures and talks about depression, suicide, and addiction to drugs amongst young teenagers. She also talked to parents and teachers, helping them with guidelines on how to be more aware of the signs of all three.' Hunter's pause was heavy ... thoughtful. 'She was trying to do good, Carlos. She was trying to turn her pain into a helping tool for others.'

'Until something changed all that,' Garcia said. 'Just over a year ago.'

Hunter nodded as he reached for another printout that was on his desk. 'This took us a little while to find it because the website has been taken down, but it's a good enough photo of her.' He handed the printout to Garcia. The image on it was of a tall woman who looked to be in her early-to-mid forties. Her straight black hair was tied back into a ponytail and her eyebrows had been professionally done. Her make-up was subtle, but it accentuated all the right details on her face. There was no question that Genesis had inherited her mother's almond-shaped brown eyes and her kind smile.

Garcia looked at the printout for a split second, and as he did, Hunter noticed the change in his partner's demeanor.

'Jesus Christ!' The words dribbled out of Garcia's lips at the same time that his eyes were filled with dread.

'What?' Hunter asked.

Garcia seemed to have frozen in place.

'Carlos, what's wrong?'

'I know who she is.' Garcia's disbelieving stare finally moved to Hunter. 'I talked to her, Robert.'

Those words crawled along Hunter's skin like an unwanted bug. *'What? When?'*

'Right at the beginning of the whole investigation,' Garcia replied, his voice almost faltering. 'She was the cab driver, Robert ... the lady who dropped Melissa Hawthorne off after she left the party at the hotel.'

Seventy-seven

It didn't take long for Research to find an address for Linda Evans. That was Genesis Williams's mother's maiden name, and the name that she had used to register as a cab driver. Research had contacted cab company's administration office in LA and they'd found out that Linda had not driven another passenger since she dropped Melissa Hawthorne off at her house in Leimert Park that Sunday morning, a week and a half ago.

But if Linda had become a licensed cab driver, it meant that she had a valid driver's license, which would show her current address, and a copy of that license would be stored in the company's database.

It turned out that Linda Evans lived in a small studio apartment in Torrance – the city immediately to the south-west of Gardena – in the South Bay region of metropolitan Los Angeles.

Two minutes after receiving that information, Hunter and Garcia were standing in front of Captain Blake's desk.

'Do we have confirmation that she's at her apartment?' the captain asked, after hearing the news from Hunter.

'No,' Hunter replied. 'But we're making our way there now. There's also an APB out on her Mazda 3 – stop and detain.'

'Alright,' Captain Blake said, reaching for the phone on her desk. 'I'll have a SWAT team ready in five.'

'Hold on, Captain.' Hunter interrupted her call by pressing down on the release button. 'We don't need a SWAT team.'

The captain dipped her head to look back at him over her reading glasses. 'You're about to try to arrest probably the most sadistic serial killer this police department has ever chased, Robert. You *need* a SWAT team.'

'I don't think so, Captain. She's not like any serial killer we've ever chased. She's not a born psychopath ... she's not after a kick ... she's not trying to satisfy some murderous instinct buried deep inside her ... she's not looking for sexual gratification ... and she's not feeding an uncontrollable urge that compels her to kill. She's after revenge for her daughter. She's not roaming the streets, searching for her next victim. She doesn't choose them at random or according to some criteria instigated by trauma. She has a specific list of names.'

The captain put down her glasses, but kept the receiver in her hand.

'With these types of murderers,' Hunter continued, 'their behavior differs greatly from psychopathic serial killers. She might try to run when she realizes that her game is over, but I don't think that she'll retaliate with deadly force.'

'You don't know that for sure, Robert,' Captain Blake challenged. 'A SWAT team would give you peace of mind.'

'Actually, it wouldn't, Captain.' The retort came from Garcia. 'A SWAT team isn't exactly a discreet unit, is it? Big black armored truck with six to twelve agents, all dressed in black, wearing masks and helmets, and carrying semi-automatic rifles. The whole neighborhood will know they're there.'

'And if she isn't home,' Hunter took over again, 'chances are that she'll find out we were there before she comes back, and if that happens, she'll be in the wind again.'

'How?' Captain Blake asked. 'How will she find out?'

Garcia chuckled. 'What do you think all the passers-by will do as soon as they see a SWAT truck pull up and armed agents jump out and rush into a building?' He nodded. 'Social media.

The whole thing will be plastered everywhere before we even knock on her door.'

'The apartment block she lives in,' Hunter added, placing a couple of aerial shots of the building on the captain's desk, 'is three stories high, with a front and back entrance, a lift and one set of stairs. There's no external fire escape stairway. Her studio apartment is on the top floor.' He indicated this on one of the photos. 'Too high for her to escape by jumping. She's only got two exits out of that building and she needs either the lift or the stairs to access them. A SWAT team would be overkill.'

The captain mulled that over for a moment. 'OK, so what's your plan? You're not just going to go and knock on her door, are you?'

'That's exactly the plan, Captain,' Garcia replied.

She glared at him.

'Every person we interview in every investigation,' Garcia explained, 'they're always told that we might need to ask them a few more questions as the investigation progresses. I really don't think she knows that we are on to her. All this will look like is that we have a couple more things to ask her, that's all. No real threat.'

Captain Blake glanced at Hunter.

'Sometimes the simplest plan is the most effective one,' he said.

'The two of you will be wearing Kevlar vests, right?' she asked.

'Absolutely,' Garcia replied.

A few more seconds of deliberation.

'Alright,' she finally said, returning the receiver to its cradle. 'No SWAT, but I want at least a couple of black-and-white units monitoring every exit to her road and two other detectives on the front and back entrance to her building. If she is as disciplined and as systematic as you believe she is, Robert, then she must have some sort of escape plan already worked out.'

'That's fair enough,' Hunter accepted.

'Take Milton and Jacob,' the captain instructed them. 'They're at their desks and they're both very good marksmen. If this gets ugly, they're the best guys to have on your side.'

'We'll grab them on our way out,' Hunter confirmed.

'Good.' Captain Blake nodded at her detectives and pointed to the door. 'You guys are on. Go.'

Seventy-eight

As Garcia merged onto Harbor Freeway, heading southwest, he switched on his car's police lights and sirens. Torrance was still about nineteen miles away from where they were, but on a freeway, the lights and sirens would practically clear an entire lane for them.

Detectives Milton and Jacob, who were travelling in an unmarked Kia Optima directly behind them, did the same.

'I should've picked up on something,' Garcia said, without making eye contact with Hunter. He sounded angry with himself.

Hunter knew that he was talking about his interview with Linda Evans, right at the beginning of their investigation.

'I don't think so, Carlos,' Hunter replied. 'Don't beat yourself up about it.'

'You know that there's always something that can give them away, Robert – a twitch, a hesitation, an odd mannerism ... something.'

'Not always. If they are unprepared, maybe, but that wasn't true in her case. She's smart and she was ready for it because she knew that she would be questioned.'

Garcia looked at Hunter through the corner of his eyes.

'She was the last person to have seen Melissa Hawthorne alive,' Hunter continued. 'She drove her home and she didn't do it anonymously. She wasn't a stranger who gave Melissa a ride on the night. She was a taxi driver taking a booking. She knew that we'd find out that Melissa took a cab home from the hotel that night, which means that she also knew that very soon we'd come knocking.' He shrugged. 'The kind of questions any detective would ask a cab driver who dropped a murder victim home just before she was murdered aren't that hard to predict, are they?'

Garcia kept his eyes on the road.

'She might've not known the exact wording you would've used, but she knew the general direction that the interview would take. She probably rehearsed every possible question you could've asked her . . . and she probably did it in front of a mirror too, checking herself for exactly what you could have noticed – a twitch, a hesitation, an odd mannerism, an eye movement . . . you name it. And I bet that she got it down to perfection. No one would've picked up on anything because she made sure that there was nothing to be picked up, Carlos. She was waiting for you.'

They drove past the neighborhoods of South Park and Green Meadows, heading toward Athens and Gardena.

'We should be there in less than ten minutes,' Garcia said into his radio.

'*We're ready, and right behind you,*' Detective Milton replied.

'Do you think she'll be home?' Garcia asked Hunter. 'At this time in the morning?'

'She's not out picking up passengers,' Hunter replied. 'She's not a trauma nurse anymore and she's not traveling the country doing single-day seminars. She's hunting down specific people. My guess is that she's getting ready . . . going over every detail . . . studying and restudying her plan for her next kill. She's left nothing to chance so far, she's not going to start now. Her apartment is probably her safest environment to do all that.'

They had just entered the incorporated city of Torrance when Hunter's phone rang in his pocket. The call was from Shannon Hatcher, at Research.

'*Robert*,' she said, as Hunter answered the call. He picked up anxiety in her tone. '*Where are you?*'

'On our way to Torrance – Linda Evans's place. Why?'

'*She's not there*,' Shannon informed Hunter.

'What?' Hunter said, as he switched the call to speakerphone. 'How do you know that?'

'*Her passport has pinged up at LAX. She cleared customs about an hour and a half ago.*'

'*What?*' This time, the question came from both detectives at the same time.

'An hour and a half ago?' Hunter's voice went from calm to ultra-worried in a blink of an eye.

'*We literally just got the data right now*,' Shannon explained. '*She's on American Airlines flight number 8649 heading to Rome.*'

Garcia looked at Hunter, both of their mouths hanging open. 'You're kidding me,' he whispered, instinctively taking his foot off the gas for an instant.

'When is the flight scheduled to take off?' Hunter asked.

'*That's the problem, Robert.*' Anxiety turned into exasperation. '*Her flight leaves from LAX in exactly nineteen minutes.*'

Unconsciously, Hunter's eyes moved to the dashboard clock.

Garcia shook his head at Hunter. He didn't even need to check the map on the onboard satnav to know. 'We need to stop that plane from taking off. Even with sirens, it will take us at least twenty-five minutes just to make it to LAX from here. Add having to rush through the terminal until we get to the gate to that time and . . . we've got no chance.' Despite that, Garcia had already veered right, getting ready to take the next exit off of I-110. He needed to join San Diego Freeway, heading north-west.

'*Umm . . . where are you going?*' The question came through Garcia's onboard radio. It was Detective Milton. '*Why are you veering right? I thought we were going to Torrance.*'

'Change of plans,' Garcia quickly replied. 'We're heading to LAX. Just follow us.'

'*Copy that.*'

'Shannon, do we know the gate number?' Hunter asked.

'Yes,' she said, '*AA flight 8649, departs from LAX Terminal B, gate 210A. Unfortunately, that gate is almost at the end of the terminal.*'

'With our luck,' Garcia commented, 'why wouldn't it be?'

'*She's seated in Economy Class,*' Shannon continued. '*Her allocated seat is seat 35H. That's an aisle seat toward the front of the Economy section. We've also checked for a cellphone number registered under both names – Linda Evans and Linda Williams. There are over one hundred cellphone numbers registered to a Linda Williams in the Greater LA area, and twenty-one registered to a Linda Evans. None of them show a registered address in Torrance, and none of the GPS on all the phones we've managed to track so far are pinging at LAX.*' She paused for breath. '*I'm sorry about this, Robert. If she had used a credit card, we would've found out about the ticket at least an hour ago, but she paid for it via her PayPal account, which is still under the name Linda Williams. That little trick cost us precious time.*'

'It's OK, Shannon,' Hunter said. 'Keep us informed of anything else you might find out, but right now, I need you to patch me straight to Captain Blake.'

'*Doing it straight away.*'

Three seconds later, Captain Blake was on the line.

Fifteen minutes until Flight AA8649 took off.

Seventy-nine

That morning, Linda Evans had gotten to LAX early – two-and-a-half hours before her flight was due to take off. An hour after that, she had already cleared customs and entered the International Departures lounge.

After spotting Garcia at Sofia Elliot's house yesterday, Linda knew that she needed a new plan ... and she needed it fast. With that in mind, it stood to reason that the LAPD would assume that either Sofia or Lucas Elliot were on the Mentor's target list. The most logical move for them would be to have Sofia's house under twenty-four-hour surveillance, which meant that the house was now out of bounds for her.

Linda had kept the card that the detective had given her when he first interviewed her over a week ago – Detective Carlos Garcia, LAPD Ultra Violent Crimes Unit. Like always, she did her research. According to everything she read, the LAPD UVC Unit was the best in the country when it came to tracking down serial and high profile murderers. Their record was superior even to the FBI.

Linda had always been an extremely organized person. She was one of those who not only planned ahead, but when possible, she would also always have an alternative strategy in place, just in case. She had spent a whole year planning her revenge ... every detail of it, including alternatives. She'd taken Krav Maga self-defense lessons, she'd changed her diet, she had taken up weight training to increase her physical fitness and power . . . she had even bought a 9mm. semi-automatic pistol and learned how to shoot. So far, everything had gone just perfectly, but this . . . this was a 'just in case' moment.

Linda had waited until the detective finished talking to Sofia's neighbor. Once he was gone, she drove back to her apartment. She needed to get plan 'B' moving, and fast.

The next flight out of LAX destined to Rome was scheduled for that same night. Too soon – not enough time to get herself organized, packed and to the airport in time, but there was a new flight from American Airlines in the morning – leaving LAX at 10:30 a.m. and arriving in Rome at 14:55, local time. The flight still had quite a few seats left. Perfect. That would give her time to visit Genesis and Michael's grave before the day was over and get completely organized by the morning, but there was something about the flight's date and time that was bothering Linda. She just didn't know exactly what it was. She needed to check her notes.

When she did, she laughed out loud as she read the name, date and time that she had scribbled down just a couple of weeks ago.

'What a ridiculous coincidence,' she said to herself, with a shrug. 'Or maybe it's a sign,' she told herself, as she purchased the ticket.

At the airport, after clearing customs, she spent a few minutes looking through the duty free shop. There was a time, many years ago, when she would've happily bought something – a famous brand lipstick for Genesis . . . a nice cologne for Michael . . . maybe even something for herself and for her and John, her husband, but those days were long gone. Instead, to help take some of the edge off once she got to Italy, she grabbed herself a bottle of Michter's Bourbon – her favorite.

At one of the coffee shops in the departures lounge, Linda ordered an espresso and checked the monitors for her flight. Not long until they started boarding.

She sat alone, lost in her own thoughts, her mind running through her new plans. Without even noticing it, she traced the large, white scars that ran along her wrists with her fingertips. They reminded her of how lost, desperate, and broken she once had become. But those days too were long gone. She had finally found her focus, and she wasn't about to lose it now.

Linda finished her coffee and looked around the area where she was sitting. Two airport police officers, who were standing by a large billboard that advertised sunglasses, were having a careless conversation. They didn't seem to be worried, or searching the crowd for anyone. That was a great sign, especially because right then, the status of her flight changed onscreen from 'Waiting' to 'Boarding'. A couple of seconds later, the call came through the airport loudspeakers.

Before grabbing her hand luggage and her duty-free bag, Linda ran her hand along the delicate chain around her neck, until her fingertips found the dainty pendant hanging from it – a tiny, golden butterfly. That had been Genesis' chain. The one she had around her neck on the day she took her own life.

Linda brought the butterfly to her lips and kissed it, gently. 'Time to go, my angel,' she said to the butterfly. 'Let's go finish this.'

Eighty

'*I don't have the authority to ground a flight from LAX, Robert,*' Captain Blake said on the phone, after Hunter told her about the new development. '*Especially an international one. We'd need a federal warrant for that and for me to get one, we'd need undisputable proof that Linda Evans . . . Linda Williams . . . whatever name she's going by . . . has murdered all those people. You know that. And proof is exactly what we don't have.*' There was a half second pause. '*The truth is, Robert, we've got nothing to place her in any of the crime scenes – no fingerprints . . . no DNA . . . nothing. You know this. No federal judge will sign a warrant to stop an international flight from taking off, based on a theory, because that's really all we have – a theory. And how long did you say we have before the scheduled takeoff?*'

Hunter checked the dashboard clock again. 'Eleven minutes.'

The captain chuckled humorlessly. '*Even if I had all the proof we needed right now, right here in front of me, we'd still have no chance of getting a federal warrant in that time. How far away are you?*'

'About seventeen minutes, Captain,' Garcia replied. 'Give or take.'

'*No plane makes it out of LAX exactly on time,*' Captain Blake said. '*There's always some sort of delay.*'

'With our luck,' Garcia said back, 'I wouldn't be surprised if they took off ten minutes early.'

'*I'll call the Chief of Police,*' Captain Blake said, sounding agitated. '*Somebody must be able to pull a few strings. If he can't ground the flight, he must at least be able to delay it. Anyway, step on it, Carlos.*'

'What do you think we're doing, Captain?' Garcia muttered. 'Pushing the car?'

'Call us back if you get any news, Captain,' Hunter said before disconnecting.

'You know that Linda Evans isn't fleeing the country, right?' Garcia asked, swerving left to overtake a VW Golf that didn't seem to care much for the flashing lights and sirens.

Instead of replying, Hunter was searching his phone's contacts for a number.

'She's going after Lucas Elliot all the way in Italy,' Garcia continued. 'I'm not sure if that was always her plan, or if she figured out that we were on to her and decided to speed things up, but either way, that is one hell of a bold move.'

Hunter found the name he was looking for.

'Hold on a sec,' he said, lifting a finger at Garcia. 'I've got an idea.'

'Really?' Garcia's eyes moved to his partner for a quick instant before returning to the road ahead. 'What idea? Who are you calling?'

'Amber Burnett,' Hunter replied, bringing his cellphone to his ear.

'Who's Amber Burnett?'

'Someone I know who used to be an air marshal. She's now head of the Federal Air Marshal office at LAX. I know that this is an international flight, but maybe she can pull something out of her hat.'

Seven minutes to the scheduled takeoff.

Garcia nodded. 'I really hope she's got one big, fuck-off hat.'

Eighty-one

Even though this was economy class, the seat was a lot more comfortable than what Linda had expected.

This was her second-ever international flight. The first had been just a few years ago, when she flew to Canada for two weeks to visit six different schools with her one-day seminars on depression and suicide amongst teenagers. Linda truly wished that she had been going to Europe in far different circumstances. She would've loved to be able to spend some time in Italy, France, the UK, Germany, Spain, and many other countries, but these were the cards that she'd been dealt. She was just playing them the best way she could.

Linda's hand luggage and duty-free bag had already been safely stored in the overhead compartment above her seat. At the plane's boarding door, two very pretty and very blonde female flight attendants were still greeting the influx of passengers coming in.

Two other flight attendants, one on each aisle – one male, one female – were helping passengers in economy class, while two more were doing the same up in first class. Boarding was being done via the mid-plane door, just a little ahead of the wing. First class passengers were directed right, toward the front of the plane, while economy went left, to the middle and rear.

Linda was doing her best to appear relaxed – sitting back on her seat, with her right leg casually crossed over her left one, her seatbelt fastened and her hands resting on her lap – but she was far from relaxed. She knew that until that plane was safely in the air, things could still go very wrong. So, despite her tranquil demeanor, Linda kept her eyes firmly on the two flight attendants at the door ahead of her, analyzing every new passenger that stepped onto the plane.

So far, no one had given her any real reason for concern.

The aircraft she was in was a Boeing 777, which was a wide plane mainly used for international flights, with three columns of seats in economy class, totaling nine seats per row – three on the left, three on the right and three down the middle of the plane.

Linda was seated on the left column of seats – seat 35H, which was on the aisle. Both seats to her left – window and middle – had already been occupied by a middle-aged couple who seemed very excited to be going to Italy. The woman had taken the window seat, leaving her husband in between her and Linda. They had said a courteous 'hello' when they took their seats, but since then, they had just been talking to each other, which for Linda was just fine.

She quickly checked her watch again – five minutes until the scheduled takeoff time, but she knew that there was always a small delay, somehow.

The influx of passengers had completely died down. No one had boarded the plane in the past minute or so. They would probably shut the doors very soon.

Linda breathed out slowly. She had to admit that she was nervous, her heart beating a little too fast inside her chest. Her eyes moved to the overhead compartment above her. She could really do with some of that Michter's Bourbon right about now.

'*Good morning, ladies and gentlemen.*' A male voice came through the aircraft speaker system. '*This is your captain speaking. It appears that we're all boarded now, which means that we'll be able to start maneuvering soon. Just waiting for the go-ahead from the tower. Please make sure that your hand luggage is in the overhead compartments and that your seat belt is safely fastened. I'll be back with more updates, as soon as I have them. Cabin crew, arm doors and cross-check.'*

With the announcement over, one of the flight attendants closed and locked the mid-plane door.

Linda took a moment to calm the rapid thumping of her pulse, waiting patiently until she could feel her heart rate settle. She closed her eyes and reached for the butterfly on her neck chain once again.

'We're on our way, my angel,' she said under her breath. 'We're on our way.'

Eighty-two

Over the phone, Hunter did his best to explain as quickly as possible to Federal Air Marshal Amber Burnett how important it was that flight 8649 stayed on the ground until they got to LAX, which would be in around thirteen minutes, give or take.

'*When is the flight scheduled to take off, again?*' Amber asked. Hunter could hear frantic typing of a keyboard on the background.

'In about four minutes,' Hunter replied.

'*Fuck, Robert, are you serious? That means that boarding is complete and the doors have been armed and locked. They might be taxiing already.*'

'There's got to be something that can be done, Amber,' Hunter pleaded, as he looked at Garcia and grimaced. 'Isn't there some sort of code that can be radioed to the pilot? The flight doesn't need to be cancelled, just delayed.'

'*Which is a major problem for the airport and the airline, Robert,*' Amber explained. '*Do you understand how takeoff slots work in an airport?*'

Hunter did – takeoff slots were all stacked up one after the other ... airline after airline. If a plane missed its takeoff slot, they'd need to wait until a new slot became available. It was true that air flight control kept emergency slots in place because flights did get delayed, it was a fact, but in a busy airport like LAX, they'd have two, maybe three emergency slots per hour. If another aircraft had been delayed before flight 8649, they'd take the next available takeoff spot first. What that really meant was that flight 8649 could be waiting on the runway for a considerable amount of time before they were given a new go-ahead.

'Yes,' Hunter replied. 'I know how they work.'

'*So you understand that any delay for an airline company means money down the drain ... a lot of it ... and they don't take kindly to that.*'

'I understand that, Amber,' Hunter said. 'I was just hoping that there was something that could be done.'

'*For me to officially radio the pilot to force him to lose his takeoff slot,*' she said back, '*I would need a warrant from a federal judge, Robert.*' There was a short pause. '*The flight is scheduled to take off in less than three minutes from now. Logistically, we're screwed.*'

Hunter closed his eyes and pressed his lips together.

'*Unless ...*'

Hunter's eyes shot back open. 'Unless ...?'

'*Just get your ass here, Robert ... pronto.*' She ended the call.

Hunter and Garcia were still eleven minutes away from LAX.

Eighty-three

After closing the aircraft door, the flight attendant turned around and entered the mid-plane galley, which was just across the aisle from the boarding door.

Three minutes past the scheduled takeoff time. They would start taxiing soon.

The second steward began closing the dividing curtains that separated first class from economy. As she did, the intercom on the wall just outside the galley beeped and a small red light, just above the receiver, came on – a private message from the pilot's cabin.

Linda craned her neck to get a better look.

As the flight attendant listened to the captain's instructions, the expression on her face changed to something that Linda could easily read. First, an unsure kind of 'what?' look, which quickly mutated into an 'oh really!' expression. Once the flight attendant returned the receiver to its cradle, she turned to look at the passengers in economy class. She didn't seem to be searching for anyone in particular – it was just a general look, but for some reason, Linda got the sense that all wasn't well.

'Ladies and gentlemen.' The captain's voice came through the speakers again. '*Unfortunately, it seems that we might have a small delay coming our way. Nothing major, or to worry about. Paperwork, really. We're just waiting for a member of our ground crew to come to the aircraft so it can all be resolved as fast as possible. Unfortunately, that means that we'll stay on the ground for just a little longer. I apologize for this small delay, but like I said, it shouldn't be a long one. I'll keep everyone posted.'*

Three seconds after the captain's announcement, the intercom outside the galley beeped and lit up again. The same flight attendant answered it. After listening to her new instructions, the attendant disconnected and switched the mid-plane door back to manual before unlocking it and pushing it open. Both flight attendants went back to the same position they had been in when greeting the passengers, looking out the door and down the retractable corridor that connected the terminal to the plane.

Six minutes past takeoff time.

Something was wrong. Linda could tell. This was not about paperwork. Paperwork wouldn't cause the flight attendants to look that anxious.

All of a sudden, both attendants shifted their weight before taking a step forward, clearly ready to greet someone whom Linda guessed was just coming down the corridor.

The anticipation made Linda's mouth go bone dry.

At the boarding door, a woman finally appeared. She wore blue jeans and a black shirt, under a dark-brown leather jacket, which seemed to be a size too large. Her black hair was cut short and neat.

That was not a member of the American Airlines ground crew. Linda had no doubt about that.

The flight attendants took a step back to allow the brunette to enter the plane, and as she did, the dividing curtains that had been pulled shut just moments earlier were pulled back open again and the captain appeared. The four of them stood in a circle, while the brunette explained something to the group. As she spoke, the taller of the two flight attendants turned to look at the passengers in economy class once again. Another general look, targeting no specific seat.

Linda also looked around at the other passengers in the cabin. Some of them were getting fidgety.

'*Maybe this isn't about me,*' she thought. Maybe she was just being paranoid – but paranoid or not, Linda convinced herself that she needed to think of something, and she needed to do it fast.

She had already clocked the nearest emergency exit, four rows of seats behind her, but getting there quickly could be a problem, especially because all three seats on the exit row next to it were taken.

Linda checked the group at the boarding door once again. The brunette seemed to be explaining something to the pilot and the two flight attendants. As she did, the pilot's attention moved to the passengers in economy class for a split second.

Linda immediately averted her eyes, pretending to be adjusting her seatbelt. That was when she remembered the coincidence – the amazing, ridiculous coincidence that she had come across yesterday, just before booking her seat on the flight.

Maybe it's a sign, she had whispered to herself then. Maybe it really *was* a sign because coincidence or not, that could work as a plan 'C'. She thought about it for just a couple of seconds before making her mind up. This would get messy, she knew that much, but as things stood right then, she saw no other way out.

Linda took a deep breath, unfastened her seatbelt, and got up. A heartbeat later, she was moving toward the group at the door.

Eighty-four

As Garcia turned right into World Way, Hunter checked the screen on his cellphone. No messages from Amber Burnett. According to the dashboard clock, American Airlines flight 8649 was supposed to have taken off seven minutes ago.

'Has she managed to delay the flight?' Garcia asked, his stare bouncing from Hunter to the road ahead.

'I don't know,' Hunter replied, lifting his phone at his partner. 'I've got nothing.'

'Well,' Garcia said back. 'Screw the parking lots. I'm driving up to the departures drop-off point just outside Terminal B. That's as close as we'll be able to get. From then on, we better run like Usain Bolt.'

The lights and sirens did clear the way, but it still took Garcia almost another minute to finally pull up at one of the departures drop-off points on Terminal B. The closest door to them was door A.

Detectives Milton and Jacob pulled up less than ten seconds after them.

In seeing the lights and hearing the sirens, airport security had already rushed toward Garcia's car to find out what was happening, but before they could get to it, both detectives jumped out with their badges in hand.

'LAPD Homicide,' Hunter yelled. 'Clear the way.'

He knew that adding the word 'Homicide' after LAPD, tended to get people moving faster, and that was exactly what happened. The commotion it created caused everyone around drop-off point A to take a big step back before looking around wide-eyed. Most of them began frantically scrambling for their cellphones to video the 'real life, Hollywood-like movie scene'.

'You can't leave your car there,' one of the security guards tried yelling back, but Hunter and Garcia had already cleared the door and disappeared into the terminal.

'It's OK,' Detective Milton said, as he and Jacob approached the security personnel to properly display their credentials instead of simply flashing them on the fly. There was no need for them to rush after Hunter and Garcia anymore. 'LAPD Homicide Division. We'll take care of this.'

At that time in the morning, Terminal B Departures Lounge wasn't excessively busy, but it was busy enough. The fact that Hunter and Garcia knew exactly where to go did help, but even with both of them yelling 'LAPD Homicide, clear the way!' every couple of seconds, they still had to zigzag around scores of people and luggage for most of the way.

As they finally approached the entrance to the mandatory TSA passenger screening, two officers from the Transport Security Administration, both built like heavyweight champions, stepped past the airline ticket counters to block Hunter and Garcia's path.

'LAPD Homicide,' Hunter said, badge in hand and half out of breath. 'We need to—'

'Detective Robert Hunter?' the first of the two officers interrupted him, his index finger pointing at Hunter.

'Yeah . . .' A heavy, deep breath. 'That's me.'

Garcia was right behind him.

'This way,' the officer said, indicating entrance 'C', on the far right, which was currently closed to passengers.

'Amber Burnett from the Federal Air Marshals Office left us

instructions regarding you,' the officer continued, leading the way. 'We need to hurry.'

All four of them broke into another mad sprint.

'Are you carrying?' the officer asked, as they cleared entrance 'C'.

'Both of us are,' Hunter replied.

'I thought that'd be the case,' the officer said. 'This way.' He once again pointed right, indicating a free pathway, which would bypass TSA screening and all metal detectors.

'Is the flight on the ground?' Garcia asked.

'For now,' came the reply. 'Amber is on the aircraft.'

That answer surprised both detectives.

Once past the metal detectors, they reached the crossing gateway – a 330-foot-long bridge that connected the departures lounge to a specific series of departure gates, and was almost as long as a football field. The four of them rushed across it as fast as they possibly could. Hunter and Garcia were both dripping sweat and Hunter could feel his lungs starting to burn.

At the end of the gateway, they turned right, to face gate 201B.

'Oh fuck!' Garcia breathed out heavily, knowing that the gate that they were after was gate 210A, on the far left end of the entire concourse – another 310 feet. 'Are we running all the way to Rome?'

They sped past crowds of passengers waiting to board on gates 202, 203, 204, and 205, but as they got to gate 206A, on their left, a little boy broke free from his mother's grip and decided to run across to gate 206B, on the right. In doing so, the boy stepped right into the path of the four running men.

'Jason!' the mother called, desperately rushing after her little boy.

That forced Hunter, who was leading the group, to swerve hard right. Somehow, he managed to avoid the mother and child by a cat's whisker, but Garcia and the two TSA officers saw the boy and his mother a fraction too late. To avoid a head-on collision, Garcia moved left, while the two officers veered right. The result couldn't have been more comical if it had been choreographed. The three of them ran into each other with full force. Garcia, who was by far the least physically powerful of the three, was thrown onto the floor, wrestling-takedown style, and he came down hard, hitting his head against the concrete floor violently enough to knock him senseless for at least a couple of minutes.

The two TSA officers, as they collided with Garcia, tripped over each other and they too hit the floor with purpose. It was a miracle that no bones were broken.

While Hunter carried on at full speed, many at the passengers waiting at gate 206A rushed to help the three men on the floor.

By the time Hunter got to gate 210A, every muscle in his body seemed to be screaming for oxygen, but the only distance left to cover was the short corridor that the passengers took to board the aircraft. He flew past the American Airline lady at the boarding gate without saying a word. He didn't have the time or the lung capacity to explain to her who he was.

The boarding corridor angled left and as Hunter finally cleared the corner, he heard chaotic, desperate screaming coming from the plane. Ahead, he could see the aircraft door wide open. That was when he stopped running.

Standing inside the airliner, to the left of the door, was a flight attendant, who looked completely terrified. To her right, Hunter saw Amber Burnett . . . covered in blood.

Then he saw the gun.

How the hell had Linda Evans gotten a gun inside an airplane?

Eighty-five

Nine minutes past takeoff time.

As Linda got up from her seat and began walking the short distance between her seat and the group standing by the aircraft door, she started coughing, pretending that she had something stuck in her throat. The group immediately noticed her.

'Ma'am,' the first flight attendant said, turning to meet Linda. 'Please go back to your seat ...'

Linda coughed harder, cupping her left hand over her mouth and extending her right one at the flight attendant, signaling that she needed a second.

'Please, I just need a glass of water,' she said, in between coughs, her voice raspy. 'I've got something in my throat.'

'If you return to your seat, ma'am,' the flight attendant countered, 'I'll bring you one right away.'

But Linda kept walking and coughing, angling her trajectory slightly left, so that she would be a lot closer to the brunette woman.

Due to how little time they had left and the urgency of it all, when Hunter had explained to Amber Burnett that they needed to delay American Airlines flight 8649 until he and Garcia got to the airport, he had kept the details down to a minimum. He had told her that a triple homicide suspect was trying to escape the country, but he never gave Amber a description, cited any names, or mentioned any seat numbers because he never thought that Amber would board the aircraft herself. What that meant was that Amber never really knew who they were after, and that had been a mistake.

From her seat, Linda had already noticed that the brunette woman was left-handed. She was also certain that the reason for the oversized jacket was to conceal a weapon – probably on a shoulder holster, which meant that she was either a police officer, or an air marshal. With the woman being left-handed, the most logical location for her weapon would be under her right arm.

As Linda got to about a step away from the group, Amber turned to face her. The turning of the body made her jacket twist and press a little tighter against her abdomen, revealing a bulge under her right arm.

Linda saw it and made her move.

It all happened fast – so fast that the flight attendants and the pilot didn't realize what was going on until it was too late.

As Linda got to the group, she pretended to trip on something on the floor and threw herself onto Amber. That caught everyone by surprise, which was exactly Linda's intention.

As Linda collided into Amber, she placed both of her hands on Amber's torso, just under her left and right arms, a move that she had learnt in her Krav Maga self-defense classes. Amber, propelled by the heavy body-bump, was thrown backwards in the direction of the open door, but Linda held her by the jacket and pulled her straight back toward her ... hard. This time, Linda dipped her chin and headbutted Amber directly across the nose.

There was a horrible, cracking noise, as if someone had stepped on a pile of broken glass. Blood spurted from Amber's face up into the air like a burst water balloon, creating a thick crimson mist and spattering against Linda, the pilot, and both air flight attendants.

The impact sent a shockwave of heart-stopping pain up

Amber's nose and into her brain, almost knocking her unconscious and completely destabilized her. Mechanically, her hands shot toward her face, cupping over her nose in a protective motion.

In the space of a heartbeat, Linda pulled the zipper on Amber's jacket down, unclipped the guard strap on her gun holster, and pulled out her weapon. With her left hand, she pushed Amber against the wall to the right of the door and took two steps back, in the direction of the galley. The whole attack lasted about three seconds.

A few of the passengers in economy class, the ones on the left column of seats and closer to the door, saw what had happened. Their reaction was to let out a unified, fearful scream, which rippled like a Mexican wave throughout the cabin, gaining momentum as it jumped from row to row. The cabin's collective, terrified scream travelled the length of the aircraft and into the retractable corridor that connected the terminal to the plane's boarding door.

Linda didn't care about the screaming, or the passengers. As she stepped backwards, she quickly grabbed the shorter of the two flight attendants by the hair, pulling her back into the mid-plane galley with her. In a blink of an eye, the flight attendant became Linda's human shield.

Standing directly behind her, Linda placed the barrel of the gun against the attendant's right temple. She was just about to give everyone an order to stand back when she saw a tall and well-built man appear down the terminal's boarding corridor. As he came to a complete stop, Linda saw the badge clipped to his belt and recognition blinked inside her head. She had seen several photos of him when she researched the LAPD UVC Unit. This was the head of the unit – Detective Robert Hunter.

'Everybody stay exactly where you are,' Linda yelled at the top of her voice, as she lifted the gun high up above her head so that Amber and Hunter could see exactly what she was doing.

She then used her thumb to flick the safety off before pressing its barrel against the flight attendant's temple. 'If anybody tries to get up off their seat, I'll shoot her first . . . then whoever left their seat. If I see a single cellphone out, trying to video any of this, I'll shoot her first . . . then the person with the cellphone.' She locked eyes with Hunter. 'And trust me – I won't miss. Are we clear?'

Eighty-six

Completely out of breath and with his legs about to give in, Hunter stood perfectly still, just a few paces from the aircraft's boarding door.

From where he stood, he could see Amber to the right of the door. Her hands were cupped in front of her face, which was an indescribable mess of blood and snot. The pilot and one of the flight attendants were standing to the left. Both of their uniforms were stained by blood splatters, but Hunter couldn't tell if it was their blood or not. It didn't seem to be because they didn't seem hurt, but what truly commanded his attention was the person standing inside the plane's mid-galley, holding a semi-automatic pistol to the head of one of the flight attendants.

For the quickest of moments, Hunter and Linda locked eyes, and all that he could see in hers was determination.

'Everybody stay exactly where you are,' Linda yelled out, before she made sure that Hunter knew that she had offed the safety on the gun in her hand.

The entire plane erupted into frantic screams, which lasted several long seconds, but as Linda explained what would happen if they disobeyed, the passengers did exactly what they were told – no one moved . . . and no one reached for their cellphones.

Police instinct told Hunter to pull out his weapon and aim it at Linda – create a stand-off until backup arrived, as he knew it would – but human psychology told him that if he pulled out his weapon, he would be making a tense situation a million times worse. He knew very little about Linda Evans's state of mind, or how fragmented her grip on reality was. Threatening an already scared and fractured mind was a risk that he wasn't willing to take with so many lives at stake. Instead, he lifted his hands at her.

'Linda,' he called, still catching his breath. 'You don't want to do this.'

Amber turned her head to look back at Hunter, blood dripping from her face, her eyes angry and bloodshot.

Hunter's stare flicked to her for just a second, and if ever anyone could say that they were terribly sorry with a simple look, Hunter did it right there.

'Is that so, Detective?' Linda replied. The determination inside her eyes seemed to intensify.

'Yes, it is.' Despite the heavy breathing, his tone was firm.

The flight attendant in front of Linda began crying. 'Please,' she said, her voice shaking and barely audible, but Hunter was able to read her lips. 'Please let me go. I have a daughter.'

'Just be quiet,' Linda said back, tugging harder at the flight attendant's hair, which made her let out a terrified yelp.

'You don't want to hurt these people, Linda,' Hunter called out, his hands still up in the air. 'I know you don't.' His best chance to calm her down right then was to use what he'd found out. 'The reason I know you don't is because none of these people . . . not a single one of them . . . ever hurt Genesis.'

On hearing her daughter's name, Linda blinked a couple of times.

'Don't you dare mention her name,' she said in between clenched teeth. 'You know nothing about Genesis.'

'I know enough . . . enough to know that none of these people ever bullied or made fun of her. What happened to her isn't their fault, Linda.' They held each other's stare. 'It wasn't your fault either.'

Hunter understood very well that the most destructive of feelings amongst people who had lost loved ones to suicide, especially to parents who had lost a young child, was guilt ... the kind of guilt that demanded answers that could rarely be found – 'Where had they failed?', 'How come they didn't see the signs?', and many more that would potentially torture them for the rest of their lives. Even if those questions could somehow be answered, most parents would still find a way to blame themselves because in essence, they were responsible for the well-being and safety of their young children. Hunter didn't need to ask to know that Linda, at least partially, blamed herself for Genesis's suicide ... for not being there ... for not seeing any signs ... for not knowing how much her daughter was hurting.

Linda blinked and this time Hunter saw nothing but pure hate inside her eyes.

'You have no idea whose fault it was.' She practically spat those words out. 'You don't know what happened.'

The tension amongst the passengers was starting to reach boiling point once again. Everyone could feel it. Hunter needed to do something, and fast. In these types of situations, he knew from experience that his best bet was to keep her talking. Conversation was always a much better alternative than a gunfight, and Hunter had the perfect opportunity right then because Linda's last statement gave him a chance to demonstrate to her that he knew a lot more than what she probably believed he did.

'So why don't you tell me what happened?' he pleaded. 'What happened at Gardena Junior High, Linda? What happened with Janet, Troy, Josie, Sofia, Pedro and Genesis? What did they do? Why are you punishing them this way? I really want to understand it, but you need to let these people go first, Linda.' Hunter exhaled, as he considered his next words. 'You can have me as a hostage, if that's what you want, but you need to let these people go and you need to do it *fast*.'

Hunter paused again, this time so that the weight of his words could properly crash against Linda's eardrums. She needed to understand that she was in as much danger as everyone else.

'A loaded weapon inside an airplane creates one of the highest levels of threat against human lives,' he explained, 'despite the plane being on the ground. I'm sure that the co-pilot has already radioed back the situation. In less than ... six, maybe seven minutes ... you'll have SWAT teams surrounding this aircraft.' He shook his head. 'And the last thing that they'll want to do, Linda, is talk.' Another pause, this time longer and heavier. 'If you let everyone go, I know I can hold the SWAT teams back. This doesn't have to end tragically for anyone, but you have to let them go. I know that you don't want to hurt anyone here, Linda. These people ... these passengers ... they're not your targets.'

'You seem to be very sure of *my* intentions, Detective ... Hunter, is it?'

'Robert,' Hunter said back.

'So tell me ... *Robert*.' There was defiance in Linda's tone. 'What makes you so sure that I don't want to hurt anyone in here?'

Hunter knew very little about Linda Evans. Research had had no real time to pull a whole file on her, but what Hunter knew for sure was that Linda was a mother struggling with grief, and the psychologist in him knew that he could use that.

'Because everyone inside that plane, Linda,' he replied. 'Every passenger ... every crew member ... is a Genesis.'

Linda's anger flared back onto her face.

Hunter was fast to clarify.

'What I mean is ... everyone in that plane is somebody's daughter ...' He allowed those words to linger in the air for a heartbeat. 'Somebody's son ... somebody's brother ... sister ... mother ... father ... They are all innocent people who were just boarding a flight. If you take their lives from them, then this isn't revenge anymore, Linda. If you take their lives from them, you'll become just like the people who took Genesis away from you. You'll have taken an innocent daughter from her family ... or a son ... or a mother .... or a father ...'

Hunter's eyes were locked on Linda's trigger finger, and for a millisecond, he could swear that he saw the tension in her whole arm relax. He needed to push further. His voice became heavy and tender at the same time.

'That's why you should take me. I am none of those things.'

Linda questioned him with a look.

'I have no family anymore,' Hunter explained. 'My parents died a long time ago. I have no brothers or sisters. I've never been married and I've never had a child. I'm nobody's husband ... nobody's father ... nobody's partner.' He pinned her down with the most sincere stare he could give anyone. 'Let them go and take me, Linda. If it so happens that at the end of all this you have to take my life ... you won't be destroying a family ... you won't be taking anything away from anyone.'

Eighty-seven

If there was one thing that Linda Evans understood well, it was psychological pain – the type that crushed your heart and paralyzed your thoughts ... the type that changed you ... the type only achievable through a great loss – and right then, every word she'd just heard coming from the detective in front of her seemed to be coated in the same sort of pain.

For a moment, Linda tried to read deeper into Hunter, but she didn't get very far, and the growing tension amongst the passengers demanded her attention.

It wouldn't be long before things started going badly inside that aircraft and when they did, they would go catastrophically for everyone.

Linda knew that she would stand a better chance if the plane were empty. She didn't have line of sight to every passenger and that was a huge disadvantage because there was always the risk of someone deciding to be a hero. But more than that – this could be the perfect opportunity for her to get plan 'C' going.

'Alright,' she finally said, her tone skeptical. 'I could let the passengers go, but before I do, you need to drop your weapon ... *Robert*.' She repositioned herself in a way that only her right eye was peeking out from behind the flight attendant's head. 'Do it slowly. If you try anything, she dies.'

'I won't try anything,' Hunter reassured her.

'Use one hand only,' Linda commanded.

'No problem.'

Keeping his left hand up in the air, Hunter used his right one to reach into his jacket and pull out his weapon. He grabbed it with his thumb and forefinger.

'Place it on the floor,' Linda instructed him. 'And kick it away.'

Hunter did, kicking it backwards, instead of toward Linda.

'Backup gun too.'

'I don't carry a backup gun,' Hunter told her.

Amber's surprised eyes widened at Hunter.

'Am I supposed to believe that?' Linda asked.

'I hope you do, because I really don't carry one.'

The stare exchange was tense.

'I guess we'll have to do this the hard way then,' Linda said. 'Take your jacket and your shirt off . . . slowly.'

Hunter nodded, finally bringing his left arm down, which was a relief because it was starting to hurt. He took off his jacket and threw it behind him. He then took off his shoulder holster and his shirt and threw them on top of his jacket.

'Hands up and turn around. Slowly.'

Hunter did as he was told.

Everyone who could see out the aircraft's door and into the boarding corridor – the pilot, the flight attendants, Amber and Linda – frowned at Hunter's scars. There were just so many of them – bullet wound scars . . . stab wound scars . . . glass cut scars . . . and scorched skin from fire.

'Looks like you just came out the other side of a meat grinder,' Linda said. The emotion inside her eyes changed, but Hunter couldn't quite read it from where he was.

'It comes with the job,' he replied. 'Are we good here?'

'Not yet. Ankle weapon?'

'No,' Hunter replied, lifting his right leg, then his left. 'I told you, no backup weapon.'

'I still don't buy it,' Linda breathed out. 'Off with the trousers.'

Hunter hesitated for a moment.

'Now, Detective.'

'Alright.'

Hunter kicked off his shoes, undid his belt and took off his trousers. All he had on then was a pair of black boxers and socks.

'See,' he said. 'No backup weapon.'

At that exact moment, Hunter heard heavy, uneven footsteps coming from behind him in the boarding corridor. A second later, a limping Garcia turned the corner. Right behind him were the two TSA officers. They too were limping.

It took Garcia a second to spot Linda and the gun. An eye-blink after that, he had his semi-automatic in hand, aiming straight ahead.

'What the hell?' he yelled. He still sounded a little disoriented from his head knock.

Linda ground her teeth and cocked her gun against the flight attendant's temple.

'Carlos,' Hunter shouted, his right arm moving back with his hand wide open, gesturing him to stop. His eyes, though, never left Linda. 'Put down the gun.'

'What?' Garcia asked, his weapon trained at Linda and the flight attendant.

'I've got this under control, Carlos,' Hunter continued. 'Linda will let the passengers go. Once she does, you need to tell Captain Blake to hold back on the SWAT teams. No teams on the runway ... no teams down this corridor.' He nodded at Linda. 'We've got this.'

Garcia glanced at Hunter. 'I thought we agreed that you wouldn't try to get anyone else to surrender by strip-teasing, Robert. Did you do your whole cop dance routine? She doesn't look impressed.'

'Tell him to put his gun down or she dies,' Linda yelled from the plane.

'No one is dying here today, Linda,' Hunter countered. 'But he has to go back so that he can stop the SWAT teams from moving in,' he explained. 'He talks to our captain, she halts them. It's that simple. He has to go back.'

Linda locked eyes with Garcia, studying his face for a moment. She could tell that he was in pain. 'No SWAT, or anyone else coming down that corridor. Are we clear?'

Garcia's stare stayed on Linda.

'Are we clear or not?'

'We're clear,' Garcia replied.

She nodded at him. 'Good. Now go.'

Eighty-eight

As Garcia and the two TSA officers turned around and limped back down the boarding corridor, Hunter restarted negotiations.

'We don't have long, Linda,' he said, using the pronoun 'we' instead of 'you' to subliminally pass on the message that they were in this together. 'We need to let the passengers off the plane, and we need to do it now.'

Linda took a step back, pulling the flight attendant with her.

'Alright,' she said in a loud enough voice so that most of the passengers could hear. 'We're going to do this nice and easy. No panic. No rushing. First, before anyone moves, I want everyone who is by a window to pull down their shades.' She allowed a second for her instructions to be thoroughly understood. 'Every shade on every window . . . down. Do it now.'

The passengers complied.

Hunter had to admit to himself that Linda was smart. *She had just removed the possibility of a sniper ending this from outside the plane.*

'Now,' Linda continued, 'we're going to do this row by row.' She made eye contact with the pilot and the second flight attendant to let them know that they were helping. 'Forget about your hand luggage. It's not going anywhere and it will just delay things. We're starting with the first row of seats in economy class, all the way to the last one. Then, we'll move to first class. Let them wait, for once. We'll be using only the left aisle, so if you're on the right side of the plane, you'll have to cross over to the left when your time comes. *Do not* get up if it's not your row turn to leave. If you do . . . trust me . . . you'll die.' Linda nodded at the pilot and the second flight attendant. 'Nice and easy. No panic. No rushing. Get them out.'

The first row of seats in economy class was row number thirty. The last one was row fifty-seven.

The pilot, the second flight attendant and the other two attendants in the economy class cabin worked quickly, doing their best to keep everyone as calm as they possibly could. The fact that the flight was just a little over half full made things move a lot faster.

As the groups of passenger exited the plane and entered the boarding corridor – between five and nine passengers per group – they were greeted by the sight of a man in his boxers and socks.

'Please just carry on straight down this corridor and an officer will help you,' Hunter kept on saying, as the scared and somewhat surprised passengers rushed by him with comments like 'What the hell?' and 'Good luck!'

It took a little over seven minutes for the flight attendants and the pilot to empty the whole of the economy class.

'OK,' Linda said. 'Let's move on to first class.' She pause and addressed the two attendants who were helping in economy. 'You two can go.' She nodded down the corridor. 'The other attendants in first class will take care of the rest of the passengers.'

The two scared attendants looked at their pilot, who quickly nodded back at them. 'Go,' he said. 'Be safe.'

The attendant who still had the gun to her head was crying again. 'Please let me go . . . please.'

'I will, but you'll have to wait just a little longer,' Linda told her, before instructing the pilot and the attendant to get the first class passengers out.

There weren't that many people in first class – twenty-one passengers, that was all, but as the fourth group of passengers got to the door, ready to deplane, Linda stopped them.

'You,' she said, pointing at an average-height man, who looked to be in his late twenties, maybe early thirties.

The man stopped and looked at her. 'Me?' he asked, in a shaky voice, his right palm flat against his chest. There was nothing else in his blue eyes other than fear.

'Yes, you,' Linda replied. 'You're staying. The rest of the passengers in the group . . . go.'

They all looked at each other in surprise and confusion.

'*Go*,' Linda ordered them again. 'Before I decide to pick someone else.'

They immediately exited the aircraft as fast as they could, leaving behind the man that Linda had stopped.

'What?' the man asked, as the fear in his eyes spread throughout his body. 'What do you mean, I'm "staying"?'

'Exactly that.' Linda's tone was firm and demanding. 'Come around to this side and plant yourself on that seat, where I can see you.' She indicated a seat on the first row of economy class, to her left.

'Linda,' Hunter called from the boarding corridor. 'What are you doing?'

'It's called leverage, Detective,' she called back. 'I'm giving you the passengers like I promised, but I need to keep at least one civilian in here. If I don't, your SWAT friends will storm the plane, guns blazing. You know that.'

'But why me?' The man had become tearful. 'What did I do?'

'Because I said so,' Linda volleyed the answer back at him. 'Now sit down.'

The man turned to look at Hunter, clearly looking for help.

'It's OK,' Hunter said, lifting his hands at the man. 'What's your name?'

'Umm . . . Phillip Maddox, but everyone calls me Phil.'

'It's OK, Phil,' Hunter said in the calmest voice he could muster. 'It will all be fine. Just . . . take a seat . . . for now . . . and we'll get this sorted, OK?'

'You're delaying everyone, *Phil*,' Linda said. 'Take a seat or I'll shoot one of your kneecaps off.' She aimed the gun at his legs.

The man was now shaking from head to toe, but he walked over and took the seat that Linda had indicated.

'You,' Linda called, her chin jerking in Amber's direction. 'Bleeding lady. Put your handcuffs on the floor and using your foot, carefully slide them this way.'

Amber was also shaking, but from anger.

'Do it now and do it slowly.'

Amber did as she was told.

'Keys too.'

Amber complied.

Linda addressed the pilot and the flight attendants. 'You can carry on with the deplaning.'

As they moved back into the first class cabin, Linda let go of the flight attendant's hair.

'I want you to grab those cuffs,' Linda said to her. 'And cuff Phil onto that chair. Do it properly and calmly and you can go.'

The attendant's breathing was heavily labored as she finally stepped away from Linda's grip to pick up the handcuffs from the floor.

'Go on,' Linda ordered her. 'Do it.'

The attendant, just like Phil had done, looked at Hunter for confirmation.

Hunter gave her a single nod.

The attendant picked up the handcuffs and walked over to the chair where Phil was sitting.

'I'm so sorry,' she said, in between sobs, as she securely closed one of the handcuff loops around his right wrist before closing the second loop around the chair's armrest. That done, she tugged at it hard to show Linda that she had done a proper job.

'Great,' Linda said, now aiming her weapon at Phil. 'You can go,' she told the attendant, who for an instant seemed unsure of what to do next.

Right then, the pilot and the three flight attendants appeared with the last group of passengers. The co-pilot was right behind them.

'This is everyone,' the pilot informed Linda.

'Great,' Linda said back. 'Now all of you can go.'

There was an uncertain look across everyone's faces, which disappeared as soon as Linda aimed her gun at all of them.

'You better get going before I change my mind. Do you want to stay?'

The four remaining flight attendants, the pilot and the co-pilot shook their heads and finally exited the aircraft, rushing past Hunter.

Linda looked at Amber. 'You too, Nosebleed. You can go.'

'I'm not going anywhere,' Amber said, her words rough . . . angry. 'You've got my weapon. The only way I'm leaving this aircraft is either with my weapon, or in a body bag. So shoot me if you like, crazy bitch, but I'm staying right here.'

Hunter's heart skipped a beat inside his chest. *Did Amber have a death wish*?

'OK. If that's what you want,' Linda said, quickly swapping her aim from Phil to Amber.

Amber dropped her arms to her sides and looked Linda straight in the eye, but she didn't flinch. Blood had cascaded from her nose, down her chin and onto her blouse and jacket.

'Don't do it, Linda,' Hunter called, taking a step forward before addressing the air marshal. 'Amber. I'm sorry I got you involved in all this. I shouldn't have. This isn't your fight. Please go. Go get your nose looked after . . .'

'Like I said, Robert,' Amber interrupted him, without even looking at Hunter. 'I'm not going anywhere.'

Linda's stare played tug-of-war with Amber's for a long instant before Linda relaxed her arm. 'You're right,' she said, giving Amber a nod. 'Stay. Maybe you can come in handy in a moment.' She looked at Hunter. 'Why don't you board the plane . . . *Robert*? And do me a favor, bring your handcuffs with you.'

Hunter turned to look at the pile of clothes on the floor behind him, where his shoulder holster was.

'Do it slowly,' Linda reminded him.

Hunter carefully picked up his handcuffs before finally boarding the plane.

'Now close and lock the door.'

Hunter brought the door to, switched the lock system to manual, and locked it.

'Now,' Linda addressed Hunter, indicating the door he had just shut. 'See the large wall-fixed handle to the right of the door?'

Hunter nodded.

'Cuff yourself to Nosebleed here through it,' Linda ordered him. 'Your right wrist to her left one. Do it slowly and no tricks.'

Hunter, once again, followed the instructions that he'd been given. Once he was done, he tugged hard at the handcuffs to show Linda that they had been properly secured through the handle. There was no way either of them could get to her now.

'Phil, are you OK?' Hunter asked. From their new position, neither he nor Amber could actually see Phil, who was now completely hidden at the other side of the galley.

'I just want to get out of here,' Phil replied, his voice unsteady.

'Here,' Linda said, throwing Amber a box of paper tissues. 'For your nose. I didn't mean to break it.'

'Is that supposed to be an apology or something?' Amber asked.

'Whatever, but I need you to call airport security, or whoever you need to call and ask them to retract the boarding corridor.'

'You know you're stuck, right?' Amber shot the question at Linda. 'There's no way you're getting out this. Even if you could fly this plane.'

'I guess we'll see about that. Now, do what you're told.'

Amber retrieved her cellphone from her pocket and made the call. After telling the person at the other end of the line to retract the boarding corridor, she looked at Linda, lifting her phone at her.

'They want to talk to you. They want to know what your demands are.'

Linda simply shook her head. 'For now, that's it. I want the corridor retracted. Nothing else, but tell them to stay by the phone. They'll get another call in due time.'

Amber passed on that information and disconnected from the call.

'Now what, Linda?' Hunter asked, his eyebrows lifting at her.

Linda smiled at him and placed her gun on the counter in the galley, safe in the knowledge that all of them – Hunter, Amber and Phil – were chained to the plane. 'Now ... *Robert* ... we finish this.'

Eighty-nine

From where she was standing, inside the mid-plane galley, Linda heard a mechanical noise coming from just outside the airplane door. It had taken them only three minutes to comply with her demand. The boarding corridor was being retracted.

'I guess it's just us now, huh?' she said, opening one of the drawers in the galley to see what she could find.

Nothing of any interest in there.

Linda tried the next drawer along. 'Now this is more like it.' She reached inside to retrieve a couple of mini bottles. Both of them whisky.

'Would anyone else care for a drink?' she asked, cracking open the first mini bottle and pouring its contents into a plastic cup. 'We've got Scotch, bourbon, vodka, rum, gin, red and white wines . . . good selection here. I'm sure that there are beers somewhere too, if anyone prefers that.'

Everyone stayed quiet.

'If I were you,' Linda said. 'I would honestly consider it, as this will probably be your last ever drink.'

Phil squeezed his eyes tight, tears rolling down his face.

'No?' Linda asked, her stare moving from Phil, to Amber, to Hunter. 'OK. If you change your mind, let me know. We've got drawers full of this stuff here.'

'Linda, what are you doing?' Hunter asked. 'I know you don't want to shoot anyone in here.'

'What am I doing? I'm having a drink . . . *Robert*.' Linda sipped her whisky. 'Sure you don't want to join me?'

'Linda,' Hunter tried again, his voice calm and calculated. 'It's over. You know it's over. You can't get to Lucas anymore. Your quest . . . your revenge . . . it ends here, whether you want it to or not.'

Linda looked at Phil before gulping down the rest of her whisky. He was staring back at her with doubt in his eyes. She opened a second bottle and refilled her plastic cup.

'Over?' she asked Hunter, sarcastically, her expression fearless. 'Let me tell you a little story about things being "over", *Robert*. Let me tell you how one stupid act ended so much, for so many. Would you like to hear that story?'

Hunter nodded once.

Linda sipped her drink. 'It all started thirteen years ago, when I arrived home to find Genesis, my fourteen-year-old daughter, floating in blood-soaked water inside our bathtub. She had cut her left wrist so deep, she'd almost severed her whole hand off. Did you know that?'

Hunter held Linda's stare. He could clearly see the pain in her eyes.

'And do you know what the most torturous thing is, Robert?' Linda didn't wait for an answer. 'I remember everything about that moment.' Her left hand moved up to her neck to grab onto her butterfly. 'I remember how she looked . . . the expression on her face . . . the lack of color on her skin . . . how her wet hair stuck to the outside of the tub . . . the odd smell of iron in the air.' She pressed her lips tightly together. 'I remember how some of the water had spilled out from the tub and onto the white-tiled floor in our bathroom. It created this horrible, red-and-white marble effect all across the floor.' Linda chuckled and had another sip of her whisky. 'Those images ... those details ... they never go away. I see them every single time that I close my eyes. *Every ... single ... time ... Robert*. For the past thirteen years.'

Hunter knew how terribly devastating the act of suicide was. Not only a life was lost, but the psychological ramifications for those who were left behind, especially loved ones, were life changing, and the most destructive of psychological effects came with 'the finding'.

When it came to damaging mental and emotional consequences, psychologists split suicides into two distinct categories – deaths where the victim's body was discovered by someone, and deaths where the victim's body was destroyed. Both were tremendously traumatic, but the mental scars created by the act of finding the body of a loved one were the kind that didn't really heal.

'That single moment,' Linda continued, her voice heavy with hurt, 'when I entered our bathroom after coming home from work to find Genesis ... lifeless in the bathtub ...' She stared at her plastic cup as she mentioned her daughter's name, not wanting to meet anyone's eyes, not wanting anyone to see that her own eyes were wet with tears. 'In that specific moment, I could actually hear my mind fracturing inside my skull. I could feel my life ... my strength ... my hope ... leaving me right then. That moment changed all of our lives ... for ever.'

Linda had another sip of her whisky, which started to worry Hunter. An angry, broken and drunk person with a loaded gun could lose control at any moment.

Linda swallowed her tears.

'We were all so lost after that,' she carried on. 'Me ... my husband ... my son ... we simply didn't know how to carry on without Genesis. None of us seemed to be able to find our place in a world she wasn't in anymore.' She laughed and shook her head. 'Do you have any idea what that feels like ... *Robert*? To enter your house and find someone who meant more to you than your own life, dead?'

As Linda said those words, Hunter blinked once, fighting the images that flashed before his eyes. Jessica.

Linda saw him blinking ... she saw the pain in his eyes and paused, her expression analytical, as she studied the detective in front of her.

'My God! You have,' she said. It wasn't a question. 'You've returned home to find someone you loved dead, haven't you?'

Hunter stayed quiet.

Amber looked at him with curious eyes.

Linda waited.

Hunter said nothing.

'That moment changed you too, didn't it?' Linda asked.

'Different circumstances,' Hunter finally replied.

'But it made you angry, didn't it? It filled you with guilt ... and doubt ... and questions ... didn't it? Questions you knew you would never get an answer to. So many of them.'

'Different circumstances,' Hunter repeated.

'How long ago?'

'A long time.'

Amber said nothing, but she gently placed her cuffed hand over Hunter's.

Linda ran the tip of her index finger along the rim of her plastic cup. 'But you remember every detail about that moment, don't you? No matter how long ago it was ... no matter how much time has elapsed. You remember everything, don't you?'

Hunter didn't have to reply. Linda knew from the look in his eyes that he did.

'So you know what it feels like afterwards, don't you, Robert?' This time, she didn't sarcastically emphasize his name. 'The nightmares ... the panic attacks ... the loss of hope ... the sleepless nights ... the tormenting questions flying around in your head ... and the guilt ... the *never-ending* guilt.' Linda breathed in through her nose and nodded at herself. 'Genesis's death anni-hilated my family. We blamed ourselves because none of us saw it coming. Genesis was always happy ... always smiling ... despite her congenital condition, which I'm sure you know about, right?'

Hunter gave Linda an almost imperceptible nod.

Amber, once again, looked at him with questioning eyes, her interest completely renewed. Neither Hunter nor Linda knew this, but Amber's stepbrother had been born with Down syndrome.

'Of course Genesis had to battle depression,' Linda explained. 'Who wouldn't? Especially at her age. She knew that she looked different. She knew that people looked at her differently, but she was loved and supported by all of us. Still, we never knew ... none of us.' Another heavy, heartfelt pause. 'It was not knowing that broke us. Little by little. We were all so close to each other ... so supportive of one another ... so how could we not have known that she was hurting so much inside? How could we not have seen the signs? Because there are always signs, right? How could all of us have missed them? How could her teachers ... her friends? How could she not trust any of us enough to talk to us? To ask us for help.' Another sip of her whisky. 'Those types of ques-tions took over our thoughts twenty-four-seven. They ate away at everything ... our hearts ... our souls ... our minds ... our lives ... our sanity.'

A few ragged tears of anger ran down Linda's cheeks. She wiped them with the back of her hands and tried to calm herself down.

'Because of the incredible guilt we all felt,' she continued, her voice, once again, controlled, 'we lost our grip on everything, especially on each other. Michael, my son, who was three years older than Genesis, was the first to disintegrate.' Linda shook her head, as she remembered. 'He was so protective of his little sister and so supportive of everything she did. Every opportunity he had, Michael would show Genesis that her disability was nothing to be ashamed of.' A single shoulder shrug. 'So maybe she wouldn't become a world-renowned pianist, or an Olympic gymnast, or win Wimbledon, but then again, most completely able-bodied people on this planet wouldn't either. We all did all we could to make Genesis understand that we couldn't solve all her problems for her, but she would never, ever have to go through them alone. We would always be there for her. All she had to do was ask. So why didn't she? On that day, why didn't she?'

Hunter knew that Linda wasn't really expecting an answer.

'They were both so intelligent,' she continued. 'Genesis and Michael. They were creative, they were funny, they were strong-willed, they were determined, but most of all, they were compassionate and forgiving. They were always trying to help others, no matter what. They both had so much to look forward to in life.'

Hunter already knew what would come next. He had read Michael's autopsy report.

'After Genesis's suicide,' Linda carried on, 'to try to numb his pain . . . to try to drown the guilt that he felt inside for letting his sister down, Michael started using drugs.' The hurt was back in Linda's voice. 'But my husband and I, we were so broken . . . so consumed by that same guilt, that we never noticed it. We had both neglected our son. We weren't there for him. One year after Genesis's suicide, Michael overdosed.'

Hunter nodded slowly. 'I'm sorry.'

Linda seemed to pick up the sincerity in his tone.

'Some of his friends think that he did it on purpose,' she added. 'To escape the agony . . . the torture . . . the pain that his own brain was putting him through. That's how much he was hurting . . . and we didn't see it.'

Everyone went silent for an instant.

'Losing both of our children in the space of one year destroyed our marriage,' Linda explained. 'That's another problem with the "not knowing". We not only blamed ourselves, but we blamed each other as well. John, my husband, started drinking heavily about a month after Michael passed. By then, we could barely stand each other. All we did was fight and point the finger at one another. Recrimination, resentment, anger, apathy . . . that's what our marriage became. The day I told him that I couldn't take it anymore . . . that I wanted a divorce . . . John jumped in the car and left.'

Full darkness blinked inside Linda's eyes.

'Two days later, California Highway Patrol knocked on my door.'

Hunter and Amber both breathed out at the same time.

'John had died in a head-on collision with a tractor unit,' Linda explained. 'The unit's driver said that John's car simply swerved out of line at the last second and collided with his truck, as if it had been intentional.' For a moment, Linda seemed lost in thought. When she spoke, her voice choked. 'There wasn't even a body for me to identify, just . . . parts of it.'

Hunter felt an endless pit open up in his stomach. This was something that he hadn't known, but it was now absolutely clear that Linda saw what had happened to her son and her husband as being a 'butterfly effect' ripple of consequences from Genesis's suicide. In her mind, her real targets – the group of students from Gardena Junior High – had been responsible for all three deaths. As Linda saw it, her entire family had been decimated simply because her daughter had been bullied.

Right then, Amber's phone rang inside her pocket.

'May I?' she asked Linda.

'No.'

'It'll either be the FBI or the LAPD,' Amber told her.

'I know. Let it ring.'

'That's a bad move, Linda,' Hunter jumped in. 'If we don't answer it, it forces them to make assumptions. Take it from me – those are never positive. They'll assume the worst, and when they do, they'll mobilize everything they have to take the plane.'

'And the consequences of that is that we all die here today, right?' Linda asked, giving Hunter an emotionless smile before quickly peeking at Phil. 'I'm fine with that. Are you?'

Ninety

'She's not answering it,' Garcia said, as he put down the phone.

He and Captain Blake, along with the Chief of Police, two FBI agents, two representatives from American Airlines, two airport officials, and an SAC – Supervisor Air Marshal in Charge – were all standing around a table inside an improvised conference room in Terminal B. All flights in and out of the terminal had been either canceled or suspended for the time being. The entire terminal had been evacuated as a security precaution.

'That's not good news,' one of the FBI agents said, shaking his head at everyone. 'We need to co-ordinate a strike and we need to do it now.'

'Well, that's the last thing we're going to do right now,' Captain Blake countered. 'We have no eyes inside that aircraft. All the shades have been shut, which means that any strike would be a blind one. There's a civilian, an air marshal, and one of my best detectives inside that plane, and we all know what a blind strike really means, right? Casualties. No, we're not going with that plan.'

'We can easily get eyes inside that plane,' the FBI Agent said. 'We can send a man in through the belly of the aircraft. He can sneak in through the galley lift and use a fiber optic camera to give us a visual. We can co-ordinate from there.'

Garcia chuckled. 'Aren't you forgetting a few things, *buddy*?'

'Like what?' the agent challenged.

'Like the fact that the plane is on the ground, with its engines turned off,' Garcia replied. 'That's problem one. Problem two is that the plane is empty, with the exception of four people, who, last time anyone saw them, were standing right around the mid-plane galley. What that really means is that the plane is *silent*. No engine noise or passenger chatter to hide the sounds that a man entering the plane through its belly and using the galley lift would create. Any noise inside an empty airplane that size would also create an echo, which would, no doubt, be picked up by the perp. If that happens, everyone dies.' Garcia shook his head. 'Like the captain said – we're not going with the "kill everyone" plan.'

'So what do you want us to do?' the agent asked. 'Just sit around and do nothing?'

Captain Blake nodded. 'That's exactly what we're going to do for the time being. Let's give it another five minutes and see if we get a call from her. That was what the air marshal told us when she called, wasn't it? For us to stay by the phone because we would get another call in due time. Maybe this isn't due time yet. Let's give it another five minutes. If we haven't heard from her by then we'll call again.'

'That would be losing time,' the second FBI agent came back. 'If there was no answer now, what makes you think that there will be one in five minutes?'

'Because like I've said,' Captain Blake replied, 'I have one of my best detectives inside that plane, who also happens to be a brilliant human behavioural psychologist. Right at this moment, I know that he's negotiating with her.' She paused and looked at the two representatives from American Airlines. 'Detective Hunter *is* the reason why we safely have all the crew members and passengers, minus one, out of that aircraft. If anyone can talk the perp into giving herself up, he can. Detective Hunter also knows that an unanswered call will give us reason for concern, and he's probably explaining that to the perp right now. He'll make her understand that if our calls keep on going unanswered, there will be a blind strike, in which her life will probably be terminated.'

'What if she doesn't care if she and everyone in that plane ends up dead?' the agent asked. 'Have you thought of that possibility?' He addressed the American Airlines personnel. 'We don't even know if they're still alive in there.'

'They are,' Garcia assured them.

'And you know that how, *buddy*?' the agent asked.

'Because there's been no sound of gunfire coming from the airplane,' Garcia replied. 'I saw the weapon that Linda Evans was holding. It was a nine-millimeter pistol.' He looked at the SAC. 'Which I believe that she somehow managed to take from Amber Burnett, the air marshal who boarded the plane. No silencer on the weapon. If any shots had been fired, we would've heard them.'

'Let's give it five more minutes and call again,' Captain Blake pushed. 'If there's no answer then, my SWAT teams have already planned a strike.'

'Why your SWAT teams?' the FBI Agent asked.

'Because the plane is on the ground,' the captain shot back, 'inside LAX, which falls under the LAPD jurisdiction. The FBI has no authority here, unless we delegate, which we haven't done. We welcome you to sit in and listen on the phone calls and the planning, if a strike is needed, but this is our case . . . our operation. Plus, everyone knows that the LAPD SWAT is the best in the country. So please, have a seat and relax.' She indicated one of the chairs. 'Who knows? You might just learn something.'

Ninety-one

In hearing Linda's words, Phil let out a strangled yelp. 'Please . . . I don't want to die.' All the color had drained from his face. 'I'm so terribly sorry for what has happened to your whole family, but I've got nothing to do with that. I'm trying to start a family of my own. Please just let me go.'

Linda looked back at him and smiled. 'Is that so, loverboy?'

'Linda,' Hunter said. 'I don't believe that you want to die either.'

'Is that really what you believe . . . *Robert*?' The sarcasm was back in her voice. Linda took off her jacket and lifted both of her wrists to show Hunter. Across them were two large, leathery scars. 'You're wrong. I think about dying all the time.'

'That was a long time ago,' Hunter countered, as he looked down at his own body. 'I know scars, Linda. Both mental and physical ones. I know how much they hurt . . . how much damage they can cause . . . and how long it takes for them to heal, if they ever do.' They studied each other for a moment. 'I also know that with psychological scars, there are no do-overs. We either deal with them, or they deal with us. And you dealt with them, Linda, because those are old scars. From a time before you found a new purpose.'

'A new purpose?' Linda tried to smile, but it came out a grimace.

'Yes,' Hunter replied, recognizing that that was his chance to remind Linda of the person she used to be. 'Despite all your pain, Linda, you did the most noble thing a human being could do. You spent years travelling the country . . . talking to students . . . talking to teachers . . . talking to parents . . . helping them understand depression in young teenagers . . . how to be more aware of the signs . . . how to approach kids who were hurting and how to help them out. You quit your job as a trauma nurse, where every day you did your best to save lives, to dedicate the rest of yours to helping others *choose life* . . . not take it away, Linda.'

Linda stayed quiet.

'So no,' he continued. 'I don't believe that you want to die . . . and I don't believe that you want to kill any more people either, and that includes Lucas.'

'You did your research . . . *Robert*,' Linda said, as she reached inside the drawer for a new mini bottle. 'And if that's what you really think, then boy will you be surprised.' She smiled at him before turning to look at Phil. 'You, loverboy, have a drink. You look like you need one. What's your poison?'

Phil began scratching the back of his right hand. 'I don't want a drink. Just please let me go.'

Linda grabbed the gun from the counter and aimed it at him. 'One drink. I insist.'

'I'll have a drink with you,' Hunter called, taking a step forward and dragging Amber's arm with him as far as the curtain division would allow.

'The hero coming to the rescue,' Linda said, turning to face him. 'What would you like?'

'I'll have a whisky.'

Linda looked at Amber.

'I can't,' Amber said, pointing at her nose. 'Whatever I drink will taste of blood.'

'Would you like some water?' Linda asked.

'If you don't mind, that'd be great.'

'Could I please have some water as well?' Phil asked.

Linda shrugged. 'Water it is. Heads up.' She threw a bottle of water in Phil's direction and one to Amber before lobbing a mini whisky bottle to Hunter.

They all caught them mid-air.

'Cup?' Linda asked.

'Please,' Hunter accepted it, while Amber and Phil just shook their heads.

Linda tossed Hunter a plastic cup.

Hunter cracked the bottle cap and poured the golden liquid into the plastic cup. When he was done, Linda raised her cup at him.

'To finding a new purpose in life,' she said.

Hunter tipped his cup in Linda's direction before having a sip.

Amber first poured some water over her face, to clean up some of the blood, before drinking the rest of the bottle down in thirsty gulps.

Phil just took a couple of sips from his bottle.

'You're right,' Linda said, addressing Hunter and placing her cup back on the counter. 'I did find a new purpose in life. Something much, much better than helping others.'

'Revenge,' Hunter said.

'Revenge. Would you like to have a guess at how I discovered that new purpose?'

Hunter stayed quiet.

'C'mon, *Robert*, you must have some sort of theory, right? You did your research; we all know that, and you did well at it because you're here. You managed to get to me before I was done, so what's your take on why I'm doing what I'm doing? C'mon, I want to hear it.'

Amber looked at Hunter as if saying: *Give her something, Robert. Make it up, if you need to, but give her something.*

Hunter pretended to have another sip of his whisky. 'The most logical conclusion,' he began, 'is that just over a year ago, you somehow found out that a particular group of students from Gardena Junior High – students from Genesis's eighth grade class – bullied and made fun of her condition – things that unfortunately kids do. Maybe it was something that happened only that year … maybe it had been going on for a long time, it doesn't matter because she never told you about it. She never told you about how much it was affecting her. In fact, she never told anyone about any of it because like you've said, Genesis was a strong girl and she knew that people looked at her differently. She thought that she could deal with it by herself.'

Linda's eyebrows lifted at Hunter. A silent sign for him to go on.

'But despite how strong she might've seemed to everyone, the truth was that Genesis was just a young teenager, whose life experiences were still very limited to be able to deal with that kind of pressure. She was just coming into a very exciting age bracket. Fourteen years old – that's when most of us start discovering so much about ourselves and about life in general. That's also the age when most of us start worrying about looks … about fitting in … about being accepted.' He paused and observed Linda biting her bottom lip. 'That overload of new information and emotions can and usually does overwhelm so many young teenagers. It makes them more vulnerable and much more susceptible to depression and anxiety. For most people who end up struggling with depression throughout their lives, that's exactly the age that its hallmarks show for the first time.'

Linda leaned back against the galley counter. She seemed to be enjoying Hunter's theory.

'Unfortunately,' Hunter said, his tone tender, 'instead of asking her mother … her father … her brother … anyone for help, Genesis kept on taking the bullying … the jokes … the abuse … she kept on trying to be strong all by herself, until it all became too much for her.'

Linda reached for her butterfly once again.

'Discovering not only what had truly pushed your daughter to end her own life,' Hunter added, 'but also the names of the students who back then were behind that bullying, was more than just a shock to you – it broke you for the last time. That was when you decided to go after every single one of them, but your revenge plan wasn't to take them out. That would be too simple, right?'

'Dying is easy,' Linda replied, her voice leaden.

'You wanted to make them suffer just as much as you suffered. You wanted them to have to carry on without someone who they loved. So you did your research and made sure that those kids, the ones behind Genesis's bullying, were the ones who'd find the bodies of their loved ones. You wanted them to break. That was why you sent them a follow-up message with a video clip the very next day – to force that mind fracture into a full-blown open wound . . . one that would never heal.'

Linda did look somewhat impressed. 'You know . . . people say that time heals all . . . time mends everything . . . just give it time, they say.' She brought a hand to her neck to massage it. 'Well, none of that happened in my case. Do you know the only thing that time has done to me . . . Robert?'

'Made you more skillful at hiding how broken you truly are inside?' Hunter ventured.

Linda's eyes narrowed at him. She clearly wasn't expecting an answer to her question, and Hunter's one did more than just surprise her.

'My God,' she said, her stare analytical. 'You're just as broken as I am, aren't you? Time has never managed to heal you either. What it did was make you an expert in hiding all your pain . . . hiding all that hurt. Just like me.'

This time, Hunter stayed quiet.

Their stares battled until Linda broke it off with a laugh. 'That was indeed a good theory, Robert. Very good, actually, but you're missing a few *spicy* details. So please, allow me to fill in the blanks for you.' She had another sip of her drink. 'Yes, I did find out about that group of students. Do you want to know how?'

Hunter's silence was a resounding 'yes'.

'Like you've said,' Linda began, 'I spent years travelling the country, trying to educate parents, teachers, students, whoever I could, on how destructive depression in young teenagers could be. I did it because I truly believed that that was what had happened to Genesis. She had lost her battle against depression. I didn't want other families to go through what I had gone through ... what my family had gone through. I wanted them to learn how to find out if their children were hurting ... if they were struggling. I couldn't help my family, but maybe I could help others.'

Amber and Phil were both listening to Linda's account with just as much interest as Hunter.

'Then,' she continued, 'just over a year ago, like you've said, while doing another one-day seminar, this one in Pomona – Claremont High School – I was approached by a twenty-six year-old man at the end of the seminar.'

'Pedro Bustamente,' Hunter said. He didn't phrase it as a question.

'One and the same.' Linda nodded. 'He looked troubled, clearly struggling with a lot – depression, anxiety, shame, but most of all, guilt. He asked me if we could talk in private. He looked so ... down and out ... so skinny that I offered to buy him lunch. He didn't accept. He just wanted to talk to me, so after I was all packed, we went out to the parking lot and sat in my car.'

This time, Linda reached for a bottle of water, cracked the cap and had a sip.

'He began by telling me that he'd known Genesis. He told me that they were friends ... that they were in the same class together back at Gardena Junior High and that he was so, so sorry for what had happened.' She ran the tip of her tongue against both of her lips. As she did, her eyes lost focus for just an instant. 'It was the way in which he said that he was sorry that concerned me. It didn't sound like a "sorry for your loss" kind of comment. It was more like a "sorry for what we've done" confession. He was shaking, his eyes were tearful and his voice was like a whisper. That was when I asked him if there was anything from back then that he wanted to tell me.'

Linda looked at Hunter with fire in her eyes.

'And here's where you were wrong, Detective. It wasn't bullying that pushed Genesis to end her own life. Not the constant kind of bullying that you referred to in your theory. It wasn't bullying that caused Michael to overdose or John to drive into a tractor unit.' A very heavy pause. 'This was a single, isolated event that they so kindly referred to as "a joke".'

'A joke?' The question came out of Hunter and Amber's lips at the same time.

From her jacket pocket, Linda retrieved her cellphone before tapping the screen three times.

'After I asked him if there was anything that he wanted to tell me, Pedro began crying. He kept on saying that he was so sorry for everything ... so sorry for Genesis ... and he *begged* me for my forgiveness. When I asked him – "forgiveness for what?" – he showed me this.' She lobbed the phone over to Hunter.

He caught it with his left hand.

'Just tap the screen,' she told him. 'It's already cued up.'

Ninety-two

Inside the improvised conference room in Terminal B, the air was heavy with tension. The shorter of the two FBI agents checked his watch again.

'It's been over five minutes,' he said, nodding at Captain Blake and pointing to the phone at the center of the table. 'Not a word from your detective. We need to enter that plane. This has gone on for long enough.' His gaze moved to the Chief of Police.

'He's right,' one of the two airport officials agreed. 'Pressure from all airlines is mounting by the millisecond. The longer this goes on for, the more money they lose. Every flight out of this terminal has been either cancelled or delayed. They all want this resolved as fast as possible.'

'We need to add a tag ending to that sentence,' Garcia jumped in.

'Which is?' the second FBI agent asked.

'They all want this resolved as fast as possible,' Garcia repeated. '*Without any casualties*. We already have three LAPD SWAT teams in place, as you know. Two on the ground and one in the boarding tunnel, just outside the aircraft door. They are ready to strike, as soon as *we* decide it's time to go ahead.'

Captain Blake disregarded the entire conversation and simply reached for the phone on the table, pressing 'redial'. 'Let's try again, shall we?'

At the other end of the line, Amber's phone rang once ...
twice ... six times before it was finally answered.

'*What part of "you'll get another call in due time" did you not
understand*?' Linda's voice boomed through the speaker system
on the table.

'This is Captain Barbara Blake of the LAPD ...' Captain Blake
tried, but Linda immediately cut her short.

'*Do I sound like I give a damn who you are? The instructions
are still the same – you'll get another call in due time. Now sit
back and wait.*'

The call disconnected.

Ninety-three

Just as Hunter caught Linda's cellphone mid-air, after she tossed it over to him, Amber's phone rang inside her pocket. She looked at Linda.

'What would you like me to do?' she asked.

'Same as before,' Linda told her. 'Let it ring.'

'Like I said, Linda,' Hunter interjected. 'If you don't answer it, they'll make assumptions.' He looked left then right, as if checking both cabins. 'SWAT teams are known for being trigger-happy. Trust me – you really don't want them to storm the plane.'

Linda considered Hunter's advice for a moment. 'OK,' she addressed Amber. 'Give me your phone.'

Amber lobbed it over to her.

Linda caught it and took the call:

'What part of "you'll get another call in due time" did you not understand?' There was a pause. 'Do I sound like I give a damn who you are? The instructions are still the same – you'll get another call in due time. Now sit back and wait.' Linda ended the call and tossed the phone back to Amber. 'There.' She told Hunter. 'Happy?'

As Amber returned her phone to her pocket, her and Hunter's attention went back to Linda's cellphone in Hunter's hand. He held it in an angle that allowed both of them to clearly see its screen.

'Like I said, just tap the screen to play,' Linda told Hunter again. Reflexively, Phil stretched his neck.

'What the hell are you doing?' Linda asked, her hand moving back to the gun.

'Nothing,' he replied in a single breath. 'Just curious. I'm sorry.'

'Boy, you better sit back and stay that way.'

Phil did exactly that, without meeting Linda's stare.

Hunter tapped the center of the screen.

As the video started playing, the first thing that Hunter and Amber noticed was that the video was soundless. The footage had been shot inside a room ... probably a bedroom by what they could see. It was also clear that whoever had shot that video was hiding behind what looked to be double doors that had been left ajar just enough – either another room, or a wardrobe. The camera kept on moving left, right and up and down, always looking for a better angle. Due to how shaky the footage was throughout, it was obvious that the camera was being handheld.

Through the gap between the double doors, about ten to fifteen feet ahead of the camera, Hunter and Amber could see two young teenagers – a boy and a girl – standing just in front of another open door that led into an en suite bathroom, the light of which was turned off. The girl was clearly Genesis. Her black hair was loose, cascading down onto her shoulders in elegant waves. She wore a white T-shirt that was tucked into a black, high-waisted, pleated skirt and low-heel open shoes.

The boy, who looked to be around the same age as Genesis, was almost a whole foot taller than her. His curly hair was as dark as the night itself, which matched his round eyes. He was wearing a black button-up shirt, blue jeans and white sneakers.

Hunter immediately recognized the boy. He'd seen his photo in the Gardena Junior High yearbook for the Class of 2009 – the same photo that had been pinned to the picture board inside the UVC Unit's office. That was Pedro Bustamante.

The two of them were talking and holding hands.

Genesis's hand malformation didn't seem to bother Pedro.

Six seconds into the footage and in what could only be described as a very tentative movement, Genesis got on the tip of her toes and as Pedro angled his head forward, their lips met. Genesis tenderly placed her hands on the sides of Pedro's face, while he wrapped his arms around her waist. The kiss was shy, lasting less than five seconds, at which point they paused, looked into each other's eyes, and then kissed again, this time a lot more passionately and for a lot longer.

Inside the aircraft, it was as if the roles had reversed because it was Linda who seemed to be studying Hunter's facial expressions.

Once the kiss was over, the two of them started talking. Due to the awkward camera angle, Hunter was unable to see their lips clearly enough to be able to read them, but he could certainly read their body language.

Genesis seemed hesitant at what Pedro was saying. She took a step back and her arms crossed in front of her body, a protective move, which meant that at that particular time, she felt vulnerable.

Pedro, on the other hand, seemed completely in control. He didn't look to be forceful, but he was certainly insistent enough, towering over Genesis. As he spoke, he repositioned his body a little to the left of where he was, putting himself in a direct line of sight with the camera, which allowed Hunter to finally read his lips.

C'mon, Gen, you promised.

Hunter couldn't read Genesis's reply.

Yes, Pedro reassured her. *The bedroom door is locked. No one is coming in here. I promise. It's just us.*

Finally, after several long seconds, Genesis's shoulders dropped and so did her head, as if she was trying to make herself even smaller than she already was. The movement indicated that she had caved in to whatever Pedro had asked her to do, but she looked awkward and somewhat embarrassed.

Pedro smiled. *OK, I'll wait out here . . . and yes, I'll go next.*

As Pedro waited, Genesis went into the en suite bathroom and closed the door.

That was when everything changed.

As the door closed behind Genesis, Pedro turned and directly faced the camera before gesturing to whoever was behind it to come closer. All of a sudden, the double doors were slid open and whoever it was that had been hiding and filming everything from behind those doors quickly approached Pedro, pausing to his left. The camera was now about four feet in front of the bathroom door . . . waiting.

'Oh my god!' Amber murmured. She could already guess what was about to happen.

The camera shook slightly, as if whoever was filming the whole thing was chuckling at the scene.

Several long seconds went by before the bathroom door was finally pulled open again and Genesis reappeared. The difference was, she was now completely naked.

As she looked up and saw that Pedro wasn't alone anymore, Genesis froze, her body seeming to recoil into itself.

In the split second that took her tiny eyes to fill with tears and dread, Pedro rounded her and closed the bathroom door behind them. Confused, lost and clearly feeling totally betrayed, Genesis did her best to cover herself, using her small, uneven hands, but the cameraman kept on expertly moving around, filming everything.

Terrified, a sobbing Genesis quickly turned on the balls of her feet and tried to re-enter the bathroom, but Pedro, who was now laughing, blocked her way. The cameraman kept on moving the camera up and down and right and left, recording everything about her naked and shivering body.

Hunter peeked at Amber, who at that exact moment had also peeked at him. Neither of them needed to carry on watching the clip.

Hunter tapped the screen to pause the footage.

'That happened just after the end of the school year,' Linda explained. 'At a party in Troy's house. His parents were away. What Pedro told me that day, in my car, was that Troy Foster was the boy behind the camera. He was hiding in the walk-in closet, inside his parents' bedroom, because they knew what would happen that night. Pedro, Troy, Josie, Janet and Sofia had planned it all out. They all knew that Gen really liked Pedro, so a week before the party, he conveniently started dating her. Genesis seemed so happy that week. I still remember it.' Linda went back to her whisky. 'The plan was – Pedro was to ask Genesis to let him see her naked so that they could film it and make fun of her, just for a joke.' She sighed. 'Those were exactly the words that Pedro used – it was meant as a joke. We're talking about a terribly fragile little girl here . . . someone who was already struggling with so much in her life. Her body was different . . . she knew that . . . and she tried so hard not to let that discourage her. She just wanted to be like any other girl her age, so when the boy that she really liked started courting her, she obviously fell for it because she so much wanted him to like her back. The plan worked because they were clever. He didn't ask her for sex. All he wanted was to see her without any clothes on, that was all. And he pushed her to do it at the party, in Troy's house.' Linda indicated the phone in Hunter's hand. 'Genesis obviously believed that if she didn't do it, Pedro wouldn't want to date her anymore, so she caved in.'

Hunter nodded.

'According to Pedro, about two weeks or so after that party, he and Troy came by our apartment building when Gen was in by herself, pretending that they wanted to apologize, but instead, they showed her that video clip and just for fun . . . just for a joke ... they told Genesis that no one would ever want to date a "freak" like her. They told her that they would keep the video because they wanted to show it to everyone in Gardena High when they went back to school in a couple of months.' Linda took a moment, visibly using the time to put her emotions in check. 'That day, after Troy and Pedro left ... Gen went back upstairs ...' This time, Linda couldn't hold the tears that rolled down her face. 'Grabbed the sharpest knife we had in our kitchen, and ended her life by almost amputating her own hand. She was fourteen years old.'

Hunter looked at Amber again. Her jaw was locked, but she didn't seem to realize she had done it.

'Pedro told me that it had all been just a joke. That they didn't really mean what they said to her. That they would've never really shown that video to anyone. It was just young boys being stupid ... having fun ... playing a prank.'

'I am so ...' Hunter began but Linda stopped him.

'Sitting in my car, that day,' she said, 'Pedro told me that they never told the girls about them visiting Gen. Only the two of them knew about what they had done. Pedro also told me that for thirteen years, he had struggled with guilt, with shame, and with remorse. He told me that Genesis's suicide had ruined his life and that he needed me to forgive him for what he'd done.' Linda chuckled. 'Ruined *his* life. Can you believe it? He said that he had always wanted to come and tell me the truth, but he'd never really had the courage. He told me that he had been to so many of my seminars, with the intention of approaching me, but in the end, he would just walk away. That day, he told me that he had promised himself that he would not walk away ... not again ... no matter the consequences for him.' Linda smiled the coldest smile Hunter had ever seen. 'He died that night.'

'Did you kill him?' Amber asked.

Linda replied with a look.

'Linda . . .' Hunter tried again, but again, she halted him.

'Don't.' Gun in hand, her arm shot up to aim at Hunter. 'There's nothing you can say . . . *Robert*. There's nothing you can say because you haven't seen it all.'

Hunter and Amber squinted at Linda.

'Better yet,' she corrected herself, 'you haven't heard it all. Go back to the beginning of the video,' Linda ordered Hunter, her voice angry. 'Top button on the left-hand side of the phone. That's the volume. Turn it up. Watch it again. It gets better . . . it gets much better.'

Ninety-four

As Hunter dragged the video 'play' bar at the bottom of the screen back to the beginning of the clip, he heard a faint noise come from just outside the airplane door. He gave nothing away – his eyes didn't divert from Linda's cellphone screen to look at the door and his posture stayed relaxed – but he knew that SWAT teams were getting ready to enter the plane.

'Go on,' Linda insisted. 'Don't be shy. I promise you, you'll like it.'

Hunter thumbed the phone's volume up full blast before tapping the screen to restart the clip.

As the footage began replaying, Hunter and Amber could now hear the voices of those who were behind the camera. Troy Foster wasn't alone.

'*Shhhhh,*' they heard Troy say. '*Don't let her know we're here,*' he whispered. '*This is going to be good.*'

On the video clip, as Genesis tiptoed to kiss Pedro for the first time, she tenderly placed her hands on the sides of his face.

'*I can't believe that Pedro is allowing her to touch his face with those hands,*' someone softly whispered. The voice behind the comment was female . . . young. '*She could kill 'im. She could hook him by the mouth like a fish with those fish-hook hands.*'

The comment generated a battery of muffled laughs from the group behind the camera.

Hunter felt a shiver gain momentum right at the base of his skull before it shot down along his spine like an electric shock.

'Would you like to guess who made that comment . . . Robert?' Linda asked.

'Janet Lang,' Hunter replied. 'Melissa Hawthorne's sister.'

As Amber frowned at Hunter, trying to understand what was going on, Linda smiled at him. She knew that he was starting to understand.

Janet's comment was the trigger for what came next – kids being kids – always wanting to outdo each other. Because everyone had laughed at Janet's comment, everyone decided to come out with his or her own remark, pushing it up a notch every time, believing that that would make the comment even funnier than the previous one.

Right on the heels of Janet's comment, came Troy's. Just another whisper.

'*And they were holding hands earlier. Did y'all see that? Is the motherfucker crazy? What if she took off running right then? Bitch would pull the motherfucker along like a tow truck with those towing hooks she's got. He'd be dragged across the ground behind her like an old slab of meat.*'

More muffled laughs.

'No points for guessing who that was,' Linda said, as Hunter paused the video. 'Since he was the only other boy in the group.'

Hunter looked up to meet Linda's angry stare.

'Please, carry on,' she said. ' The comments get better . . . the "joke" gets funnier.'

Hunter, reluctantly, tapped the screen again.

The remarks died down until Genesis disappeared into the bathroom and the group was ushered out of the walk-in closet by Pedro. As they waited for Genesis to come out, no one said a word, keeping it dead quiet until the door was pulled open again.

'*Surprise!*' they all yelled out before bursting into laughter, as a terrified Genesis froze in front of them.

'*Good thing that you didn't ask her for a handjob, Pedro,*' came the comment from one of the girls, as Pedro got behind Genesis to close the bathroom door. '*She would've probably sliced your dick and balls clean off with those lobster claws she's got – clack, clack, clack.*'

Another round of animated laughs.

Hunter knew that that comment had come from Josie.

'*Yeah, I wouldn't even put a finger inside her,*' one of the girls said. '*Who knows if she has a claw in there too?*'

'That was Janet,' Linda clarified.

Hunter allowed his chin to drop to his chest and his eyes to close for an instant.

In all three aftermath video clips, Linda had used their own words to taunt them . . . to push them to remember.

'All I did,' Linda said, matter-of-factly, as she finished another mini bottle of whisky, 'was follow their suggestions.' She nodded at the phone in Hunter's hands. 'Admit it, *Robert* – I didn't do a bad job, did I?'

Amber looked completely lost.

Hunter's attention returned to the video clip.

As Genesis tried to get through Pedro and back into the bathroom, she placed her hands around Pedro's abdomen to try to push him out of the way, but he was too strong for her.

'*Careful, Pedro.*' Once again, the comment came from one of the girls. '*With those Edward Scissorhands of hers, she could cut you in half, easy. Your insides would just fall out like mincemeat.*'

More laughs.

Hunter paused the clip. The comment had clearly come from Sofia Risoli, now Sofia Eliot. That must have been Linda's plan – to cut Lucas Elliot in half and probably spread his insides all over the floor, like mincemeat, for Sofia to find.

'So there you have it, *Detective Hunter,*' Linda said, gesturing for Hunter to toss her phone back to her.

He did.

'Mystery solved,' she said, as she returned the phone to her pocket. 'I bet that answered a few questions about your investigation, didn't it?'

'Linda,' Hunter began. 'I can understand your anger, because I was once as angry as you are. I wanted revenge on the people who had taken someone I loved from me . . . and that has happened more than once.'

'Good. So you should really help me out here and let me go, so I can finish my business.'

'Let me ask you something about your revenge, Linda,' Hunter risked. 'Has it worked? Has it made you feel any better? Has it made you miss Genesis, Michael and John any less? When you were brutally extinguishing those people's lives – those completely innocent people's lives – did it appease your heart? Did it take away any of the pain . . . any of the hurt that you've been carrying inside you for so long?'

'You see . . . Robert.' The sarcasm was back in Linda's tone. 'That's where you got it wrong. This isn't about me, or how it makes me feel. This isn't about appeasing my heart, or ending my pain. The pain I feel will only end when I'm gone. I know that. This is about people being responsible for their actions. This is about people not getting away with whatever the fuck they want, just because they call it a joke.' She shook her head, angrily. 'To every action there's a consequence. You know that, right? Some actions have a third step, which is the "reaction". Genesis's suicide, followed by Michael and John's death is the consequence of their action.' Linda stabbed her index finger against her chest. 'I . . . am the reaction. And believe me . . . Robert – I am happening.'

'But the people you're murdering,' Hunter said back, his tone far from condescending, 'are innocent of the action you're talking about, Linda. I know that you can see that. They weren't, in any way, related to that video.'

'Innocent?' Linda asked through clenched teeth. 'You want to talk about innocent, do you? OK.' She drew in a furious breath. 'Genesis was innocent. Michael was innocent. John was innocent. They're all gone, *Robert*. My whole family. Everyone I loved . . . *gone* . . . because a group of fourteen-year-old kids wanted to have a laugh . . . just for fun . . . just a joke.' She put on a silly, childish voice. '"Oh, I have an idea – just for a joke, let's trick a vulnerable and fragile little girl into exposing herself, just so we can film it and humiliate her to the point of despair." As if Genesis didn't already have a life-long battle to fight against her own body, her mental state, prejudice, and let's not forget ignorance.' Linda took a moment, using her hand to emphasize her point. 'And do you know what else is just incredible? Five kids in that group . . . *five*. Three of them girls. Not one of them said, "Well, this is a fucking mean, dumb-ass idea. Let the poor girl be. She never did anything to any of us, so why do you guys want to break her down like that? Would you like someone to do that to you?"' Linda used both hands to point at herself. 'Well, retribution is an ugly bitch, isn't it?'

'But the people you've murdered, Linda. They never even knew Genesis.' Hunter was trying to appeal to her human side once again, which he was sure was still there – hidden behind all that anger, but still there, nonetheless. He just needed to reach it. ' In fact, other than Melissa Hawthorne, who was Janet's stepsister, if you go back thirteen years to when Genesis ended her life, all the other people you've murdered didn't even know the people who you've murdered them for. Kirsten Hansen only met Troy Foster three years ago. Oliver Griffith only met Josie Moss seventeen months ago.' He paused for effect. 'You took their lives away from them, Linda, for something they had absolutely no fault in . . . something that happened when they, themselves, were just kids, like Genesis.'

Like Genesis – two words – and just like that, Hunter's thought process found a whole new gear, as a brand new idea exploded inside his head.

'I know you did phenomenal research in finding out everything you could on all of these people,' he said, testing the water. 'You spent months collecting data on all of them. Your research was impeccable, but let me ask you this – did you research their younger lives?'

A flicker of doubt flashed inside Linda's eyes.

Hunter saw it. He knew the answer even though Linda didn't give it to him. This could work.

'Well, we did,' he lied. 'We had to find out everything we could about the victims to try to understand why they were being murdered. Do you know why Kirsten Hansen left Denmark to come to America?'

Linda's eyes narrowed at him.

'Kirsten Hansen was born with a speech impediment,' Hunter made that up right there and then. 'Submucous cleft palate. In school, she was made fun of by most of the other kids because of how she spoke.'

Linda paused and all of a sudden her whole demeanor became unsure.

'She came to America for an operation to correct it. She ended up staying. Oliver Griffith didn't suffer from any physical disabilities, but when he was fourteen years old – the same age as Genesis – he was toothpick-thin. He was bullied all the time for his lack of muscle, for how awkward he was, and for not being into sports. He was pushed around, beaten up, made fun of, pranked . . . all of it. It was only after he left high school that he decided to do something about it. That was when he joined a gym and bulked up.'

For the first time, Hunter thought that Linda looked like she was questioning herself inside her head.

'Lucas Elliot is dyslexic,' Hunter carried on. 'He still struggles with it today, but when he was a kid, in school, he was made fun of because he couldn't read or write properly. His nickname was "dumb & dumber".'

'Can I . . .' Phil tried asking a question, but Linda immediately shut him down.

'Shut up.'

'All the people you've murdered, Linda,' Hunter continued. 'They struggled when they were kids. They were bullied . . . they were made fun of . . . they were humiliated . . . they were pushed around and beaten up.' Hunter's pause was, once again, heavy. 'They *were* Genesis, in their own way, trying to fit in . . . trying their best to be accepted . . . struggling with their own imperfections . . . fighting their own wars against prejudice. The big difference is – they didn't end their lives, Linda . . . you did. Do you truly believe that that was justice for you . . . for Genesis? Do you really believe that Genesis would be OK with her mother murdering people who just like her, had fought so hard to overcome ignorance . . . fought so hard just to be themselves.'

Linda's stare flicked to Phil, then to Amber, then to Hunter. She was clearly struggling with something inside of her. Guilt? Shame? Both? Hunter couldn't tell. Her reaction was to reach for the gun.

'Somebody had to pay,' she said, her voice unsteady with emotion. 'We all lost our lives thirteen years ago – Genesis, Michael, John, and I. I had to avenge them.' She shrugged. 'An eye for an eye. An innocent life for an innocent life. So what?' Her voice went steady again. 'This world isn't fair, Detective. This life isn't fair. I'm sure you've noticed that already. If this life was fair, Genesis wouldn't have been born with ectrodactyly.' Her eyes moved to the gun in her hand for a second. 'I've done my suffering. Now it's their time, and if some innocent people had to die for it . . .' She shrugged. 'So be it. Tough luck.'

Hunter could have been wrong, but right then, he felt that Linda's words lacked conviction.

Linda took a deep breath, as her gaze moved from Phil, to Amber, and finally to Hunter.

'There's something else you've got wrong today ... *Robert*. You might not understand it right now, but I know that you soon will. It's all out there, waiting for you.'

'What else did I get wrong?'

Coincidence or not, plan 'C' was all that Linda had left. She just needed to execute it.

'You said that no one would die here today.' She gave Hunter and Amber a dead smile, void of every emotion. 'You were wrong.'

Linda aimed her weapon and fired two precise shots, sending a new, thicker mist of blood up in the air, this one filled with bone fragment and brain matter.

Ninety-five

In the boarding corridor, LAPD SWAT team Alpha was anxiously waiting for their green light to take the plane. All the aircraft window shades had been pulled down, including the one on the boarding door. That had allowed the team to sneak up through the corridor until they reached the articulated bend, located just a few feet from the opening that would extend to connect to the airplane.

When Linda had asked the airport officials to retract the connecting corridor, they'd done just that, but they hadn't retracted it all the way. In fact, they only moved it back just a few feet.

Full retraction of the connecting corridor took somewhere between fifteen to twenty seconds, but they'd only retracted it for three seconds – less than five feet. Since the taking of the aircraft seemed to have been something that Linda had to improvise, they had guessed that she wasn't exactly aware of the details of how the boarding corridor properly worked.

They had been right.

What that meant was that with the green light, it would take SWAT team Alpha three seconds to extend the corridor to the aircraft, one and a half seconds to use the external release latch on the door, and one second to pull the door open. In total, almost five seconds until they could storm the plane. Not ideal, but much better than twenty.

Bang.

Bang.

The loud shots, muffled by the door and the pressurized interior of the aircraft, sounded like two popcorn pops from the outside, but all five of the SWAT team members knew exactly what they were.

'Shots fired, shots fired,' Jose Alvarez, the leader of the SWAT team, whispered down his radio.

'*Go – now,*' Captain Blake's voice exploded through the SWAT team members' earpieces.

Four and a half seconds later, they were pulling the airplane door fully open. As they did, two M84 stun grenades were lobbed into the aircraft. They exploded on impact.

Upon detonation, the M84 grenade emitted an intensely loud bang, together with a blinding flash of light. This was designed to cause immediate flash-blindness, deafness and inner ear disturbance, which would cause confusion and loss of co-ordination.

With the explosions, the team immediately boarded the air-craft – all of them with their MP5 submachine guns in hand and searching for a target. As they stepped into the plane, team Leader Alvarez saw Hunter straight away. He was standing to the right of the door, with his head down and his left hand up against his ear. He was wearing only boxers and socks. To Hunter's right, Alvarez saw a woman, who was handcuffed to the detective through a large wall-fixed handle. Her face was covered in blood. Her eyes were shut, her right hand pressed hard against her ear. They were both a little disoriented.

'Detective Hunter,' Alvarez called, 'are you alright?'

'We're OK,' Hunter shouted back.

Both Hunter and Amber knew protocol. They'd known that if any SWAT team was to take the aircraft, the first thing they would do would be to lob a couple of stun grenades into the plane. As

soon as they saw the door opening, they both closed their eyes
and used their free hand to cover one of their ears.

Bang . . . bang.

The grenades exploded, sending two flashes of more than one
million candela each rushing through the plane.

It took Alvarez, and his second in command, Portnoy, less than
a second to identify Hunter and Amber as hostages. In doing so,
their MP5s moved left and right, searching for Linda Evans.

'Phil?' Hunter yelled, as he opened his eyes. 'Phil, are you OK?'

There was no reply.

Ninety-six

Just a few seconds earlier.

'You said that no one would die here today.' Linda gave Hunter and Amber a dead smile, void of every emotion. 'You were wrong.'

In a movement that no one had predicted, Linda extended her arm left, aiming her weapon not at Hunter or Amber, but at Phil, who had his feet up on his seat and his knees pulled up against his chest.

It all happened so fast that it didn't give Hunter or Amber a chance to react. By the time they realized that Linda hadn't pointed the gun at them, she had already squeezed the trigger.

Bang.

'*No,*' Hunter shouted at the top of his voice, thrusting forward with all the strength he had, but the handcuff that connected him to Amber, together with the fixed-wall handle, prevented him from getting to Linda by at least six feet.

It didn't matter.

A millisecond after Linda had shot Phil, she brought the barrel directly under her chin and once again squeezed the trigger.

The bullet, a 9mm soft point round, entered Linda's skull through her lower mandible, before ripping through her tongue and the roof of her mouth. It then penetrated her brain, destroying everything in its path, before pulverizing the top of her cranium.

Somehow, Hunter caught Linda's stare, just as her finger applied the necessary pressure to the trigger.

He saw nothing in them – no emotion … no anger … no life … as if her soul had left her body even before the round had left the weapon.

As Linda's lifeless body fell to the floor, Hunter's shock at what had just happened paralyzed him for a heartbeat. He simply stood there, eyes wide-open, jaw dropped, breathing held on his throat.

'*This shouldn't have happened.*'

It was then that Hunter heard the aircraft door being pulled open. SWAT teams were coming in. That forced his brain to finally re-engage.

Ninety-seven

'Phil?' Hunter yelled one more time, trying his best to angle his body as much as he could to get a visual on the young man, but being handcuffed to Amber didn't allow him to see past the galley, no matter how much he tried.

Phil had been sitting across the plane from where Hunter and Amber were. He was to the left of the galley, while Hunter and Amber had been chained to the curtain divide to the right of it.

After identifying Hunter and Amber, Team Leader Alvarez veered right into the mid-plane galley. That was when he saw Linda's body on the floor. Skin, hair, bone fragments and brain matter were splattered across the aircraft wall just behind her, as well as on the seat to her right and on some of the galley cabinets.

'Target down,' Alvarez called out, as he rushed to Linda. 'Target down.' He kicked the gun in her hand away.

Since Alvarez and Portnoy had gone left, as they'd entered the plane, the remaining three members of SWAT team Alpha had veered right at the door.

From the corners of his eyes, Hunter saw two new SWAT teams appear. They had used the front and rear doors of the aircraft to board the airliner.

'She's gone,' Alvarez informed everyone.

'You think?' Hunter shouted back, his ears still ringing from the detonations. 'Half of her brain is on the wall behind you. Phil, she shot Phil first.' He pointed to the left of the galley. 'He's cuffed to the seat just past the galley.' Hunter's voice faltered. 'Tell me he's not dead.'

'He's non-responsive,' came the reply from one of the SWAT team members, who had been the first to get to Phil.

'Get the medics in here,' Hunter ordered them.

'He's not shot,' the SWAT team member announced. 'He's passed out, but he's uninjured.'

'What?' Hunter looked at Amber, who was just then beginning to recover from the stun grenades. 'She shot him. We saw it.'

'She shot *at* him,' the SWAT team member replied. 'But she missed ... by a lot. The bullet hit the seat next to him. Like I said, he's just passed out. No wound ... no blood. He's unhurt.'

Ninety-eight

Five hours later – Linda Evans's apartment in Torrance.

Hunter and Garcia stood still, their eyes wide with surprise, as they stared at the walls inside Linda Evans's small studio apartment in the South Bay region of Los Angeles. The walls were plastered from floor to ceiling with photographs, schematics, and written plans.

On the table, which folded out from one of the walls, Linda had left her laptop. Surrounding it, evenly spread on the table surface, were more photographs and a target practice record book from a shooting range.

At the airport, once the whole stand-off was over, Hunter and Garcia had both been seen by EMTs. Hunter was fine. The effects from the M84 stun grenades had long worn off. Garcia, on the other hand, had a badly sprained ankle from his collision with the two TSA officers. His whole left foot had been bandaged and for the time being, he was walking with the assistance of crutches.

From LAX, they were supposed to have gone straight back to the Police Administration Building to file the paperwork and face whatever was coming from Captain Blake and the Chief of Police, but Hunter was driving, and he decided that he first wanted to have a look at Linda Evans's apartment. He had retrieved her keys from her handbag when no one was looking. Garcia didn't object.

'This is insane,' Garcia finally said. They'd been looking at everything in silence for the whole five minutes that they'd been in the apartment. 'It looks like she's left everything out here, Robert. All of her research – surveillance photos, schedules, names, addresses . . . everything.'

You might not understand it right now, Linda had said on the plane. *But I know that you soon will. It's all out there, waiting for you.*

Hunter said nothing back. Instead, he started looking through a series of photo printouts that he had found inside an envelope, which had been tacked to one of the kitchen walls.

Garcia limped over to the table and began flipping through the target practice record book. The more he flipped through it, the more he frowned.

'Robert, come have a look at this.'

'Just a sec,' Hunter called from the kitchen.

'No,' Garcia's tone was firm. 'You need to come have a look at this.'

Hunter brought the envelope with him.

Garcia indicated the book on the table. 'Skip the first fifty pages or so,' he said. 'Have a look from then on and tell me what you think.'

Hunter flipped through it, starting from about halfway, quickly studying the figures on the pages, including the dates. Once he got to the last figure, he looked back at his partner.

'Those are some impressive scores, Robert.'

Hunter nodded. 'She practiced almost every day for six solid months.'

'Exactly,' Garcia agreed. 'Now how do you suppose that somebody with these sorts of scores, would miss a shot at a target that was merely six feet away? And miss by about a foot?'

'She wouldn't,' Hunter replied. 'She missed on purpose.'

There was something in the way that Hunter had delivered his sentence that intrigued Garcia.

'So she shot at that passenger – Phillip, right?' Garcia said. 'Why? For effect? Just to scare you?' He shook his head. 'That makes no sense.'

Hunter breathed out. 'She didn't shoot at Phil for effect. I think that she changed her mind at the last second.'

Garcia grabbed a chair from the corner. His leg was hurting again. 'Changed her mind?' he asked, as he took a seat. 'That makes even less sense, Robert. Yes, sure, she killed innocent people, but those innocent people at least had some sort of a connection to the group of students behind that video clip.'

Hunter had also taken Linda's cellphone from her jacket pocket before leaving the plane. The only two other people who had seen the video clip that Linda had showed Hunter and Amber in the aircraft had been Garcia and Captain Blake.

'Phil had nothing to do with that,' Garcia continued. 'He was just an unlucky passenger on a flight.'

Hunter handed his partner the envelope with the photo printouts that he had found in the kitchen. 'No, he wasn't.'

'Huh?' Garcia took the envelope and began leafing through the printouts. There were over fifty of them, and they all showed Phil in the company of an attractive brunette woman. They clearly had a romantic attachment. Some of the photos showed them holding hands, some showed them kissing.

Garcia immediately recognized both people on the photos – Phillip Maddox and Sofia Elliot. 'What the fuck?'

Hunter nodded. 'Phil was having an affair with Sofia.'

Garcia dropped the envelope onto his lap. 'No fucking way.'

Hunter stayed silent.

'Hold on,' Garcia lifted his hand at Hunter. 'This is unbelievable. How come you're not freaking out over this shit?'

'I would be . . . if I didn't already know it.'

'What?' Nothing seemed to be making sense for Garcia. 'How did you possibly know about this?'

'In the plane,' Hunter explained. 'When Phil told Linda that he was trying to start a family, Linda called him "loverboy". She did it again when she was pushing everyone to have a drink.'

Garcia's eyebrows arched.

'I thought that that was odd,' Hunter continued. 'The nickname came out of nowhere and it didn't fit the whole scenario. And then, when I told her that Lucas was dyslexic, Phil tried to ask a question, but Linda shut him down. Things didn't fall in place in my head until we were with the EMTs. That's when I went over to talk to Phil.'

'And he confessed.' It wasn't a question.

'I had to push it,' Hunter said, with a nod. 'I told him that we would find out, one way or another, so he decided to come clean. They've been seeing each other for five months.'

'And that was why he was flying to Italy?' This time, it was a question.

'Yes,' Hunter confirmed. 'Lucas is coming back home on Saturday, remember?'

Garcia chuckled. 'So husband comes back, wife stays a few more days, pretending that she's going to hang out with her family or whatever and *boom*, in comes the lover for happy days.'

'Something like that,' Hunter agreed.

'How did Linda know that he was on the plane?'

Hunter broadly gestured at the entire studio apartment that they were in. 'I don't think that she missed anything with her research, Carlos. Do you?'

'Do you think that Phil was the target all along?' Garcia asked. 'I mean, if Linda had found out that Sofia was more in love with her lover than her husband, then it makes sense.'

'Yes,' Hunter agreed. 'And I have a feeling that once we're finally done here ... however how many days it takes ... we'll know for sure.'

Garcia looked around at all the photos on the walls for an

instant. 'That's what this is. That's why she left everything here the way she did . . . everything organized. She could've easily had destroyed all of this.'

Hunter nodded again. 'I don't think that she knew that we were on to her yet, but she knew that eventually, we would get there. She wanted us . . .' He paused and thought better of his words. 'She wanted everyone to know why she did what she did.' He indicated the laptop. 'I bet that we'll find a copy of that video clip in there.'

'So she knew that she wasn't coming back,' Garcia said. Once again, it wasn't a question. 'Her plan was always to take her own life at the end of her crusade. Once it was all done, she had nothing else to live for anymore. Everyone she loved was gone. Talk about a ripple effect.' He shook his head at the thought of so many wasted lives.

Hunter turned to face a large photo of the Williams family – Linda, Genesis, Michael, and John. They were sitting together at a restaurant table. All four of them were laughing, as if someone had just cracked the funniest joke in the world. They all looked so happy together.

That was the only photo in the whole studio apartment that was in a photo frame – the only image Linda had left of her family.

'I think you're right, Carlos. I think you're absolutely right.'

Ninety-nine

One day later – Police Administration Building.

Linda Evans had disabled the security protocol on her laptop. There was no password. As soon as Hunter turned it on, it loaded her desktop. It contained only one folder, named 'Genesis'. Hunter had slowly been reading through every file for the past three hours.

'Incredible,' he murmured, as he sat back on his chair.

'What is?' Garcia asked, looking at Hunter over his computer screen.

'How bold Linda Evans really was.'

'Why? What else have you found out?'

'She visited them all before the attacks . . . all of them.'

'Visited them?' Garcia asked. 'What do you mean?'

'Janet Lang is a beautician, right?'

'Yeah.'

'Linda had two beauty sessions with her,' Hunter explained.

'What? Really?' Garcia got to his feet.

Hunter nodded and pointed at the laptop screen. 'Both of them last month. She used a different name, though.'

Garcia got to Hunter's desk and studied the screen. 'Grace Bauer?' he read.

Another nod from Hunter before he loaded a new document

onto the screen. 'Last week, on Wednesday, three days before she took Oliver Griffith's life, she had a therapy session with Josie. They talked for a full hour.'

'I'll be damned,' Garcia chuckled.

'And check this out.' Hunter loaded yet another document onto the laptop screen. 'She bought her weapon, the 9mm. pistol that we found in her apartment, from Troy's shop. The shooting range where she practiced for six solid months was the same shooting range that he went to. They met at the range several times.'

Garcia looked completely lost for words.

Yet another file onto the screen.

'At the beginning of the month,' Hunter said, '"Grace Bauer" visited Sofia Elliot in her house to discuss the possibility of Sofia becoming her accountant. The meeting also lasted about an hour.'

'Why do that, do you think? Why go visit them?'

'Linda knew that she would end her life when all this was over,' Hunter explained. 'I think that she just wanted to meet the people who caused her and her family so much pain . . . so much destruction. She wanted to look into their eyes, talk to them, maybe even get a feel for how much they really loved the person that she was about to take away from them. Her frame of mind was truly psychopathic by then.'

'That's just . . .'

Garcia was interrupted by a knock to their office door.

'Come in,' he called.

The door was pulled open by a man in his mid-forties dressed in a dark suit. His thick, dark beard softened his jawline and disguised his cheekbones.

'Detective Hunter?' he asked.

'That's me,' Hunter replied.

The man approached his desk. 'A few days ago you ordered a DNA and fingerprint test on a wine glass, do you remember that?'

Hunter grimaced. 'Oh, I'm so sorry. I forgot to cancel that

request. Things have been quite crazy lately and it completely escaped my mind. That person isn't of interest anymore.'

'Not to you, maybe,' the man said, showing Hunter his credentials. 'I'm Agent Wilson Reeves, with the Sex Crime Division for the California District Attorney's office. The DNA on the wine glass you handed in flashed up as a match for a rape/murder investigation that we've been running for five years.' He placed a photo on Hunter's desk. 'Suzy Black – twenty-two-years-old – a student from San Francisco.'

Hunter and Garcia studied the photo for a few seconds.

'We have reason to believe that in the past five years,' Agent Reeves continued, 'the same perpetrator that raped and murdered Miss Black has done the same to at least three other women.' He placed three new photos on Hunter's desk. 'Helen Austin – twenty-one-years-old – a student in San Diego ... Martha Driscoll – twenty-four-years-old – a kindergarten teacher in Oakland ... and Alice Pearson – also twenty-four-years-old – a bartender in Sacramento.'

'Reason to believe?' Garcia asked.

'The circumstances, the MO, and the signature on all four rape/murder attacks were practically identical, but the perp got better at it. His only mistake came with his first murder, five years ago.'

'The DNA left behind in San Francisco,' Hunter said, tapping his index finger against the first photo Agent Reeves had place on his desk. 'Suzy Black.'

'Exactly. No more mistakes after that. We've been chasing this sick sonofabitch for five long years, Detective Hunter, so please tell me that you have a name you can give me?'

Hunter reached for his cellphone, called up his image gallery and thumbed through a few photos. 'I have something better than a name.' He showed Agent Reeves his phone screen. 'I have his face.'

Acknowledgements

As always, my heartfelt thanks goes to a few special people – my agent, Darley Anderson, for being the best agent an author could have. Darley's Angels – Mary Darby, Kristina Egan, Georgia Fuller, and the whole team at the agency, for simply being amazing. My editors at Simon & Schuster UK – Katherine Armstrong and Bethan Jones – who, with their amazing suggestions, have improved this book ten-fold. My editor at Ullstein, Germany, Monika Boese, for all her incredible work and support.

Thank you so much also to all the readers and everyone out there who have so fantastically supported my work and me for so many years. Without your support, I wouldn't be writing.

I would also like to say a very special 'thank you' to Amber Burnett, who won a competition to become a character in my next novel back in 2019. Thank you so much, Amber, for being so patient. I'm so sorry it took me so long to complete this project. I truly hope you like your character.

FIND OUT MORE ABOUT
CHRIS CARTER

Chris Carter writes highly addictive thrillers
featuring Detective Robert Hunter

To find out more about Chris and his writing,
visit his website at

www.chriscarterbooks.com

or follow Chris on

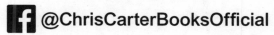 @ChrisCarterBooksOfficial

All of Chris Carter's novels are available
in print and eBook, and are available to
download in eAudio

Helplines

If you've been affected by any of the issues raised in *Genesis*, here are details of organisations that offer advice and support. You can also call these helplines for advice if you're worried about someone else.

Websites and phone helplines

Samaritans
Call 116 123
https://www.samaritans.org/
jo@samaritans.org

Campaign Against Living Miserably (CALM)
Call 0800 58 58 58 – 5pm to midnight every day
https://www.thecalmzone.net/

Papyrus – for people under 35
Call 0800 068 41 41 – 9am to midnight every day
Text 07860 039967
pat@papyrus-uk.org
https://www.papyrus-uk.org/papyrus-hopelineuk/

Childline – for children and young people under 19
Call 0800 1111 – the number will not show up on your phone bill
https://www.childline.org.uk/

SOS Silence of Suicide
Call 0300 1020 505 – 4pm to midnight every day
support@sossilenceofsuicide.org
https://sossilenceofsuicide.org/
https://supportaftersuicide.org.uk/

Message Helplines

If you do not want to talk to someone over the phone, these text lines are open twenty-four hours a day, every day.

Shout Crisis Text Line
Text "SHOUT" to 85258
https://giveusashout.org/

YoungMinds Crisis Messenger – for people under 19
Text "YM" to 85258
https://www.youngminds.org.uk/young-person/youngminds-textline